Praise for *Snowbound*

"A haunting novel about hubris and its consequences."
—Larry McMurtry, Pulitzer Prize–winning author of *Lonesome Dove*

"A dramatic and colorful epic." —*Publishers Weekly*

"Wheeler . . . has fashioned a dramatic character study while staying faithful to the outline of events. Frémont had a fascinating career . . . [and] Wheeler carefully draws the Pathfinder true to history, unafraid to expose his foibles." —*Historical Novels Review*

Praise for *Eclipse*

"A riveting recreation of the tragic final years of an American legend." —*Booklist*

"A wonderful biographical fiction . . . vividly described."
—*Midwest Book Review*

"[Wheeler] has forever branded Western literature with his presence. [His] characters . . . are not the people who win every showdown . . . Instead [they] struggle for their lives, and often their souls." —*True West*

"A riveting novel by [a] master storyteller . . . Wheeler brings readers a stunningly told and hitherto incomplete story of the tragic, final chapter in the life of Meriwether Lewis, one of American history's most famous and lasting characters." —*The Denver Post*

BY RICHARD S. WHEELER FROM TOM DOHERTY ASSOCIATES

Aftershocks
Anything Goes
Badlands
The Buffalo Commons
Cashbox
Easy Pickings
Eclipse
The Exile
The Fields of Eden
Fool's Coach
Goldfield
Masterson
Montana Hitch
An Obituary for Major Reno
The Richest Hill on Earth
Second Lives
Sierra
Snowbound
Sun Mountain: A Comstock Memoir
Where the River Runs

SKYE'S WEST

Sun River
Bannack
The Far Tribes
Yellowstone
Bitterroot
Sundance
Wind River
Santa Fe
Rendezvous
Dark Passage
Going Home
Downriver
The Deliverance
The Fire Arrow
The Canyon of Bones
Virgin River
North Star
The Owl Hunt
The First Dance

SAM FLINT

Flint's Gift
Flint's Truth
Flint's Honor

SNOWBOUND

· AND ·

ECLIPSE

RICHARD S. WHEELER

A TOM DOHERTY ASSOCIATES BOOK / NEW YORK

This is a work of fiction. All of the characters, organizations, and events portrayed in these novels are either products of the author's imagination or are used fictitiously.

SNOWBOUND AND ECLIPSE

A Forge Book
Published by Tom Doherty Associates, LLC
175 Fifth Avenue
New York, NY 10010

www.tor-forge.com

ISBN 978-0-7653-8364-8

Our books may be purchased in bulk for promotional, educational, or business use. Please contact your local bookseller or the Macmillan Corporate and Premium Sales Department at 1-800-221-7945, extension 5442, or by e-mail at MacmillanSpecialMarkets@macmillan.com.

First Edition: August 2016

Printed in the United States of America

0 9 8 7 6 5 4 3 2 1

CONTENTS

SNOWBOUND

To Tom Doherty,
who asked me to write about the Pathfinder

PROLOGUE

Senator Thomas Hart Benton

I shall never forget the months I spent as a spectator in the Washington Arsenal watching the fiendish glare that Brigadier General Stephen Watts Kearny directed at my daughter's husband, John Charles Frémont. I had never seen anything like it. General Kearny had fixed his unblinking scowl upon my son-in-law with the full intent of intimidating the young man.

The court-martial of Colonel Frémont began on November 2, 1847, and ran eighty-nine days. General Kearny had brought the charges, including mutiny, disobedience, and conduct prejudicial to good order. These sprang from the period when Frémont and his battalion of irregulars, along with Commodore Robert Stockton, had largely conquered California with little help from the regular army. Commodore Stockton, the senior United States officer in the region, had appointed Colonel Frémont the governor of the newly conquered province, a position he ardently defended against the meddling of Brigadier General Kearny, until the malice-soaked Kearny stripped him of the office, accused him of insubordination, and then hauled him east as a prisoner.

Kearny must have seethed, for the young and celebrated conqueror of California was neither a veteran line officer nor a West Pointer but a junior officer, an explorer and mapmaker with the Army's Corps of Topographical Engineers, who happened to be near the Pacific coast when war broke out. Not only that, but Frémont and Stockton had won California with minimal bloodshed, and Frémont had made a generous peace with the conquered Californios.

It didn't end with that, either, for the young man was also a national hero, well known to his countrymen as the Pathfinder. In previous explorations he, along with a company of gifted scientists and cartographers, had mapped large portions of the little-known West, and the accounts of these journeys had been published by the government and made available to pioneering Americans bent on settling the West. Thus the Pathfinder had been a great instrument of westward expansion, an enterprise dear to my heart, and one to which I had devoted my entire career in the Senate.

But all this success, which seemed to wrap my son-in-law in a golden aura, was too much for the old guard in the army, and in General Kearny it found the means to ruin the most celebrated young officer in the republic. I knew, even as the two sides prepared for the trial, that Colonel Frémont would have to endure a special burden, the rage of envious senior officers who vented their rank hostility and contempt toward my son-in-law at every opportunity, sometimes stating their case in the sensational daily press.

I took steps in my own fashion to salvage my son-in-law's career, one day interviewing President Polk about the matter. I noted his tepid response, and I marked him as a pusillanimous opponent of the Bentons, though we had made common cause for many years. I took to the Senate floor, where I still commanded a faction of my Democratic party, and did not hesitate to let the whole body know of the malign effort to disgrace Colonel Frémont, and by extension, bring ruin upon my family.

How I ached for my daughter Jessie, who was forced to

listen day after day to the most disgraceful and base accusations against her beloved husband, even while she bore his unborn child. It was plain to the whole world that the charges against my son-in-law were utterly without merit, concocted by a vindictive old general who had arrived in California too late and with too little force and had suffered the mortal indignity of defeat by the Californios. Was it any wonder that a bilious stew began to boil in the bosom of the old soldier or that it was soon to spew over the true conqueror of California?

I took my own measures as I watched the trial progress through the weeks and months. When General Kearny took the witness stand, I stared back, as relentlessly and unblinkingly as he had glared at my son-in-law, and my steadfast gaze had its effect. The general exploded in rage, and the tribunal directed its attention toward me, even as I sat with glacial calm among the spectators. But the conduct that was perfectly acceptable to the tribunal in Kearny's case was not acceptable to them in my case, and I suffered the rebuke of its presiding officer, Brevet Brigadier General G. M. Brooke. That gave me the measure of the thirteen members of that tribunal. I knew where the Bentons stood with them, and some things I do not forget or forgive.

I like to think that the whole lot of them were recollecting an earlier utterance of mine that still follows me around, much to my advantage: "I never quarrel, sir, but I do fight, sir, and when I fight, sir, a funeral follows, sir."

They found Frémont guilty on all charges and directed that he be thrown out of the army. The miserable Polk affirmed the charges but remitted the sentence, permitting my son-in-law to remain in the service. But that additional rebuke was too much for the young man; he resigned in deepest sadness, and thus the Pathfinder, the young republic's most honored young man, found himself tarnished and alone. Those were hard days for my daughter Jessie and her husband, and I ached for them.

It mattered not that the American people, along with the press, were solidly behind Frémont for it was plain to the whole country that sheer spite among senior army officers had brought the Pathfinder to his ruin. It mattered not that this vindictive verdict caused grave illness in Jessie and threatened the life of her unborn child. It mattered not to the Polk administration that it had wrought an injustice and that the American people were aware of it and outraged by it.

But I have my own ways and means, and I thought of an enterprise that not only would regain Frémont's reputation for him as the nation's foremost explorer but also would open a way for Saint Louis to funnel the entire commerce of the West and the Pacific into the States and to hasten the day when the republic would stretch from sea to sea. I proposed to several Saint Louis business colleagues that they fund a private survey along the 38th parallel, with the intent of running a railroad to San Francisco along the mid-continent route. I received somewhat hesitant backing because the gentlemen feared that Frémont might once again fail to use sound judgment, but in the end, we raised enough to finance Frémont's fourth expedition. It would be up to the Pathfinder to restore his name and reputation. But in this case he would not be defying a superior officer; he would answer only to himself. This time there was no one looking over his shoulder.

CHAPTER ONE

John Charles Frémont

General Kearny killed the baby. I would never say it publicly, but I knew right down to my bones that it was true. Jessie would come to it also; she thought that Benton was sickly because of the court-martial.

Ten weeks was all the life allotted my firstborn, named after Jessie's family. The ordeal in Washington City was more than Jessie could endure, and it afflicted the child she was carrying, and now the bell tolls.

Stephen Watts Kearny and his cronies brought the charge, mutiny and disobedience in California; put me and my family through the ordeal; and triumphed. He who was a friend of the Bentons, supped at their table, could not contain a raging envy of me, and now the bell tolls.

Benton was a sickly infant, delivered by a worn woman, though Jessie was but twenty-four. Even Kit Carson, almost a stranger to children, said as much. He had visited Jessie in Washington only a few weeks ago, having completed his courier duty for the army, and thought that Benton would not live long.

I watched the pewter river slide past in the dawn. We were aboard the *Martha*, plying its slow way to Westport from Saint Louis. Most of my men were there, awaiting me, receiving and guarding the expedition's materiel and mules.

I didn't much care to go on this expedition. It would not be the same. A great weariness has afflicted me ever since the verdict—no, ever since General Kearny marched me to the States as the rear of his column, in disgrace.

I had read in the press that I have changed: "Colonel Frémont looks weary and gray since his ordeal," according to all reports. I have not changed and nothing bends me, and soon the republic will see what I am made of. The army will see what I am made of. So will President Polk. And their brown claws will not touch me this time.

The *Martha* vibrated more than most river packets do, and I wondered if Captain Rolfe knew his main bearings were out of true. The hooded shores, heavy with mist-shrouded trees wearing their yellow October colors, slid by. I would need to talk to Rolfe; I would need to help Jessie out of her world and into the real one. I had left her in the gloomy stateroom, sitting in her ivory nightclothes on the bunk, crooning to Benton at her breast. The boy was dead. Sometime in the small hours his weak heart had failed. Kitty, her colored maid, had discovered it. Now the infant hung limp in her arms, while she whispered and sang and clutched the still, cold infant.

I would have to disturb her. It is not in me to flee from any duty.

I retreated from the deck rail and entered our dank stateroom. Jessie sat on the edge of the bunk, rocking softly, the child still clamped to her breast. She eyed me, and then the shadows, where Kitty sat helplessly.

"Jessie, it's time to let go."

She nodded. "He's dead, I know."

"Yes. May I take him?"

"I had him for such a little while."

But she handed the cold infant to me. It didn't resemble anyone I knew. I stood, holding it. She turned away, not knowing what to do or caring to see what I would do with the dead boy.

I found the blue receiving blanket and wrapped it around Benton. The boy should have weighed more. He weighed almost nothing. Did souls have weight? Did a living infant weigh more?

"I'll have the cabin boy bring you something. Tea?"

"It was the strain," she said. "All the while you were under a cloud, the little baby knew it. It shrank him up."

"Jessie—you are a beautiful mother."

She smiled fleetingly. "I wanted him to be like you," she said.

"Rest a while. I'll be back."

"I'll never see my baby again."

I nodded. Then I slipped out on the dewy deck and made my way forward, the bundle in my arms. Below, the side-wheeler shivered its way upstream, gliding over murky water, leaving a gentle wake behind. A quiet rhythm punctuated the dawn as the paddles splashed and the great drive piston reciprocated.

The grimy white wheelhouse was ahead. I knocked, and was shouted in, but I saw only the helmsman steering the boat's slow passage. "Captain Rolfe, please. Frémont here."

The helmsman simply pointed at a door behind the wheelhouse. I opened it and found myself staring at the half-dressed captain eating breakfast in a small galley. The man wore blue trousers and a stained gray union suit.

"It's you, Frémont. I knew you were aboard."

"Captain, we have lost our boy."

Rolfe stared at the small bundle. "I am sorry. Was it cholera?"

"He was sickly and died in the night."

Rolfe nodded. "I'll have the carpenter's mate build a box. Have you plans? We can stop and bury him . . ."

"Can the child be shipped to Saint Louis?"

"We're coming on to Jefferson City . . ."

"I would like to do it that way."

"I'm sorry, Colonel. It's a hard thing."

"Hard on Jessie, yes." That was less than I intended to say. "Hard on both of us," I added.

Captain Rolfe dabbed his chin whiskers, wiping away the remains of oat gruel, and tugged a cord. A cabin boy materialized.

"Take Colonel Frémont to the shop."

I followed the youth down a gangway to the silvery rain-soaked boiler deck, and finally to a noisy room aft. It took only a moment. The carpenter's mate eyed the quiet bundle, nodded, and set to work.

I was glad to escape and headed forward until I stood at the rounded prow. This ship was heading west. I was heading west. I was going to California, but going the hard way. Jessie would meet me there, after crossing the isthmus of Panama. She had come to see me off.

I watched ahead as the riverboat wound its way around lazy curves, scything deer from the riverbanks and alarming ravens. The bankside trees clawed at us. An overcast hid the sun and hushed the wind. This was level country. Far away, where the Rockies tumbled up to the sky, I would chop a hole through the wall. That was what this was all about as far as any other living soul knew. But I knew it was about much more. The West Pointers would eat crow, every feather and claw, beak and brain. They would rot unknown in their graves; the nation would decorate its public squares with statues of Frémont.

But of that I said nothing, especially not to my wife. She was my ally, prized from the Benton family by our elopement. I acquired the most powerful father-in-law in Washington, and we have put each other to good use, he in his dreams of westward expansion, and I in my dream of decorating every village square. These were unspoken but ever present. He doesn't like me, and I've never cared for him. But we make common cause.

We docked at Jefferson City, an indifferent city of indifferent people, and I watched the roustabouts heft the small pine casket ashore to a waiting spring wagon, and that was the last I would see of my son. The Bentons would bury him. Jessie did not join me at the rail, and I supposed she lay abed. I am made of stern stuff, and I watched what passed for a coffin removed from the vessel. The *Martha* did not tarry long, but it did take on some dripping wet cordwood, and then we shuddered west once again, and I would have it no other way.

I put my son out of mind.

This, my fourth expedition, had formed swiftly. It had been privately financed by that old fur trade entrepreneur Robert Campbell, along with O. D. Filley and Thornton Grimsley, but all told, they had not pledged a third of what the government would have given me. There were those in Saint Louis who saw the virtue of steel rails to the far Pacific, spanning the unknown continent, and funneling the whole commerce of the Pacific and the Orient through the gateway city. I was indifferent to that. Success would merely line other men's pockets. But I was not indifferent to other facets of this trip. I would do it without the leave of the army, without the hindrance of government. And I would do it in winter, the very season requiring the most strenuous exertions and posing the greatest risk. Let them absorb that.

I would be my own commander, exempt from court-martial, and my only judge and jury would be public opinion and my private esteem. I supposed there would be some obligation to my backers, most particularly my father-in-law, who contributed his skills and his purse to all this. And

I would provide it. They would receive the cartographic results for which they anted up.

There were other things on my mind; I wished to look upon the great foothill tract in California, Las Mariposas, that had been purchased for me by the American consul, Thomas O. Larkin, from the Mexicans. It was not anything I wanted, and Larkin had violated the trust I had placed in him. So I was stuck with a huge tract of rolling land, good for little. Perhaps something lucrative could be made of it, though I wasn't sure what. I knew it would do for the grazing of cattle or sheep, because that was how the Californios had exploited it. But it might yield more under good Yankee management. I had sent an entire sawmill around the horn, knowing that sawn lumber is in short supply in that remote province. I planned to discover how best to line my pockets.

The Mediterranean climate of that far shore appealed to me, and I imagined it would appeal to Jessie as well, but it fostered indolence in the natives. She could not endure the transcontinental trip, so she would travel to the Pacific across the isthmus of Panama after seeing me off and meet me in a remote place recently renamed San Francisco, destined by geography to become a fine city someday. Thus she would accompany me to Westport Landing, where my corps of exploration would assemble and depart, and then return to Saint Louis and New Orleans, and we would have a rendezvous some unimaginable distance away, at some unfathomable moment to come.

It was just as well. She might be brimming with youth, but she was not fit.

I returned frequently to the stateroom where Jessie secluded herself. She seemed uncommonly stricken, and I did my best to cheer her, along with her maid, who was quartered below. By the time we reached Westport she was up and about, wearing gray wool, taking tours on the boiler deck, studying the ever-moving panorama as we shivered our way west.

"I am very nearly the only woman on board," she said on one of our tours, her arm locked in mine.

"The wilderness offers no closets," I said. "Men go west first."

"Oh, fiddle, Charles. There are women in the wagon trains, and no closets for two thousand miles."

I enjoyed her renewed brightness. She might have an entirely unrealistic perception of the strength and weaknesses of the sexes, but at least her lively spirit was returning, along with a healthy blush to her cheeks. She took great delight in me, which I found flattering. She certainly had her pick of men, being a senator's daughter, but all those high-bred swain were felled before they knew they had been hewn down. On my part, I prided myself in offering her the utmost consideration.

This was not her first experience of steam travel, and she eyed the roustabouts with a knowing eye. Most were freed blacks, rawboned ragged men in ceaseless toil. The furnace required enormous amounts of wood to wrestle the packet against the steady current, and that meant that the deckhands sweated through long days, lifting three-foot logs, nimbly swinging them into the firebox, somehow avoiding burning themselves, only to draw yet another log off the great piles stacked on the boiler deck, only two feet or so above water. It was steam that wrestled with gravity and nature, but the sinewy legs and arms of men fed the furnaces that wrought the steam.

"They are so thin," she said.

"They move tons of wood each day," I replied.

"They would be good men for you to take with you."

"I have better men," I replied.

Indeed, I had assembled a fine lot of volunteers, many of them men from my old corps of exploration who knew the wilds and how to survive in it. To these I had added a few adventurers, who would travel unpaid. There was no money to pay wages, and not even enough to equip them, but my father-in-law planned to introduce a bill that would cover costs. His first efforts along those lines had been roundly rebuked, with the court-martial looming as the obstacle to any further consideration. But the senator and I thought that on the successful completion of the railroad survey, some funds would be forthcoming from a grateful Congress. So I did not hesitate to assure our company that one way or another, they would be paid, and in any case they would have safe passage to California. Thus did we finally dock in Westport, where the Missouri River bends north, and we were met by most of the men of my company, who were waiting for their leader.

CHAPTER TWO

John Charles Frémont

I grew anxious, as we approached Westport, that there should be an appropriate showing of my men. I wanted Jessie to see with her own eyes the enthusiasm of the company, so she could report favorably to her father and my backers when she returned to Saint Louis. It would suit me ill if few of my stalwarts showed up to greet us.

I was not disappointed. When we rounded a leafy bend and Westport suddenly hove into view under an opaque pearl sky, I noted the compact crowd at the levee awaiting the *Martha*. Westport was a tangle of temporary gray structures in a sea of mud; its denizens had not yet acquired the civic spirit that fostered grace. The disorder of the town reflected the disorder of their passions.

The ship's passengers crowded the rail as the shuddering subsided and the steam whistle emitted an eerie howl like a wolf's cry. Then came deep silence as the packet slid against the thumping current toward shore. Deckhands had pike poles and hawsers at the ready, and soon the stained boat would be snubbed fast to thick posts set in the mud.

This was Westport, famed entrepôt where the Santa Fe caravans and Oregon trains and most overland companies outfitted and then vanished into the unknown continent. There was a last weird silence, broken only by the slap of waves on our prow, and then the boat thumped against the piles and a dozen brawny blacks made it fast.

But my gaze was on my company. There they were, the motley crowd I had recruited over the past several months. I was gratified to find cheerful ruddy faces among them, men who had been with me during previous expeditions. Men who were in my California Battalion. Men who had climbed the Sierra Nevada with me in midwinter, proving it could be done. Some of them were ready and willing to try it again, loyal to their commander through all kinds of weather.

"There's Godey," I said to Jessie. "He'll be my second. And there's Preuss, the topographer, grouchy old German. And there's the Kern brothers. Philadelphia people. They've come to greet me. Ned Kern was with me on the third expedition. I'll have two artists this time. They'll catch every landscape. Railroad men like sketches best of all. See what's ahead, where the trouble is."

"They look very competent," Jessie said, as the sweating roustabouts slid a long gangway over a small span of water to the muddy bank.

"They are, when taking direction," I replied. "But they

need to be welded into a company, and that's what I do best. Ah! There's Vincenthaler, another of my stalwarts. With me in California. Oh, and Taplin! With me on the second and third expeditions, army captain then, and I made him an officer in my California Battalion. Ah! Raphael Proue, a Creole, with me on all three of my trips. And Tabeau! Morin! Voyageurs, my dear. Men born to the wild."

"They've spotted us," she said. "Oh, capital!"

I eyed her sharply. Her face had lit, and I saw a bloom in her cheeks that belied the somber gray of her stiff woolen dress. Good. She would take the good impressions back to Saint Louis and convey them to her skeptical father. When it came to Senator Benton, Jessie was my best advocate. He listens to her but expects me to listen to him, and I play the lesser part in his company.

I waved cheerfully at my men as they crowded the gangway but said nothing. I would have more than enough to say once we had alighted and our luggage had been hauled ashore, along with several leather-bound trunks filled with cartographic and navigational apparatuses.

It is my style to address people with a level tone, avoiding the extremes of passion at all times. That is a quality of leadership I possess, this steady calm that wins respect and quiets all turbulence. Such was my conduct now as we descended the gangway, Mrs. Frémont on my arm, and found ourselves surrounded by smiling bearded men of various vintages. Our servants, Kitty and Saunders, would take care of our things.

I turned at once to Alexis Godey, another of the Saint Louis Creoles and a thoroughly able man, one who understood me.

"Alex! You've paid us honor with your presence. I am honored to introduce you to my wife, Jessie."

"Mrs. Frémont," he said in flawless English.

"My wife has suffered a great sorrow, Alex, which I will make known in due course, so we will refrain from taxing her."

Godey stared, blank as to what that was about, but he would learn soon enough. He was discreet, which is more than I could say of most Creoles.

A wiry man unknown to me stood before us. "Andrew Cathcart at your service, Colonel Frémont. Captain, Eleventh Hussars, off on a little adventure." He spoke with a burr, and I disliked him on sight. I didn't want adventurers, and I don't care for Scots.

"Ah, yes, you're the one who wrote me. I'm glad you'll be with us," I said, somehow concealing my thoughts. The Scot was simply larking his way west. "Captain, this is Mrs. Frémont," I said.

She offered her hand and a curtsey.

"Honored indeed," Cathcart said. "You're the toast of the regiment."

Jessie did not smile.

I found myself shaking the hand of Ned Kern, my artist during the third expedition, and an officer in the California Battalion. A good hand. Kern introduced his brothers, Richard, also an artist, and Benjamin, a medical doctor, both the color of bread dough. I introduced them to Jessie, but without enthusiasm. These Philadelphians didn't look hardy enough to stand up to what was coming. Not even Edward, who had topped the Sierra Nevada with my company two years earlier, looked the part for this trip. Both Richard and Benjamin looked so pale I wondered if they had spent even an hour in the natural world. I decided to keep a sharp eye on them, and if they proved too fragile, I would dismiss them before we ascended the Rocky Mountains. Tough old Preuss could sketch if he had to.

We met the others one by one, even as other passengers

and freight drifted away from the levee, until at last only our own company remained. Several of the company had already slid our trunks into a spring wagon.

"Let's go, Godey. You're driving, I take it. Along the way, you can tell me what's here, what's missing, and what needs doing. I want to be off as soon as it can be managed. Also, you can rehearse what you know about these gentlemen. And don't mind Mrs. Frémont. Anything private for my ears are for hers also."

The company drifted apart, mostly to the saddle mules that had been tied to a lengthy hitch rail. Westport had returned to its slumbers. It was plainly a town that woke itself up with the arrival of a wagon company or a riverboat, only to doze under the pewter skies.

"You'll take us first to Major Cummins's house, won't you now?"

"As you wish, Colonel." He slapped the lines over the croups of the gray mules, and they sullenly pushed into their collars and started us rolling. I did not like the looks of these mules and wondered about the rest.

"Colonel is it, my friend? I'm an ordinary civilian now, Godey." I said it with that certain quietness of voice I knew commanded respect.

"Always Colonel to me, sir, but I'm at your command even if you call yourself mister. It was a pity."

Had Jessie not been sitting there, and her maid on the seat behind, Godey might have called it something stronger than a pity. I never used oaths or words that gave offense and rebuke such language uttered in my presence. And that is a part of the hold I have on my men. I have studied on it.

"We will install Mrs. Frémont there; by day she will occupy a tent I will raise for her at Boone Creek, whilst we put our company together. The major has generously offered to board my wife and her servant."

Cummins was the old Indian agent there at Boone Creek, outside Westport, and had in his charge the Delaware nation. It would be a good thing; Jessie under a roof by night, in camp by day, where she would observe and take her impressions back to Saint Louis men who counted. I had brought her this distance for a purpose.

"Very good, sir."

"And Alex. Mrs. Frémont is grieving the loss of her infant."

The Creole tugged the lines, slowing the mules. "Loss, Colonel?"

"Our boy, Benton. On board."

Godey hawed the mules forward. "I'm sorry, Colonel. That is a hard thing. It's a bad omen. Should the company be told? Maybe not a word?"

"I will, at the proper time," I said.

"Then my lips are sealed."

That was Godey, I thought. No man more reliable, and none more faithful to me.

The burdened wagon creaked through rain-softened lanes, past gloomy oak groves and sullen wet meadows. West of Westport little existed except those copses and creeks where the wagon companies fitted themselves for the great haul west. Ours would be entirely a pack-mule expedition once we reached the mountains, and we would need scores of them to carry ourselves and our truck. But where I was going no wagon could go. I would take a few horses but would trade them if possible. They were no good in the mountains and flighty on the plains.

I planned to take a good look at the men, several of whom were entirely new to me. I have good instincts. It is a gift. I know in an instant what a stranger thinks of me and am prepared for him even before he opens his mouth. Cathcart, now, he might be alright even if I didn't much care for him.

An officer in the Queen's hussars would understand command. But those Kerns. They would take some study. Ben's surgical tools might be a valuable asset, but the man hadn't the faintest idea what this trip would be about. Fine Pennsylvania family, privileged sons. Not a bit like their leader. I had never known a day of privilege.

I shifted uncomfortably on the seat. Would a day ever go by, in all my life, when I wasn't reminded of my origins? We drove through swelling hills clothed with tawny grass and copses of trees. The air was chill and more autumnal than it should be in October.

"Last night, Colonel, we were treated to northern lights. No one had ever seen them this far south," Godey said.

"It is a good omen," I replied. It was my habit to turn superstition to my advantage, lest it work against me. "Now, what is our condition, Alex? Are we ready?"

"Alors, non. A lot of green mules need to be broken to pack saddle, and only half of our equipment's come in. We're lacking tack, pack and riding saddles, those India rubber sheets you ordered, some kettles and kitchen goods. Most of the provisions are here. Flour, sugar, molasses, all of that. We're not ready, and it'll be a week or two."

"That's fine. Winter passage is to our advantage."

Godey eyed me sharply, but I meant it.

We reached Major Cummins's Delaware Agency midafternoon. It proved to be an odd assortment of shabby log structures, strung in a row on a flat devoid of trees, which had all been sacrificed to the woodstoves within. The gouty old agent greeted us effusively and set several nubile maidens to work settling Jessie and Kitty in an empty cabin. I saw at once how it was with the major, whose face bore the rosy hue of dissipation. He did not lack for comforts.

"Ah! Colonel, I'm at your service. We're all at your service here," the major announced. "Whatever you need, anything at all, any little thing, you have only to call on me."

"Mrs. Frémont will be here nights only," I said. "She'll be in camp by day."

"A most admirable arrangement," Cummins said. "We will entertain her accordingly. I'm available late afternoons for libations and devote myself to my duties at night."

The man either had laryngitis or his tonsils were ruined.

We clambered to the ground while the Indian agent sent his charges scurrying about. Jessie and her servant found themselves in a primitive cabin with a puncheon floor, a fly-specked window, and a fireplace for heat. I examined it and thought it to be adequate for women.

I continued on, with Godey, to the Boone Creek camp a mile distant. It was spread through a cottonwood grove and showed signs of hard use. It had been a favorite marshaling place for wagon companies heading to Oregon or Santa Fe for years. But it was convenient to Westport; merchants could deliver the last of our equipment easily, within an hour after it was taken off the boats.

Now at last I could see what sort of company this would be. There would be no blue uniforms here; these were either civilians or else soldiers on leave, such as Cathcart. But still, many of my men were formerly enlisted, and this was a military camp, with tents formed in a square and the mule herd under guard. The men had divided themselves into four messes, each with its cook fire.

Even as Godey reined the mules to a stop, the company flocked to our side. It was grand. I am not one for displays of feeling, and these men knew it and greeted me courteously. But I could see they were pleased to receive me in camp. And with amiable handshakes we either resumed old ties or took the measure of one another. I was particularly anxious to meet the newcomers and assess their feeling for me. It would not do to have dissenters and soreheads in the company, and it was important to me that my command be acceptable to them all. So I paid close attention as I met them one by one, at least those who had not come to the river's edge earlier. Take Micajah McGehee, for instance, a Mississippi man, more literate than some, son of a judge, gentle in nature. I was delighted to see evidence of his respect for the Pathfinder, as I had come to be called, and knew that if the man's health held up, he would be a good addition to the company.

In due course I gathered them close, because I never raise my voice.

"Mrs. Frémont will be here by day, whilst we organize ourselves," I began. "She has recently suffered a most grievous loss, the death of her infant son Benton, and any courtesy extended to her at this time would be most welcome."

My company fell into deep silence.

After a few moments, I smiled. "Now, then. We'll begin. I intend to reach the Pacific coast early in the spring, having found an easy way across the middle of the continent. I understand that last night you all witnessed northern lights, a great rarity here. That is a splendid omen. And all of you will share in my good fortune."

CHAPTER THREE

Jessie Benton Frémont

He was so buoyant before the trial. He was certain the court-martial would come to nothing; the malice of General Kearny and his West Point cronies would be exposed and the charges dismissed. Was Frémont not the conqueror of California, a national hero? Had he not been celebrated and fêted in every village and city from the frontier to Washington City?

He was buoyant then, eager for the trial to begin so he could clear himself and shame his accuser. My father, Old Bullion they called him, was already roaring in the Senate, buttonholing officials, lecturing the uninformed. Between my husband and my father, nothing bad would befall us.

When we finally reached Washington to await the trial, John and I slipped away from my family for an idyllic week I shall never forget. It was heaven. For five of our six and a half years of marriage, he had been away on his expeditions, but now he was there every evening, every dawn. We slept late each morning, breakfasted in bed, hiked through red-brick Georgetown, drove in the pearl moonlight, and returned to our rooms to share all the pleasures that can ever befall a happy husband and wife sharing a reunion.

And from our joy that week, we would bring a son into the world. But the trial did not proceed as we intended; that wall of stiff-backed officers in blue and gold and white glared malevolently at John and even more acidly at my father. And in the end, they won: they found John guilty on all three of the charges: mutiny, disobeying the commands of superiors, and conduct prejudicial to military discipline. And President Polk betrayed us by largely accepting the verdict, though he commuted the sentence. John resigned.

He has not held me in his arms since that hour. How often I held my arms open to him, invited him into the circle of my love, only to have him say in that polite, courteous way of his, that no, my illness forbade it; no, I was too tired and it would not be healthy or wise for me to surrender to my passions just then. How polite he always was, how much withdrawn from me, and how he had veneered it all with his innate courtesy. But the truth of it was that I yearned for my lover with all the hungers in my twenty-four-year-old heart. Now, at Boone Creek, I yearned for one last embrace from my husband before he once again vanished from my presence.

But he always had a courteous answer. At first it simply was too soon—too soon after Benton's birth, too soon after Benton's death. And so my beloved husband seemed to grow distant and not to need me or want me. But all this I set aside. It was more important to help him and the fourth expedition in any way I could.

I was in the presence of my rivals. For I had come to understand that John enjoys the company of men, in wilderness, far more than the company of my sex, in cities. I had been slow to come to it, thinking only that his duties took him far afield and that soon he would return to the bosom of his family. But it has never happened in that fashion. No sooner is he back among us in Saint Louis or Washington City than he is restless, his gaze west, yearning for the campfires and wilds I could never share with him.

He grew a beard after the court-martial; the clean-shaven handsome man I had married now hid behind sandy and luxuriant facial hair that made him all the more distant from me. To be sure, a beard is a utility in cold and cruel weather, but there is more to it. For the beard is yet another layer between Mr. Frémont and me; between Mr. Frémont and his company of adventurers.

If I have been unwell, as has been my case ever since the trial, it has much to do with this deepening gulf between him and me. I sense at times I am losing him, only to enjoy other moments when his old warmth and love reappear, as if rising from some ocean bottom. I have not known how to cope with this. One moment I am desolate; the next I think I must do whatever I can to advance his life and career; and yet at other moments I feel I must pull a little free of him and return to the hearth of my own family. One thing I know: Frémont has changed, and I wonder whether I play a role in his life.

But all these dark thoughts were only something to abolish from mind and heart and spirit as we settled in Boone Creek. I knew what I must do. I would help the colonel any way I could, and I would so master the nature of his company that I would make a good report of it to my father, and the colonel's Saint Louis backers.

I put Kitty to work settling us in the log cabin that the Indian agent, Major Richard Cummins, provided. She opened my trunks and set my clothing out to air, shook the brown bedclothes for bedbugs, and laid a small fire in the stone fireplace against the night's chill. There was a marital-sized bed with an iron bedframe and a narrow bunk for her across the room. It would have been Benton's, and Kitty would have made herself comfortable on the floor, but now it was hers.

Major Cummins had shown us in, blandly inquired after our needs, and departed, along with the colonel, who headed at once to the encampment along with Alexis Godey. The major was no surprise to me; his gouty body and ruined face informed me at once of his prodigal appetites. His bland good cheer was the patented atmospheric of a man dependent on the government for his stipend and fearful of losing it. His lithe Delaware handmaidens bespoke his appetites, and it took no imagination to see how things stood with him. But he was our host, and I would endure, so long as his gaze did not rake me too finely.

"Major, I would like some stationery and the means to write," I said.

"At your service, madam. There will be a slight charge, which I'll enroll to the colonel's account."

No sooner had Mr. Frémont settled me in the cabin than he rattled away in the wagon, and I was once again alone.

This was the first moment since Benton's passage to a different place that my husband was not with me, but I always had Kitty, whose angular dark face and shrewd gaze were ever a comfort. I never mistook her silence for a lack of awareness. She seemed almost to know my thoughts and found discreet ways to tell me so. She belonged to my father, but he had lent her to me. Neither the colonel nor I believe in involuntary servitude, but I welcomed her comfortable presence, especially when I ill cared to feed myself and my mind was adrift with thoughts of the coughing and blue infant whose lips barely caught my breast before he was taken away.

"I suppose the colonel, he's at Boone Creek now, just meeting the gents," Kitty said.

"He's a shrewd judge of character. He may be meeting his company, but he's doing more. He's sorting them out," I said.

"Imagine he's got some mighty fine ones," Kitty said, gazing from the tiny glassed window across empty fields and wooded watercourses. "He'll need himself some fine ones, I do believe."

"Oh, it's not going to be much of a trip this time, Kitty. Not like crossing the Sierra Nevada."

Kitty responded with an odd sharpness. "Miss Jessie, this heah trip, that's night curtains we been seeing in the sky."

"Night curtains?"

"I never done seen anything so cold."

I didn't encourage Kitty's superstitions and turned instead to hanging two woolen dresses, a suit, several skirts, and some flannel nightclothes. There wasn't an armoire, and we would make do with some pegs driven into the log wall.

A rap at the door brought the desired stationery and inkwell and a quill, though the major had not included a blotter. It would do. I meant only to write to Lily, and a letter to a girl not yet six could not be long. I thanked the shy Indian maiden who proffered the items.

"I'm going to write a note to Lily," I told Kitty.

The maid retreated into herself. This was magic she knew little about.

"My dear Lily," I wrote. "We miss you very much and hope Grandfather Benton is taking good care of you. I know how sad you must be at the death of your baby brother. I hope you said good-bye to him when he was laid to rest. It hurts not to have a baby brother, doesn't it? But we must swallow our grief and face the future as best we can.

"Soon I will be home, and then we will take a long boat trip to a warm place called California, and there we will see about what to do with the tract of land your father purchased. Maybe we will put cows or sheep on it. It is very big. Seventy square miles.

"Meanwhile, my dear, I am daily with your father as he prepares to go to California overland. And after our sea journey we will all be together again on that distant shore. I hear it is a very pleasant place, with smiling people, and we will begin a new life there.

"My darling Lily, we both miss you and love you and hope that you are doing well with your lessons and that your grandpa is taking good care of you."

I signed it, "Your loving mother." It was the first letter I ever wrote to her, and my father would have to read it to the girl. I missed Lily terribly, but not so much as I missed Benton. I wondered fleetingly whether I was not giving Lily her due or dividing my love in a proper manner. But I can do only so much.

I slid the letter into the envelope Major Cummins provided and addressed it to Miss Elizabeth Benton Frémont, care of The Honorable Thomas Hart Benton, Saint Louis. Then I sealed my letter with a drop of candle wax and handed it to Kitty, who held it as if it were a hot potato, her fingers barely able to clasp this mysterious thing.

"I told Lily we would be seeing her soon," I said to Kitty.

Kitty nodded, slid into the late light, and returned empty-handed.

I felt trapped that evening. The major's ladies eventually brought us a meal of sorts—moist, rich corn bread and a stringy beef stew, but I wasn't hungry. In truth my mind was a mile or two distant, where my bearded husband was preparing to flee from me once more. It did not feel right this time. It felt as if he was avoiding my company.

I retired early and doused the tallow candle even before the last light had fled the western skies.

That night I had a terrible recurring dream that felt worse than it really was. Over and over I dreamed that Frémont and I were at the moment of reunion. I awaited him with opened arms, aching for his embrace and his kiss. He was in his blue army uniform, clean-shaven, young and vibrant, and as he rushed to me I took him into my arms only to have him vanish. Simply vanish. He was gone, and I would awaken briefly and cry out. But then I slid back into the arms of Morpheus, only to experience the dream again. And again.

I was awakened before full light, this time by Alexis Godey. I peered at him through the cracked-open door.

"Madam, forgive the intrusion. The colonel sent for you," he said.

"We haven't done our toilet," I replied.

"I am at your service whenever you are ready," he responded.

It took a while to shake a bad night from my body. But I am young and stronger than most of my sex. We were ready in a few minutes, though not properly washed, and stepped into a lovely chill half-light. The day was no more than a promise, with a streak of blue along the eastern horizon and not a breath of air moving. We clambered into Mr. Godey's spring wagon and were soon rolling past dewy meadows, and my heart was brimming because in a few minutes I would embrace my beloved, and he would not vanish just as my arms enfolded him.

The colonel's camp was bustling as we approached. I saw several fires blooming and knew them to be the separate messes. The colonel always assigned several men to each mess, the meals divided into small companies within the larger one.

But Mr. Godey drove us past the crowd of men, straight toward a small wall tent out beyond the camp, and then drew to a halt.

"The colonel's put you here, madam," Godey said.

We stepped down upon a grassy sward and discovered a small abode with a camp cot and canvas chair.

"He'll send breakfast over directly, and if there's anything you need for your comfort, let me know," Godey said.

"Where's the colonel?"

Godey smiled. "Here, there, everywhere."

"And will he join me for breakfast?"

Godey paused, smiled, and nodded. It seemed no answer at all. He flapped the lines over the rumps of the mules, and the wagon jarred away.

"Land sakes," Kitty said, surveying our austere quarters.

The brightening heaven did at last reveal Colonel Frémont. He was dressed in a gray flannel shirt, black woolen trousers, a blue cotton bandanna about his neck, and a flat-brimmed slouch hat.

He would come to us eventually. I loved watching him. He was compact and lean and lithe, and moved with grace and ease, unlike so many men who seemed barely to command their own bodies. I could hear nothing, for all of this occurred some yards distant, but I could read events even at that distance. I had become an expert at extracting meaning from the way people approached one another at Washington City balls. And now I could see my husband in easy triumph, quietly turning this band of adventurers into a disciplined company that would soon plunge into wilderness, mapping, sketching, observing flora and fauna, studying gradients, finding a way over the spine of the continent.

It was lovely seeing him so alive, not at all broken as he had been. And soon he would welcome me.

CHAPTER FOUR

Benjamin Kern, MD

I was expecting to like Colonel Frémont. My brother Edward had been with the colonel during his third topographical expedition, the one that resulted in the conquest of California. Indeed, Ned played no small role in that affair and commanded Sutter's Fort for a while.

It was Edward who lured me into this adventure with his vivid depictions of the unknown West and his absolute trust in the sublime competence of Frémont. Edward was the artist/cartographer on that trip, who along with the brilliant German topographer Charles Preuss, mapped the unknown continent.

So enticing were his tales that I was seduced. Come along on the next adventure, Edward urged, and so I did, along with my other brother, Richard, also a fine artist. Frémont had no funds to pay us, this new expedition being privately financed, so we outfitted ourselves with all the best wares and agreed to join him at Westport. We would go along for the sheer joy of it and supply Frémont with services as well.

Edward and Richard would provide valuable sketches of unknown country, of great importance for a railroad right-of-way survey; I would bring my surgical tools and skills as a healer.

I was on hand when Frémont and his lovely young wife debarked at Westport Landing, and I watched as the pair were immediately surrounded by admiring colleagues and friends from the previous expeditions. It spoke well of Frémont that many of his old command had signed up for the new one. I noted at once that they addressed him with deference and affection and that he had a quiet and easy way with them—I'd say a natural authority, though in this case his command did not rest on rank but simply on his personal qualities.

I scarcely had the chance to take the measure of the man at Westport but intended to when we reached Boone Creek, because we three Kern brothers were putting our lives and our safety squarely in the hands of this leader. There were certain aspects of his conduct, such as the perilous crossings of the Sierra Nevada in winter and his actions that led to a court-martial for mutiny and disobedience of General Kearny's orders, that invited scrutiny.

The camp itself was actually sprawled over a vast tract of lush Missouri meadow and woodland; it takes considerable pasture to nourish well over a hundred mules and a few horses. So I was curious as to how this celebrated conqueror of the Mexican province would conduct himself. I should not have worried. No sooner had he settled into a small tent at Boone Creek than he was inventorying his equipment and listening to his lieutenants about what needed doing, always in that quiet, civilized manner that seemed to be inbred in the man. Some men are born to command, and he was one.

I knew nothing about expeditions and how they are assembled, so I had the advantage of seeing everything fresh.

I gathered that the mules were a major problem; some large percentage of them were entirely green and required breaking either to saddle or packsaddle. Missouri may be a well-populated state, but it cannot on short notice supply a hundred thirty trained, docile, reliable mules, plus a few horses, especially so late in the year, after countless companies heading for Oregon or Santa Fe had depleted the market.

The mules were largely left to Frémont's old command, plus a few Missourians, who, I gathered, prided themselves in the art of reducing quadrupeds to usefulness. That would be no easy task for this gang of adolescent animals. This enterprise was, I fathomed, under the direction of Charles Taplin, late of the United States Army and a veteran of the California campaign. His able assistants included some Missouri frontiersmen, also veterans, such as Josiah Ferguson, Henry Wise, and Tom Breckenridge. Another pair, Billy Bacon and Ben Beadle, also lent a hand. They were getting some additional help from Elijah Andrews of Saint Louis and Raphael Proue, an older Frenchman. I learned later he was the oldest man in the company. I can scarcely tell an aged Frenchman from a young one.

These worthies had a formidable task: half the mules in the herd had never known a saddle on their backs, and a few were little more than frisky yearlings. The muleteers proceeded, I thought, in a no-nonsense fashion, dealing with each animal according to its nature. If the animal was docile and accepted a halter and didn't struggle against a rope, it was rubbed down, saddled with a folded blanket and a crossbuck, and allowed to absorb the novelty of weight anchored to its back. But if an animal was recalcitrant, it was swiftly thrown to earth by various devices that I marvel at, hobbled, haltered, tied to a snubbing post, and allowed to learn the authority of stout manila. What struck me most as I watched this massive recruitment of animals was that the muleteers devised a method for each mule, reading its nature in its responses to its steady subjugation. The quiet ones advanced easily; the outlaws learned about their future life the hard way. I have come to an admiration for this skill, heretofore unfamiliar to me. I saw some lessons in it for the medical profession.

But there was plenty of other work undertaken at Boone Creek. The voyageurs were expert with all manner of equipment and were inventorying kegs and cases of picks and shovels, axes and rifles and little brown casks of gunpowder and pigs of lead, along with awls and knives and hatchets and coils of rope. All these had to be counted and divided into separate packs. Since several of those on this trip were unpaid volunteers, including the Kern brothers, we looked to our own equipage. We each had good woolen underdrawers and shirts, but we found we lacked stockings and tanned leather to repair or resole boots.

It was a day or two before Colonel Frémont found time to acquaint himself with me, and this happened not at one of the messes, as I had expected, but because he sought me out. I knew exactly what to expect: an assessing gaze, absolute calm, quiet and cultivated voice, and a certain distance.

"I'm pleased you'll be with us, sir," he said. "I always worry about calamities to my men. You'll be a comfort."

"That's all I'll be, I fear. There's not much a man can do out in the wastes. But I can set a bone or amputate. And I have a few powders. I have some cathartics that may ease some distress. Edward says that's a complaint."

"They'll take heart from it."

"And you, sir?"

"I'm fit. Nothing like that ever befalls me. I thrive out there, and the farther I am from settlements, the healthier

I am. I'm fated to prosper in wilderness, so I'll have no need of your services."

There are men like that, and I supposed this one was one. "Will the trip be taxing for someone like me? Or my brothers?"

"A trip is as easy or taxing as one makes it. If you learn your lessons along the way, you'll walk comfortably into California. The secret is to economize everything."

"I'll make a point of it."

"Very good, sir. If you have any difficulties, talk to my second, Alexis Godey."

With that, he drifted away. We had not gotten past the barest acquaintanceship. But of course there would be a whole trip ahead to form friendships. And yet my instinct was that this man had no intimates. Since he arrived, I had seen him address most everyone in that quiet manner but also stay distant from them. Yes, he kept space between himself and his command. His emotions were unreadable. At night he vanished into his own tent, permitting only his man Saunders to enter, and no one saw more of him until the next dawn.

He struck me as a man apart. That was just as true for his old comrades of the California Battalion as it was for newcomers like me. I found myself wondering if the man had ever had friends, men who could be called intimates or confidants, because I saw no sign of it nor did it seem obvious from my cursory examination of his character. In time I rebuked myself for invading his privacy. Whether he had friends or none was not my business. But the puzzle would not leave my mind, and the more I observed Frémont, the more curious I was about him.

I wondered what hold he had on these men. He obviously had some sort of grip on them, and it was plain that his veterans looked up to him. Was it the quietness of his voice?

His civility? Was it something assumed? He expected full obedience to his wishes and received it without cavil. He used no profane language, unlike some of his veterans and his Creoles, who had their own French scatology. That was part of it. He was a gentleman from a powerful American family, and the company knew it. I thought it must be caste. He somehow let them know he belonged to a higher order.

I felt a little useless there. Save for the Kerns, every man had been put to work. Even the California Indian boys, Manuel and Joaquin, who were being returned to their people by Frémont, were assigned tasks such as leading the haltered mules or building fires for the morning and evening messes or scrubbing kettles. I noted with approval that Frémont's freed black servant, Jackson Saunders, was treated exactly the same as the rest, except that Saunders had rather less to do and spent time attending to the colonel's wardrobe.

The camp had the quality of a military bivouac, but there was that notable exception of Mrs. Frémont, sitting quietly before her tent hour after hour, absorbing the autumnal sunlight. The colonel had told us all that she had suffered a great loss en route here and was in fragile health. But he added that she would welcome us and was eager to acquaint herself with every member of the expedition. That seemed to be the case. Young as she was, Mrs. Frémont rarely drifted from her tent and was content to receive members of the expedition, one by one. And at the end of each day, Alexis Godey would harness the mules and take Mrs. Frémont back to her log quarters at Major Cummins's agency. But the Pathfinder never accompanied her. I found myself curious about their relationship and rebuked myself for it.

That seemed excuse enough, and I drifted to her each midday, eager to acquaint myself with the wife of the Pathfinder and the daughter of the most powerful senator in

Washington. I was never disappointed. She mastered my name and vocation instantly and always invited me to join her for tea kept hot on a charcoal brazier. Even without being asked, her maidservant, Kitty, would pour a steaming cup of oolong and present it to me.

"Well, Mrs. Frémont, it appears we'll be on our way in a day or two. And you'll be heading back to Saint Louis?" I asked.

She smiled faintly. "Briefly. I'll take my daughter, Lily, with me on a riverboat to New Orleans, and then to Panama, across the isthmus, and meet the California steamer on the Pacific side. The colonel and I will meet in Yerba Buena, they call it San Francisco now, in the spring."

"That's a perilous trip, madam. The jungle fevers . . ."

"I have never fled from peril and don't intend to start, Doctor."

"Chagres is famous for them. You'll want to move overland as fast as you can. Avoid the swampy places."

"The colonel and I are destined, Doctor. Absolutely destined to meet as planned in that distant land."

"You see little of him here," I said.

For an instant her face clouded, but it took a sharp eye to notice. Which I have. I am insatiably curious about people, and especially these people. "It is my daily pleasure to observe him organizing this enterprise," she said primly. "I marvel at it. How rare is this chance? What woman in similar circumstances may observe a commander and his men? I count myself lucky."

"I'm glad he invited you to come here," I said.

"I invited myself. He was all for saying good-bye in Saint Louis and said my health wouldn't permit something as strenuous as this. I think perhaps he now feels a woman can travel across the isthmus without difficulty." She smiled wryly.

"What awaits you on the Pacific shore?"

"It's like Italy but scarcely settled, he tells me. Have you never yearned to see another world, Doctor?"

"Many times. That's why I'm here. Curiosity is my vice. What's it like to walk across a continent? What's between here and there? What awaits me on the coast? Who on earth would join an expedition like this? Are we all madmen?"

"Then you know the joy of a challenge. We'll be together in California, and we'll head for his estate. He's never seen it. It's called Las Mariposas, The Butterflies. What a lovely name! The consul, Larkin, purchased it, and it wasn't what the colonel wanted but we're stuck with it. It's mostly meadows or foothill forest land, you know. It'll pasture thousands of cattle or sheep. So, we're in the livestock business, it seems. We'll know more when we see it. I'm rather taken with the idea. Perhaps my destiny is milkmaid or goatherd."

"You preferred not to go overland?"

"The colonel wouldn't think of it, sir. He's fully occupied with finding a rail route, and a woman would be in his way."

"Did he fear for your safety?"

"The overland journey will be safer than passage through the jungles of Panama, sir. No, safety was not among his considerations. He did feel it would be inconvenient to be taking a wife and daughter with him." She smiled suddenly. "He says I'd put most of his men to shame."

I wanted to probe further but dared not. For a girl of twenty-four, she was as seasoned and shrewd as someone much older. She had been born into a powerful political family, had entertained presidents and secretaries and all sorts of dignitaries, and she would know instantly if my gentle probing transgressed the bounds of decorum. A pity. I really wanted to find out what sort of man Frémont was, and the truth was that I hadn't the faintest idea. And I suspected that she didn't have the faintest idea, either. I had gotten one thing out of it: he believed he lived under some sort of star and that his fate was not in his hands.

CHAPTER FIVE

Captain Andrew Cathcart

I was heading for Cathay, actually, and thought to shoot a few buffalo en route. When I heard about Frémont's expedition I signed on, thinking to have a sporting holiday. I'd been in the Eleventh Prince Albert Hussars for a decade and grew bloody weary of it, so I sold my commission. I prefer to rove. It's a habit of the Scots.

This chap Frémont, when I looked him over, seemed a thoroughly competent officer who had rambled all over the American West and pocketed California for the Yanks. Still, there were the shadows cast by the man. What sort of officer was it who could get himself in trouble on charges of mutiny, insubordination, and conduct prejudicial to military discipline? The fellow would take some observing, he would.

What I found, when I first met the man in Saint Louis, was a perfectly civilized fellow, mild of manner, who obviously didn't care one way or another whether I joined his party. I saw no rebel in him. Neither was he rigid. In fact, I saw not much of anything when I was sizing him up. It was as if he lived on some distant shore. But I saw nothing to alarm me, either. He had manners, an odd gentleness, and seemed quite at peace. I decided to ramble with the fellow and told him I'd join him at Westport, which I did. The arrangement suited me: I had made no commitment, and neither had he. If I didn't like the way he was commanding his men, I could walk away.

He told me he was going to hunt for a railway route to the coast along the 38th parallel, something his father-in-law ached to see and that some Saint Louis businessmen thought might bring prosperity to that frontier city. That parallel should take a traveler straight to the bay of San Francisco, which those visionaries saw as the Pacific portal of the American republic, but there were a few bumps along the way, according to the scanty charts available, mostly from Mexican sources. He said he knew of a way and was destined to tie the republic together.

I outfitted myself with the best that pound and shilling could buy, because Frémont would not do it. This was a private survey, he had informed me. I didn't mind. I prefer my own kit and gear. I have lived in the field and was not afraid of cold and rain, wind and sun, and misery. Those are a soldier's lot. When we all were settled at Boone Creek I saw no evidence of luxury in Frémont. His gear was as simple as the rest, though he did prize some scientific instruments, half of which I could not fathom. He had the usual sextants and magnetic compasses and thermometers. He also had two chronographs that should give him good longitude readings from the Greenwich Meridian. He was equipped to survey, with a theodolite, quadrant, transit, and Gunter's chain. He had altimeters and barometers. He also had a morocco-leather portfolio of charts and tables. I scarcely grasped the half of what he was carting west, but I knew it would burden a dozen mules. His topographer, Charles Preuss, would be well equipped to map the rail route and all the surrounding country. If Preuss and Frémont didn't know where they were at all times, no one would.

I've known officers to bivouac with wall tents, Brussels carpets, enough ardent spirits to stock a pub, wagons to haul all their truck, camp cots, canvas chairs, and a staff of orderlies and chefs. Frémont showed none of that, and I gave him credit for it. He did have a considerable wardrobe. Some of it was simply his blue uniforms stripped of the marks of rank. He was a button-up man. If he wore a coat, he buttoned it right to the chin. If he wore a flannel shirt, it was buttoned to the neck.

Of course there was the oddity of Frémont's young wife, receiving the men as if she were the Queen herself. She had dark circles under her eyes, and I learned that on board the *Martha* she had lost an infant son. I pitied her but also admired her bravery. She put on a good front before all of us, no matter how she hurt within. Frémont rarely visited her; he seemed much more absorbed with sorting out the gear and putting his mules into service. But I was glad to see the men cosset her; she certainly wasn't getting much attention from her lord and master.

That mule operation I watched closely, drawing from my own years as a cavalry officer. We didn't much truck with mules in Great Britain and took far more time perfecting our mounts, employing a patience acquired over generations. The Yanks' methods were rough but effective, and in a matter of days the green stock had become serviceable and would probably settle into usefulness on the trail. I did see them accidentally lame a mule they had thrown to the earth, so their rough treatment was not without its toll. And I had the sense that some of those mules would prove to be outlaws. Missourians are mean by nature and that only breeds mean livestock.

I volunteered to help, being a cavalryman, but was turned down. It soon became plain that Frémont's old hands, veterans of his previous trips, were a circle unto themselves, and we newcomers were regarded as baggage. That was particularly evident at the messes. His veterans formed their own messes; the rest of us found ourselves thrown together. I could understand it. The veterans knew one another's abilities and limits; the rest of us were jokers in the deck. One thing I did learn, though: those veterans could cook. Any one of them could produce an adequate meal, without scorching the stew or spilling the oatmeal or burning the side pork. I wished we had a few blokes with such skills in the hussars.

One of Frémont's regular chaps, a Mexican War veteran named Lorenzo Vincenthaler, seemed particularly eager to isolate the rest of us, which worried me because he was one of Frémont's obvious favorites.

There were other peculiarities about this company that soon emerged as we prepared to leave. We had an array of specialists of one sort or another with us, and I was hard put to connect this with the practical business of locating a railroad route to the Pacific. Take the German, Frederick Creutzfeldt, for example. He was a paid botanist. Why a financially strapped, commercially funded expedition whose sole purpose was to establish a rail route needed a paid botanist was something that kept tickling my curiosity. Who hired him? Was it Benton, maybe? And for what purpose? Was he looking for coal, or for plants that might have crop value? Assessing timber resources? The more I studied on it, the more likely it seemed to me that this private expedition was to be staffed as closely to the military ones as possible. Here were a renowned topographer, Preuss; an established cartographer and artist, Edward Kern; Creutzfeldt, a botanist; Rohrer, a millwright; and Stepperfeldt, a gunsmith. The Pathfinder intended to explore, and railroad building was merely the scaffold for his larger ambitions. I supposed I'd learn much more on the trail, when men thrown together in wilderness usually discern the truths and realities that are masked in more civilized places.

Meanwhile, I did not at all mind being thrown in with the newcomers. One of our chaps came from Mississippi and had the impossible name of Micajah McGehee. Now how do you pronounce that mouthful? I reduced him to Micah, and he cheerfully accepted it as long as he could call me Cap. He was along entirely for the adventure, as fiddle-footed as I am. So our mess was almost entirely adventurers, save only for Edward Kern, a Frémont veteran. I had the hunch that it was going to be better this way than if we had been roped into the other messes. The Creoles had their own mess, which included the black servants. I took that as a sign of social status here in the States.

By some mysterious process, the company completed its preparations, and on the eve of October 19, 1848, the Pathfinder announced that we would break camp in the morning and travel only a few miles, the purpose being to test our mules and packs and deal with any difficulties. I had supposed we would be at Boone Creek another week or so and was delighted at the prospect of leaving. As usual, Godey drove Mrs. Frémont back to the Delaware agency that evening, and I wondered whether we would be seeing Mrs. Frémont again, at least until we should meet on the Pacific shore. If the colonel and his lady said any private good-byes, these were invisible to the rest of us. He seemed concerned, instead, with assigning saddle mules to each member of his company, trying to gauge which mule best suited which rider.

As Godey drove Mrs. Frémont away, she turned to look at us one last time, her expression obscured by her bonnet. But I knew exactly what passed across her face; it was an inexpressible yearning and a grim determination not to show the slightest feeling. I felt an odd pity. We were her rivals. As for the Pathfinder, he seemed not to notice. And in a few moments, Godey's wagon and its cargo disappeared around a tree-carpeted slope, and I never saw Jessie Benton Frémont again.

I felt just then an acute homesickness. I have felt it often, but those smudges under her eyes set it off in me, a longing for Ayrshire, from whence I came, that I could scarcely endure. For it was there, facing the western sea, that I grew to manhood, and it was the sea that lured me ever westward and was still taking me away from my people. I don't know what makes me roam, what it was about the western seas and the mysteries beyond them that lured me away from my hearth; from the kind and sometimes reproachful eyes of my mother; from the settled world of Ayr, its hardy cattle, its sere slopes and mild winters so gloomy at the time of the solstice that a cheery fire lighting our parlor seemed like heaven. Why had Jessie Benton's departure plunged me into that secret melancholia that I have struggled so long to ignore?

I was suddenly angry at this man Frémont.

We raised camp rather late that morning of the twentieth, coping with the usual difficulties. Some of the greener mules had other notions than to haul our goods. Some of the company proved to be inept at saddling. Others discovered they had too many goods and too little space in panniers and packs. One mule bit a man's finger, and Ben Kern applied a plaster.

We arose before dawn, actually, and completed our morning mess in darkness with a steady breeze chilling us. A simple meal of gruel sufficed, and we soon had our kettles and tin bowls packed away. Frémont wandered freely, at ease, and I never heard a command issue from his lips. His veterans seemed to anticipate what he wanted. An occasional question was all it took for him to make his will known. At least among his old companions of the wilds there was great jubilation, as if this were the beginning of something sweet, a nectar that befell only the most privileged of mortals. I marveled at this.

The break-in trip was not without its mishaps. A girth strap loosened, sending a pack of macaroni and sugar and coffee southward until it hung beneath the quivering beast's legs. But these things were swiftly remedied, and no harm was done. Here on the backs of a hundred-odd mules was grain for the stock, tents, tools, flour for ourselves, rubberized sheets for wet ground, and a myriad of other items too numerous to detail. All those mules were transporting a miniature city as well as thirty-three men heading west into the unknown to look for a place where shining rails might span the midcontinent.

I found mule transportation much to my liking. A mule's gait is dainty compared with the gait of a horse and gives the rider the impression of floating. It was in perfect ease that I spent my hours in the saddle. Mules can be uncommonly stubborn, but mine seemed determined to keep up with the rest, and I had no need to deal with insubordination. I thought that maybe the Queen's hussars ought to weigh the benefits of mule travel.

The five miles proceeded peaceably enough through grassy country under a variable Wedgwood sky, and Frémont called a halt for the day in ample time to inspect the mules for sores on their withers and for the evidences of all sorts of troubles. It had been an easy day's travel, wisely shortened to permit adjustments to the tack and equipment and to break in the mules for what would be a long haul. The hunters, Godey especially, had proceeded ahead of us and left two does and a buck on our path, ensuring us a fine venison dinner that eve. These bloody carcasses had been loaded onto skittish mules, which alarmed them, but eventually our parade resumed.

"Easy trip, eh?" I said to Doctor Kern, who was unloading his truck from a mule.

"No worse for wear," he replied. "I must say, Frémont has a way about him."

That was the very thing that had struck me through the entire day. I had never seen a commander less conspicuous or more effective. I wondered what his secret was. Whatever it was, he induced men to see to their appointed tasks without ever addressing them. It was as if he had a secret finger signal for every whim.

I chose not to raise a shelter, it being mild and with little sign of rain, and settled into my Hudson Bay blankets at some distance from the fire. I did vaguely remember that well into the night a horseman left camp in some hurry, the rapid gait conveying some urgency to me just as I drifted into sleep. I gave it no further thought until morning, when Frémont appeared out of the east, on a worn horse.

He had, it seemed, decided to spend one last hour with Jessie and had returned to Major Cummins's agency well beyond Boone Creek, awakening her and her servant in the small hours. She had welcomed him happily, he said, and had set Kitty to making some tea, and there the lovers whiled away an hour before he saw fit to return to his company.

It had been a cruel night for her, apparently. Cummins had found a wolf den nearby and knocked the pups in the head. When the wolf bitch returned and found her pups gone, she began the most pathetic howling and mewling and whimpering and coaxing the dead to return to her bosom. This dirge did not cease. The forlorn wolf did not surrender her hope but continued through the deeps of the night to lure her pups back to her breast. All of which stirred the most dire melancholy in Mrs. Frémont, who was aware that the major had destroyed the wolf pups. She felt the wolf's suffering within her own bosom, as only a mother who has recently lost a child can do, and so passed a night of torment and sadness, broken by the startling arrival of Frémont.

All of this he told us in his usual offhand way, while we listened silently. His veterans thought all the more of him for his romantic journey back to see his wife and to comfort her in her moment of sadness. My own instincts were otherwise. I wondered why he was telling us about this night passage. Frémont's trip was an attempt to salve his neglect of his wife, and the man was a bastard.

CHAPTER SIX

Henry King

We started west with great ease. The company's outfitting was so perfect that we had no difficulties and proceeded steadily along the Kansas River, making twenty-five or more miles each day across frost-nipped grassland. The whole company was at ease and in the finest of spirits. I could not have been happier myself. Just being with Frémont once again was enough to fill my days with delight. No man ever led a happier band.

Our mules were in good flesh and carried us easily as we progressed across the plains, rarely encountering any serious climb or descent. There was yellowed grass waiting for them at the end of each day, and our skilled muleteers put the mules out on it. We maintained a light but ready guard against thieving Indians but didn't expect trouble.

The timing of this expedition worked out perfectly. I was afraid that Frémont might leave a fortnight earlier, which would have been awkward for me because it would have interrupted or postponed my wedding. But it was all just fine. We married, Beth and I, and I enjoyed a few days in the bosom of hearth and home before I set off for Westport Landing, even as the restlessness in my heart was growing unbearable. I could not, under any circumstances, avoid this trip, which I had fastened on ever since I heard that Colonel Frémont was planning it. I was with him in the California Battalion, rising to captain in an irregular armed force that was composed of the army's topographic corps and civilian Yanks in Mexican California.

There were several veterans of that campaign with us now, the memory of our easy conquest of California glowing in our bosoms. Without half trying, the colonel had welded together the most powerful armed force on the Pacific Coast, drawing on a motley crowd, whether regular soldiers or Bear Flag rebels or settlers. Most of us were irregulars, but it didn't matter. It wasn't only that we took California with ease; it was that we had such a good time doing it and achieved it without much cost in blood. We were a terror, bearded men in buckskins, and I never forgot it.

I was eager to renew an old friendship. Charles Taplin had been with Frémont during the conquest, rising to captain in the colonel's irregular army. We had been through the whole campaign together. I spurred my mule forward to catch up with him. Fortunately, our mules were gaited much the same. It is next to impossible to conduct a conversation when two beasts have different gaits and one or another rider must always rein in or spur forward.

"Ah, Henry, I was hoping you might join me," Taplin said.

"This brings back the old days for sure," I replied.

He smiled wryly at me. "And you abandoned a wife for it?"

"She can wait," I said.

"I don't know that I would abandon a wife after just a fortnight."

"She's the picture of domesticity," I returned, enjoying his needling. "She's especially skilled at mending my socks. But her cooking is still wanting."

"Probably an improvement on the cooking around our campfires," he replied.

"No, sir. I don't think any woman can achieve the perfection of good cow buffalo hump, nicely blackened on the outside, or buffalo tongue, well roasted on the outside and pink within."

"I take it you're not done with adventure, Henry. I'm done with it. I'm going to settle in California. I was greatly smitten by the climate. It's like living in perpetual springtime. When I resigned my commission, I had in mind heading west. This seemed the way to do it." He touched heels to the mule, evoking a slight spurt before the sullen animal settled back to its indolent walk. "I should like to find a Californio lady. It strikes me that a diet of chili peppers yields a hot nature in them." He eyed me again. "But of course, that doesn't interest you."

I laughed. I was not going to let Captain Taplin make me the butt of this company's humor the entire trip. A bridegroom was considered exotic in this crowd.

"I love this country," I said earnestly. It stretched ahead to a distant brown horizon lost in fall haze, mile upon mile, with naught but wind and sun and cured yellow grasses. This time we would climb over the roof of the continent and make our way to the far coast again. It was that ridgepole part of it that excited me. The colonel could inspire his men to achieve anything, summer or winter, desert or mountain.

"An improvement over the fair sex," Taplin agreed.

He was not going to let go of it, so I simply grinned at him. Silence was the best reply I could offer. I knew then and there that I was going to hear about this the entire journey, and the day we topped the Sierra Nevada and beheld California, they would still be asking whether this was an improvement on Beth. The joke was going to be on Captain Taplin, once he discovered that those chili peppers he yearned for were volcanic in more ways than one.

Even as we rode, I saw Frémont's veterans taking their ease, enjoying the trip while the greenhorns were struggling, sore in their saddles and worn out by the middle of the day. I supposed they would harden eventually, and then life would become easier for them. I didn't know what a botanist was doing on a railroad survey, but maybe the colonel wanted to achieve the very thing he accomplished the previous times as an army officer, making a major contribution to science. He always had his eye on the public, like a man planning to run for president. A few more laurels wouldn't hurt. Still, since this was an underfinanced commercial expedition, I didn't quite fathom it. Every businessman I'm acquainted with wants to cut unnecessary expense, and here we had an odd German named Cruetzfeldt with us whose task was to pluck flowers. I supposed he didn't leave a new wife behind. That sort of man never marries.

I could understand Preuss. He was along on the previous trips, doing his mapmaking and reading the instruments and furiously writing notes, pretending not to enjoy himself. The man wouldn't smile. It always ended up a sneer or a grimace. I always wondered what he put in his diaries. If you're going to run a railroad, you need a map and some topographic knowledge, what kind of grades you'll be facing, things like that, and that's what he supplied. And I could understand Ned Kern, too. He was with us in California. He could sketch, and a railroad needs to have drawings of the terrain if it's going to run a line through it. I supposed I could even understand Kern's brother Benjamin. A doctor is handy to set a bone or fix a mule, but he'll not be doctoring the veterans. Only the newcomers will get snake bit or fall off cliffs or get kicked by a mule.

Some of us weren't getting paid, and I didn't know if that's because the colonel was laying out fancy salaries for these newcomers. Some things about this trip didn't make much sense, and one of them was the whole idea of a railroad to the coast. Who needed it? It would be a lot of rail to nowhere. Where were the customers? This railroad would pierce through two thousand miles of wilderness, buffalo, Indians, and mountains, with scarcely a settlement along the way. I thought the colonel was doing this trip at the behest of his father-in-law, who had the power and money and also a dream about a railroad. It would have made more sense to push it south or north of here, but I have never underestimated the power of politics. Old Senator Benton called it the middle route and believed it made more sense than one farther north or south. Actually, it was simply a ploy to bring trade to Saint Louis.

Four days out we ran into a prairie fire, a wall of smoke rising from a lick of orange flame from south to north, and managed to get through, our keg of powder and all, without getting ourselves blown up or scorched. The grass was high, which didn't help. It was odd, because we'd had some rain off and on. But that day we made twenty-five miles and camped in a little valley with good grass. The next day we made twenty-eight miles and stopped at the Potawatomi Mission. We got some butter from the agent, a bloodsucker named Major Monday, and spent the rest of the evening looking over the Pott Indians, just as they looked us over. We put an extra guard on, but these Indians were tame enough.

We were getting into buffalo country by then, and we would see how the greenhorns could shoot. When you have buffalo, you also have wild Indians; the two are wedded together so tight that if one vanishes, the other will too. We were going to have plenty to eat, good hump meat or tongue at the messes. But I expected all that to disappear when we hit the mountains. There would be deer and elk up there, not the big shaggies.

The colonel said he'd follow the Smoky Hill branch and then cut down to the Arkansas River and stop at Bent's Fort, where he hoped we could improve our livestock. We had a few laggards and one or two half-lame, and maybe we could trade them off, along with the horses, which are no good in high country because they panic.

There was one thing I was noticing and that was the cold. The wind was tough on some of us, and we weren't seeing much sun, either. The pools froze up at night. No one was complaining. The cold was better than summer heat and horseflies. I didn't mind the cold so much, but the wind got mean and there was nothing here to slow it. There was hardly a tree between here and the British possessions.

I heard some shots, and pretty soon Godey came back to us. He had been ahead, hunting, and shot some buffalo bulls. I didn't look forward to the meat. Bulls are tough and sometimes stringy and not good for much except some stewing if you've got the time to boil the meat senseless. But at least we were getting into buffalo country, and we'd have us a cow or two now. Still, it would be entertaining to see how the greenhorns dealt with some bull meat, so I decided to join their mess.

That was morning, and it was up to each mess to hack meat for supper, so I kept one eye on the greenhorns. It was a sight, alright. Chopping meat out of an old bull was about like sawing the trunk off an elephant. Ned Kern knew enough, but his brothers didn't, and the rest had never seen one and hardly knew where to begin. But Ned began slicing into the hump, and it took a deal of work even to open up a hole. Not even the surgeon was doing much good. Of course the rest of the messes had gone for the tongues; not much else worth putting into a cook pot. By the time the greenhorns got enough meat for supper, they had put hatchets and an axe to the task and were plumb worn out. I could hardly wait for supper, when they would get another lesson.

That eve we camped in the shelter of a clay cliff beside Smoky Hill, and a few of Frémont's veterans lent a hand to the greenhorns, getting a big fire going and getting that sawed-up meat on green sticks to broil on the lee side of the flames. I think the doctor, Ben Kern, figured it out long before they began to chomp on those slabs of shoe leather they were about to down for dinner. When the moment came, he tackled one or two bites of the brown ruin on his tin plate, sighed, and gave up.

He never complained; I'll give him credit, but McGehee was whining.

"Fat cow's what we want," I said to the doctor.

"The other messes have tongue. I think I'll remember that."

"Say, whiles I'm here, do you have powders for anyone bound up?"

"Salts, yes, purgatives. I have ample."

"That's good. I get bound up on buffalo. Sometimes we go a week without seeing a green, and then it's misery."

"See me, Mister King."

"I guess a doctor's worth something after all," I said.

A faint smile spread across his face. "I have my instruments. If you break a leg, I can amputate. A saw cuts right through bone, and I imagine your leg would be a good bit more tender than this old bull." He was smiling blandly, obviously enjoying himself.

"I'm a young bull, alright."

"Watch your tongue," he retorted.

I had to admire the doc; he had some wit.

It was getting colder than I wanted. The wind smelled like December. It had a whiff of the Arctic in it. But the chill was nothing compared with the sheer pleasure in being hundreds of miles from the nearest shelter. That was the plains for you. A norther could blow out of the north and there was nothing to slow it down, and sometimes it plowed clear into Mexico.

We set off the next day in cold weather, a mean wind adding to our misery. I thought that pretty soon we'd hear some whining, but the greenhorns didn't emit a peep, and we made our grim way west through an increasingly arid country, broken now by gullies and slopes but utterly treeless. Ere long we'd be using buffalo chips for fuel.

The colonel seemed oblivious to the lancing wind and everything else and simply led us along a route that he did not share with us, content to let nature supply us. And it did. Godey shot a cow, and we feasted on good hump meat, plenty fat, and this time the greenhorns got a taste of prime buffalo meat. It made an impression on them, for sure. The whole trip, Frémont had scarcely given a command, and the slightest suggestion was all it took to remedy or achieve anything he wished. I didn't know, and probably will never know, what the man's hold was on others.

The Delawares left us the next morning. They had agreed to accompany us a way but didn't want to tangle with some of the tribes we were facing ahead. The colonel continued up the Smoky Hill fork for the next days. These were exposed stretches, with a howling wind that burrowed into a man's clothing and chilled him fast. The temperatures were mostly in the twenties and thirties, but it felt worse. There wasn't a tree in sight most of the time, nothing to break the gale that whipped through our straggling party.

Despite good cured shortgrass, some of the mules were weakening, and I wondered whether the colonel was aware of it. He wasn't stopping to let them recruit. Sometimes one day on good grass is all they need. But the colonel plunged on, through increasingly barren country, in weather that did nothing to lift the mood of the company. If the greenhorns needed hardening, they were getting it sooner than expected.

At least there were buffalo. For some reason, our hunters continued to drop bulls instead of good cows, but we made do with tongues and boiled bull stew, at least when we could find enough deadwood to build fires. There were places where the plains stretched to infinity and not one tree was visible. The messes were fed with some antelope and even some coon meat the hunters felled here and there, but the staple was bull meat, boiled until it surrendered.

Then one day Frémont turned us south, and we headed over a tableland that divided the drainages of the Missouri and Arkansas and plunged into a lonely sea of shortgrass that probably would take us to the Arkansas some hard distance away. But the winds never quit, and now they brought bursts of pellet snow, which settled whitely on the ground and on the packs, shoulders, and caps of our men. It was early and wouldn't last, but it was snow and it brought on chill winds that never quit and drove me half-mad. I just wanted to find a hollow somewhere, an overhang, a cozy place where that fingering wind didn't probe and poke and madden me. For the first time, I began to wonder about this trip. It made no sense at all to travel this time of year.

The colonel didn't seem to notice the cold or the wind. He rode without gloves and didn't hunch down in his saddle the way most of the men were hunched, trying to rebuff the cruel wind. I wondered what sort of god-man Frémont was, riding like that, as if he was unaware of the suffering around him, unaware that others were numb and miserable.

But he didn't choose to see what I was seeing. He had no eyes for the hunched-up mules that stopped eating and put their butts to the wind and hung their heads low. We sheltered where we could, sometimes under a cutbank, other times in a gulch, but it didn't help much. The wind always found us. The wind found everyone except Colonel Frémont. I swear, the wind quit dead when it came to him; I swear he rode in an envelope of calm warm air, never knowing what other men, mules, and horses were going through.

CHAPTER SEVEN

John Charles Frémont

We reached the valley of the Arkansas River in perfect ease, and I was satisfied that the exploration would proceed without difficulty. My outfitting had never been better despite limited funds, and we were proof against the worst that nature could throw at us. We entered the wide sagebrush-covered valley and found it largely denuded of trees on its north bank, so we crossed at a good gravel ford and then the travel was more comfortable and there were ample willow and hackberry and cottonwood to feed our fires and build our shelters. The road was excellent, not so churned up as it is on the north bank, where the Santa Fe trade had wrought quagmires.

I was satisfied that we had located a good rail route across the prairies, and Charles Preuss was, too. I trusted the man, dour as he may be, simply because he drafted excellent maps and kept unimpeachable logs during my first two explorations. His readings, both at high noon and of the polestar at night, were finer than any before attempted, and he could tell me within a few feet how high we were above the sea. Now he was daily advising me about how far we wandered from the 38th parallel. He had a certain irony in his eye, knowing full well that by all Hispanic accounts there is no practicable route over the Rockies at this latitude or even anywhere close by. South Pass on the Oregon Road offers an excellent route along the 40th parallel and is much used now by the Oregon bound. And of course, the Sangre de Cristos peter out off to the south, offering unimpeded passage west. But we had been commissioned by men who want to run rails straight over the top, so we would find a route for them, even if it meant turning high mountain saddles into benign passes and impossible chasms into placid valleys.

The visionaries in Saint Louis thought there might be a practical route and had set me to find it. Preuss just shook his head, an ironic gleam in his eye, saying nothing and yet telling me everything on his mind with little more than an arched eyebrow. I tended, privately, to agree with him but could not confess it publicly, nor did I wish to refute my father-in-law or bring him bad news. Better to find a route of some sort and let them decide whether it will break the United States Treasury or bankrupt all the merchants of Saint Louis to build it. In any case, it is my fate to achieve the impossible. I have known all my life that I am destined to do what other men cannot do. It is out of my hands. If it is my fate to find a new route west, through the middle of the continent, then it will happen no matter what I may choose to do.

No sooner had we reached the south bank of the Arkansas than we ran into an encampment of Kiowas, old Chief Little Mound's people. Their tawny lodges were scattered through cottonwood groves. They seemed entirely friendly, and I saw little menace in them. And some of them were handsome, which pleased me, for I take them to be a noble race. But I did halt my company and let them know that I had the utmost respect for Indians, and I required that all my men treat the savages with kindness and discernment. Of course I doubled the guard, not wanting my mule herd stolen.

They seemed an impoverished people, and I imagine they were verminous. Certainly they were unwashed. They mostly stood beside our trail, examining us one by one as we rode past. Who knows what thoughts were festering in their heads? When we camped that eve, there they were, collected silently around our perimeter looking for something to lift when we were occupied with other things. I brought few trade items because trade was not our business, which meant I could engage in little commerce with those people. And now I wished I had a few gewgaws.

But, oddly, Doctor Kern came to the rescue. They found out that he was a medicine man and were soon seeking him out. Godey and other of my veteran Creoles are pretty good sign talkers, and so the consultations proceeded. Kern hung out his shingle, examined the patients, and prescribed from his cabinet. In one case he compounded salves for some skin lesions. The Kiowas watched the compounding with wonder and took away these ointments as if they were gold. That made Ben Kern a very popular man among the Kiowas. The good doctor told me later that many of the Kiowas were flea plagued and he dreaded any contact with them because fleas are hard to get rid of.

The next days we traveled with the Kiowas, who were our constant companions, all of them curious about our ways and observing our every act. Apart from losing a saddle blanket, we suffered no losses, but it took constant vigilance to keep what was ours. I was especially zealous in protecting my instruments, which we needed to measure latitude and longitude as well as elevations and temperatures. We had several instruments whose sole purpose was to give us an altitude above sea level. The mercury barometer was the simplest, but it was variable in its results because of shifting air pressures. It was a fragile device, a thirty-inch glass tube partly filled with quicksilver, and we took special care of it. So I put these things under guard at all times and kept the mules under watch.

We had lost several mules en route, and I intended not to lose more. It was a puzzle. None of our stock was so heavily loaded as to give out, and all fed themselves nightly on the nourishing grasses that stretch endlessly in every direction, and yet some of our animals faltered, stumbled to earth, and would go no farther. I ascribe this to bad blood. There is bad blood in human beings and bad blood in animals, and the weak are constantly being culled out, both by nature and by man. I see even in my company some bad blood, men whose weakness will tell on them. I have good blood, and passage through hard country is as easy for me as a stroll down Pennsylvania Avenue in Washington City is for my father-in-law. I can't help those who cannot help themselves, and if any feel foreboding about our passage across the mountains, I hope they will withdraw from the company and not wait until they become a burden and liability.

We were well supplied with meat. Godey and several others are expert hunters and discovered a few buffalo in most every ravine, taking refuge from the wind. One could wish that we could feast on cows, but that was not to be our fortune this trip. We ate bulls. There was always ample meat for us and plenty to give to the Kiowas, who were tagging along with us. It seemed a good way to preserve a tenuous peace, but the constant presence of these half-starved people did not elevate the mood of my company. It didn't help either that it snowed off and on and that the thermometer swung wildly up and down. Give us a southerly wind and we rode in comfort; give us a northerly one and the weaker men in my company wrapped themselves in their blankets and grumbled.

The farther upstream we progressed, the more excited the Kiowas became, and I could not fathom what was exciting them until we arrived at a large camp of Arapahos, and among them was my old friend Tom Fitzpatrick, Indian agent for these southern plains tribes. He was in the midst of a great gifting of the tribes, a peacemaking process intended to secure their friendship. Major Fitzpatrick (all agents receive that honorary rank) was well known to me as Broken Hand Fitzpatrick, a veteran of the fur trade, a mountaineer without equal, a man who had survived numerous scrapes involving Indians, weather, animals, starvation, and cold. Indeed, he had been a part of my company on the second expedition when we made a winter foray over the Sierra Nevada into California, refurbished our company at Sutter's Fort, and returned to Saint Louis unscathed except for one small loss. He had done his work without complaint, constantly using his experience and skills to help the distressed.

Were he not employed by the government as agent, I would have approached him about the prospect of guiding us over the mountains ahead. But that was not a possibility, especially since my party had no official status and I had no way to loosen him from his duties. I thought to ask him who, in his opinion, would be the ideal man to guide us over the mountains lying to the west. If anyone would know, he would. But whether or not I could find a guide familiar with the country, I never doubted that I would succeed. I knew my fate, and I knew I would reach California no matter what lay ahead.

We had clearly arrived on the eve of a powwow of some

sort. There were smoke-blackened lodges scattered through the bottoms, amply supplied with firewood from the groves of hackberry and cottonwood scattered across the valley. Some of the lodges had gaudy medicine art painted on them. Fitzpatrick, and an assistant who was probably a breed of some sort, had a wagon loaded with gifts from Uncle Sam, which after some treating with these chiefs and subchiefs would be dispensed. There would be something or other for every lodge. These were simply bribes. Don't attack white men and stay at peace, and your father in Washington will give you these things. A blustery wind blew through the valley, scarcely broken by the copses of trees. I smelled snow on the breezes.

Major Fitzpatrick recognized me at once as we rode through the loose-knit campground, and he waited patiently. I was glad we were not in blue uniforms, which might have upset the tribesmen. Plainly, the lot of us were ordinary citizens. We seemed a larger force than we were because of the hundred thirty mules and a few horses, most of them bearing our provisions neatly stowed in the reinforced duckcloth panniers I prefer for mountain travel. The major eyed us knowingly, perhaps even recognizing a man or two, especially the Creoles.

"Colonel Frémont, I believe?"

"So it's you, Tom," I said. "I see you're busy."

"Oh, not so busy that we can't delay matters. I heard you were coming. Moccasin telegraph."

"Then you know about our mission."

"I do."

The response was so abrupt that I eyed the man sharply, aware that this was not the usual effusive greeting of this veteran of the mountains. Fitzpatrick had made his name in the beaver trade and had been a partner in some of those companies. He had guided me on my second venture into

Oregon and California. Indeed, he was with me at the time of one of my most celebrated moments, a December crossing of the Sierra Nevada that we attempted, with great success, even though the local Indians warned against it. Broken Hand Fitzpatrick had roamed across the West, but from that trip with me he acquired a knowledge of country previously unknown to him, and I fancy he appreciated it. Now he was an experienced Indian agent.

"Railroad survey, thirty-eighth parallel."

"It's rather late in the season," he said.

"That's the object. Trains run year around."

"But summer's the time to look for a route."

"I do things my way, Major."

He nodded and motioned me off my roan. My company was drawing up, studying the Kiowas and Arapahos, tribes that were not exactly friends in other circumstances. The Indians were wrapped in bright striped blankets and brown buffalo robes, and sometimes their breaths were visible. The major himself had a buffalo-hide coat wrapped around him and a heavy scarf at his neck.

I dismounted and shook, careful to grasp his undamaged hand, and I clasped it awkwardly. The hand was cold.

Fitzpatrick introduced me to the assembled headmen, using tongue and hand signs I could not follow. The chiefs stood gravely, acknowledging our presence with a nod.

"This isn't the best time to visit with you, actually," the major said. "But I tell you what. Tomorrow we'll be through here and heading for Bent's Fort. I suppose you'll lay over for a time?"

"We will, sir. I want to do some trading."

"There's not much in the place. It's late in the year."

He was saying that the Santa Fe wagon companies had depleted the fort's stock of goods, but I had hope of improving my stores anyway.

"We're well provisioned, except for stock," I said.

He smiled wryly, his gaze on our herd.

"I tell you what, sir. I'll see ye at the fort before sundown tomorrow, and we'll palaver. Just now, you see, I have a deal of work. We're going to powwow, and I'm going to hand out peace medallions, a few muskets, some powder and lead, some red blankets for the blanket chiefs, lots of knives and awls and trade beads, and five hundred plugs of tobacco. And for that we want friendly treatment for the wagon companies. Now I'll see ye off."

This interview was more abrupt than I had hoped, but we would have a time to talk things over on the morrow.

"Very well, Major. Until tomorrow, then."

"Oh, and by the way, Colonel. When ye get beyond the trees yonder, ye'll have your first view of the western mountains."

"I'll tell the men."

"They stretch like a white line across the western horizon. A lot of snow, sir, this early in the season. I'm told that no one has seen the like." He stared evenly at me.

"It's nothing I am worrying about, Major."

"Nothing to worry about, then." He lifted his beaver hat, smiled, and waited while I boarded the horse I hoped to trade for a mule at Bent's Fort.

I signaled my company, and we rode west once again, while several hundred bronze faces observed our every move. Pretty soon we passed through the entire encampment and found only a few squaws beyond, collecting firewood. And then we were free.

Alex Godey rode up and joined me at the van. The column had assembled behind us and was snaking its way up the valley along a trail hemmed by the silvery sagebrush that grew rampant in the area.

"Did Major Fitzpatrick have any news, Colonel?"

"No, but we're going to have a good talk at the fort tomorrow evening."

"He was busy."

"He was something more, which I intend to get to the bottom of. He did not seem eager to see us. Oh, and he did make a point of something. There's a lot of snow ahead. More than anyone's ever seen this early. It seemed important to him. It doesn't worry me, but it troubled him."

"Alors, he's a man to listen to," Godey said.

"If I'd listened to every caution well-meaning but timid men offered me, I'd not be here now, leading my own expedition. I'd not be known."

"Ah, bien, sir, but you have the lives of many men to think about now."

"They have signed on voluntarily, and I will see them through, Alex. Now that you've raised that subject, I am hoping that the fainthearted will abandon us before we begin the ascent into the mountains. In fact, I plan to invite them to do it."

Godey smiled. "I doubt that anyone will, sir. They have their eyes on the history books, eh?"

"Well, I don't. What the world thinks of me is of no consequence to me. What I think of myself is all that matters."

We rode silently, following a river trail that gradually rose from the valley to the open plains. And there, when we topped out on the plains, lay a white wall far to the west, a brooding blue and white rampart barring our way.

CHAPTER EIGHT

Thomas Fitzpatrick

I am not very good at concealing my private opinions, but when it comes to John Frémont I make the effort. He is well connected. He is also a national hero, idolized everywhere for his contributions as an explorer and as the conqueror of Mexican California. It behooves me to keep my silence, especially because his father-in-law is the most powerful man in the Senate and can do me mischief.

Indian agents serve at the whim of presidents and with the consent of the Senate, and an agent's security rests on the most precarious of platforms. So is the case with me. I happen to like my office. I am at ease with the Indians, many of whom I know well and count as friends. I am able to mediate the conflicts rising between the advancing tide of white men and the tribes, and so far, at least, I have preserved the peace and made allies and friends of these people. I think a less-experienced man in my office would cause mischief.

All of which is my way of saying that when Frémont showed up with yet another exploring company and a large mule herd, I chose to conceal whatever lay within my bosom and deal with the man as best I could.

My own views were formed during the second expedition, the one in which he first invaded Mexican California. I was a well-paid guide on that one, along with Carson. Frémont's instructions were to proceed out the Oregon Trail, mapping it thoroughly, and then link up with Naval Lieutenant Wilkes on the Pacific Coast, in order to link the two explorations by land and by sea. Those were his instructions and what I thought I had contracted to do. He did as much but then struck south from the Oregon country, contrary to any army instruction but probably with the connivance of Senator Benton, until he came to the eastern flank of the Sierra Nevada. Then, on January 18, 1843, he attempted a winter passage of the Sierra Nevada, a course so reckless that he narrowly averted disaster. He managed to invade Mexico without leave of their authorities, risking an international incident, and eventually refitted at Sutter's Fort on the Sacramento River. From there it was a relatively easy journey home. Never did the man have a more reluctant guide than I, and I count myself lucky to survive a winter passage of the Sierra Nevada. I was duty bound to complete my contract with him, and I did. But I never again permitted myself to be engaged by him.

It was all portrayed in his subsequent report as a triumph, and the perils he exposed us to were blandly bridged with cheerful rhetoric. I knew better.

Even by the time he reappeared in my life, that November of 1848, I still remembered the starved, cold, miserable, and desperate hours high in the Sierra Nevada, in the dead of winter, in which our lives depended not on Frémont but the merciful cessation of the storms constantly rolling in. We were spared from the man's folly by a random turn of weather, but at terrible cost in terms of the ruin of men and animals. I believe that the miraculous respite in the weather only strengthened his belief that he is fated to succeed at whatever he does.

After we had topped the Sierra Nevada and were heading into mild California more or less unchastened, I chanced to remark to him that we had been extremely lucky that the weather held.

"It wasn't luck; it was destiny," he replied.

That alarmed me then, and it still does.

But how could one find fault with a brave national hero? His journals were published by the government itself and became the guidebooks of westward expansion, and the young topographic commander became a celebrated and rising man. But I would never celebrate him. Ever since that journey, I knew I was living on borrowed time.

And there he was once again, wandering into my powwow, as powerful and protected in 1848 as he had been in 1843, despite the court-martial and conviction on all counts and his resignation from the army. Standing behind him were the most powerful men in Washington City.

I am not very good at hiding what lies within me, but I put a good face on it and welcomed him. There is no man alive who is more obsessed with the opinion of others. Frémont looks into the eyes of others not to see what others are about but to see what is mirrored back to him. And so it was with me. We met there, at the hour of my council, and he was not so much interested in me or the tribesmen but in my view of him. I had not seen him in the intervening years, and he was eager to fathom my perception of him. I fear I did not conceal my private thoughts adequately.

If I was a bit chilly, I don't doubt that he registered it instantly.

However the case, I reluctantly agreed to see him at Bent's Fort as soon as I was done with the Indians. If he was still unsure about my approbation, he would not be unsure when we had finished there. I concluded my business with the Kiowas and Arapahos and started to the fort with my hired boy, Tito, and the empty wagon, from which I had distributed a goodly number of muskets, blankets, knives, awls, and trinkets, along with peace medallions.

The unsettled weather turned into yet another snow that evening, and we rode the wagon through six or seven inches of fresh white powder. That was an uncommon thing so early in the season on the southern plains. But maybe it could be used to promote some prudence in the Pathfinder. I would try, both for his sake and mine—or rather, for the sake of those men he was about to put in harm's way. Even as the tribes dispersed, going off to hunt buffalo and settle into wooded river bottoms for the winter, so did we ride wearily west along the sage-carpeted valley, well bundled against bitter winds. It was my hope that these very winds might impress themselves on the explorer, but I somehow knew they would do just the opposite. The promise of adversity was the siren song in John Charles Frémont's bosom, and that was how it would play out.

Two miles east of the fort and south of the river, I spotted their camp, located in the shelter of trees. Three campfires glowed. Frémont had chosen a good place, and judging from the messes he was keeping nearly all of his men there to guard the mules and supplies, which was wise. In the early twilight, the orange fires wavered through the spidery screen of brush, under a cast-iron sky. The adobe fort with its generous fireplaces would be a good place to stay this wintry night, and I welcomed it.

We raised the post as we rounded a low shoulder. The tan adobe rectangle on the north bank welcomed me with its promise of warmth and safety. That's what civilization was about. There were never-used bastions and a portcullis leading into a yard surrounded by warehouse and living quarters. Since the twenties, it had served as a great entrepôt on the Santa Fe route as well as the depot where southern tribes traded thousands of robes and tongues for blankets and pots and arrowheads and knives and sweets. As lavender twilight engulfed us, we could see that the post was worn and ill kempt. It had seen its day but still was the great comfort of the southern plains. Where else was there so much as a roof? or safety?

Frémont was waiting for us, standing alone in the yard. Whatever passed between us would be unknown to his company, I supposed. That was fine. Tito looked to the four mules and harness, and I stepped down to the clay yard wearily. I was not so young as I used to be, and a life outdoors had settled rheumatism in my bones. Still, I was far from the grave, or so I supposed.

The place seemed oddly empty; the post was ill manned now, almost as if the Bents had lost interest in it. And that pretty well summed it up. Charles Bent, governor of New Mexico, was murdered in a Taos uprising in early 1847; his brother, William, didn't much care about his great post anymore and had let it deteriorate. Maybe it was only age filtering through William, just as it had filtered through me.

The Pathfinder greeted me cordially, and I motioned him to the billiard room upstairs, a sort of observatory that once was filled with good company but now stood silent and gloomy. The place was William's stroke of genius. He had a billiard table hauled clear out the Santa Fe trail and put in there, and then added plenty of Taos Lightning and some imported beer, and for a few bright years that upstairs billiard room and its crowds of rowdies and drifters and mountaineers and hunters and tradesmen were the center of the whole universe.

We ascended creaking wooden stairs, trekked around the fort's perimeter, and then entered the chill room, protected from the wind by tight shutters. The billiard table was gone but some chairs, remnants of more hospitable times, remained.

"I've been wanting to talk to you, Tom," he said while I laid a piñon fire and lit it with a lucifer. The kindling caught, and small yellow flames began to lick to sticks of wood. The room would warm soon. "This is my good fortune. You're the one man here who knows this country. I tell you, Tom, out there's the future of the country, the road to Cathay."

"Well, I have in mind some talking," I replied. "Let me show you something."

I threw open the shutters on the west side, exposing a twilight panorama that embraced vast distances. Off to the west, lit by a blue band over the horizon, the remnant of the day's light, rose the Rocky Mountain front, a stern white wall as far north and south as the eye could see.

"That's where you're going?" I asked.

"Straight west, as close to this latitude as I can manage."

"You see any notch or gap ahead?"

"Well, those Wet Mountains are no great obstacle. It's the ones beyond that might give me some trouble. We'll be hunting for a good pass. All I need from you is some direction. You've been through there. Where can you take wagons? If I can find a wagon road, I can find a road for steam cars."

"There might be a wagon road. I don't know the country as well as Uncle Dick Wootton. He's a hunter here, and, if anyone can steer you across those mountains, he can. But that's not what I want to talk to you about."

Frémont had already guessed my mission, and his wry amusement was a dismissal even before I plunged in. But I would anyway. I would because lives were at stake. I had been with this man through a January crossing of the Sierra. One small change in weather would have destroyed Frémont, his topographic corps, Kit Carson, and me.

"Worst snow in memory," I said. "No one here's seen anything to match it."

"All the better. If I can negotiate a route through the roughest winter known, then there'll be no argument about it back east."

"Is that what they say back there?"

"Well, not exactly. They say that we need a practicable route. I'll give them one."

"You plan to find coal or timber this time of year? Steam engines need fuel and water."

"I'll find the route, grades that steam locomotives can handle, and worry about that some other time."

"You want to locate a route that might be under twenty feet of snow now? Where you can't see the true bottom or whether it's rock or marsh or talus?"

His wry amusement was all the answer I would get. But I pursued it.

"What can you report? That you've found passage to the Pacific but haven't seen the terrain itself because it's under drifts?"

"I'm not concerned about that. We can use poles to measure snowpack and terrain."

"And you expect to find coal seams in the dead of winter?"

"I'm not concerned about fuel in the mountains."

"Well, what do you expect to report?"

"That there is, or there isn't, a way west on the thirty-eighth parallel."

"So you're going to look just where the Rockies are highest and widest?"

"All the better, wouldn't you say, Tom?"

"And the most lethal?"

"There's not a man on earth who would attempt what I am attempting."

There it was, and it didn't surprise me. This wasn't about finding a rail route.

"There's a way around the Sangre de Cristos below Santa Fe," I said. "There's South Pass on the Oregon Trail. Neither of them would cost much compared with laying rail over trestles and gulches and rivers and canyons out there." I waved a hand westward.

"I told my backers I would do it."

The billiard room had heated well now and recovered some of the cheer it possessed back when Bent's Fort was a great oasis and men from all over the West collected right there in that room to share a cup, tell yarns, exchange vital information, and plot out great enterprises. The great stone and adobe hearth threw light and cheer into this haven, and with every degree of additional warmth Frémont's determination expanded. He wanted to achieve the unheard of.

"It's not the railroad, it's the challenge, isn't it?"

"What do you mean, Tom?"

"I mean that even if you succeed in getting over the top, three tops actually, in snows and weather like this, you still won't give them a rail route along the thirty-eighth parallel."

He shrugged. "I'm on my way to California. Jessie's probably headed for Panama now. We're going to meet in Yerba Buena on the big bay out there. I've got some property to look at, and this is the way to get there."

"What's beyond the San Juans?" I asked.

"I imagine we'll find out," he said.

"Well, let's see now, Colonel. You make it to the valley of the Rio del Norte after scaling two ranges in winter, and the first thing you'll hit is sand dunes, dunes everywhere. And if you continue, you'll cross miles of barren land without a tree for firewood. There'll be snow. And when you cross that, assuming you still have your company, you'll face maybe the roughest country in the region, and all of it under the worst snow in memory. It's no place for a railroad.

I don't think a transcontinental railroad will ever be built there."

"You know it well enough to say that?"

I hesitated. "Not well enough. But there's a man who does, and he's around here. That's Richens Wootton. He's run wagons up in there. He told me once there's a place he calls Cochetopa Pass that takes a man across a northern corner of the San Juans. You have to know where to turn off from the Rio del Norte, some stream called the Saguache, a tributary of the Rio. You find that, maybe you have a route in summer. In summer, John."

"And winter," Frémont said.

"You won't find it without a guide. I've been in those mountains, and I can pretty well tell you, one creek looks like any other, and one peak like another, and that's in the summer. It'll be worse when everything is white."

"But Wootton knows?"

"I don't know of any other. He's hunting meat for Bent, but he pretty much steers his own course."

"I want to talk to him."

"The kitchen, I suppose," I said.

"You lead the way," he said.

"I wish I weren't," I replied.

CHAPTER NINE

John Charles Frémont

We made our way down the stairs, the treads hollow under our boots, and into the vacant yard. Bent's Fort had an eerie silence about it. The great doors had not been shut for the night, and I wondered whether they would be.

"Where's Bent?" I asked Major Fitzpatrick.

"Who knows? Probably with the Cheyenne."

"Who's running the post?"

"No one is. There's a dozen engagés here—Mexicans, Creoles mostly."

"Wootton?"

"I wish I knew, Colonel. He's a meat hunter and a trader here, and that's all I know. Bent's not the same. Charles was murdered, and then George died. He's buried just outside the walls. William's Cheyenne wife died in childbirth. Cholera's cut the Cheyennes in half."

"Someone must be running this place."

"Unofficially, I am."

I wondered why the major was so reluctant to say it.

We crossed the somber yard toward the sole source of light, which bled from a small window on the south side. Within, several men in buckskins and rough wool sat around a plank table. There were Anglos and Mexicans and breeds, all so weathered a man couldn't tell them apart. Some had bowls of stew before them. Most were done eating and were smoking pipes. The change in mood was palpable. Here was fire and cheer and comfort. William Bent's melancholia had not reached this corner of his great fortress.

"Major," said one, eyeing me.

"Colonel Frémont here," Fitzpatrick said.

They looked me over, their gazes neither friendly nor hostile. No one was introducing himself, but they were curious about me. I took them to be laborers mostly and wondered whether there was a trader around. It was plain that none recognized the Pathfinder.

"I'm looking for Richens Wootton," I said.

"Wootton here," one replied. He was a big fellow, with a pulpy nose and an unkempt look. "Stew in the pot. Not much to eat around here except buffalo."

"I'll have some," I said. I hunted for a clean bowl, found

none, and finally realized one served one's self here. I espied a kettle of water, found a dirty bowl, scrubbed it clean, and then ladled stew from the iron pot suspended by rods over the fire at the hearth. I repeated the process with a metal spoon. Fitzpatrick pursued the same agenda, and we settled at the table with the rest.

The stew proved to be corn gruel with some unknown meat in it, probably boiled bull.

"Not much to eat here," Wootton said. "I haven't shot a buff for three days and we're down to old bull."

"You're the man I want to talk to," I said between bites. "You know the country west of here?"

"No, I wouldn't say that. A man could spend a lifetime out there and not know it."

"But you've cut through a few times."

He shrugged. "Pretty rough. I go through there to get to the Utes and trade for pelts."

"You know the passes."

"What passes?"

"Through the San Juan Mountains."

Wootton looked faintly amused. "Twelve thousand foot peaks and a few saddles is all. I wouldn't call them passes."

"Streams flow from there. Water goes downhill."

"Through canyons. I hear you're looking for a railroad route. Forget it."

"I'll find a way."

Wootton turned silent on me, so I ate quietly and assessed the rest. There wasn't a man among them I would want with me. They were mostly inscrutable, their faces masks. They struck me as a little slow. I wished I could follow their thoughts, if they had any.

"This is the worst place on the continent to run a railroad," Wootton said. "Three ranges of mountains and where are you? A land of canyons, and then more mountains, and then desert—and all that before you hit the Sierra Nevada. You run rails up grades and over trestles, and then down the other side over more trestles, and you hit canyon lands, trenches so deep and wide you can't bridge 'em. It makes no sense. Anyone could tell you that."

"Do you know the entire country?"

"Not by half," he replied.

I smiled. His response was answer enough. But he wasn't through. Wootton was a stubborn cuss.

"Suppose you find some sort of pass. Does it make sense? What about all those trestles and bridges and tunnels and grades, eh? You could run a rail line to the coast south or north of here for what it'd cost to do these mountains."

"I welcome skeptics," I said.

"And why do it in winter?"

I started to give him my stock answer, but he rudely interrupted.

"You can't get through. Don't even try. The Indians, they're saying this is the worst. Snow's higher than a man in those ravines."

"I don't base my decisions on faulty memories and superstition."

Wootton seemed aroused, as if some anger were simmering just below the surface. "You want a guide? You got one. I'll go take a look. If I don't like what I see, I'll quit and walk out. Maybe I can help, maybe not. You can pay me in advance. If you get trapped up there I'll never get a dime."

The offer was so startling after all his truculence that I barely could digest it. I didn't agree to it, though he was the only man around, apparently, who had even been in the San Juan Mountains. But he looked like trouble. The sort who wouldn't take direction. I marveled that he didn't see opportunity and public esteem when it was placed before him. The less ambitious weed themselves out of the race.

"I'll consider it," I replied.

"What are you paying?" he asked.

"I haven't said I would pay you anything."

He laughed suddenly, his truculence a thing of the past. "I'll go to Pueblo de San Carlos with you and see what they're saying. Believe me, they'll know. Maybe I'll hire on, maybe I won't."

"You won't persuade me to stop," I said. "I don't stop."

Wootton simply chuckled and stretched.

That was how I acquired a guide, or so I believed. Fitzpatrick had remained as silent as the rest of Bent's crew. The whole lot seemed to be unmanned. My very presence had plunged them into wariness. Wootton seemed to be a boor, but I didn't doubt I could reduce him once we were underway.

I turned to other matters. "We've some worn-out stock to trade, three saddle horses and two lame mules. We're also looking for provisions."

I waited, wondering who was in charge, who might be the post trader, and it turned out to be Wootton. "We've some small Mexican mules in good flesh. Left behind by the last company through, eight, ten days ago, and pastured a few days. I'll trade three for your five. But provisions, we've got none. We're scarce on fodder here. And the buff, they've hightailed out. We're about reduced to eating pack rats."

"Anything else for sale or trade?" I asked.

Wootton smiled. "Cupboard's empty, but have a look if you want. You want some trade beads? How about Green River knives?"

"I'm well equipped, but for some staples."

"You'll be eating mule meat," Wootton said.

He was no fool after all. I was taking my commissary with me, on the hoof. A hundred thirty mules could feed thirty-three men for whatever time it took to cross those mountains. Mule rawhide could build snowshoes, keep feet shod, yield caps and vests and pantaloons. These ruffians knew all that but had talked themselves into huddling around the fireplace in a comfortable post. I wouldn't have hired a one of them.

I thought that Bent's engaged men were a debauched lot, especially Wootton. The rest had the good sense to remain silent so as to preserve my respect for them. As for Fitzpatrick, I wondered where the man's reputation had come from. He was just another frontier soak. The red veins in his nose told me all that I needed to know. None of them had the vision to see what I was about. Carson would have. He thinks highly of me and has no envy in him. I thought for a moment I should send for him. He was in Taos, not far away, and I could have summoned him and he would have come at once. But Carson knew less about the barriers ahead than Wootton did.

I headed back to camp alone, crossing at a ford just below the fort they showed me. It was a taut moment, pushing my roan into inky water that threatened to sweep him, and me, downstream, but soon he clambered up a gravel beach, and I rode toward the distant orange dots of my camp with the bitter wind at my back.

Godey was waiting up for me; the rest had built barriers against the wind and settled as low to the frozen ground as they could get.

"Any news?"

"The usual. Don't go. Too much snow. Bad winter. No place for a railroad."

"It's all true," Godey said, and laughed.

"I agree with them. It's no place for a railroad," I said.

"Then, why?" Godey asked.

"To prove that we did it," I replied. "If I'm going to say no, don't go that way, I've got to show them why. I've got to walk the ground. So we're going."

"You are very peculiar," he said. "A human locomotive."

"Maybe it's not in my hands," I said.

Godey stared at me and smiled slowly.

I traded stock the next day. The new mules were tough but not in good flesh as promised. They proved to be small and wiry and they looked useful, no matter that they were skinny. As for the horses, I didn't want them in the mountains where they would spook at any cliff and bolt at the sound of a hawk. I don't have much use for horses in any country higher than molehills. We left Bent's Fort on a raw morning, straight into a mean wind. Wootton came along, driving a freight wagon drawn by four mules. The man meant to do some hide business for Bent, one way or the other. I intended to ask him a few things en route. I didn't even know where he hailed from or whether he had a wife and family. It seemed unlikely.

That was an easy leg of the trip despite icy winds that never quit, day or night. We were following the Arkansas River, where there was ample wood and shelter. My efforts to find out more about Wootton came to naught. Instead, I was the one being interviewed.

"What's the good of this trip? You'll be chest deep in snow. How do you find a roadbed for the railroad under twenty feet of white stuff, tell me that, eh?"

"I leave that to engineers," I said.

"Even if you get through, and I'm not saying you can, mind you, you won't have a railroad line. What can you tell anyone about a canyon whose floor you never see because you're walking on twenty feet of snow?"

"I agree, Mister Wootton."

"Then why? The senator, is that it?"

"That, sir, is neither here nor there. I'll engage you if you know a way; if not, it's time to dissolve this arrangement."

We sparred like that off and on all the way to Mormon Town, as they were calling the place. Some Mormons were farming it. Some old mountaineers had settled there, along with their Mexican concubines, and were living far beyond the reach of law. Wootton ended up learning more about me than I about him, which nearly decided me to look for someone else.

In the final stretch, as the Rocky Mountains loomed whitely before us, I settled again beside Wootton. We needed to come to an agreement.

"You see that snow?" he asked, pointing upward. "You see it's smooth and white and nothing is sticking out of it? No rocks, no trees, just white? That's the sign of a lot of snow. Lighter snow, there's gray and blue spots all through. It's sort of speckled. But not up there. See how the wind's whipping snow off those peaks—a regular plume, like a cloud? That tells me the snow is cold and powdery and not melted in."

"I've worked through worse," I said.

"So I've heard," he said, eyeing me.

"What would change your mind?" he said.

"You mean, at what point would I quit? I can't answer that because I have no intention of quitting."

"What if it becomes plain that no railroad can go through, eh?"

"I'm on my way to California, sir," I replied.

"That's a dandy place," he said. "If you can get there."

We reached the pueblo midday. There wasn't much by way of lodging for thirty-three men, but we finally sheltered in an adobe house with a good hearth, and my men could enjoy four walls, a roof, and some warmth. Pueblo wasn't what anyone could call a town, not even a village. It was just a disorderly patch of adobe houses with snow-covered squash gardens, full of heaven-knows-what sort of people, all male except for a few leathery ladies of Old Mexico. But people crowded around, unbidden, eyeing us, our string of burdened mules, and our armaments, which largely consisted of Hawken's mountain rifles. The arrival of thirty-three travelers and a hundred-thirty-odd burdened mules was the social event of the season. The only question was whether they would dance with us or massacre us.

These poured in until the house could hold no more. They were rough cobs, old mountaineers with Hispanic wives and a few Mormons who had settled only recently, many of them dressed in farm dungarees.

When they scouted out my intentions, it didn't take them long to come to a unanimous conclusion, and to advise me of it. "Worst winter we've ever seen, and it's a death trap. You go on up there, and we'll find your frozen carcasses in the spring, what's left after the wolves have done you."

That was the consensus, as expressed by an old trapper named Ephraim.

Wootton looked me over and announced his pleasure: "I can see what they see, and what I see is snow and cold. I'm not going to leave my bones up there, and I hope you don't either, Colonel. Count me out. A man needs to take heed of the way things are."

I had expected as much and nodded. "You know of anyone who's a competent guide here? I'm going ahead, and I'll hire the right man."

"There's one, and only one. His name is Williams. Old Bill Williams. He's an odd duck, living alone too much, but he knows that country," Wootton said.

That was bad news. I knew the man all too well.

CHAPTER TEN

John Charles Frémont

I could scarcely imagine a worse choice for a guide. I knew the man. Old Bill Williams had signed up for my third expedition, lasted two months, and quit. I had employed him for a dollar a day, and he seemed glad enough to get it. I supposed I might employ him now for the same amount, and he still would be glad enough to get it, being an improvident sort who was always out of pocket.

Old Bill Williams was memorable. He was a tall beanpole, well over six feet, all whipcord and without an ounce of fat. He had lived a lifetime out of doors and was weathered to the hue of an old saddle. His private toilet was nonexistent, and he apparently wore whatever came to hand until it fell off. He was bent at the waist so that his nose preceded his toes. He walked with an odd wobble, almost spastic, and shot his rifle in the same manner, but with deadly effect. The old border man, who was probably in his sixties, was no one's fool when it came to surviving in wilderness.

"Where do I find him?" I asked Wootton.

"He's around here somewhere."

I cased the crowded adobe house, examining a wild collection of mountaineers and their concubines, but I did not see him.

"He's not a man to get into a crowd," one of these people said. "Try over at the Paseo, yonder."

The Paseo was the closest thing the pueblo had to a store. There was a plank bar of sorts, a few shelves of goods, and plenty of benches. Sure enough, Old Bill was perched on a log stool all alone and not wanting company, his face caught in shadow. A dying fire at the hearth supplied the only light. I waved away the others, wanting to talk to the old mountaineer myself, without the crowd.

"Colonel Frémont here," I said, extending a hand, which he did not accept. He was sipping something amber from a tin cup he held in hand. I took it to be aguardiente, Taos Lightning, which had a way of scouring a man's pipes.

"Do you think I don't know?" he replied. "I was doing my best to be scarce."

"I'm not interested in the past," I said, although I had found his previous conduct instructive. "I'll get right to it. I'm taking a company to California and need a guide. We're going to cross right about here, thirty-eighth parallel."

"No, no you's not gonna do that," he said, and sipped at whatever was in his tin cup. "You're gonna go around, like any other sensible man. Thirty-eight parallels, what is it? Why not forty parallels, or twenty-three? Is thirty-eight your age, maybe? I don't care if it's parallels or rectangles or triangles, you ain't going straight over."

"Up and over. As close to this latitude as I can. I'm looking for a rail route." The man seemed abysmally ignorant. "Parallels from the equator. Invisible lines marking distances from the center of the earth. It's round, you know." I waited to see whether he knew that. Men of his station couldn't imagine the earth as a globe.

"They's no such thing as a straight line," he said. "God slides a curve into everything."

"You have some theology?"

"I'm a minister. I've got the Good Book measured and weighed and sawed into parts, ready for a sermon or a funeral."

I scarcely knew how to deal with this vagabond. "You

know this country, and I need someone who'll show us the right pass."

"I know every square foot, but I'm not agoin' so you better think of someone else."

"We've a large company; we're well equipped."

"Those are big mountains and I never seen such snow. And what sense is it? That's no place for a railroad. You go around. Me, I'd take her south of the Sangre de Cristos. You can cut through there, not much trouble."

"Up and over, without you if I must. But that's where I'm going."

That was bravado, but I intended to do it. If I could not find a guide, I would proceed without one. It wasn't so hard, really. There were some ancient Mexican charts to guide me. Follow the Rio del Norte north until I found the Saguache River, and go up it and over Cochetopa Pass. If I missed the right creek, I'd try the next one.

"My bones hurt just thinking on it," he said. "I'm too tired."

"I need you. A dollar a day would fatten your purse."

"What good would that do? All I'd do is leave my frozen carcass up there."

"A dollar a day and a ten-dollar bonus when we got past the Rocky Mountains."

He stared morosely into his cup.

"You're the devil is what," he said. "I'm glad I didn't go get myself froze and shot on your last one."

"It's snowy, sure. But with good mules and good men beating a trail, we'll be over the top in a week or two."

He grinned malevolently. "You wouldn't know that pass from a piss ant's jaw."

"That's right, but we'll find a way no matter what, and you can earn some good money or not."

He grinned, wiped his mouth, and said nothing. I am a close observer of men, and I knew he would soon come around. Even now, he was looking past me and at the opened door, where Alexis Godey and several others waited.

"Not me, no way, you don't even know what cold is. How are you going to feed all them mules up there? You think there's one stick of grass? You think there's one cottonwood they can chew on? It's under fifty feet of snow."

"We'll be looking for grain here."

Williams sipped, coughed, and cackled.

"Go on, get away," he said. "I'm warm and I'm not about to freeze my butt, not for some . . . old railroad."

He turned his back to me, his dismissal.

I fired my parting shot. "We're going to bed down here. We'll raise camp here before sunup. You'll join us or not. Try God. He'll tell you to join up."

He presented me with his full back, which wasn't much wider than a fence post.

I signaled I was done, and the rest flooded in. If they could buy some brandy here, they would. They wouldn't be seeing spirits for a long time.

Godey pulled me aside. "Did you hire him?"

"He'll come around. I told him we're leaving before dawn, with or without him."

"He didn't like the snow, oui?"

"He says grass will be fifty feet under it."

Godey laughed, but uneasily. "He's right, Colonel. You'll find out soon enough. The trick is to turn around and get out when the moment comes."

I didn't reply.

I had things to do. I wanted fodder of any sort. Grain, corn, whatever I could get for my mules. If I couldn't get Old Williams, then I wanted Wootton to draw me some charts and tell me where to turn off. I was headed for Cochetopa Pass, but I'd heard that there was another pass, slightly higher but with better railroad grades, called Leroux Pass—or Williams Pass. Maybe Wootton could pencil it in for me.

The whole mob was rushing in now, abandoning the little adobe I'd rented for the night to house us. An old gap-toothed mountaineer was pouring from a small cask behind his plank counter and raking in whatever he could. I watched coin, bills, a knife, a blanket, and a box of precast bullets cross the counter. I wanted to stop this but thought better of it. Let them enjoy a sip. It would put them in good spirits for the struggles ahead. They lit up pipes, and soon a blue haze hung over the place, disturbed by gusts of icy air pumping in from the open door.

I made inquiry about fodder and discovered that the denizens of this pueblo were an improvident and lazy lot, barely staying alive with household gardens and constant hunting. It was probably too much to ask of an old mountaineer to work his land and make it bear fruit. And even at that, it was the Mexicans who were providing for themselves. I retreated into the icy night to peruse the area, letting a quarter moon be my lantern. But a considerable walk on snowy ground revealed little agriculture here. I spotted no corncribs, but I did see some haystacks. Hay would be of little service to me.

I would need to do what I did in the Sierra Nevada: find open southern slopes to graze the mules. These slopes caught the sun, melted off the snow, and exposed grass. If the tactic worked in the Sierra Nevada, so would it work in the southern Rockies. By the end of my foray, I noted that my company had already retired to their bedrolls, with which they filled the little adobe house. A rank odor marked their presence. I chose to bed at the store, where I was welcomed cordially.

"Would you know of any place we can obtain feed for my mules?" I asked the keep, a grizzled veteran named Whipple.

"You shouldn't be crossing them hills without it," he replied. "They've got some corn in cribs up to Hardscrabble."

That was promising.

I awakened my company well before dawn that November day, and they lazily made themselves some corn gruel in a fireplace pot and packed their blankets. It was another blustery day, the sort that would pump cold down a collar or up a sleeve or up a pant leg no matter what. I didn't mind. I had discovered that I am made of tougher stuff than most men, an accident of birth.

Williams was nowhere to be found, and I imagined we would vault the Rockies without a guide. I had maps and counsel enough. I had the old Mexican charts. Carson knew the country and had shared all he knew with me. This was the plan he proposed: find the Saguache River, a tributary of the Rio del Norte, head up it to Cochetopa Pass, and descend into the Colorado River drainage. I didn't need a guide for that. Godey hastened my men through their morning rituals and into the icy predawn darkness. There were, after a few trades, one hundred thirty sound and healthy mules to load.

We raised camp about nine, and only then did Williams show up.

"You can't top those peaks without a guide," he said.

I was in no mood to haggle and ignored him. He peered at me slack-jawed. I steered clear, if only to avoid getting louses.

"Day wage. You pay me every night," he said, "and you got a guide."

"So you can run when the going is tough?"

"You put your digit right on her. You is going to leave your bones up there, frozen up solid until it all melts come June, and I'm not gonna leave mine there. One dollar each night."

I shook my head. No deal.

"Why're you going up there now? It's a head scratcher," he said.

"We will do what no one else has ever dared to do."

He cocked his head. "That all, is it?" He yawned. "If I go, I go. If I quit, I quit. If I come back here, I come back here."

I had him. "You lead the way," I said. "We'll follow."

He grinned, never said yes, but hightailed to a grimy bedroll and a scabrous old rifle he had stacked nearby.

"Can't let you go freeze your arses," he said.

I didn't trust him and intended to correct his progress if he steered too far away from the route. Just by staying with the Arkansas River we could put ourselves on the west slope of the Rockies without difficulty, climbing some benches to avoid a gorge. That would put us on a grassy valley leading to an easy pass to the Colorado River drainage. It had been traversed by Stephen Long and Zebulon Pike, so I wasn't interested in it. We wouldn't go that way. Why follow others' footsteps? And we were already too far north.

We reached Hardscrabble without difficulty and found plenty of dried corn in a crib. It took little to persuade its owner, a Mormon named Hamel, to part with it. The only trouble was that it was dried ears and the man didn't have a sheller. But I put the men to the task, which they undertook eagerly, knowing that corn would feed man and beast alike in the high country. They set to work with their skinning knives, and ere long we harvested a hundred thirty bushels of good feed, ample to keep the mules in good condition during our week or ten-day crossing of the three chains of the Rockies. All this golden treasure was carefully loaded into panniers, and I made sure each pannier was tied shut and the loads were balanced.

Hardscrabble was as miserable as the pueblo farther downriver, a shantytown full of lazy mountaineers plus a few hardworking Mormons. It was also hard against the flanks of the Wet Mountains, the first range we had to negotiate, and stood at the confluence of the river and Hardscrabble Creek. It was here that I made my first decision. Once again I rented an adobe house and once again my men slept warm. It would be the last time they would see walls and a roof for some while. The next morning, we loaded early. I was itching to be off.

"We're going up Hardscrabble Creek," I told Old Bill. "And then over. There's a pass there."

Williams blinked at me so long I thought maybe he was slow witted.

"Huerfano Road. Mosca Pass," I said.

"Oh, is that what you call it," he said, slouching so much he was actually staring up at me, even though he had six inches of height on me. "You wanting to make a railroad there?"

"It's closer to the thirty-eighth parallel."

"Why this parallel, eh? You bought this parallel from Uncle Sam? There's a lot of them parallels."

"It's where we're going."

"Why don't you run your railroad where it's halfway level, eh? Follow a buffalo trail. The buffalo got it all worked out."

I smiled and turned away. I'd heard enough of that.

On the afternoon of November 25, we finished with the corn, broke camp, and Old Bill led us up the creek, through a deepening snow-packed canyon. We were now headed straight south, in the direction of the pass I had heard much about. But we were also running into snow. Half a foot at first, no trouble.

Then we were pushing through a foot of it, even as we gained altitude. Williams rode a mule we had given to him, his old rifle across his arms, his body slouched so deep in his saddle he looked bent in the middle. He wore an odd cap made of skins, with earflaps he could pull down if needed, but the temperature was mild.

Some of the men thought the cap made him look like he had fox ears. The rest of his ensemble was just as odd, but I decided not to worry about him. He'd spent a life in the mountains, and he would see us through. I wondered why I didn't really believe it.

CHAPTER ELEVEN

Micajah McGehee

We abandoned the Arkansas River valley the afternoon of November 25, having loaded the mules with shelled corn. We had all enjoyed pumpkin and chicken and sheltered beds that night, a luxury we would be dreaming about the rest of the trip.

Colonel Frémont was taking us south, up Hardscrabble Creek, to some pass he and the new guide, Old Bill, knew about. I didn't know the route and was a simple foot soldier on this trip. Back in Saint Louis I discovered that the colonel was recruiting for a California expedition, and I thought to join it. I was footloose and California intrigued me. I have that itch. He said there would be no pay, although his father-in-law would introduce legislation to subsidize the trip. A rail line at midcontinent would satisfy both the North and the South, Frémont said, and Congress might come through. It sounded plausible enough.

Most of the recruits thought that the government would eventually pay them, but I never took it that way. The way I calculated it, I should be shelling out a few coins to the colonel for a guided trip west. This would be my ticket to California, and that's as much as I needed. So I had signed on. I found myself enjoying the company of the three Kerns, Andrew Cathcart, and Frederick Creutzfeldt, all well-educated men like myself, and so we made something of a party to ourselves.

Hardscrabble Creek soon plunged into a gloomy canyon lined with white oak and pine as well as cactus aplenty, and as we veered westward toward the Wet Mountains the snow increased. Still, it wasn't bad, and I saw that once a trail was broken through the pillows of soft snow by the leaders, the rest of our heavily laden mules followed easily enough on the packed snow. If this was winter, I would have no trouble with it, even though I had been reared in Mississippi. We were all in fine spirits. The corn did it. That golden wealth stuffed into sacks and panniers was, for us, more assuring than metallic gold.

There were storms aplenty just before. En route to Hardscrabble, an overcast sawed off the mountains, and we no longer could see the snowy reaches of Pike's Peak. That and the brutal wind made that leg of the trip worrisome and hard. There's no way to fight the wind. No matter what a man wears, the wind finds its way through, shooting icy fingers down your neck, pushing up your trousers, bullying in at the waist, and nipping at ears and noses and chins. The men made rawhide throatlatches to keep their slouch hats from flying away and eventually made their own leather caps with earflaps. We hunted for momentary relief any way we could, pausing under cutbanks, stopping in a copse of trees, hunkering low behind a rock.

Darkness caught us only three miles from Hardscrabble, but it was a start. We made a good camp under a cliff, out of the wind, where there was plenty of dead pine to fuel our fires. We could find no grass, but put the feedbags on the mules and gave them all a quart of shelled corn, something we had to do in shifts because we had only twenty bags. One quart went down those mule throats in a hurry, and they looked just as hungry when the bag came off as before. But there wasn't a blade of grass in sight. Frémont introduced us to his rubberized sheets, big tan waterproof affairs that let us settle into our bedrolls on top of muck or snow without getting soaked. The colonel divided up the watch, two guards, two hours apiece, and so we settled down. The night was mild enough, though I could never sleep outside in a bedroll as well as I could on a good stuffed-cotton mattress in a house. In that I was lacking, for Frémont's veterans were soon sawing wood, their hulks quiet near the several wavering watch fires.

Before dawn Godey was rousing us, and we shook the sleep out of ourselves, packed our kits, huddled around the breakfast mess fires to down some gruel, and began harnessing the mules. I yearned for some golden johnnycakes fried from cornmeal, but those weren't on the menu. The flour was already gone, and we would be surviving entirely on game soon. We were low on grains.

Now Godey was a man to inspire confidence. I pegged him as the more sensible of the two leaders, and I knew I wouldn't start worrying until I saw Godey worry. The veterans of Frémont's previous trips didn't share my views. For them, Frémont was a man of uncanny destiny. I can't say why I distrusted Frémont's judgment, but I did. As long as Godey thought things were alright, I would, too. I supposed my views were colored by the court-martial and conviction. I had followed the case closely.

It had turned cooler, and soon we were trudging up the canyon, still on foot, past giant red boulders topped with snow, following a twisting path ever higher. We had the drill down now, even without the colonel's orders. A few of us would break trail until we wearied and then fall back, and a few more of us would pick up the lead, and so on, as we rotated the hard work and spared the mules as much as we could. The mules had enough to worry about on slippery ground with a heavy load on their backs.

The only peculiar thing about all this was that this wasn't a route for a railroad. There was evidence of a crude wagon road out of Hardscrabble, but it forded the creek constantly, and I suspected that during certain spring months the whole canyon bottom would be flooded.

I spurred my mule, Betsy as I called her, up to Ben Kern.

"Do you think a railroad could run thisaway?" I inquired.

"I'm a doctor, not an engineer," he replied. "But it's a mystery, isn't it?"

"It's the thirty-eighth parallel, that's what it is. Frémont's going to stick with it. What's so sacred about it, do you know?"

"You know what it is?" he replied. "It's a golden highway across gentle grades with tropical weather to either side, coal seams every hundred miles, ample water, and easy connections. I hear it runs straight to California, without any detours. Once we're on it, friend Micah, we'll just race right along. You just ask the colonel, and he'll tell you."

That's what they called me. Micah McGee is how they shortened it. I was used to that; it had started about when I was old enough to notice. Doc Kern was smiling.

But what we were getting into was no tropical highway. The creek had swung west and was tumbling out of the Wet Mountains now, splashing over boulders, and we were breaking through two feet of snow. We were climbing through gloomy pine and aspen woods. Word came back to us that we should dismount, save the mules, which were burdened with all that corn. I slid down into the snow, hoping I had used enough neatsfoot oil to keep my boots tight against leaks. Up ahead, I saw Frémont shifting leads. He would put one group of men and mules up front for a while, and then another, thereby spreading the hard work of making a trail among as many men and animals as he could. I supposed he would call on me soon, though so far he was using only his veteran men.

The man was the least like an army colonel as I could imagine. Did he bark orders, demand instant obedience, dress down fools and knaves? No, he never raised his voice, never even seemed impatient, and somehow won the allegiance of his men. Not least, he broke trail himself for a spell, off his mule, kicking open the snow. Old Bill, I noticed, did no such thing, but hung back in the middle, staring amiably at the rest of us and hawking up great gobs of yellow spit now and then. For that he was earning a wage.

I'd come to admire Frémont, in a tentative way. So far as I could tell, he was a gifted man in the field and a natural leader whose very presence seemed to make this journey easier and more secure. And yet something nagged at me and wouldn't let up. Maybe, someday when I knew Doctor Kern better, I'd ask him why I kept pushing aside doubts that swarmed like horseflies in my head.

The men ahead of me showed signs of wearing down. But we continued, one step at a time, and because most of the party was ahead of me I was less worn than most. Still, I had to admit that we were making progress. Snow or not, we were snaking through the Wet Mountains, a lengthy line of men and animals.

All in all, we made good time that day, maybe nine miles, and darkness caught us near the summit. I suppose one could call it a pass. But I just kept wondering how you'd get twenty tons of iron horse up there, especially if that horse was drawing a dozen steam cars.

The next day we started downslope, which was harder because the snow was heavier on the western side of the mountains. Men kept stepping into the unknown and taking a tumble. We were wet and cold ere long. The canyon narrowed until its walls vaulted up on either side of us and we were caught in a creek, fighting through pines and white oak. Giant red rocks hemmed us, and I thought that a railroad company would be detonating tons of powder to break through all that. We made only a few miles through deep snow and finally retreated up a side canyon and camped away from the gorge we were descending. We fed the mules more corn, since there wasn't a blade of grass in sight.

Colonel Frémont seemed perfectly relaxed, as if all this were the most ordinary passage in the world. And somehow the men seemed just as relaxed. He had a way of pacifying our worries. We boiled up some beans, having trouble keeping heat under the kettles because the wood was so wet and we were so high up. The mules were restless; a quart of corn a day didn't appease their hungers a bit, and they were primed to cut and run toward anything that looked like fodder. It was hard to drive them through an aspen grove, because they had a hankering for the smooth bark of the younger trees and could peel it off with their teeth.

Frémont's veterans taught me something one night when the wind had died. They built pole racks next to their campfires; stripped out of their soaked and cold duds, right to the buff; and then hung their wet, water-stained clothing next to the roaring fire to dry out. They wrapped their blankets around themselves for the hour or two they were drying their duds. Most of them had woolen undershirts and drawers, and these absorbed campfire heat and some smoke too. But they dried. When I tried it, the first in my mess to do so, the Kerns eyed me askance, but they saw the merit of it. After a couple of hours beside the cook fire, my duds were bone dry and felt good when I clambered back into them. I marveled. The dry clothing lifted my spirits. It took the Kerns a few more nights to attempt it, but Captain Cathcart saw the merit and soon was drying his clothing whenever he could.

I did notice one thing. Frémont himself never toasted his underwear. In fact, he stayed buttoned up in that blue overcoat he wore constantly, a military coat without any insignia on it. His conduct was entirely private. He had his own tent, and inside that canvas, shielded from our eyes, he did his toilet, arranged his clothing, slept, ate, trimmed his beard, read his law books, and hid from us. I gradually realized he was a true loner, and this nightly retreat from us was a need in him, just as staying buttoned up to the chin was a need in him. He didn't want us to see anything of him but his dressed-up self, even in the worst weather. Dry clothing was so valuable to me I marveled that Frémont didn't dry his. But his manservant, Saunders, never brought any duds out of that tent to dry by the fire, so either the colonel's clothing never got wet or he chose to wear wet clothing. It sure set him apart from his veterans and also from those of us traveling with him for the first time.

The weather was mild enough, and little wind caught at us that night, so I didn't hear much complaining. Indeed, Frémont and his vision of a new path west seemed to have infected us all, and we could only think of the magical railroad that would be constructed in our wake. The only worrisome thing was that Godey and the hunters weren't finding any game, not even a track in the snow. The deer and elk had retreated to bottomland for this hard winter, and we were working through a silent country without so much as a crow above us. I thought little of it, because we were heading down the canyon and at its foot we would find game, and the thirty-three men in the company would enjoy some elk or venison.

We could not see what lay below the snow and kept stumbling over hidden logs and rocks and obstacles we could not fathom. The burdened mules were lamed by sudden plunges into the snow, when there was no footing. Sometimes we had to dig one out. Mules virtually vanished, plunging into snow so deep that it was all we could do to keep their heads clear so they could breathe. Then the company would halt while the few with shovels dug around the trapped mule until we could drag the wretched, overburdened beast out of its snow prison. Thus our progress came nearly to a halt, and we lost precious time.

But then we reached the western foothills. The canyon widened out, the snow lessened, and the worst was over, or so it seemed. Ahead lay an arid anonymous valley, and beyond its broad reaches, another white wall, which we understood to be the Sangre de Cristos, which stretched from this general area deep into New Mexico. We gathered on a plateau for a rest, having utterly exhausted ourselves and our mules in that miserable canyon, and our mood was not lightened by what we beheld. Those brooding peaks presented a wall much higher than the range we had just traversed, and we understood that beyond these lay yet another range, wider and higher and more rugged than the one that was evoking such dread in our hearts.

We had managed one range, fed out half our corn, and there was not a blade of grass anywhere to be seen. Colonel Frémont seemed to think nothing of it. After a brief rest, he set us on our course once again, and we descended the rest of the way to the intermountain valley without great difficulty.

The weather turned warm, and we were heartened by an

occasional bare patch covered with sagebrush. Never had bare earth looked so friendly. We were further heartened when Godey's hunters shot a deer; we would have meat for supper, which somehow gave rise to our hopes. This wasn't so bad; the colonel's calm was entirely justified. The Pathfinder knew exactly what he was about. The valleys were full of game; we would stock up, find grass, recruit our mules between assaults on the slopes, and so pass through the difficult country.

By the time we had reached the valley floor, an icy wind was billowing out of the northwest, and that stung us to hasten along. Old Bill Williams had taken command here, and he steered us south.

"Why do you suppose he's doing that? Just to keep his back to the wind?" I asked Doc Kern.

"He knows of a pass, easy as a hot knife through butter. Robidoux's Pass is what they're calling it. And we'll slide across this range as if it hardly existed."

I stared at Kern, wondering whether he believed this monstrous proposition, and caught a wry turn of his lips.

"That's what they're saying up ahead," he added.

The Sangre de Cristos did not look very hospitable.

"You see any railroad prospects here?" I asked.

"Here, there, everywhere," Kern retorted.

We camped in a wind-sheltered spot in the valley. Godey's hunters fanned out, but I knew beforehand they would come back empty-handed. There wasn't an animal track to be seen. The next day was arctic, and between the bitter wind and the low temperatures, I wondered how I would endure. The valley had snow up to four feet in some places, bare ground in others, and no feed for our mules. What looked like grass here and there proved to be the tips of sagebrush. They couldn't find a thing to eat except a little cottonwood bark where we camped. It was odd, watching them gnaw at green limbs of the younger cottonwoods, peeling off the tender bark with their big buck teeth. The mules had thinned badly; they had no flesh left to burn off and nothing to fill their empty bellies.

I wondered whether they would survive the next mountain range. The only people enjoying any of this were the colonel and Bill Williams. The guide meandered through the camp, pausing at the various messes, saying nothing. I had the distinct feeling he was enjoying our anxiety, and maybe even plotting ways to make the trip as miserable as he could manage it.

I dismissed the notion as the sort of thing that didn't deserve serious consideration, but the notion kept burrowing into my head, until it lodged there. Old Bill scared me.

CHAPTER TWELVE

Captain Andrew Cathcart

I was much intrigued by our guide, Williams. He affected a rusticity that was belied by his command of English when he chose to display it. I learned that he had intended to become a preacher but had long since digressed from that goal. Still, he was a man who had mastered the scriptures and sometimes resorted to them. I learned also that he had taken up Indian religion, though I could not discover which beliefs, since each American tribe seemed to possess its own theology. I gathered, from campfire talk, that Williams believed he would be incarnated as a bull elk with white chevrons on his flanks and had cautioned all and sundry never to shoot such an animal, lest they shoot him.

But if there were remnants of a high calling in the man, they had largely vanished as a result of a quarter of a century as bloody border riffraff, trapping, roaming, somehow avoiding the worst of the perils that afflict those who venture far beyond the safety of civilization. Here was the man in whom this company was placing its trust. He had proclaimed his knowledge of the country and told us that he knew every pass and river on sight. We could blindfold him and he could take us west.

So of course I was interested in this odd ruffian who dressed in layers of gamey cottons and wools and in an even gamier leather tunic and britches that held his ensemble together. He was subject to both silences and voluble moments when one could scarcely stop the flow of words issuing from him. But on this trip he remained silent, never doing any work he could avoid, and making the passage as easy on himself as possible. Unlike the rest of us, who dismounted and walked our burdened mules through the worst drifts to spare them, Williams rode steadily, his long frame dwarfing the mule that bore him, so that his moccasined feet sometimes dragged in the snow. He sat hunched, incapable of straightening the bends of his body, but I did not make the mistake of thinking that his bad posture signaled an oafish man. He took in everything, with a keen eye. One of the things I noticed from the beginning was his fascination with the company's equipment. Preuss's instruments absorbed him. Frémont's field equipment, including surveying instruments, intrigued him. But Williams never asked a question about any of it; he simply meandered through the camps, observing, and vanished as silently as he appeared.

These particular days we were on a southerly course, having worked through the Wet Mountains, and we were now heading toward a gap in the Sangre de Cristos known as Robidoux's Pass, which I was given to understand was the only one of consequence through the formidable cordillera before us. Williams avoided Colonel Frémont as much as possible, or was it the reverse? The man might be guiding us, but rarely did he consult with the colonel. And Frémont seemed content to let Williams steer the party his own way.

We were traversing the valley between the two ranges, but the going was little easier than it had been passing over the first range. We encountered snow up to three feet in places, which wearied the company. We were so exhausted that we often didn't break camp until nine or ten in the morning and surrendered to our weariness by three or so in the afternoon, when we all hastened to gather firewood before the December night engulfed us. The temperature varied from pleasant to bitter; Doctor Kern told me that one morning was eight degrees on Fahrenheit's scale. Add wind to that and not even a Scot like me could enjoy the day. But for the moment, no storms engulfed us with snow, and so we made our way, hour by hour.

Doctor Kern's boots gave out, and the experienced men in the company showed him how to create moccasins of rawhide, which they said were better in snow anyway, and so the Philadelphian was able to continue with us. Loss of footwear on a trip like this is a serious, even fatal, calamity. He would repair the boots with an awl and thong when the chance came to him.

As we struggled through the valley, with the Sangre de Cristos forming a grim white barrier on our right, I thought maybe Frémont would let me hunt. I had superb English steel and powder. I had come to North America to hunt. I wanted to try my hand at buffalo and elk. I had sold my commission in the hussars and set out to see the world, and here was the world. Frémont obliged me at once, and I found myself with a small hunting party that included Alexis Godey, Raphael Proue, and Antoine Morin, all Creoles, as they were called in these parts, and all of them veteran hunters.

We spurred our mules ahead and drifted off to the left, where the bottoms of the frozen and unnamed creek wound along. If there was game, it would be sheltering there in the red willow brush, close to whatever feed might be found amid all this bloody white. They all spoke English, but so accented and ruined by Yank perversities that I could hardly make out what they were saying. Still, a smile or two was enough. We would make meat for the whole company here in this snowy valley, where every hoofprint would lead us toward our quarry.

Our mules soon exhausted themselves in belly-high drifts. We separated, spacing ourselves two hundred yards apart or so, giving us a wide sweep that should drive the beasts before us. They wouldn't get far, weakened by starvation and fighting drifts. I wanted meat badly. Unlike some of the others in that company who were more trusting, I had calculated what it would take to feed thirty-three men over two more mountain ranges, and the sum of my calculations became my inspiration. Ten buffalo would not suffice.

Our mules gave out all too soon, and we found ourselves walking, fighting through drifts that sometimes reached our waists, keeping our rifles high and out of the snow and wet. We reached the creek and found it mostly frozen, but with an occasional open rapid. But worse, we found not a single hoofprint. I spotted plenty of bird tracks, rodent tracks, and the tracks of small creatures I could not identify. If there was game in these thickets, it was laying low, not moving an inch. But there was no game. I was keenly disappointed. I had thought to line up a fine shot or two. Where had the game gone? Had it all been driven to some sheltered valley to graze peacefully whilst we toiled by?

"Alors, we will soon boil shoe leather," Godey said.

"Are you serious, sir?" I asked.

He laughed. "Mule meat, mon ami. It tastes like smelly shoes."

I hadn't given much thought to dining on mule for breakfast, lunch, and supper.

The mules were hard to handle in the thickets because they tore at cottonwood bark and wouldn't be led or spurred or whipped. I thought to let my mule get himself a mouthful and then tug it ahead, but the beast was planted next to a green-barked cottonwood and was gnawing that bark as neatly as if it was a beaver, peeling it off and downing it. So were the rest. This was the first meal they had enjoyed for days. A quart of corn each day had been their entire sustenance, and a poor one at that. I had kicked apart their pitiful spoor and found most of the yellow kernels intact, having passed through with no effect. That bloody guide Williams had better find a pasture soon, or there would be a price to pay. If he knew the secret havens of game of this country, he didn't show it but plodded onward, oblivious to the suffering around him.

We hunted as late as we dared, fearing the early December dark would engulf us before we could find our company. We had not seen an animal. This accorded exactly with what the hunters had faced the previous days. The game on which we depended was somewhere else, perhaps driven by those north winds to some sheltered refuge far to the south.

This trek was proving to be more adventure than this Scot had bargained for, but in for the ha'penny, in for the pound, as they say. I should be trusting the Yanks. They knew the country and knew how to get through. Only the whole business gnawed at me. Frémont expected to find game and knew that his company would suffer without it.

Godey found a relatively barren patch that led back to the company, and we forced the mules along. They were all ready to break for the bottoms where they could feed on bark. What I was mulling in my head was to suggest to Frémont that he camp there, put all the mules into those thickets, and let them put some fodder into their gaunt bellies. I don't know what stayed me, other than professional courtesy. He was a lieutenant colonel, albeit a slightly tainted one, and I a resigned hussar captain, and it didn't seem to be my office to counsel him. This was his fourth expedition, and he knew what he was about.

Or so I hoped. A man needs some flexibility. If there's no pasture at hand, one heeds the mules' own signals, and what our mules were telling us as we fought them was that we were stealing their dinner from them. By the time we caught up with the company, they had built fires and were setting up tents and were unburdening the mules.

It turned out to be an odd moment. Every man in that company stopped whatever he was doing to study us as we rode in, and what they saw was our empty hands and empty saddles. We had hunted most of the day and returned without so much as a rabbit.

I suddenly felt their gazes studying me, their hunger visible in their faces. It didn't seem right; we had meat on the hoof, a hundred thirty edible mules if we should get into trouble. Mule meat was, I knew, stringy and unpalatable, but it would boil into stew, and it would sustain us. So why, then, was I seeing a hooded bitterness wherever I looked? These were bloody veterans of the wilds, and they could conjure up a meal from roots and things I could not imagine.

I made my way to Frémont's mess, past men who were pulling off soaked boots and setting them to bake next to roaring fires. Others were scraping snow away and raising tents. It seemed a pleasant camp, with mild air lifting spirits.

There would be a corn stew this night, I learned. Boiled up maize with some crumbled jerky thrown in. Off to the west, the sun dropped below the white lip of the brooding mountains, plunging us into a fearsome lavender shadow that crept across the ground like death.

I found the colonel on a log outside his tent, working neatsfoot oil into his boots.

"Why, Captain Cathcart, it's my pleasure," he said.

"And mine, sir. I don't wish to intrude on your plans, but I did have an idea cross my mind, sir. A mile and a half from here, where we were hunting, a lot of willows and cottonwoods and box elders formed thickets along the creek, and I noted that the mules thought the bark was a repast worthy of kings. They took right to it, colonel, and we had a time keeping them in hand. I just thought it might be a chance to feed the whole lot, sir. Put them in that bottomland; let them feed all night."

Frémont smiled easily. "You're an observant man, and a cavalryman, too, captain. That's not very good fodder, and the animals don't profit from it, which is why it's not worth the trouble. A mile and a half through these drifts is no small trip. No, we'll give them their ration, good feed."

"They're looking gaunt, Mister Frémont."

"Ah, you have eyes for the animals. I've noticed that, too, Cathcart. But here's something I've learned from my previous trips. There's always south slopes, cleaned off by sun and wind, where the animals can feed all night. We haven't come upon one because our route hasn't taken us to the right sort of slope. But I assure you, sir, when the moment arrives, I'll call a halt and let the mules recruit themselves on the grass."

"As you wish, Mister Frémont. I wonder if you'd permit me to take my own mule and put him out on that feed."

"You're free to do that, captain. I'm not a commander

but simply an organizer of a private company. But I would strongly suggest that you stay here. There is safety in company. If a storm should blow up, we'd not see you again. This country swallows people."

I saw how this was going and left the colonel to his oiling.

I passed the depot in the snow where the saddles and panniers were collected and noticed that many of the corn-stuffed saddlebags were now empty. And we weren't a third into our passage. The mules had been herded into a piney woods where they could shelter from night wind, but there wasn't a stalk of grass in sight, and nothing edible in those woods. I thought they would have been better out in open country, where they might paw down to a little grass. I wondered about the keep of mules here. In the British Isles, where livestock is scarce and keeping them is costly, every beast is fussed over and fed as well as possible. But these Yankees seemed content to wear the mules out. It didn't rest well with me. There were chances not taken.

I joined my mess, where the Kern brothers and McGehee had put things in good order, collected ample wood for the night, and were relaxing comfortably on sheets impregnated with India rubber, one of Frémont's better ideas. If passage could be no worse than this, we would clear the Rockies in a fortnight and enter what Frémont called the Great Basin, which supposedly had level, grassy valleys.

"You see any hoofprints today?" Micah asked.

"If we had seen even one track, even an antelope track, we would have followed it and kept on following it until we caught up with the game."

"Where did the game go? It just doesn't disappear from country."

"I've a theory," Ned Kern said. "When it snows, they stand still. It costs them too much to plow through snow, and what they find to eat doesn't make up what they lose getting there. So they just stay put in thickets. You just have to stumble on them, and you'll have meat."

"I wish I could believe it," I replied. I was thinking of the way our mules had bulled into the thickets, quite beyond our control, to gnaw at bark. They did not stir up any game.

The hunt had left me soaked. I changed into my reserve drawers and tried to dry my duds, but the wind and blowing snow and fickle fire defeated me. Tonight, I would crawl into my bedroll wet and cold, and so would every other man, excepting maybe the colonel himself.

I meditated before the wavering fire, for the first time wondering whether I had played the fool, signing up with these Yanks. I was consoled at last not by Frémont's studied ease but by Godey, the calm voyageur, used to grave hardship. If Godey wasn't worried, there was no need for a displaced Scot to be worried.

CHAPTER THIRTEEN

Tom Breckenridge

I'd been with Frémont in California, and when I heard he was heading west again, I signed right up. So did lots of others who had been with him. That's the sort of man Frémont was. Old John Charles did more to win California than the whole U.S. Army and Navy together, and we had a smart time doing it, too. I always figured the West Point brass couldn't stand it, and that was what got him court-martialed and convicted. Well, hell, a Frémont just don't come down the pike every day.

This winter trip was turning into some real mischief. But I like to grab a tiger's tail. So does old Frémont. So do all his veterans, those rough cobs like me. We even got that old kraut Preuss back, even though he had moaned and groaned and muttered through the two previous jaunts. He was just as addicted to Frémont as the rest of his old hands, even if he liked to sneer at him behind his back. Preuss was the topographer, always out there with his bulky black instruments, squinting at the polestar or the sun and consulting his chronograph and his barometer and his thermometers, figuring the height of every goddamn molehill and tit, and jotting it all down with a pencil.

But old John Charles, he wasn't content with just having one scientific genius along. He went and got him a botanist named Frederick Creutzfeldt. Now go ahead and ask yourself, what was a leaf collector doing on a midwinter trip like this one? Anything he could botanize about was buried under ten feet of white stuff. Unless he planned to study the tops of trees to look for bark-beetle damage, he was without a task, and extra baggage. But that's old Frémont for you. If you're going to have yourself an expedition, you're going to equip it in the latest style, so we had a botanist from Germany along for the ride. If old Johnny couldn't nab Alexander von Humboldt, Creutzfeldt would have to do. That plain tickled my fancy. When we got up to the summit of those mountains, yonder, I planned to ask old Freddie what sort of lichen he's scraping up.

I thought some of those new gents would quit, with all the cold and wet and heavy going, but they were game. I'll say that for them. Maybe they didn't break trail, the way we did, but they plugged along behind us breaking wind, and I never heard a whimper. But some day, maybe I'll get a peek at their diaries and see whether they wrote out their whines.

All of those new people, they didn't know much, but we showed them the tricks: how to build a snow cave to get out of the blow, how to stay clean, how to cook your drawers on sticks beside the fires until they're hot and dry, how to grow a full beard to keep your ugly snout from freezing.

We all looked pretty grim at times, with icicles dangling from our beards like chimes and ice collecting in our eyebrows and a rime of frost around our nostrils. They learned quick, those artists and botanists and hoity-toity farts like that. That settled a wager or two. Half the veterans were betting the artists and pansies would hightail south at the first chance, but that didn't happen. We all were looking shaggy after a few weeks of cold, but all that hair kept us halfway comfortable. If you don't want a frostbit chin, you grow some fuzz.

Old Bill Williams, he was a card, slouched on his mule and letting the rest of us do the work. He was being paid for what was in his noggin instead of what his muscles could do, though I sometimes think there wasn't any difference between his brain and his belly. He wasn't wearing himself out any, and that made for a little grumbling. But I didn't care. The man had roamed these parts for a quarter of a century and knew every trail and every pass and every bear's den on a high slope. So he claimed, anyway. On the borders, reputations grow faster than a pecker in a parlor house. I always figured that if we got into trouble, he'd lead us straight to a denned bear, and we'd get meat, fat, a pelt, and shelter out of it.

On December 3, after weathering a bitter night with ornery temperatures and an unsociable wind, we pushed into the canyon that would take us up the road and over Robidoux's Pass and into the valley of the Rio del Norte. Or so they said. Me, I just tag along. What the hell? For days we had been pushing south, the forbidding massif of the Sangre de Cristos looming on our right like a jailhouse wall. Those shoulders formed a rampart such as I had never seen before, the cloud-wrapped peaks forbidding us passage westward. Even old John Charles kept staring at that white wall, while icicles dangled from his beard and eyebrows. Our burdened mules didn't like that wall either; they might be dumb beasts, but they knew enough to shy away from those fatal highlands, and the slightest westward passage brought them all to a halt. Only curses and whips set them on our path.

When we did enter the yellow canyon, everything improved at once. We were out of that icy wind. The creek had snow piled along its banks, but back a little there were bare patches we could traverse without trouble. The mules beelined for every spidery cottonwood and quaking asp to gnaw at the bark, and it made me aware how starved they were. We could barely keep them on the trail. I was all for letting them gnaw a meal out of the bark and twigs and leaves for a day or so, but old Frémont, he would have none of it. It was almost balmy in there, with sun heating the south-facing slopes and making the sun-heated rock friendly for an hour or two midafternoons. But later on, snow showers skidded over, wetting us and making our passage treacherous. Still, this was easy, and our spirits soared as we gained altitude.

We made the divide about noon, and were once more exposed to the howling wind, which stole our hats until we treated it with more respect. Doc Kern, he had to toss his rifle onto his hat or he'd have lost it forever over a precipice. I spotted Herr Preuss trying to set up shop on that barren ridge, with the wind battering him so violently he could hardly stand. I knew what he wanted: the altitude of the pass, and he was not going to get it in that gale.

"Hey, you old bastard, you want some help?" I asked.

He unbent his bundled body, stared up at me through

wire-rimmed spectacles, and glared. "If I vant help I ask for it, ya? If I vant help, I make every man here help me. I don't vant help. I do this myself."

A touchy sort, I thought. Me, I don't know Germans from Spanish and barometers from sextants. But I'm good with a Hawken. I braved the wind, curious about how the topographer would deal with it. He scraped away a crust of snow until he found bedrock and then set an instrument on it. The device was little more than a long upright glass tube full of quicksilver.

"What's that, Herr Preuss?"

He glared at me. "Mercury barometer, that's what it is called, and not a good way to do this. Wind bad. Air pressure, ach!"

He got on his hands and knees, ignoring the icy gale, and studied the mercury in the glassed column, muttering to himself.

"How high are we?" I asked. I wanted to skedaddle off that ridge fast, but curiosity got the best of me.

"Stupid Yankee question," he said. "Where you from? Missouri? With wind like this, we could be below sea level, ya?"

I laughed. Old Preuss, he was one to make some sport.

He pulled off a glove, extracted a notebook, and began making calculations in it with a stubby pencil. "Nine thousand seven hundred seventy feet, give or take," he said. "Don't ask any more questions."

"That's why I'm out of breath," I said. I wanted a lot more air in my lungs than I was getting.

He stuffed his instrument into a rosewood chest and hurried away. He had converted barometric pressure to height above sea level, all he could manage there. He didn't look happy with himself.

I hastened off that ridge myself and hurried down a barren blue rock slope, with mules in front of me, finding precarious footing. Every living creature among us was in a hurry to get off that damned ridge and into some shelter, any goddamn shelter. We followed a vee downward, with Old Bill steering us as if he knew what he was doing. I saw no trace of a wagon road, but that didn't mean much. Railroads could go anywhere. Railroads could climb Mount Everest, right?

So far, we hadn't had much trouble on the alleged road to Robidoux's Pass, and I told myself that Old Bill, he knew what he was about. He wasn't just making this up. We were sailing right along. Up high, on that saddle, I saw naught but white, grim, and desolate ridges and peaks with a plume of snow streaming off of them. And of course no game. Animals had more sense than we did.

That was a moment of elation. There we were, midway on our passage across these chains of the Rockies, the divide of the middle range, and nothing more than some hungry animals were plaguing us. The canyon on the west side of the pass had been cut by a rill that sawed furiously into the mountain slopes, and we hurried into it, wanting to escape that gale. This was different. For one thing this canyon was choked with snow. I thought maybe we were walking on top of fifteen or twenty feet of it. Truth to tell, I had no idea how far down we would strike rock. One moment we would be carving a trail through snow; the next we would be stumbling over crosshatched deadwood, giant logs lying every which way a foot or so under the snow, which halted us and stymied the burdened mules. This here was no cakewalk.

This was a twisty, narrow defile, filled with giant boulders and slabs of rock that had tumbled down from above, gray and red barriers we had to work around.

"Some road, eh?" King said. "Robidoux must have been three sheets to the wind."

"There's no wagon road here," I replied. "Impossible."

"I wouldn't take Bill Williams's word for anything. The stupid bastard. Maybe this isn't Robidoux's Pass at all," King said.

We were, at that point, trying to ease one mule after another through log-strewn narrows, when the slightest misstep sent a mule to its knees. Sometimes we had to pull off their packs before they could get themselves up and out of those miserable little holes hidden by benign-looking snow. Now, too, the snow showers increased. The sky would darken and spill thick flakes, and then the shower would blow off and we would enjoy a moment or two of bright sun, which hurt our eyes. Every time the snow blew, I'd get a dose of it down my neck.

I swear, some of us had so many icicles dangling from our facial hair that we rattled and chimed with every step. If the trail up the east slope had been easy and warm, the trail down the west slope made up for it. We plunged into snow so deep we had no idea of the contours of the gulch beneath our feet. Our lead men broke the crust, and those who followed stamped a deepening trench in the enormous drifts, until we were progressing through a virtual tunnel whose walls reached many feet above us. I dreaded what a cave-in or avalanche could do. The mules didn't like it and had to be goaded ahead. Old Bill Williams, he just nodded and let us do the work.

Still, we were out of the goddamn wind, which counted for plenty.

The rill we were following twisted every which way, and once we got below timberline we faced new obstacles—heaps of deadwood, logs, and brush—that frustrated our descent. Snow showers added to our tribulations, but we worked grimly forward until we rounded a bend and caught a glimpse of a vast, arid, naked valley ahead.

"It's the Rio," Godey announced. He actually slapped old Johnny Charles on the back, which I've never seen done before or since.

That was a cause for rejoicing. We had conquered the second range. Ahead would be grass prairies, warmth, escape from wind, comfort, and game. I could hardly wait to climb onto one of those mules, Hawken in hand, and go after some juicy red meat. We might even find some big shaggies down there, and surely plenty of deer and elk.

The rest of that blustery day we fought the narrow defile, working around tight corners, staring up at giant orange rock slopes, which were often sawed off by clouds. More and more, we could glimpse the peaceful valley ahead, looking like the promised land, and that inspired us to move our hundred and thirty mules and ourselves with haste. After a tough descent, we reached the foothills.

Godey settled us in a willow grove not far from some giant gray sand dunes that formed an unexpected barrier to our passage. But that would wait for the morrow. We turned the mules loose in cottonwoods, where they began gnawing ravenously on bark and leaves and whatever roots they could pry out of the frozen earth. I watched those wretched animals do everything in their power to feed themselves. They worked at bark and twigs frantically, as if they knew that worse would follow. It troubled me some. Them mules knew more than we knew, and no one was paying them any heed.

It was snowing again off and on, but this would be a comfortable camp, and we rejoiced. By dusk we had ample deadfall at hand for the mess fires, and we settled down for an evening of rest and recovery. Two ranges down, one to go. Men built towering fires and dried their outfits as best they could, but blowing snow didn't help none. A man would get his drawers half baked dry and a gust would pelt fresh snow into them.

I discovered old John Charles before his tent and thought to ask him a question that had been burning in my bosom.

"That's no canyon for a railroad, is it?"

"No, of course not. This pass won't work," he said. "I'm not sure it's Robidoux's Pass. There wasn't a sign of a wagon road."

"Herr Preuss told me the ridge measured almost 9,800 feet."

"He did, did he? I'll talk to him about it."

"Do you think maybe Old Bill got himself turned around?"

The colonel didn't like that and stared at me for an answer. I was getting into some kind of politics there.

I drifted back to my mess. This would be a macaroni night. At least we had some of that to feed ourselves. But later I discovered that Frémont had lit a bull's-eye lantern and had settled himself in front of his tent with a book. A book! What manner of man would park himself outside of his tent on a wintry eve with a book? He had pulled his spectacles on and was quietly reading away.

I edged up to him and discovered a massive tome in his hands, with dense type on every page.

He gazed up at me and fathomed my curiosity. "It's Blackstone's commentaries," he said. "Common law and cases. I should like to practice law when I reach California."

I stared at the book, at him, at the whirling snow that blew across its pages.

Later, when I was back among my mess mates, I told them that the colonel was reading Blackstone, and they marveled at it.

"Other men would be looking after the animals, checking supplies and all," King said.

"It's all for show," Vincenthaler said.

But Godey objected. "Why would a man of his repute do anything like that, mes amis?" he asked.

CHAPTER FOURTEEN

John Charles Frémont

All my life I have been cognizant of the impressions I have made on others. There were multiple messages in my reading of Blackstone. I could just as well have pursued the jurist's ideas in the privacy of my tent, but that would have accomplished nothing. So I settled myself outside, where my study would be seen and considered. I wanted my company to draw proper conclusions, and I don't doubt that I succeeded.

They would marvel, of course. There we were, deep in a snowy wilderness, where common law was the last thing on the minds of these men, and there I was, toiling at my book by the light of a bull's-eye lantern. I considered it a most efficacious moment.

It signaled, of course, that my thoughts were now on life in California and that our present problems were surmountable—indeed, nothing to dishearten good and valiant men. It was an acknowledgment that we were two-thirds through the cordillera that had posed the principal barrier to our westward progress. It expressed my calm, and my utter absence of anxiety. To be sure, we were in some peril, but it was important to let the entire company know that these perils would be dealt with. It was never far from my mind that we had a larder of one hundred thirty mules, meat on the hoof.

So I chose to read the Blackstone, knowing the galvanic effect it would have on my men. They would cease their fretting and be well armed in spirit for the final assault on the Rocky Mountains. Ahead lay the vast, arid valley of the

Rio del Norte, whose headwaters collected near where we were camped and wound their way south and east, clear to the Gulf of Mexico. We were not far from settlements. Down that drainage lay Abiquiu, northernmost of the Mexican hamlets, and below these, Taos and eventually Santa Fe. Ahead lay a fertile river bottom chocked with game, filled with grasses and brush and a few trees. By the time we were ready to ascend the San Juan Mountains, we would have fresh meat, the mules would be well fed and even fattened, and we would be in prime condition for the last alpine assault.

To be sure, just west of us was a bleak sea of sand dunes, mostly covered with ribbed snow, but the wind had whipped against their sides, exposing a desolation devoid of all vegetation. We would need to cross that wasteland, and I supposed Bill Williams would know where to do it. I had found myself less and less sure of the man. Was that really Robidoux's road he took us over? I didn't see any sort of road at all, especially on the west side, which was deep in snow and crosshatched with fallen timbers, making wagon passage impossible. The grades were too precipitous for a wagon road in any case and were probably beyond what was acceptable for a railroad.

A dark suspicion of the man flared in me. Maybe he was an utter knave. But I set it aside as unworthy. He might be unprepossessing, but by all accounts he was the foremost master of this country. I didn't need to like the man; I needed only to respect him.

The dunes ahead would have to be skirted. They were constantly in a state of wind-driven flux, and no rails could be laid across them. It was plain that the 38th-parallel route was not practicable unless it strayed considerably from the parallel. But it was my duty to finish what was started, and I would continue to pursue a rail route as close to the 38th parallel as possible. If the passes ahead proved to be as difficult as those we had traversed, I might be forced to disappoint Senator Benton and his colleagues. But I had no intention of doing that. I planned to force a passage by whatever means, and this of all my expeditions would be long remembered for going where no company had gone.

I set the book aside, blew out the lantern candle to save tallow, and returned the Blackstone to its oilcloth case. Then I hurried through the bone-cold night to Godey's mess and found him unrolling his blankets atop one of those rubberized sheets that were the salvation of my men.

"Alexis, tomorrow you take the lead. Straight across the dunes. If I ask the guide to steer us, he'll take us around to the north."

"I'll do it, sir."

"There'll be neither food nor fodder nor water in those dunes, and that will be Williams's argument against the direct route."

"We can save a day or more, colonel."

"That's how I see it. And Godey, kindly put your best hunters out. I don't suppose they'll find anything in those dunes, but put them two or three hours ahead of us, and they'll reach the valley floor in time to make meat. That's what I have in mind. When we reach camp tonight, I want the men to discover some elk haunches roasting for them all."

"I'll send our best hunters, colonel. But it doesn't look like game country to me, sir."

"You're quite right, Alex. But it's something that must be done. The men expect it."

"As you wish, sir."

"The mules are feeding well tonight on the bark. They should be fine tomorrow."

Godey's hesitation told me he disagreed. I have come to

read men well and can sense disagreement in them almost as fast as ideas form in their heads. But he smiled. "We'll have them on good pasture soon," he replied.

That's what I liked about Godey. He read my mind. He understood my deepening disillusionment with Williams. And he accepted my instructions without cavil.

The weather cursed my designs that night. A wind arose out of the north, bringing snow squalls with it and severe discomfort to my men, who could not stay dry. The icy blast rattled canvas shelters, raked cook fires, chilled the mules, drove men to cover, and even whipped the mules farther and farther from our bivouac. By dawn there was a thick layer of white upon us. Men were numb. Mules had vanished. The dunes to the west had a new layer of snow over them, to make our passage harder. But I set an example, expressing good cheer, even amusement at our plight, and soon enough a thoroughly chilled party was out, wading through snow, to recover our strays. Others were attempting to ignite cook fires, without much success in those Arctic gusts. And once again, icicles dangled from beards and eyebrows, and a rime from our breaths covered our leathern coats.

I heard that Ben Kern was both frostbitten and attempting to treat some frostbite in others with stimulants. Some of the wretches had stockings frozen to their feet, and getting flesh and cloth thawed and separated was no easy task. They should have known better than to let themselves suffer needlessly. There are canvas shelter cloths and blankets for all. But some men just won't perform the tasks that would spare them trouble. Later I would find out who had let himself suffer frostbite and keep the lapse in mind.

But it would all work out. By noon of a blustery and bitter December 4, with the thermometer's mercury hovering low inside its bulb, we set out across the sand hills, the hunters well ahead of us, the balky mules fighting our whips and kicks. It was all we could manage to drive them into that blast of air, and they fought us as if their lives depended on it. It was odd. The mules clearly did not want to leave the protection of that cottonwood and willow forest, which offered fodder and warmth, and this time they resisted frantically, looking for any opportunity to turn tail and head east. We had to maintain utmost vigilance.

"Drive them ahead of us," I suggested to Godey, but that didn't work either. They all simply quit. I am always one to learn from my mistakes, being flexible in nature, so we put several men and mules in the van, to clear a path through the drifts, and in that manner we won the reluctant cooperation of the rest of the mules. But they were not a happy lot and trudged with heads down, brushing as close to one another as their packs would permit, for the sake of whatever warmth could be gotten that way.

We saw not the slightest sign of game, but neither did I expect to see any in an area of shifting sands. In all, we made only five miles that day and camped in the lee of a great dune, which gave us a little protection from the furious wind. I was disappointed. I had planned to reach the river. It would be a miserable camp, without water, save for whatever snow we could melt, and without much fuel for our fires. The mules would be hard to contain, and I decided to double the guard. One slip and the whole lot would head back to that grove.

Bad as the camp was, it was better than what lay ahead, a featureless plain covered with snow, without shelter or wood or feed. Beyond, looming in the West, was the jagged white wall of the San Juan Mountains, the last great barrier we faced until we reached the Sierra. The tops were sawed off by cast-iron clouds, but I knew that the San Juans probably contained peaks in the fourteen-thousand-foot range, if my informants were right. I scraped away snow until I reached naked sand and put up a tent, feeling the heavy canvas flap in the Arctic wind. I hoped my tent stakes would hold in the soft sand, and I drove them as deep as I could, not liking the softness beneath my feet.

Nearby, my men struggled with firewood. There was naught but sagebrush, which they harvested ruthlessly. It would barely heat water, and their porridge or macaroni would be tepid, more glue than food this evening. I didn't mind it myself, but I had long since learned that I am more resilient than other men and can endure most anything. I ascribe it to good blood. The mules lost no time crowding east and had to be checked forcibly. I feared we would need to picket all of them. I watched my Creoles and California Indian boys, Manuel, Joaquin, and Gregorio, wrestle with the animals, finally picketing some in the lee of the dune where there was a little brush. I was returning the boys to California; the army had brought them east as curiosities and to let them get a glimpse of civilization and the great father in Washington. They had been docile and useful to me on the trail.

I was not yet settled when Old Bill materialized. He was permanently bent and walked with his northern half leaning forward and his southern half backward. But now he hunkered down on the balls of his feet, a form of rest common among mountain men who knew no chairs in the wilderness. Carson often did it. I could never find comfort in it.

"Hard night on the mules, no water or feed," he began. When addressing me he spoke a fairly educated English; among the men his inflections were rustic, even quaint.

"They'll eat snow," I replied.

He snorted. "Warming a mouthful of snow costs them more heat than they can get from eating," he retorted. "And they hardly get a spoonful."

"I know that."

He stabbed a crooked index finger west. "See that? It's death. It's plain death to anyone that goes into there."

"I know a pass," I replied. "Cochetopa. It's on the Mexican charts."

"So do I, and it's death, I'm saying."

"We have come this far without loss, Mister Williams."

"There's a way around. I've taken it plenty of times, just ease around the south of this range here. Cuts some foothills, plenty of valleys likely to have game and grass. Takes an extra day or three, but I'll put you all beyond those hills yonder, and you'll be glad we did."

"There's a path heading north; that's the one I plan to take. It leads to Cochetopa. It cuts off of Saguache River. It's an old Spanish route, and it's where we're going."

"It's where you're going to get into trouble like you never did see before, Colonel."

He was riling me, so I smiled pleasantly. I cared less and less for the oaf. He squinted at me and began an amazing monologue.

"You see the Rio del Norte out there, that winding bottom? Well, that's all sagebrush flats, not grass, and there's no feed worth a damn. You think you'll put some iron back into these mules? You'd better take stock. You're about out of corn and they're about to start stumbling and tumbling unless you get them on some good pasture.

"It gets worse, even before you start into that wall." He paused dramatically. I enjoyed his theatrics. He could run for the Senate and win. "Beyond that river, where those brushy flats lie, that's the strangest country you ever knew. It's where all the waters off those mountains have collected, just a little under the surface. It looks like naked arid land, don't it, sir? It is, for sure. But just below, it's wet like a sponge, like a hidden marsh, and if you think it's tough to pull and push mules through a lot of snow, wait until you push them through that. They can't hardly step without each foot sucking up and oozing in. If you take off their packs, maybe you can help them a little, but that means the men'll be carrying the load on their backs through the same swamp. This time of year, Colonel, they'll soak their feet and their boots; they'll freeze, and their feet will be so frostbit you'll likely perish the whole party, men and mules, before you even reach them hills you're planning to leapfrog over. I'm saying, Colonel, it's not the way to go; you'll be wearing the last out of the mules before you even step into the first gulch taking you up to where the gales blow constant and kill a man in five minutes."

"I don't want to stray from our plans, Mister Williams." I smiled, wanting him to see there was no hard feeling between us.

"Yes, sir," he said, unbending his hairpin frame until he was upright again. "I suppose it'll be for us to see."

That was an odd observation.

It was something I was very familiar with, the undertone of people trying to deflect me from my plans. I would have the honor of crossing the Rockies in December and intended to see to it no matter how much carping I had to endure. No one had ever done what I was about to do. I would alert Godey to be aware of conspiracies and disloyalties and to report these to me in confidence.

As the day waned, I could see the cook fires blooming, perfidious light and heat that would vanish for lack of tinder even before the supper was warm. It was something for them to endure; it would strengthen their manhood and prepare them for the travail ahead, when we toiled across those subterranean wetlands on the other side of the Rio del Norte.

CHAPTER FIFTEEN

William Sherley Williams

That man Frémont, he was the serpent that tempted Adam and Eve, no doubt about it. I reckoned it when I looked him over close. I can sometimes see right through, to the inner spirit, and inside of the colonel was the serpent himself, same as got Eve to eat the apple.

That next day, mean cold and blowing again, we raised camp late and worked out of the sand hills through some gray snow, and I climbed up on a ribbed dune to watch until the wind blew the heat out of me. It was the serpent all right, snaking through a trench in the dirty sand-topped snow, single file, the head of the serpent out front, and the tail most of a mile behind, one hundred–some worn-out mules, a hairy man here and there, all in a snaking black line. The corn was most gone, so the Creoles had adjusted the loads, but them mules were still hauling heavy goods, canvas shelter cloths, and all of that, and now they were looking like scarecrows, caved in, muscles ridging on their flanks like hogbacks.

They knew their fate, I could tell. I can see right inside an animal, and they knew they was about finished and soon they'd die. They knew that, so they didn't much care. They stopped fighting the wind and snow and just didn't much care, and I knew they'd all but given up on this earth, anyway. Maybe I'd see them down the road apiece. I have that vision so I know I'm coming back as a bull elk. Animals got no clock; it's all here and now. Only us mortals got time. But animals know what's coming where we don't.

There was a lot of nothing to eat in that naked flat of the

Rio del Norte, just a little sagebrush poking from the dirty snow, and the mules toiled past it, knowing they would die soon. I got inside the skull of one of them, and he was saying he was worn out and cold and he hurt and no one cared and pretty soon he would stumble and die. I have the ability. I can even get myself inside the head of a squirrel. I can converse with a chipmunk if I'm of a mind. I told that mule I was going to cash in, too, mighty quick now, but not this trip. I plain knew. Once you get to talking with animals, you see how they think. I picked up on it.

This was a solemn day, mean black clouds, mean wind, mean sleet spitting in our faces, and the serpent's men had froze-up beards again, icicles dangling and clanging off beards, and eyebrows pasted with ice. They was all cold and wet down inside, round the waist, over the belly. The colonel never took the lead, never broke a trail himself, but let shifts of his men do that, busting up the crust and making a path. It was all done without an order. The men seemed to know when to quit, and another bunch would bust up crusted snow and the serpent would snake along, heading for the river that ran betwixt naked banks where the wind never slowed or quit. If the serpent thought to feed the mules there, he would be surprised.

Ahead loomed the worst heights a man could fathom, a white death so high it vanished into the cast-iron sky. I knew that country; it was bad enough in the summer, and now I couldn't tell one part of it from another. White canceled out everything. I would go in there as much a pilgrim as the next fellow. But it didn't matter to the serpent. He would go in there and drag the whole company to its doom. And what for? Not a railroad. No. He was looking for the tunnel into hell, is what he was trying to find. The more I thought upon it, the more I thought I should help him to the tunnel of hell. Why would a sane man do this?

We proceeded out on that vast flat, with nothing but snow and sagebrush and greasewood and wind. They told me it was Thursday, December 7, but I never know one day from another. For once we made good time, though the wind was bad and the temperature was worse and the air scraped heat out of me. I entertained myself by watching the spirits of the mules hovering just above them. When animals are fed and healthy, their spirits climb back inside of them and stay there, but now their spirits rode their backs along with the packs, and that told me what I wanted to know. The mules plodded listlessly, but we made time anyway.

Godey sent hunters ahead, but I heard no muffled shots on the wind and doubted that we would feast on deer or elk that night. Most of the day we were wrapped in a gray cocoon, with ice crystals stinging our faces and melting down into our beards, where the moisture froze, until we clicked and clanked as we progressed. We could not see the looming mountains, except at rare intervals, and our only companion was silence that day.

We camped on an open plain that night; there was absolutely no shelter for man or beast, and the miserable mules huddled together for warmth. Occasionally the mules on the outside burrowed into the center, for a moment of warmth. The mule herd seemed to understand this process, and periodically there would be a great shifting as mules on the outside, exposed to icy blasts, would burrow toward the middle of the herd for respite. We laid our bedrolls on iron ground and pulled stiff canvas over us. There was no fuel for fires, so we went nearly hungry, but for a few pieces of jerky the colonel had stashed away for moments like this. I never heard such silence. The company said nothing, each man caught in his private thoughts.

My thoughts were on the mules, which declined to eat snow for moisture, knowing somehow it would only chill them worse than the icy gales were chilling them. Men lay restlessly in bedrolls, which did little to stay the cold, and the night passed interminably, each man awake and locked in his private thoughts.

I suppose the serpent slept. Like the rest of us, he huddled in blankets underneath flapping canvas. He knew no suffering, saw it not in others, and blamed all suffering on the sufferers. A true Beelzebub, I thought. Parson Williams, as I am known, saw the man through and through and saw the need for exorcism. By the light of a gray dawn there was another few inches of snow on the ground. The company, without firewood for coffee or food, trembled itself together, threw packsaddles over the wretched mules, pulled the cinches tight, loaded the panniers, and departed on a compass course because it was impossible to fathom direction. I've been fair uncomfortable, but that night tested my endurance and made all my wounds and scars howl at me. I loathed the serpent, who acted as if everything was normal, and contemplated shooting him where he stood. Instead, I took some satisfaction in the certainty that he would do the job himself.

Once again, wordlessly, we slogged west through crusty drifts and treacherous mounds of grimy snow, a giant serpentine string of men and animals coiling toward the Rio del Norte, which we struck in the middle of the day. Here the serpent sent us north along the east bank, thereby signaling to me that he would not bring us safely around the southern flanks of the mountains, as I had proposed. I saw naught but horns on his skull and spent the day conjuring up ways to shoot him in the back, one wobble of my rifle, and thus to prevent what soon would befall us.

But I didn't. It was odd how I didn't. I would fix it all up in my head and had it exact. I'd ride forward a piece, wait for a ground blizzard to veil me, and plant a ball between his shoulder blades. I thus kept myself entertained for hours, whilst the company stumbled toward hell and finally dropped into a thickly timbered pocket beside the river, a haven for man and beast. That was December 8, 1848, and it had snowed in fits all day. The famished company made haste to free the wretched mules of their burdens and turn them loose, and I watched the beasts head for the river, there to slake a cruel thirst, and then to the willows and cottonwoods and red brush, where they tore at the bark and twigs and anything organic they could put their buck teeth around and strip free. It was poor fodder and would not put an ounce on any of them. But it would comfort them, the sticks and bark in their gut.

The hunters brought no game in; I knew they wouldn't. I have the vision, and I warned away the deer. "Make haste!" said I. "The serpent wants you." I watched them hasten away and watched the snow swiftly fill their hoofprints until not a dimple remained. I saw it as clear as other men see a rock or a tree. Two does and two yearlings warned away, and now the serpent would never touch them.

We would eat more macaroni. It would do. If the mules might enjoy cottonwood bark, I might prosper on pasta. I watched the company drag deadfall and shake the snow off of it and build huge mounds of it. There was no lack of firewood in this forest. Somewhere above us, the wind raced, but in this wooded pocket under a cutbank we found a little peace. Then I saw fires bloom, bright orange in the lavender light, yellow in the gray darkness, and not just the usual three mess fires, either. They were building bonfires at every corner, fires to drive away darkness; fires to vanquish the serpent; fires to turn this cold wild into a bright parlor for a night; fires to soak heat into the frozen ground, heat a man's backside while another fire heated his front; fires to dry out their soaked duds. And now they were talking, too.

I heard shouts and cheer and relief. I have hardly heard better in a saloon, with a dozen men enjoying their cups and a good fire warming the pub. Fires circled the camp, and it was better than having a wild woman.

There would be no guard this night; no two-hour shifts. Those mules wouldn't stray from the bottoms and would eat all night, never pausing. Me, I drifted toward the dark river, which tumbled out of the mountains and flowed south and east. Snow lined its banks, eerie in the half light. I saw where an elk had descended its banks and crossed only recently.

"Go on, escape the serpent," I said. "Old Parson Williams will have you for supper some other day."

The next day, the serpent marched us up the Rio del Norte, but snows choked our progress and we made only three miles, finally camping in a piney wood. The mules would have nothing to eat once again. They never touched the resinous pine, which was poisonous to them. Godey spotted the elk tracks, got his five best hunters, and took off after the elk, which had retreated upslope into foothill forest. It didn't take long for the hunters to return dragging two elk over snow.

"So you stayed to feed the serpent," I said, angry with the elk. "But now I will feed my empty belly on you and be glad because you were stupid."

"Meat!" cried Stepperfeldt. "Meat tonight!" The man was a gunsmith, no hunter but handy to have around.

The elk, two young bucks, lay quiet in the snow, even as fresh flakes fell on their still-warm bodies. One had been shot through the neck; the other in the chest. The company rigged hempen ropes over limbs and slowly tugged the great four-foots up where they could be gutted. It took a gang of men to hoist an elk. I saw the elk spirits hover for a moment, and then gallop away, never looking back. It made me angry. Expert butchers soon peeled back the supple elk hide, which would be valuable, especially for men whose boots were falling apart. I wanted the little two-point antlers. A bit of elk antler could make a man lusty. In time, every mess had thick elk cuts broiling or stewing, and the smell of it drifted through the air. But the butchers never stopped, because they wanted the elk cut up before it froze, and the rest of the meat would be carried with the company.

Old Parson Williams was well fed that night, in a camp scraped out of four feet of snow and surrounded by pines. Once again the mules were fractious, wanting to retreat downriver to the cottonwoods and a meal, so the serpent posted two-hour guards to check the poor beasts. It would have been better to let the mules feed and collect them in the morning, but it wouldn't make any difference. The serpent would snake up the mountain, and the mules would die.

I suffered that night from fits of Christianity, and the next morning when the serpent showed his face, I squatted next to him. "Cross the river here, and go back down, and I'll take you around these peaks safe and sound," says I.

"That's a detour," he said.

"It be more like a safe passage," I replied, full of holy righteousness.

"Take us to Saguache River, and then up Cochetopa Pass," he said blandly. "That's how the Spanish did it and how we'll do it." He smiled kindly. I thought maybe to kill him on the spot but decided to wait.

I saw how it was with him and nodded. I had me some elk shoulder and coffee for breakfast, put a well-cooked piece in my possibles bag, and hied me down to the mules, which were standing in snow. Their backs were coated with the latest snowfall, and icicles dangled from their manes and bellies, jaws, and tails. They hadn't been grained and were gnawing on one another's manes and tails. But even as I stood there, some of the serpent's Creoles began doling out a little maize and putting a few mouthfuls in nosebags and feeding the animals twenty at a time.

I watched one mule, one I fancied because it was plainer than most, sigh, eye me wearily, and stuff his hard-frozen snout into the bag, and soon I heard the quiet crunching of corn succumbing to molars. Half of it would go down that throat and emerge untouched a few hours later. That old mule's spirit hovered there and told me what I wanted to know. It wouldn't be long now.

It was cold again, that morning of December 12, but clear for a change.

This time the serpent sought me out. "You know the way to Saguache River?"

"I've walked over the hull country," I said.

"This is the most important day of all, then. We must find it. I'm depending on you."

"Well, it's not so hard. Just go wherever a railroad would go."

He laughed softly. I don't reckon I'd seen him laugh much. I had made a good joke, I thought.

There were no thoughts of railroads these days. We took off late, but in sunlight, with intense blue skies overhead for a change. Serpent's luck, I called it, as we worked up a deepening canyon that would take us once again into mountains.

CHAPTER SIXTEEN

John Charles Frémont

The guide was steering us ever westward instead of northwest. I pulled out my brass compass and checked, not liking it. We were leaving the headwaters of the Rio del Norte, a place of pine-clad hills and sloughs, where creeks and rivers tumbled together to form the great river.

By some mysterious fashion Old Bill had assumed the lead, working us away from the larger stream and up a branch I knew nothing about. I had sketches to work from. So had Preuss. Some came from knowledgeable mountaineers in Saint Louis and Westport. The most recent one had been drawn by Richens Wootton, who knew this country as well as Bill Williams.

This was a tumbled and rocky land, with giant gray outcrops, steep slopes, somber pine forests, groves of spidery cottonwoods and aspen, fierce, cruel creeks. And snow lazily smothered the country. It had caught and settled in every valley and dip, so that we were crossing spots that were ten or twenty feet deep, perilously working upslope in a tamped-down trench that reached over our heads.

This creek was not the Saguache River. I was sure of it. That stream was formidable, according to my informants, and had carved a broad valley that could support a wagon road—or a railroad. And it ran north and west, not straight west.

Yet there was Old Bill, perched on his bony mule, putting the beaters to work pounding a trail up this creek running within a narrow defile guarded by gloomy slopes. It was no easy task, and progress was slowed by steep grades, deadfall, giant boulders blocking the way, and a perilous drop to our right, which threatened the lives of our burdened mules.

I pulled aside until Preuss drew up.

"Do you know where we're going?" I asked him.

The topographer smiled wanly. "All I have is rough maps, sketched by men with bad memories."

"What do you call this creek?"

"I don't call it anything. How should I know? Maybe we should call it Old Bill Williams River, eh?"

"I need to know. I need to stop this."

"Why don't you talk to him, yah?"

"Where is Saguache? The river?"

He shrugged. "It is maybe twenty miles north. But that is a guess."

"And where is Cochetopa Pass?"

Preuss grinned evilly. I had the sense that he was enjoying this side excursion and maybe enjoying my discomfort, too. I have a way of reading men.

"It's not here, that much is what I say to you. It's off that way." He waved a hand in a vaguely northwestern direction.

I wheeled my mule away. I would never again hire that man. He couldn't even say where we were. Mapmakers were a dime a dozen. I waited in the snow while more of my company rode by single file, and then pulled Creutzfeldt over.

"Where are we?" I asked.

"We are proceeding up an unknown valley with slopes of fifty and sixty percent on each side. I am thinking we will enjoy an avalanche."

"Have you a name for that creek down there?"

He smiled blandly. "I will put it down as Frémont, yes?"

I laughed softly so that he might know that I appreciated his humor, but only mildly. I would prefer that the Pathfinder's name be used sparingly and to good effect.

"We might climb to that ridge and see," he said.

The ridge was five or seven hundred snowy feet up. I shook my head. It was already too late to do that. We must either proceed where the treacherous old guide was taking us or turn around at once. It was time to confront Williams, but the trail was narrow and the snow-trench in which we walked did not permit me to work forward, so I pulled into the middle, between two weary mules, whose every step betrayed exhaustion. They were receiving one pint of corn morning and evening. My hope to find grassy south slopes to feed the mules had so far been dashed by the heavy snowfall this year. We were lucky on this day, the first in which we had not suffered yet another dumping of snow.

The company halted ahead at some stony shelf where the forest parted, and I carefully worked my way around the drooping livestock and reached a bench where Williams had paused.

There was little in sight but snow: snow climbing the valley walls, snow burdening pine trees, snow capping giant claws of rock that had tumbled from above eons ago. Just off to the right was a steep abyss and a creek tumbling below, mostly ice-capped but here and there open.

I waited for a moment while the old man relieved himself.

"What is this place? That's not the Saguache River."

"Never said it was," he replied.

I smiled and bit back a retort. "The Saguache River is where we're going. I want you to take us there. If that means turning around here, we'll turn around."

He sighed. Breath steamed from his nostrils. "I don't think that's the way to go. It's an extra three or four days, and this is some shorter."

"What place is this?"

"Mexicans, they call it Carnero Creek."

"Why are we here; why didn't you consult with me?"

"We're here because we're here, and I brought us here."

"We're climbing a tributary. We're climbing a cleft in the mountains. That could be fatal. What's on top?"

"Saves two days. Mules there are mighty poor, your honor. How much corn's left? Three, four days?"

In truth I couldn't say exactly.

"So ever' day counts, don't it now?"

"Where does this creek take us?"

"Up and over, then we're coming onto Cochetopa Pass to the other side."

"Are you sure? How do you know?"

"Getting higher. Lot of snow around," he said.

His evasiveness was maddening, but I smiled. Somehow, I had to deal with this renegade.

"The route I wanted was a wagon trail," I explained with great patience. "The Mexicans could wagon over to the far side. It's in their records. That's important. Railroads follow old wagon trails."

"Yep, that's right. It's a wagon road, and it'd take rails, maybe. I don't know why not. But this here's shorter, and I took it to save time. That all right with you?"

I found myself facing the most anguished decision of my life: go ahead or go back. He stood there insolently, solemn, but I could read that man's heart, and I knew he was enjoying it.

"It's what you want, isn't it?" he asked. "Snow, heaps and piles."

The question puzzled me. "I'm sure I could do with a lot less."

"But then it wouldn't be a challenge, your honor."

I didn't like the tone in his voice. He meant to reduce me. "In my own humble way, sir, I am seeking a rail route across the middle of the continent. And that's all. And this narrow defile is not a place to run rails."

"I reckon I showed you one around the south. Waved my finger right toward it. It weren't to your liking."

I heard the amusement in his tone. I also knew I was utterly at his mercy. He knew the country, and I didn't. I had only one choice. Stick with him or turn back. "All right, we'll go straight up and over. Show us the way, Mister Williams. When we get to Cochetopa, we'll be back on the rail route."

He grinned slowly, and I sensed he had somehow bested me, though I couldn't say how or why. He clambered back on his mule and sat more bent backed than ever, as if sitting straight in the saddle would give offense.

It was now out of my hands. Whatever fate befell us would be laid on him alone. I intended to make much of that in my reports.

We fought our way up the narrow gulch, which rarely exceeded two hundred feet in breadth, working back and forth across the icy creek, wherever the trail might take us. The mules so resisted stepping into the icy torrent of water and making their way over the treacherous rock that we had to drag them by the nose through each crossing. But the guide paid no heed and imperturbably proceeded ever higher. We were climbing the streambed, there being no other trail, and often we were caught in drifts several feet deep, which required breaking a trail for the burdened mules.

This was a piney canyon, not a quaking asp in sight, and the mules feared it, unwilling to move forward, which put a great strain on the company. Sometimes the thick snow covered holes, into which mules tumbled and had to be dug out. Other times the snow covered a perfect cross-hatching of downed timber, over which each mule had to step delicately, one hoof at a time, sometimes faltering on a slippery grade.

I eyed the steep walls uneasily, noting the burden of snow lodged on them, snow that our very passage might unloose as an avalanche. There were great escarpments of snow just waiting to roar down on us and carry us all into the gulch below. One good thing was the clear blue sky above us, which promised no new snows for the moment. We labored in constant shade, because no sun penetrated to the floor of this defile on this twelfth day of December. We made only a few miles that day and eventually camped late in the afternoon on a steep slope, there being no level ground anywhere. We were well above the creek, on a timbered shoulder that made no proper campground at all, but time was against us and we could see no level place ahead as the darkness thickened.

The mules stood trembling, unable to go farther, as my men stripped the packs and saddles off of them and stowed them on the upslope side of trees to keep them from tumbling into the gulch below us. Men made level beds only by felling trees and setting the logs on the downslope side and covering the scaffolds with pine branches. There was naught for the mules to graze on, and they clung to the slope, the very picture of dejection, too weary to roam. The men attached the feedbags, with the pitiful pints of corn in them, which some mules ate at once, while others barely seemed to care. Most were up to their bellies in snow, trying to find some small comfort on that cruel slope. At least there was no wind in that defile, and as the icy stars appeared, it was plain the enemy that night would be bitter cold instead of a gale. Even as we prepared to endure the night, we could feel a draft of heavy air slide down the gulch, numbing every creature.

We could not manage shelters or cook fires in that snowbound place, so men wrapped themselves in canvas and struggled to find a little warmth as the night settled in. I stumbled past men, looking for Godey, and found him near the rear of the column. There were no messes this night, and I could not find half the men I needed.

"Sir?" he said, peering up at me from a mound of canvas and blankets, nothing but his beard and a pair of eyes and a red nose showing.

"Alex, how much corn is left?"

"One day. Tomorrow we run out."

"One day! What about our food?"

"We still have some frozen elk. Macaroni. Jerky. Sugar, coffee, salt."

"How long will the mules endure?"

"They're chewing on one another's manes and tails, sir."

"Tomorrow, work ahead as much as you can. Find a south slope for the mules."

The night was thick enough to hide his face but not his skepticism. He didn't respond. We had seen not the slightest sign of a meadow or hillside in this defile. Trees crowded the creek bottom, only to give way to heaps of talus and blocks of rock, vaulting upward and plastered with snow. The chances of putting the mules on grass were so poor that I found myself casting about for other prospects.

"Look for quaking asp or cottonwoods or any soft-bark tree."

Godey did not reply. There would be none at this altitude, barring a miracle.

"We'll make it," I added. "Call it Frémont's luck."

"Round the next bend, who knows?" Godey said.

Did I detect amusement in his response?

I was getting chilled and hurried forward to a hollow I had found, a tiny cavity located in the slope that afforded me some comfort. I cleaned away the snow, settled some pine boughs in the hollow, used some limbs to create a sort of hut when I draped my tent over them, and crawled into my nest. I permitted myself two sticks of jerky, which I wished to eat privately from my personal stock, and settled down for the night.

I wondered what all those diary keepers were scribbling this night. When I commanded an army exploration party, I forbade diaries, but I could not do that with these civilians, and I suspected they were scribbling things about this camp and this expedition that would not please me. Preuss was keeping one in German, and probably it was riddled with his own sour comments. I didn't care what the man thought. But I wished I might see what the Kerns were writing about Old Bill. I felt sure they wouldn't fault me for taking them up this anonymous gulch.

I had been too occupied on this trip to keep my own diary but had made mental notes along the way, which I would form into a record when I had the chance. I might need it to correct the impressions of those greenhorns, who had no experience of the mountains and might suppose that we were embarked on a foolish or dangerous course. I would, of course, set all that straight later.

The camp was very quiet, very cold, and a certain foreboding hung in the icy air.

As I lay huddled under the canvas, I reached toward something just beyond the horizons of my mind, and then it came to me: this was Frémont's providence. We'd be up and over in two days, hit that Cochetopa Pass in three, get down to feed and game in four. Saguache River might take a week. A week of starving, dying mules, and hardship. Old Bill had delivered me.

CHAPTER SEVENTEEN

Benjamin Kern, MD

We broke camp about eight thirty the next morning. A brutal west wind was ripping straight down the gulch, but the sky was azure, what little we could see of it in that mountain trench. A certain foreboding had grown within me, a feeling that I did not wish to share with my brothers for fear they would think I was pusillanimous. But the behavior of the mules was evoking alarm in me.

They were now so worn they simply stood mutely, as if they had surrendered to fate. We groomed and saddled them as usual, while they stood with bowed heads, no longer caring. I had seen that all too often in my practice: mortals too far gone to struggle, too worn to breathe, too weak to grasp at life.

That is how the mules struck me as we slipped the feedbags over their muzzles, each filled with a pitiful handful of corn. Yet, one by one, we blanketed and saddled them, slung their burdens on their frosted backs, and slid icy bits into the mouths of those we would ride and halters over the heads of those we would lead or drive. They had not watered that night, and those who had gnawed at the caked snow had only drained a little more heat from their gaunt bodies.

As I studied them, with the growing dread that we were getting into grave trouble, I wondered whether the others were feeling the same thing. I eyed them sharply, but to a man they were cheerful and brimming with confidence. Was I the only one in the company filled with foreboding? Was I the coward, dying a thousand times before my death?

I dared not reveal my anxiety to anyone, least of all Ned and Richard, who seemed oblivious of the plight of the mules and eager to proceed.

We managed to boil a little macaroni, which took a long while at that altitude, and so got some nourishment in us before we began, but soon we had the mules and the company lined out and were struggling upslope once again. We encountered a steep hill, maybe three hundred yards, slick with snow, and the mules could not manage it. We pushed and tugged. We removed packs and skidded them upslope through heavy snow. Then we yanked and whipped and shoved the mules up. And once we reached the top, we loaded the packs onto the mules. What should have been an easy three hundred yards of climbing took hours and left us diminished and weakened.

But the climb had brought us to the lip of a hanging valley. It lay broad and open and level, with receding slopes. There were noble prospects in all directions from here, including one back to the Rio del Norte, far behind. I should have been elated. Instead, I fell into the most painful sort of melancholia. The mules clustered in the snow, at least on level ground, not wanting to move at all. I saw nothing for them to eat, not even brush along the creek. There were only needled branches poking through the snow.

We had consumed the morning wrestling the mules that small fraction of one mile, and we spent the rest of the bright day working up the valley, and then a low hill, to a second broad valley, where we would camp. These hills were snow choked, but we would be able to scrape snow away and make a level camp and feed some roaring fires with deadwood.

But all I could think of was the mules, which would this evening receive the last small bait of grain. I thought that it was still not too late to retreat down to the Rio del Norte and the cottonwood groves along its banks, where the mules might rip and chew some sort of miserable living, though bark made poor fodder. That icy eve, the company fed out the last of the corn as if no one had a care in the world. The mules ground the kernels between their molars, sipped at the creek, nipped at the few stalks of brush poking from the blue-shadowed snow, and then stood stock-still, their heads low, awaiting their fate.

Did no one notice? Did no one pity these animals? Did my companions fear to reveal their true feelings to the others? Was Colonel Frémont so forbidding that no one of them might approach him? There was, in a few of those panniers, a good bit of macaroni the colonel had brought along. I didn't doubt that the mules would make a feast of it. There was also some sugar, which might be poured into the feed bags with the last handfuls of corn. Maybe feeding them hot water laced with sugar would help. Maybe on the morrow I would see about these remedies.

I found myself waiting for something. I thought surely some of the company would at least consult with the colonel, tell him how it was with the mules. But not one man did. His authority reigned so supreme among his veterans and retainers that not the slightest dissent manifested itself in the purple twilight. I cursed myself for being as subservient to him as all the rest.

Maybe the harbinger of bad news ought to be me. Maybe I ought to brace the colonel and give him a medical opinion about the mules and urge him to retreat to safety whilst he still could and before his mules and maybe his men perished. I sat before the crackling pine fire pondering it, phrasing words in my head, making arguments, urging him in my mind to do what was needful. And yet I didn't. I will never know why I didn't. Nor will I know what sort of magical hold Frémont had on the rest, so that not one of us approached him with a warning. What was it about Frémont? I gazed at my brothers, who seemed perfectly at ease, though they were as aware as I that the mules were about to fail. Fail! That's a weasel word. They were about to die. I believed that on the morrow, with no breakfast in their bellies, the mules would falter, one by one, and tumble into the snow, too far gone to rise up.

The fires that evening were particularly cheerful. The pine knots snapped and shot sparks into the firmament. There was warmth enough to warm our front sides or our backsides, mend clothing, dry our underclothes, apply an awl to our boots and moccasins, and bring a kettle of macaroni to a cheerful boil.

"I imagine we'll be having mule meat soon," I said to Ned.

"It's not an improvement on elk," he replied. "It's on the menu, though."

"We've seen our last elk until we're off the mountains," Creutzfeldt said. "No game here."

"I haven't seen a crow for a week," my other brother, Richard, said. "I could eat crow."

He thought it was amusing.

But we did fill our bellies that night with boiled macaroni spooned into our mess cups. It tasted remarkably good for something that was nothing but boiled-up wheat.

I could not stand my sense of foreboding anymore and restlessly cleaned out my cup and packed it in my kit, and then I worked through the snow, past the other messes, toward Frémont, all the while rehearsing what I wanted to say. It was an odd thing: no one was alarmed about anything. I was the sole worrywart in that camp.

I found Frémont at a well-executed camp, with three feet

of snow carefully scraped aside, a bright small fire warming the tent and the earth before it, and Frémont sitting in a camp chair I didn't know he possessed. He was fiddling with an instrument.

"Ah, so it's you, Doctor. You're just in time to see me take a measurement with my barometer. Actually, I'm taking two measurements, and I'll compare my observations with Preuss."

I recognized one as a mercury barometer. It contained a tall column of mercury that would rise or fall in its glass cylinder with variations of air pressure.

"A barometer," I said.

"An altimeter. Air pressure declines with height. This other device measures altitude another way, by recording the boiling temperature of water."

Indeed, this metal cylinder sat on legs just above a small kettle of boiling water, and baffles caught the steam and steered it through a jacket around the cylinder.

"There's a thermometer inside that cylinder. The cooler the steam, the lower the boiling point of water, and the higher the altitude. It's all calibrated on the Celsius scale, of course, and so is the mercury instrument, which makes it easy to calculate heights."

"Subject to weather, temperature, and so on."

He smiled. "Your science serves you well. I always am glad to have learned men with me on these little trips."

"And have you reached any conclusion?"

"Why, tentatively, 8,742 feet above the level of the sea, if the mercury device has it right, and I am waiting for the boiling-water device to heat the thermometer beyond all possibility of error, apart from climactic variations. It requires a little patience, does it not?"

"We're very high. No wonder I grow so weary, with air so thin."

"We'll be going higher, my friend. The pass will be close to ten thousand."

I dreaded the very thought of it, and it must have shown in my face.

"Cheer up, my friend, we'll be up and over in just a few hours, let's say forty-eight at the outside."

I found myself unable to say what I wanted to say, which is that some of the mules would not survive even that span. What was it about Frémont? Why could I not raise the issue that was causing me great anguish?

"But of course you didn't come here to talk about altitude, I imagine."

"The mules are on their last legs," I blurted.

"Of course, of course, Doctor, and some will perish."

"I was hoping that wouldn't be necessary."

He smiled softly. "They are our commissary, Doctor. There will be mule steaks, boiled and fried and roasted mule over the top and down the other side, and we'll keep our bellies full no matter what."

"Yes, surely."

"That's why we have so many."

"I imagine you've answered my questions, sir," I said, feeling a great need to escape.

"Well, have a restful night, then. Preuss and I'll keep on with our measurements. Altitude is a tricky thing to get right."

I nodded and hurried into the bitter night. Away from his fire I felt the flood of icy air that was quietly settling over this camp. I made my way back to my mess, sat in the warmth of the fire, and pulled off my rawhide moccasins. My stockings were frozen to my feet because of the snow that had worked in. I dared not pull the stockings loose, for fear of tearing my own half-frozen flesh, so I carefully laid my feet close to the crackling fire, which my brothers watched silently. In time I felt a tingling in my feet, the sign of life returning to them, and after an interval I was able to draw my stockings off and warm my white, frozen flesh in the radiance.

"I am lucky," I said to Ned. "A while more and I would be disabled."

To be disabled there, at that time and place, would have been fatal.

I endured the prickly sensation in my feet as life returned to them, and then put on my spare stockings while the others were laid close to the wavering orange flame to dry. I was heartily sick of winter, sick of hardship, and worse, I didn't know why we were here in this cold place or why we needed to be.

"You went to see the Colonel?" Ned asked.

"He told me about his instruments and altitude and barometric pressures."

"About the mules," Ned persisted.

I nodded, even more melancholic than before. "They are, it seems, our dinner."

"It's been in the back of my mind," Ned said.

"The Colonel said we'd be up and over, descending the west slope in forty-eight hours. That's how he put it. In hours rather than days."

"To make it seem shorter. How many mules will survive that long without a bite of food, carrying us, carrying loads?"

"They're so starved now that one mule can't feed thirty-three men. Not even one meal," I said.

But all this talk about mule meat didn't sit well with me. As I warmed my feet beside that cheerful flame, I knew that the source of my melancholia was pity. Poor, dumb beasts dragged where they would not go, yanked across streams, whipped up slopes, mauled and pushed and pulled and burdened. And now all of the hundred and thirty faithful and trusting beasts were so famished, so empty in their bellies, they could hardly make the heat that kept them alive. I knew all about cold, how cold kills warm-blooded things, how cold this night would be ten times worse for these mules because their bodies couldn't make enough heat to keep them alive.

I also felt embarrassed. Other men cared little about the comfort of their animals; they were simply beasts to be used, discarded, eaten, pitched aside. But there I was, wondering what sort of man John Charles Frémont was that he could be so indifferent to the suffering of animals. I realized then that a man who had no sensibility about animals could have little or none about other animals, namely the human animals who were the beasts of burden of his insatiable hunger for fame. How many living creatures would be sacrificed on the altar of his ambition?

CHAPTER EIGHTEEN

Captain Andrew Cathcart

I could scarcely remember a worse night. Sleep was impossible. A bitter wind tormented us, piercing through every fragile barrier we had erected, crawling under canvas, probing through caps and mittens, making a mockery of blankets. I had never known such cold, relentlessly fingering me as I lay abed. I wanted to be anywhere but there, half-frozen, my body as wretched as my soul, my mind filled with black thoughts.

It wasn't my plight alone that haunted me but that of every other man and the miserable mules, which had started to give out. Yesterday they stumbled, and we could scarcely put them on four feet. This morning there would be not a stitch of feed to warm them after a night of brutal wind that would steal life from them. I wondered, as I lay there in that bitter dark, whether we would see one mule alive at dawn.

A plague on Frémont. We should have retreated from this icy mausoleum long ago, whilst we could. In the dawn, if I lived through the rest of the night, I would watch. There was yet one remedy for the mules, a great deal of sugar the colonel was hauling to flavor his tea, I imagine. In the British Isles we knew all about sweet feeds and how they perk up an animal. This dawn I would see whether Frémont would spare his mules or let them perish. He had enough sugar and some macaroni, too, to fashion a hot meal for them, a meal heated up with boiling water. I could show these Yanks a thing or two. We'd see.

I tugged blankets this way and that and dug into my kit for more woolens, only to find I was wearing all that I possessed. I wanted more gloves, layer on layer to pull over my numb hands, and more stockings to cover aching feet, but there were none. I could lie still until dawn or brave the subzero air and walk and stomp about and maybe bring some prickles of life back to my aching limbs. I chose to lie still. That bloody wind would kill me if I left my bedroll for long.

Dawn came slow in that time of year, but the men didn't wait for it. They were in the same condition as I and chose instead to build fires under the flinty stars and warm themselves. It took some doing to start a blaze with wood so cold, but a little gunpowder and some pine shavings and a lot of shelter from that gale finally did the trick. But it was as if we had no flame at all. The wind raked away the heat faster than the fires could burn, and the whole predawn exercise was a worse misery than lying in our icy robes. I was no warmer after a half hour beside the roaring fire than I had been in my miserable blankets.

We could not see the animals, and as we sat about trying to boil water for tea, all of us keeping our thoughts to ourselves, I grew aware of their silence. No coughs, no snorts, no wheeze or shuffle in the blackness. I wondered if most were dead. When the reluctant dawn did finally arrive, and we could gaze through the murk into the pinewoods where the mules had attempted to shelter from the gale, we could see that most lived. But here and there were dark lumps half-buried in snow, the gale swiftly burying them. I counted five. Several of us tramped through the thick snow to look the herd over. Those that lived stood stock-still, heads lowered, and most of them jammed together to share whatever heat they could offer one another.

The dead mules were frozen solid. So much for mules as a commissary, I thought. We'd have to kill a living animal for food. The dead mules were rock-solid, and cutting meat from one would be like cutting steaks from a bronze equestrian statue. With saws and axes we might whittle away some meat, but I knew that if it came down to sawing and hacking a dead mule or slitting the throat of a live one for dinner, these weary men would take the easy way. The colonel's much-heralded food supply in extremity was not a good supply at all without live animals.

This morning we would saddle these half-dead animals and make them carry us up a wintry slope until they dropped. It took an hour to get some water boiling for coffee or tea, and I hoped the first act would be to give these animals a hot drink. But the Americans simply ignored the stock, as if the mules didn't exist, and went about readying themselves for another assault on the mountains.

Frémont appeared, smiling, restless, enjoying his morning coffee, saying little. I soon realized he would do nothing, absolutely nothing, for the mules this morning except grind them to death. I was too cold to hate the man but full of schemes to give a furtive handful of sugar to the beasts, preferably with hot water. In the end, I did nothing. Old habits of command prevailed. It was not for me to give orders or to disobey the man in charge. It haunts me that I did not rise up and do what I had in mind, without the leave of Frémont. I had been in the hussars too long.

The bitter wind never quit, and I knew this would be one of the worst days of my life. And yet the camp was uncommonly cheerful. We stood at the very base of the ridge that would take us into the drainage of the Colorado River and ultimately the Pacific. The ridge was not half a mile distant, though this last assault would be steep and cruel. There was, among the company, a sense of victory. Beyond, we could tumble our way west, into warmer climes, where grass grew and a man could pull off the layers of leather and wool that now kept him alive.

So we saddled the mules, which stumbled stupidly as we brought them in one by one, brushed the snow out of their coat, and threw packsaddles and loads over them once again. One mule simply went down, and no tail twisting could wrench him up. He had played out, lying inertly in the snow, too worn to resist the bullying. I watched it lying there, its lungs pumping irregularly, its neck arched back, its mouth open. And then with a shudder, it ceased to breathe. And even as it died, snow was filtering into its hair.

No one came to butcher it while it was possible to do so.

I saw Ben Kern staring, mutely, and he saw me, and a faint shake of his head told me his every thought. I felt an inconsolable sadness. The mule had died even before we raised camp and tackled that terrible grade. What would the hard day ahead do to the rest? So there they were, the Creoles and Missourians and the rest, offering not even some heated water to these miserable beasts and loading them with all the tons of gear and our own remaining fodder before leading the stumbling creatures up the valley once again, one slow step at a time, the men in front wielding giant clubs made of deadwood to hammer a trail through thick snow that sometimes reached the shoulders of men sitting on those mules.

I counted it a miracle that the mules walked at all. They are noble beasts and were giving their last breath to the task. But as soon as the grade rose dramatically, they could go no farther and simply stood in that trench cut into the drifts, heads hanging.

"We'll pull them up. Then it'll be downhill," Godey said, so we dragged out our hempen ropes, fashioned cruel halters over the snouts of the mules, and tugged them upward, one step at a time. But the mules were beyond walking and simply stood where they stood. It became a great exercise of force, men in front of and behind each animal, pulling and pushing, yanking and shoving, as we climbed the last few hundred yards toward that treeless summit not far ahead.

Then Godey's own mule, Dick, gave out. He had treated it more severely than the rest, and now it folded to its knees and would not budge, its half-frozen body blocking the trench trail. Godey saw at once it was over for Dick and swiftly unsaddled the animal, and we pushed it into a drift, where it expired, one last sad rush of air, and then lay inert, its mouth open, tongue hanging out, neck crooked back. Godey said nothing, which was the only decent thing to do, and set off on foot, dragging the mule that had stood in line behind Dick. And so we spent a whole morning and midday struggling up the last few hundred yards to the barren summit.

And when we got there, we saw grass, a whole slope of it that the wind had whipped free and clear. But when we finally emerged on that great cap of the world, the subzero gale blew heat out of us so swiftly that no living creature could survive there for more than a few minutes. To put the mules on that grass would be to kill them all within the hour.

We paused up there to look about. There we were, on top of the world. The distant valley of the Rio del Norte was behind us, and beyond it, the white peaks of the Sangre de Cristos. To the north and south, range after range, peak after serrated peak whitened the landscape, beneath a bold blue sky. I saw cirrus clouds to the west, heralding another storm, and knew we were in for worse than this cold day. But that is not what stopped my heart. To the west, some miles distant, stood another wall of mountains, with a notch in them well above the one from which we all gaped at this alpine world. We had not crossed the divide. The valley into which we would now descend was yet another drainage of the Rio Grande and led to the Atlantic.

But in this bright, eye-smarting place we could not tarry, not for an extra second, because the icy gale was plucking the last heat from us and further destroying our mules. We studied the mountains and hastened across the ridge, dropping into a gulch so steep we could not keep our footing, and floundered our way downslope through giant drifts higher than we could stand, amid yellow pines. And there more mules simply halted, too worn to proceed, but we could not stay there in that awful place and hurried on, needing all that was sustaining about lower altitudes and escape from wind and perhaps fodder for the mules, which were now clearly in extremis. My own mind was filled with terrors now. We had not crossed the divide, as Frémont had promised us, and we could see nothing to the west or north that suggested descent or cessation of this towering range.

It was as if, up there, we were witnessing our death warrant. Or so I thought. We were all too numb ourselves to say a word to one another. We slid and stumbled and plowed our way down that steep slope for as long as we could endure, never reaching any sort of bottoms that might yield feed for our wretched animals or game for ourselves. I felt trapped.

Finally, in the last hour of December light, the colonel decided we would camp in a wind-sheltered bottom, in four or five feet of snow. There would be plenty of firewood but not a bite for the mules. We unloaded the mules and heaped the tack in a single place where we could get at it in the morrow. We had to keep our tack from the mules, which were gnawing at leather and canvas and rope and trying to break into the panniers for whatever would fill their bellies. Most of them had lost manes and tails, which had been gnawed away by other mules.

Some of the men attempted to dig out a camping place, while others wearily spread a rubberized sheet over the snow and collapsed onto it. I had never experienced such silence in a bivouac, each man among us entirely private. If their thoughts were similar to my own, it was no wonder. They dared not utter what they were thinking. So deep was Frémont's grip on his veterans of previous journeys that they would follow Frémont to their doom rather than wrestle him or set themselves loose from the rest of us. I could not fathom it, and yet I was doing the same thing. There I was, in probably fatal circumstances, meekly accepting my fate.

The mules stood stock-still in the bottoms. A little brush poked through, and a few of them found the energy to nip at stalks and twigs. But most had given up and numbly awaited their death. No one seemed to care. I was weary, but I made my way to the bottoms and flailed away with a piece of deadwood, gradually exposing more brush for a few mules to masticate. I was satisfied to see several of them begin to nip and chew. I hoped that my example would stir the others to open some of the snow fields to the forage, but I made no progress there, though most of the men had watched me carefully, and all of them knew my purpose. It was as if they needed a command from Colonel Frémont to undertake the labor, and that command was not forthcoming.

In time they did complete a makeshift camp, and mess fires burned in holes in the snow, their heat glazing the walls of the pits. The company could find warmth in those protective circles, which reminded me of the walls of an igloo, and there the men congregated as a lavender darkness descended, and along with it an icy downdraft from that ridge above, which was ladling killing air down that draw, air that would murder the weakened mules.

Some men, it turned out, did go upslope, and they recovered eight of the beasts and herded them down, arriving in camp at dusk, the mules stumbling and sliding so slowly that they barely made it while daylight lingered. These eight were simply herded in with the rest, to live or die as fate saw fit. I once again felt a great loathing for men who would not make every effort to sustain their beasts. And yet these same men were so weary they could barely sustain themselves, so I supposed my judgment was harsh.

The bright fire down in that snow pit cheered me that night. Our mess had the greenhorns, the ones who had never been out on an expedition before, the ones unknown to Colonel Frémont, the ones least familiar with the arts of survival. Some boiled macaroni cheered us. It was good to get something solid in our bellies. The glazed walls caught the heat, until it seemed we were in a parlor instead of high in the Saguache Mountains, as they seemed to be called by these men. I peered upward uneasily, suddenly aware that

the ice-chip stars above had vanished, and I knew that w
would soon be inundated once again. The night would nc
be so pleasant.

"How much food have we?" Ben Kern asked. "Does any
one but the colonel know?"

"I know. I looked in the packs," his brother Richar
said. "We have three packs of macaroni, maybe fifty pound
of sugar, salt, and some frozen elk that the colonel i
saving."

"Just that, for thirty-three men?" Ned asked.

"That and the mules."

"What good are frozen mules, that's what I want t
know," Creutzfeldt asked. "I couldn't hack them up with a
axe."

"How far to the Continental Divide?" Ben asked.

No one could answer him. That next ridge west could b
days away, with the mules so broken down.

"The mules could be helped with warm water mixed wit
sugar," I said.

None of them responded at first.

"We'll need the sugar ourselves, I am thinking,
Creutzfeldt said.

That's where it ended. Later, it began to snow, thic
flakes that soon buried us as we lay in our bedrolls. Th
snow had become a prison, shackling me. Now there wer
walls rising in every direction. We could not return fror
whence we came. We could not go forward. The silent snow
ruled us.

CHAPTER NINETEEN

John Charles Frémont

I wondered how Jessie was faring. She probably was still in Saint Louis, readying herself for the Panama trip. She was made of sturdy stuff, and I little doubted that she would negotiate a successful journey to California. A lesser woman could manage it. I felt no qualms about consigning her to the fates of the traveler, knowing she was a Benton. I supposed she was pining for news of me, but I had no means of telling her that I was somewhere close to the Continental Divide, being guided by a lummox who might or might not know the way, and only time would tell.

I had strong men with me during the army expeditions, and some of them were with me this trip, having left the service or taken leave. They were from good stock and had weathered all the adversities of life lived in raw nature. Preuss was a tough little German who knew how to keep himself comfortable. Godey, of course, is the very prototype of his sort, as strong as they come, and a veteran. King is another one, a veteran who was with me in California and who is made of sturdy stuff. Add my California men Taplin, Martin, Stepperfeldt, Ferguson, Wise, Vincenthaler, and Breckenridge, as well as my veteran Creoles, Proue, Tabeau, and Morin, and there is my cadre of hard men, good stock, who never urged on me the counsels of despair. It was the rest who concerned me, but I didn't let them know it. They were soft city men, unused to hardship.

We were being guided by a degenerate, and that caused me some difficulty. It was plain to me that Williams had been a poor choice, though the only one available, so I can scarcely fault myself. He had not lifted a finger the entire trip, reasoning that a guide need not concern himself with food, firewood, saddling and grooming and feeding the mules, breaking a trail, or making and breaking camp. He assumed no responsibility, not even for the mule we provided him, letting my company do every lick of work whilst he meandered about.

That he had led us into a perilous circumstance high in the San Juan Mountains did not escape my attention. He had barely said a word, and I knew he was avoiding me as much as he could. Now we had topped a saddle Old Bill had assumed was the divide, only to discover that many miles distant rose another chain, higher than the one we had topped, and we were far from crossing over to warmer and safer climes. Indeed, I found myself wondering whether this odd degenerate had the slightest idea of where he was leading us, and that morning I decided to find out.

After my morning toilet I sought him out. He was lounging on one of our rubberized sheets watching my company once again prepare to tackle massive drifts and to hack a passage for our weary mules.

My men were busy; the mules had this night eaten saddle blankets, ropes, manes and tails, woolen clothing, belts and shoes and canvas, in the process damaging such tack and equipment as we had at hand. It was almost impossible to keep them out of camp.

I squatted down beside him as he lounged, picking his teeth with twig. I seethed with contempt for the lout but carefully set aside my private thought and smiled.

"Well, Williams, we obviously have a long way to go to cross the divide," I said.

"Goodly way, yes."

"I wonder if you could show me the pass. I see nothing but another wall of white mountains off to the west."

He grinned, his tongue working the gaps in his teeth. "Oh, she's there. I always know it when I see it."

"Is there feed for the mules ahead?"

"Oh, could be, depending on how she blows."

"How steep is it?"

He lifted his cap off and scratched his hair, or maybe it was a cootie he was scratching. "Depends on which way we go," he said. "It don't make a difference."

I found the answer maddening. I espied a knob to the right and saw how it might offer advantage.

"My friend, we'll go up there," I said, pointing. "Then you may enlighten me."

He studied on it. "That's a far piece and full of snow."

"I'm sure it's of no consequence to a man of your abilities."

He offered me no resistance save for some mumbling, and we struck through heavy drifts, sometimes waist high, ascending a rough slope that revealed only the tops of the pines growing on it. In no time he was heaving air in and out of his ill-used body, whilst I ascended easily, the steam of my breath dissipating in the icy air. It was a clear and sunny morning with a cobalt sky, and that would help me accomplish my purpose.

He followed along in my path, daintily avoiding what labor he could, but that was the inferior nature of the man. The last portion was a steep ascent over unknown obstacles underfoot that tripped us, but in time we arrived, blowing, atop the knob, which afforded us a breathtaking view west and north and south. It was at once brilliant and forbidding. The heavens were a bold blue, and before us lay hundreds of square miles of whitened country. In the immediate foreground was a rolling plateau, but beyond was a great range of whited peaks. Overall, the snow lay so thick that it obscured all else, so one could not tell whether forest or plain or rockslide or brush lay underneath.

It was too bright; my eyes leaked tears, which froze in my beard.

"Ah, Mister Williams," said I, "this gives us a view."

He blinked, said nothing. The glare didn't seem to affect his vision at all, and I wondered whether his eyes had dimmed with age.

"Now, sir, we can peer into the future. Where are we going?"

"I don't rightly know from this distance, but I know close at hand, as we pass by," he said.

It was not a response that gave me comfort.

"Now, where is Cochetopa Pass?"

"Oh, yonder there." He waved an arm vaguely north, toward a formidable white range.

"Is that where we're heading?"

"I got my own way."

"Well, then, kindly point it out to me."

He eyed the distant ridges to the west, which probably were the actual divide, and finally shrugged. "I'll know her when we get there," he muttered.

"This was the route you recommended because of its ease and good fodder?"

He smiled cheerfully. "Trust me or not," he said. "It's better than the other."

"What choice have I?"

He laughed, a low muttering that finally broke into an odd giggle. And yet I saw no alternative. He would lead us through, or not. Ahead of us were two or three or four days of passage over a rolling plateau, but it was snow-blanketed open country that afforded little shelter and no fodder unless we could turn the mules into a watercourse somewhere ahead.

We descended in a small avalanche, which in fact bruised

my shin, and I proceeded into camp, where my old stalwarts were waiting, having watched our ascent.

"Old Bill assures me that the pass is just ahead," I said. "We have some snowy country to cross, mostly level, and then it's up and over. By Christmas, we'll be down in warm and grassy country, celebrating our deliverance."

"We lost eight mules last night," Godey said.

"And we'll lose more, I'm sure," I replied. "The hardy stock will pull through. The inferior ones will surrender."

I did not see skepticism in their faces, which was good. I've learned over the years that candor is the most excellent means to keep spirits high, and that is what was required at this crucial moment.

"Let's be off," I said.

The men cheerfully finished loading the mules. They had rebalanced the loads, making sure that as our stores diminished the burdens were lighter. Godey took the lead, having fashioned a club of deadwood that would hammer a trail for the mules, and so we proceeded down the canyon where we had harbored ourselves from the icy gale of yesterday. At the van, half a dozen good men hammered the drifts into submission. It swiftly became plain that this day we would work through snows that could well be twenty or thirty feet deep. The V-shaped trench in the soft snow soon blotted out all horizons, save for a narrow strip of blue above. We fell into a world in which the surface of the snow was above our heads, even those of us who were riding the mules.

My men rotated the trail breaking frequently, gangs of four or five slowly making progress through the morning. Scarcely did we see more than the slit of heaven, and at no time did any of us observe the vast, chilling panorama of the San Juan range. I thought it was just as well that no man caught a glimpse of the larger world. This was a mild day, with open skies, and no wind pierced into our trench to chill us. I thought in a way it was rather jolly, though some of my men were fearful of those looming walls of soft snow on either side of us.

A mule gave out, and it turned out to be Ben Kern's. He had urged it forward, only to feel the beast shiver and slowly capsize. Nothing he did could arouse it, and finally he abandoned it. He is an overly tender man but took it stoically. The remaining beasts had to step over the dead one, which they did unhappily, with ears flattened back. But in time we left our troubles behind and completed our descent, heading out on rolling plateau country, with great rounded shoulders of land driving us south and north as we kept as low as we could. The winds had swept some areas fairly clear, and sometimes we could peer over the lip of our trench upon a blank white world, a landscape without landmarks, perfectly submerged by the snows.

We made three and a half miles across that tumultuous tableland, but the plummeting sun compelled us to halt and make a dry camp on a slope. We had scrounged some deadwood and made use of it, for there was none at hand. There would be wood enough to boil some macaroni, but not enough to sustain a fire all night. It would be an unpleasant night for man and beast. I knew the sturdiest would never complain, and I heard not one word of distress. But the silent complaint rising from the mess of the greenhorns was palpable, and I could well imagine what the Kerns were scribbling in their diaries. No matter. I have learned to shrug off the mosquito droning of small men. I would set things straight in my own journals when the time came. My stalwarts soon had their rubberized sheets spread, affording them a dry place to unroll their beds, and I heard no more of trouble. I knew the night would claim more of the inferior mules, and I knew there was no help for it. Let them perish. We did not need them.

I sent Saunders to fetch Godey to me. My deputy commander appeared at once.

"Some stew?" I asked, motioning toward the kettle. Saunders had boiled some jerky and cornmeal from my private stock.

Godey shook his head.

"A few quiet words, eh?"

Godey squatted beside me, mountain style.

"How are the men, Godey?"

"Doing well, sir. I don't hear any complaints."

"What do they think of me?"

"Not a complaint, Colonel."

"Do they know who got them into this difficulty?"

Godey paused. "Old Bill eats by himself, sir. That says all that you wish to know."

"Ah, then they do know where the fault lies. Now, what about the Kerns' mess? That's where trouble will come."

"Quite valiant, Colonel. Doctor Kern was severely frostbitten last night, but he carries on without complaint."

"Yes, but what do they really think?"

Godey eyed me and finally shook his head. I didn't know how to interpret that but let it pass.

"Soft men are a burden to me, Alex."

"I think Doctor Kern would like to save the mules. He headed for the creek and pushed snow aside until he opened up some brush, and pushed a mule into it."

"They're poor stock. We're better off eating them."

"We've lost twenty some and haven't butchered one, sir."

"Choose the weakest," I replied.

I dismissed Godey and watched him hurry into the darkness. He was my most reliable man.

A cruel north wind arose in the night, probing once again into men's bedrolls, ruining hope as well as comfort. My men were already badly frostbitten, with patches of white flesh on their hands and feet, their ears and noses and chins. They had endured these things stoically, as I did, but this night of December 16 seemed to herald a shift in the weather. We awoke to a sullen sky, as dark as the underside of a skillet, with polar air gliding relentlessly past us. Godey lumbered out into the snowfields and came back with the count. Another eight down, but several more so stupid with cold he doubted they could survive another hour.

"Butcher one," I said. It was easy enough to butcher a live and warm animal, and I thought to take advantage of it. He nodded and summoned Sorel, who selected an animal that was barely standing and slit its throat with one sweep of his Green River knife, and we watched the beast sag into the snow with a final spasm as blood gouted from its throat. The butchering was left to the Creoles, who seemed to have a knack for it, and soon they were peeling back hide and slicing skinny loins and rib roasts from the half-starved beast. I wondered whether there would be meat enough to feed thirty-three men one meal.

The rest watched silently. It was so cold that the Creoles had to work swiftly, and soon their hands were covered with frozen red slush. Not even stuffing them under their coats or into their armpits helped much, but in time they did crudely butcher perhaps a hundred pounds of stringy meat and load the freezing red meat into panniers. The head of the mule, now severed from its body, was half buried in snow, its sightless eyes staring at nothing and its sliced-off tongue an open wound between its jaws. It would go hungry no more, and I had done it a favor.

CHAPTER TWENTY

Henry King

I was settling a blanket and a sawbuck on a mule when I spotted Colonel Frémont and Old Bill struggle up to that knob. I thought I knew what that was all about. I grinned and nudged Godey, who was overseeing the loading.

He winked. Pretty soon the rest of the colonel's men were observing the two climbers who were stumbling up that snowy grade. Old Bill could hardly keep up with the colonel. I nodded slightly to Breckenridge, who in turn nudged Scott, Bacon, and Beadle, and that caught the attention of Ferguson, Hubbard, and Carver. Pretty quickly, most of the colonel's veterans were staring up that slope, plainly entertained by the sight.

"Colonel's heading up there to get the Ten Commandments," Ferguson said.

"No he isn't. He's going up there to give God ten or twelve commandments," Hubbard said.

"Saddle those mules," Godey said, but no one paid the slightest heed.

Frémont and Old Bill Williams reached the crown of that knob and began an animated conversation or maybe a dispute, with plenty of arm waving.

"I guess I know what's being said," I announced.

"Maybe you don't," Tom Martin retorted.

"That old coward Williams, he's calling it quits, and he's telling the colonel to turn around and head back the way we came," I said.

"Could be, but I'd suppose they're just looking at the way west. All this snow, it gets hard to see what's what."

"I've been watching that Williams," I said, reaching for the girth that Martin was handing me under the mule's belly. "You know what he is? A loafer. He hasn't done a lick of work, but that's not what's galling me. He don't know the way, and he's pretending he does, and now the colonel's seen right through him and giving him what for."

"I think he wants the colonel to turn around," Joseph Stepperfeldt said from behind the next mule over. "He's half-crazy. He told me once he can see animal spirits. Maybe the mule spirits are telling him to turn around." He laughed. It was a good joke.

I tightened the girth and buckled it. Martin began lifting panniers onto the trembling mule, who stood with locked legs, head low. They were all like that. They had gone three days without a meal, apart from a few twigs.

The wind was howling again, and cirrus clouds ribbed the sky. It would be snowing soon. It entertained me. I'm always wondering how bad it can get.

"I'd bet my last dollar we'll move ahead," I said.

"Of course," Martin said. "The colonel's commanding. There's not one soul over him now that he's out of the army. There is no one to say nay."

I hadn't thought of it that way, but I saw the truth in it. I'd always seen the colonel as a man who let nothing stop him. Our gentlemanly commander would take orders from no one, not even God. And he would succeed in his design, even if he left the entire company behind him. I have the same nature. We were going to go over these mountains no matter what the cost, and that was already decided. We were going to do what no others could do. The Conqueror of California would conquer the San Juan Mountains.

"He's got him a wife waiting out in California," Martin said. "If I had me a wife, maybe I'd be in a hurry, too."

I smiled. "Mine's back East, but you don't see me high-tailing it out of here."

"It ain't a wife that's itching old Frémont," said Breckenridge. "He's got some other kind of itch."

No one had a reply to that.

Iron-bellied clouds were scudding in, and we faced another mean day. Breckenridge noticed the clouds, too. "Don't know where we'll be spending Christmas," he said.

"We'll have a feast. Mule-meat pudding, with mule soup," I replied.

He eyed the trembling mules, who stood lock legged with the packs on their backs. "It'd do them a favor," Breckenridge said. "What's the new missus going to do this Christmas, Henry?"

"Pine for me," I replied.

"Like you're pining for her, eh?" Breckenridge retorted.

I laughed. A gust of air wormed through my buckskin coat. I was already frostbit in half a dozen places, two fingers, my earlobes, and there was plenty of dead flesh around my ankles too. "She's not frostbit," I said. "She's with her parents, I imagine."

A burdened mule shivered and slowly buckled, slowly collapsing, resisting its own weakness to the last, but it went down in the snow, half-buried even as it shuddered and died.

"I suppose we ought to butcher him," I said. "I'll ask Godey."

I found the headman loading a trembling mule.

"We just lost one. You think we should butcher before he freezes up?"

"Leave him. We'll butcher another tonight," Godey said.

So Breckenridge and I tugged the packs off the dead one. It was hard work, and I kept feeling I wasn't up to my usual. Sometimes I felt plumb faint. Half the men felt the way

I did. Maybe it was altitude, or bad food. We hadn't seen a green in weeks. But some of the company didn't seem affected at all. Preuss, the wiry German, seemed the way he always was, furiously measuring everything, getting the height of every peak in sight, making pencil sketches and notes, and ignoring every hardship. But others, like that Scot, Cathcart, seemed to shrink down every day, and now he was parchment over bones and had great hollow sockets around his eyes. You never knew about those foreigners, whether they could take it.

A fresh gust of bitter air boiled past us, firing pellets of ice into our beards.

"Goddamn the wind," Martin snapped.

I had rarely heard oathing in this company. The colonel's utterances were free of it, and there was an unspoken rule that the rest of us would follow his example. But the colonel was up on that knoll, talking things over with the rotten guide.

I felt the slivers of ice melt in my beard, work down, and then freeze. This would be another day of icicles hanging from our beards and hair.

About then, Frémont and Old Bill skidded and tumbled down that knoll, barely remaining upright. Frémont surveyed the company, the loaded mules, the newly dead one.

"On our way," he said. "We'll walk."

Some of the company seemed irritated by the command and reluctantly slid off their wretched animals. But it was a valuable request. By now the outliers of the approaching storm were overhead, and the wintry sun vanished behind an iron overcast. The trail beaters once again hacked our way westward, this time through windswept country that harbored only two or three feet of snow on the level. The wind jammed so much drift into our faces and eyes we couldn't tell what was descending from the clouds and what was being lifted by the gusts.

It took the heat right out of me, even though I was walking, and I knew ere long I'd be frostbit again and again, and this would be a hard day. I wondered if a man could get frostbit in the privates. What would that do to me? Now that was something to think about. I thought I'd ask Ben Kern about it, not that a greenhorn would know anything. There sure are places a man doesn't want to get himself frostbit, especially me. I've sure got an itch to get to California with all my parts ready and willing.

We rotated the trail breaking, three at a time. When my turn came, I found myself with Stepperfeldt and Ferguson, each of us armed with a deadwood club, which we used to break through the skin of the drifts, hammer down a wide-enough trail to pose no obstacle to the weary mules. Usually I didn't mind the work. It was a way of keeping warm, keeping the blood up, but now a mysterious lassitude gripped me, and it was all I could do to lift the deadwood, smash through snow, and lift it again. And instead of getting warmer, I found myself getting so chilled I thought to find my bedroll and wrap myself. Not that blankets would do much in a wind like that.

So, step by step, we proceeded on. I was glad when Godey sent our relief forward, and I turned over my driftwood snow club and waited for the train to catch up. The rest were a long time coming, and I could see why. The mules were quitting, and even the efforts of several men tugging and shoving couldn't get them to move. So time was flying by and the company was stalled, right in the first foothills on the far side of that plateau. There wasn't a mule that would climb up that trail.

Godey shouted a few things, his voice lost in the wind, and I watched as the company stripped the packs off the mules, tied ropes to the panniers, and began skidding them forward. Even then the mules had to be yanked and shoved, but now the company was struggling up slopes again. I watched Preuss wrestle two panniers up the icy slope, his precious instruments in them. He would not allow anyone to touch the packs and was uncommonly careful whenever he came to a hump or a protruding rock. Well, I didn't blame him one particle. Tough old bird, doing what had to be done. We all protect our jewels.

Godey handed me a rope, but I was so worn from beating a trail I didn't have the strength to drag a pack. But I did. There was no help for it. Drag a pack or give up. Quit. Sit down in the snow and die. And I was damned if I would do that and let them think I didn't have the temper in me. So I learned to drag for twenty yards, pause a while, and go another few yards, and pause, and let my heart settle down.

The snow fell now, driven by the gusts, but these were thick flakes, and in moments they were filling the trench the beaters had pounded up that slope. More mules quit. They would stop, tremble, and slowly collapse into the snow, and we would leave them there. In two minutes they were buried by snow, just a white lump blocking our snow road.

There went more dinner, I thought. Mule meat wasn't much for eating, and the mules were down to bone anyway. But we managed, mostly by cutting the meat up fine and boiling it to a sort of mush. Some of the messes tried slicing it thin and roasting, but it was like eating leather, and pretty soon we were all eating mule stew, mule mush, mule soup, because that was the only way we could get any mule into our innards.

But now we were running through mules in a hurry, and I wondered what we would be eating in a week. I'd heard that Frémont had put aside some frozen elk for Christmas dinner a few days before, and I supposed that would be mighty fine, if we got as far as Christmas. The way things were going, I didn't know whether we'd make one more day or not.

I'd heard there were some Mexican settlements down the Rio del Norte, but that was some piece away, and that wasn't the direction the colonel was heading. He'd gotten his compass set on west, and west was how he'd go. California or bust. He was stubborn, I'll grant that. That's what I liked about him. There's a type of man who won't quit, and he'd rather die trying. That's what I am.

We didn't make much progress, and by afternoon, with the peril of darkness drawing nigh, the colonel halted us on a slope in a pine forest where deadwood abounded and there would be some shelter from the gale. We had lost mules all day; an animal would simply quit, stand stock-still, and slowly fold into the snow. I surveyed the new camp hopefully and did see some grass on an exposed southerly slope, and I hoped we could put the mules onto it, even though we would have to beat a path through perilous slopes to reach it. Some weary men started at once, while the rest of us collected deadwood and tried to save the mules by rubbing them. The mules either stood inertly, an inch from death, or sought blankets and ropes and leather to eat, making life difficult for us because there was little they would not gnaw on, including what was left of our tents and clothing and tack.

I watched the Creoles slit the throat of the weakest of the living mules, watched it sag into the snow, blood gouting from its neck. They set upon the animal before it was entirely dead. We would have mule stew this night, and mule hide with which to fashion patches for our ruined boots. The prospect offered me no comfort.

Somehow, we made camp and got some fires going in protected snow pits where the wind would not snuff them. The snow had diminished, but the heavens scowled at us, and I had the sense we were trespassers, invaders of a place sacred to others, where no mortal should pass by. I got from gossip that ahead, at the top of a bald hill, one would only find more of the same, no relief in any direction.

The men were all done in. I had thought myself alone in my weakness, but now I saw horror everywhere, men so skeletal and worn they seemed half alive. The sole exception was the colonel, who was calmly erecting his tent, scraping snow away, building a private fire—he always camped apart from the rest of us—and making himself comfortable. I could not fathom it. He had pulled away from us for several days, rarely saying a word to any of us, and never a word of encouragement. It was as if he were indifferent to our fate, or maybe he simply felt helpless to change anything or admit to a mistake or terrible judgment. And if pride stopped him from changing course, his fate was our own, for there was nothing we could do about any of it.

We did get a few of the mules over to that grassy slope, but most could not be budged and stood mutely near our mess fires, waiting to die. I imagined that within a day or so, not a one would be standing. The question that had us all brooding now was whether any of us would soon be standing.

CHAPTER TWENTY-ONE

Benjamin Kern, MD

White on white on white. We called it Camp Dismal, but that understates the case. We huddled on the north slope of a great bald mountain at around eleven thousand feet, in a deluge of snow that lasted for days. There was only misery and foreboding.

We settled in some vast depth of snow, whiteness so deep we could see only the tops of trees, making them seem like needle-bearing shrubs. But below us, buried in snow, were scrub pines, all that grew at this altitude. We could not pitch a tent, for there was no ground under us to take the stakes, so we erected huts of deadwood and canvas, and that was all the shelter we could manage. Each mess managed to build a fire in a pit, which allayed the wind slightly but added smoke to our misery and did little to warm our numb flesh.

Now, at last, we could go no further. We were walled by white, by endless snow falling upon us, a foot or two or three a day. We could neither retreat from the bald mountain nor push forward, so we were trapped there. Preuss led a small party westward, intending to find a way down, but not even that wiry, hardy man, a veteran of Frémont's earlier campaigns, could manage it, and in time he retreated to our camp, where we all sat helplessly, awaiting our fate with each tick of the clock.

Snow engulfed our messes, and we could scarcely find firewood to keep a blaze going in all that stinging white downfall. The misery was compounded by the wetness of our clothing, which permeated every layer of our wool and leather and rendered us so miserable that we wondered how we might endure yet another minute of another hour of another day. We could not dry ourselves or our clothing in that constant blizzard.

We scraped away snow with our tin mess plates, struggled into the treetops to hack at limbs for the fire, retreated into our huts chilled and soaked, our beards dangling icicles, our eyes smarting from the smoke. And lost from us was hope, for the extent of our horizon was a white wall blotting out even the closest scenery, so that all we had before our watering eyes was ten or fifteen feet of whiteness.

But that was only one facet of the horror. Through this whole white nightmare, we heard the piteous whickering of the dying mules, summoning one another for help, telling one another they were departing. I swear, all that first night, the mules we had managed to drive to that windswept dome where a little grass broke through wailed miserably. I swear what I heard was sobbing, the weeping of the mules as they trumpeted their distress to one another, and then the heavy silence that overtook them in the night. I knew they were gone. I knew that the murderous wind had clubbed them senseless, even as they frantically pawed and dug for the thin brown strands of grass that might sustain them in kinder climates.

Thus did the ghastly night pass, and in the gray light of dawn, after we had scraped away new feet of snow with our mess plates, we searched for them and saw none standing on that slope. They had vanished, and we could not find their carcasses even if we had tried with a pole, for merciless nature had mercifully hidden them from our eyes under a white blanket. Yet a few still stood in the woods, protected from the wind, a foot of snow on their backs, icicles dangling from their every hair, rattling under their jaws. Old Bill Williams swore he could see their spirits hovering over them, waiting to fly away, but I could never fathom such a thing. I knew only what my medical training and senses told me: their body temperatures barely sustained life. They had not eaten for days and were surviving on the last of the fat they carried. They were too weak to walk, much less plow through drifts as high as they were. But those few lived, if only for the moment.

At some of the other messes, live mules were being slaughtered. I would hear one last pitiful bleat, and then the thud of an animal capsizing. But it was odd. These messes never dressed out the entire carcass, making the most of it. Those men were as worn as we were, numbed by cold, struggling for breath in the thin air, and soon the slaughtered and mostly intact mule was blanketed by merciful snow. The last mules were simply targets of opportunity and were not systematically butchered to give us as much meat as possible. I had come to love those mules, knew many of them well, and could hardly bear to see them tumble, never to rise again.

I sat mutely as the sun rose and set somewhere above the gray blanket of clouds, too stupefied to write a thing. I'm not sure my numb fingers would have enabled me to write. I didn't have anything to say. Richard managed a few words. I saw him laboriously scribbling some little thing in his bound ledger, probably thinking what I was thinking: those who found us in the distant future would at least have an account of our last hours.

I confess I gave little thought to what transpired elsewhere, in the other messes. We were all wrapped in our misery. But some distance away—it seemed miles away but it was only a few dozen yards, Colonel Frémont was making his own plans. His object, I was soon to learn, was to move our camp from this exposed north shoulder of the bald mountain to the southern side, where we might escape the wind, find forage and a shred of warmth. It was not a bad plan except that without capable mules, we would need to drag our worldly goods to the new locale by brute force, mostly along a snow path of our devising. He sent some of our stronger men to break a trail, and soon we found ourselves slowly dragging panniers and tack over the powdery snow, pausing every little way for breath in the thin air, hoping the ongoing storm would not close in and blind us or strand us. This wretched task consumed two days, and even after that we would need to return to Camp Dismal for the last of the packs. I can't remember a worse time, when I felt so faint and dizzy that I thought I would topple at any time and vanish in a drift.

And yet we succeeded and found ourselves in better circumstances, out of the icy blast and able to collect a goodly supply of deadwood to feed our fires. Such mules as were still standing were scattered behind us, unable to walk the three miles, and we ended up with none at our new refuge. I knew, with heavy heart, that we were now afoot.

In all this I saw Frémont consulting with our guide, Williams, over and over, but the colonel never made me a party to his decisions, preferring to consult only with those veterans of his California expedition. He avoided those of us who were newcomers to his cadre. So I didn't know what was being discussed so ardently, and the others were too weary or breathless at that altitude to inform me. But it was mostly about topography. When we finally settled on the southwesterly slope, we were in a new drainage, which I took to be another tributary of the Rio del Norte, but one more precipitous than what we had traversed to reach this upland of the San Juans.

The brutal cold lessened, and some fragments of a coy sun caught us up, and we heartened at the better prospect.

But I soon learned through the camp grapevine that the divide, which might take us to the waters of the Colorado River, still lay many miles west. It was apparently beginning to sink into the colonel that he was nowhere near Pacific waters and his company was now stranded in high country and had only enough food to last a week or so more. We set out to consolidate the new camp and drag the last of our packs over the ridge, a task so exhausting we could manage only a little at a time. But at last we left the north-slope Camp Dismal behind.

We were more comfortable out of the wind, which lifted our spirits enough so that we could begin talking to one another again. I began to make diary entries. But despite the slight improvement, we were feeling hard used, caught on a mountain top and subject to an ambitious man's whim. Our very lives depended on Colonel Frémont's decisions. Those in my mess knew nothing of his plans.

My artist brother, Richard, wondered aloud one night while the three of us huddled in the cold under a canvas hut, whether there would be any good in escaping the company and making our way to the Mexican settlements down the Rio Grande. He seemed reluctant even to bring it up, lest it seem an act of betrayal and cowardice.

"Maybe we could gather a party and leave," he said. "Take some frozen mule meat and head down this drainage. It will take us to the river, to whatever game is along it, and to firewood and warmth."

"How would the colonel take it?" I asked.

"We don't need to give him any choice."

"We signed on," Ned said. "We gave our word."

That's what was bothering us all. We had bonded ourselves to Frémont and could not simply pull away from the company.

"None of us can hunt," Ned said.

That was one of the most telling arguments.

"We could enlist a few, maybe Micah McGehee," Richard said.

"We lack equipment. This tenting; the axes and mess ware; rifles, shot, and powder—it's all his, not ours," Ned said.

In truth, if we started off on our own, we could take only our personal gear, which didn't come to much and wouldn't help us sustain life for the long trek off the mountain and down the river. We were honorable men; whatever we did had to be done in a proper fashion.

But the speculation came to nothing. We knew we wouldn't. Frémont had some sort of hold on us I could not fathom, a hold on all of his men. It was as if the slightest resistance to his command would be betrayal and leaving the company would be treason. I could not endure it.

"We're at his beck and call," I said. "Our fate is his."

The recognition of our bondage to the colonel did not lift my spirits a bit. Those bitter hours left me feeling trapped and helpless, as if there was not a thing I could do, out of my own free will, to mitigate or avoid the impending disaster. I was yet a greenhorn and ought not to be forming judgments, but I could not help but feel that something in Frémont's nature was leading us straight toward our own doom, and he was not quite right.

"I don't trust him," Richard said.

"I do. I was with him in California, and he was splendid," Edward said.

"All his veterans think so," I said.

Through all this misery I had not heard a word, not a hint, of antagonism or even skepticism about Frémont in the company. It had become a phenomenon that caught my attention. How could a commander, and a civilian one at that, win such total devotion and obedience? I had never seen the like. I had never been in a company so devoid of grumbling. I had never been in a schoolyard or in a town meeting or at a party without some sharp-tongued criticism of some leader or politician or magistrate. The more I studied on it, the more puzzled I became. Something about Frémont was either miraculous or horrifying. The only clue I had was a sense that he was really indifferent to all of us, and if he had no great affection for us, it didn't matter a bit to him what we thought. His perpetual calm was not the mark of a quiet nature, but it reflected his utter indifference to all but himself. Was that the source of his strange power over us?

I knew I wasn't alone in my brooding. But there was little time for it. We were trapped on a mountaintop, Christmas was nigh, we did not know from hour to hour what our fate might be, and our food supply was swiftly diminishing. I heard that we still had some packs of macaroni, some sugar, a little cornmeal, salt, and a few odds and ends. And I had heard rumors that Frémont had put aside some frozen elk meat, which he intended to give us at Christmas.

And there was still mule meat, at least if we were willing to dig through several feet of snow, dig out the carcass, and hack at the frozen animal. During this entire pre-Christmas sojourn on the mountaintop, I had seen no more living mules. Now they were all ghostly remains, white lumps swiftly vanishing in the almost daily snow showers, and it would not be long before we would find no carcasses at all because there would be six or ten or twenty feet of snow over them. If any lived, it would be a miracle.

I found Bill Williams and remembered his peculiar brag that he could see animal spirits.

"Are all the mules gone?" I asked.

"Ever' blessed one," he replied. "I watched them go. I watched them hover above each of them mules, and then slide away."

"How do you know that?"

"Why, Kern, I did sure enough see their spirits fly up into the sky, fly with one sad look back, and vanish up yonder, into the mysterious."

"How can you be sure, Mister Williams?"

"Mister Williams, is it? That's a doctor for you. I'm Old Bill, a renegade preacher that went Indian, and anyone calls me mister's no friend of mine."

I retreated a little, but I did want to know what he saw.

"What do animal spirits look like?"

"How can I tell you that? Like nothing you'd ever see."

"Human spirits, too?"

He clammed up fast. "Ain't saying," he said.

"Are any of our spirits hovering above us?"

"Listen here, you go back to your powders, and I'll just git some firewood, understand?"

Rebuffed, I did. I continued on my way. I also sensed that his occult gifts had somehow given him a foreknowledge of what our fates might be, and his sudden silence about that filled me with unspeakable dread.

CHAPTER TWENTY-TWO

Captain Andrew Cathcart

They called this place Camp Hope because Frémont had announced that he would send a relief party to the Mexican settlements. We had dragged most of the packs over the saddle to the southerly drainage in two days, but even on Christmas Day a few men were trailing the three miles between camps. Ben and Richard Kern were among them and reported seeing two or three surviving mules at Camp Dismal, miserably awaiting their fate.

So much for Williams's claims about seeing spirits, I thought.

Alexis Godey became *chef de cuisine* on Christmas Day, preparing a wondrous feast, given the paucity of our stores. We did enjoy the elk that the colonel had set aside, along with minced mule pies that reminded me of haggis. Godey spread remarkable cheer through the camp, wandering from one mess to another. These were located in snow holes so deep we could not see the neighboring messes or the men at them.

But the good cheer was a damnable fraud. There was not a man among us who did not wonder whether this would be his last Christmas or whether we would ever get off that mountain. The cheer was an artifice, a sweet jam spread over the stark reality of our circumstances. The truth was that this company of scarecrows sat on a mountaintop a hundred miles from the nearest settlement and was running out of food. Its men were weakened by altitude, cold, and poor diet, for none of us could eat enough to replace what was burned away in our labors. We were shod in decrepit boots that shipped snow with every step. Such mules as might still be alive at Camp Dismal were useless.

I kept my thoughts to myself, not wanting to be unseemly. I also didn't want to spoil such miserable pleasures as the men might find on that Christmas Day. What troubled me most was that we were Frémont's prisoners. He held our fates in his hand. And now, having decided to send for relief, he turned to Blackstone's commentaries, once again choosing to impress his eerie calm on us by this means, rather than take an active hand in overcoming the crisis. I was not impressed. I could see that his regulars, those veterans of the previous expeditions, were awed. There Frémont was, reading a law book, while the rest of us wondered whether on the morrow or the next day or the day after that, we might perish.

I both admired and loathed the man, and I itched to make my feelings known but chose instead to honor the birth of the Prince of Peace. I wanted to find the good in the man, but I could not bring myself to it. I wanted to seek peace on earth that Christmas and give Frémont my peace, but it was beyond me. At least I could bury my private thoughts behind a wall of holiday cheer. I had always kept my feelings to myself. I kept to myself in the Queen's hussars, and I would in this place and among these Yankees, no matter how I might seethe inside. Let other men whine; Captain Cathcart would not. By God, I was a Queen's man and I would act like it.

It was a cheery camp, with ample deadwood to feed our fires and good elk steaks to fill our bellies, cut from a frozen haunch the colonel had kept for this moment. It seemed luxurious after the hardships we had endured. But I could only think of those dead mules, whose ghosts would celebrate no Christmas ever. This was an odd sentiment in a born hunter, but it gripped me as I stood there, studying our distant and bland leader who was poring over his law texts in the most theatrical manner he could manage.

He deigned to join us when Godey had the elk roast well seared and sliced for us, and I watched him slowly put the ribbon betwixt the pages and close his leathern volume, smile benevolently at his underlings, and drift toward the nearest mess, Godey's own, where Frémont's manservant, Jackson Saunders, and Godey's young nephew, Theodore McNabb, made their home. With a soft wave of his bare hand, he summoned us. We gradually collected there, around that snow pit where Godey and his nephew were cooking meat.

Frémont stood at the far edge, smiling, scarcely bothering to bundle up. His veins ran ice water, and one rarely saw him smothered in leather and fur and wool.

"We'll take a little detour from the thirty-eighth parallel," he said.

The very idea of it startled me. Was this man still thinking of a rail line over the 38th parallel? And not about his weakened men, his dwindling food, his lost mules, his perilous camp?

"We're not far, actually, from whatever help we may need. Our friend Bill Williams tells me help is available down the Rio Grande, not more than a hundred miles distant, and most of that downslope and over flat river bottoms, which should be full of game. We'll need to reach lower altitudes where we may find game, and tomorrow we'll begin. I'm sending a relief party to the Mexicans at Abiquiu on the Chama River, and the relief party can also continue to Taos on the Rio Grande if more help is needed. I'll appoint Henry King its commander, and he will be accompanied by Frederick Creutzfeldt, Tom Breckenridge, and our guide, Bill Williams. I'm also sending Godey partway, to find a way down the mountain for us. While this takes place, we will begin moving downslope by stages. In short, we'll be moving toward the relief party that will be coming for us."

So the obsessed colonel had finally decided to do something. It seemed sensible enough.

This was indeed a Christmas gift. I looked at the colonel benignly and thought maybe even a testy old Cathcart could endure the man.

They debated how long it would take for the relief party to reach the settlements and return with mules and supplies. It seemed no great trip, and Old Bill Williams supposed it might take four days, and then the relief could be back in a dozen days, sixteen at the outside, given that the company would steadily be descending this drainage and heading into the Rio Grande Valley. It heartened the men, and they plunged into their Christmas repast with relish.

The next morning, after we had scraped away the usual six or eight inches of fresh snow with our mess plates, we prepared to break camp. But before that, we helped ready King's relief party. Frémont gave them four days of rations, enough to see them to the settlements, or so everyone thought. These consisted of a pack of macaroni and some sugar and some mule meat. There was nothing else to offer. Godey supplied himself and made sure his rifle was in good condition. He was a born hunter, and these men would descend to the river bottoms, where game might be found.

Four days, twenty-five miles a day. We watched them slide and skid down this drainage, along a nameless creek that tumbled through a steep and difficult gorge.

"All right, we'll build sledges," the colonel said, and we set about doing that, using axes to shape runners and fashion crossbars, which we lashed in place with rawhide. The progress was slowed by snow. It was no easy task to hack down limbs and shape the runners into anything we could use, but we were inspired by the knowledge that the relief had left, and we would soon follow toward safety.

I was optimistic. We would load the packs and drag them downhill without great difficulty, benefitting from the tug of gravity. Little did I know. But we toiled at that sledge-building project for days, watching our macaroni and mule meat diminish to the point that I wondered where our next meals would be coming from. Then, amazingly, the Creoles managed to drive three live mules over the saddle from Camp Dismal, and we all were heartened. The wretched mules were no good for packing, but we would have meat on the hoof.

On December 27 we set out, dragging the sledges down the creek bottom. The day was mild and we were in high spirits. But the canyon ahead was narrowing and forested right to the banks of the rushing creek. Still we kept on, believing that the relief party ahead of us was making faster time and was now probably out of the mountains and onto the great plain marking the Rio del Norte. What fools we were.

The mild weather held, and we proceeded down the drainage with little difficulty and amazing good cheer. The brooding sensation that we were at the margin left us. We were alive, had food enough, and would soon be in the Rio Grande Valley with its game. I even found myself revising my opinion of Frémont a little; not that I admired his judgment, but at least he had not plunged us over the brink, and it seemed likely that we would soon be enjoying the comforts of the New Mexicans. We made a cheerful camp that evening.

Then we encountered Godey, slogging his way up the drainage. We collected around him, eager for news. But what he imparted was entirely dismaying.

"We can't get through down there," he said. "It's a narrow canyon, choked with downed timber and boulders. You have to cross the creek a dozen times an hour. There's no other way except through this choked-up maze."

"You're saying we can't use the sledges?" Frémont asked.

"No. It's too steep, jammed with boulders, and the only passage is the creek itself in places. Sledges are worthless. And the creek drops so fast, with rapids, there would be no hanging on to packs."

We stared at one another. We were three days down a steep-sided canyon with no way out. What Godey was saying, though no one wanted to put it into words, was that we would have to retrace our steps, drag the sledges back to the top of the mountain, and find another way down—that or leave our equipment behind.

The Creoles responded first. Without a word they turned the sledges and began the weary climb that would take them toward the Christmas camp, and then over the first saddle into the next drainage.

The silence was palpable. I was determined to wrestle my way up that slope, but some of the men just wilted.

"Where are the relief men now?" Frémont asked.

"I'm not even sure they're at the bottom of that canyon. They were crawling over deadfall and rock and wading the rapids."

"They were to reach the settlements today," Frémont said.

"They're hardly on their way," Godey said.

"Did they find game?"

Godey simply smiled and shook his head.

They had a pack of macaroni to hold them. I calculated that they would take two weeks or more to reach the settlements, and food would run out long before, unless they made meat. Still, they had Williams with them. He might make meat. But why had he let them descend that morass? Did he know less about this country than he let on? It was a mystery.

I eyed Ben Kern, who was feeling poor, and wondered if he could make it up that trail. I thought maybe the altitude was weakening him. Whatever the case, he was utterly unable to drag a heavy sledge uphill.

"I'll help ye, Ben," I said.

He simply shook his head and began to drag a sledge mounded with packs up the snowy grade. I watched, worried. His every step was labored. The air was still rarefied, and he had been struggling for breath.

Round and about, the company was turning sledges around and starting the weary hike uphill, through heavy drifts. At least we had broken a trail, but if it snowed, we would be fighting our way up the mountain through massive drifts once again.

No one spoke, but I knew the cheer that had pervaded the company only minutes before had fled it, and now we were all privately pondering the odds and wondering whether fate would visit us after all.

The mild weather held, and that was a blessing. But this climb seemed longer and harder than any I had ever known in my life. Frémont strode ahead cheerfully, oblivious to the suffering behind him. What good was it to haul all this stuff? Most of it was mule tack, though scarcely a mule lived and the last of them would soon be food. He could have cached the tack, but didn't. He plainly was determined to haul it up and down the mountain to save himself the purchase of replacements later. But now we were human mules, and the halters were over our own snouts, and no one objected.

Ben Kern was so weak and gray that now and then I took hold of the cord he used to drag his sledge.

"Take a breath, Ben, and I'll keep us up," I said.

He didn't object but sat in the middle of a snowbank, his lungs rising and falling, his bluish face haggard. Still, the doctor was game, and soon enough he caught up and relieved me of my double burden.

Little by little we ascended that mountain, worn and melancholic and silent. There yet was hope. Down below, somewhere, four experienced men were working steadily toward the settlements. Frémont had entrusted King with some sum of money, the exact amount I did not know, with which to purchase whatever was needed. There would be gold to offer to the New Mexicans, and gold always spoke loudly.

We arrived in Christmas Camp and surveyed the ruin

mutely, pausing only to see whether there might be anything to salvage. But such carcasses that existed had vanished under several feet of fresh snow, and we could not cut another mule steak from any.

We needed still to top the saddle to the next drainage, and we did, though I am not sure how any of us managed it. Sheer grit, I would say. Ben Kern was so gray I feared for his life. But we somehow descended to a suitable campsite and quit. We were falling behind the colonel's party, but we could go no further. It was December 30, 1848.

CHAPTER TWENTY-THREE

Benjamin Kern, MD

We were falling behind, and it was my failing. Colonel Frémont and the other messes had worked down the new drainage, finding the way easy. They were even riding their packs on the slopes and enjoying the sledding. I watched them vanish far below, around a bend where the forest projected into the creek bottoms, and then all was quiet.

It was a grand, mild winter day, the sort when the sun warms not just the flesh but the heart and soul. The wind had died away, and only gentle zephyrs played with our coats and hats that last day of 1848. I had never seen a bluer sky. A vast sea of white stretched serenely in all directions, dotted only by what seemed to be scrub forest except that what we were seeing was the needled tips of fifty-foot pines, which now lay buried.

I ascribe that benevolent weather to my survival, for surely I would have perished had another storm raked us just then. My brothers, Ned and Richard, and Captain Cathcart had observed my distress. At the worst of it on the thirtieth, when we were struggling upslope and over the saddle, I gave out after a couple hundred yards and could do no more than crawl on hands and knees. They soon gathered around and lifted me up and took my packs, and slowly we worked our way up that awful incline and down. We had to go back once more to collect our rifles, but finally we were settled in a pleasant woods. The next day, the last of the year, was much better. The sun, while making only a brief appearance because of the towering cliffs to either side of us, warmed the air, and we walked and tumbled down the watercourse, enjoying ourselves. And yet Frémont's main party continued to gain ground on us, and all we saw was the swath of disturbed snow marking the colonel's passage.

We were joined by two of the three California Indian boys Frémont was returning to their people, Manuel and Joaquin, whose cheerful countenances added to our levity. Ned and Richard were especially solicitous of me, asking often if I was doing well. In truth, I was feeling a bit better, and the lower altitude was helping me along. My heart was not so labored as it had been during the climb to the saddle.

I am a worrier by nature, and the deepening distance between ourselves and Frémont troubled me. We knew of his passage only by what the snow told us. Still, I am a man of faith, and I assured myself that soon the colonel would send for news of us and make sure we were not in trouble.

"I'm sorry I'm holding us back," I said to Cathcart at one point while we were resting in afternoon sun, which playfully warmed my face.

"We're doing better than they are," he said. "Gaining strength as we go."

We reached the colonel's previous camp that New Year's Eve and found that it offered exactly what we needed: ample firewood, level ground, shelter from the night wind offered by coppery cliffs, and the comfort of sun-warmed rock. Best of all, there were only two feet of snow. So we settled there, knowing the main party would now be several miles down the slope. I looked for messages for us, hoping for instruction from the colonel, but saw none. Perhaps it was a compliment. He was assuming we were fit and able and would find our way as well as we could. But any sort of message stuck in an obvious place would have comforted me.

Ned and Richard were in a gay mood and soon built a warming fire and prepared a comfortable hutch out of limbs and tenting for me. We had rubber ground cloths to keep the wetness from creeping into our bedding at night, and these proved once again to be among the most valuable of Colonel Frémont's provisions. When I examined Cathcart with a medical eye, I was certain he was sicker than I but concealing it. He was down to a skeleton. His face was so drawn that his eyes bulged. It was not just that we didn't eat enough; it was not proper food for good health, and no matter how much mule meat we demolished, it didn't renew us.

We would have mule haunch that night. The colonel had seen to it that all the messes got the last of the meat, and we had received enough to feed us that festive evening and New Year's Day as well. Ned minced the mule meat, which was by far the best way to cope with that stringy stuff, and added macaroni and baked some minced-meat pies for our celebration, which we consumed with gusto. It seemed a grand feast, and for once I was full up, warm, and content as the last light faded and we plunged into the night that would bring us to the new year.

We explained to the Indian boys what all this was about, and they grinned back. I am not certain how much of it they mastered, but it mattered not. They were soon joining us as we sang a few old favorites, and then we crawled into comfortable bedrolls content.

New Year's Day was much like the previous one, mild and quiet. We broke camp after eating the last of the minced-mule pies and dragged our packs down that long slope, which at times became precipitous. But we never lost control, and eventually we reached another of the colonel's camps, this time at the confluence of a creek. This too had little snow. We had passed gulches where snow lay a hundred feet deep or more, burying tall pines. But now, well down the mountain, the snow was thin. We had made steady progress but were uncommonly tired, and I knew I needed rest. There were more worries to trouble me, the worst being that we were now at the very gates of starvation.

"I wish I had a mousetrap. A few mice would look good to me now," I remarked to Captain Cathcart.

"We're not far from the colonel and the rest," he replied.

"They may be worse off than we are."

"They have excellent hunters."

"You're a fine hunter, Captain."

"There would be no game here, not after twenty men passed through. And we're still miles from the San Juan Valley."

That was true. The whole descent from the mountaintop to the valley was eight miles, but in our enfeebled estate it seemed three times farther. This, too, was a pleasant camp, and Richard sketched it. He had somehow sketched through the entire journey, carefully placing each sketch, carefully labeled, in his portfolio.

I was feeling cautiously optimistic in spite of the grave want of food. The relief party would be closing in on the Chama River settlement by now and would soon be back with provisions and pack animals. Still, I began wracking my head, wondering what we might eat from nature if we had to. We had descended to an area of brush, where there might be rose hips, and perhaps we could find trout in the stream or pine nuts, a famous staple of the local tribes. It might be that Manuel and Joaquin could help us with that. We had but a little macaroni, and our trusty rifles if we could shoot most anything that flew. And that was a real possibility. The lower we descended, the more crows and hawks we spotted. But my eyesight was poor now. Bad food and snow blindness had taken their toll, leaving me blurry eyed. I was hoping Cathcart, a fine shot, was in better condition.

"Are your eyes good?" I asked him.

"I can't see a bloody thing," he growled.

Only Richard's eyes were unaffected, and he could barely manage a rifle. It was a fix I had not anticipated.

The second day of January we struggled once again down the drainage, but we were about done in. The packs were too heavy. Sadly, we went through our books and journals, saving only what was absolutely essential and burning the rest. I had ceased writing daily entries in my journal and couldn't say why. Some of those evenings when we were high up the mountain, I lacked the strength even to put a few sentences down, but there was more to it. I had intended from the start to record only those things I would not hesitate to make public someday. Then the day came when every thought in my head was a private one, so I wrote nothing. I had been observing our leader for a long while and realized one day that I did not wish to record the true nature of my thoughts of Colonel Frémont's character. And the worse our condition, the less I felt like writing. But both Edward and Richard pursued their journals, managing to take a moment each day, even now, no matter how exhausted they were. Their journals would be worth something someday; mine, poor dishonest thing, would not. But I didn't discard it, and I included it in the bundle we were putting together to drag over snow to the next camp.

I watched the pages of a botany text darken, curl, and burn.

"There goes my only plant guide," I said.

The weakening of our bodies was insidious. We discovered we lacked the strength to carry all our truck in one trip, so we started down the broad valley, knowing we would have to come back. The day was warm and sunny, but I was dispirited, and so were the rest. We were all diminished by the constant hardship and miserable food. I couldn't remember when last I had some greens. We kept our rifles at the ready, knowing what a folly that was, but the thought of game gave us a thin thread of hope.

At the next campsite we found ample evidence that the colonel's whole party had spent the night. A fire still smouldered. Not all the deadwood had been used up. It was a fine place, a level flat where two streams joined, with abundant wood and plenty of shelter and not enough snow to trouble us. But we were still behind the colonel's party and feeling more and more isolated. We began unburdening ourselves of our packs, and Richard began constructing a shelter, because we had seen mare's tails across the sky and knew another white fury would soon descend on us.

He stayed in the new camp to build us a shelter and collect wood and tend the fire, while Captain Cathcart and I and the Indian lads struggled back to the old camp, which was at a much higher elevation. There were more packs to drag down, packs we could not abandon. But none of them contained food. The others were soon ahead of me, and I found myself giving out. I hadn't gone but a quarter of a mile upslope when I lost the rest of my strength and toppled into the snow. I felt my heart labor, and my muscles quit me, and I lacked the strength to get up. I would have to retreat to the lower camp but didn't know how. I rested until the chill of the snow had worked through my rags, and then began to crawl on hands and knees, a little at a time, grateful that I did not have to cope with a drift. The trail was well worn. I continued in that fashion, resting when I had to, until I reached the lower camp. Richard spotted me, helped me up, and dragged me into the pine-bough hut he was building. I was soon lying on the rubberized canvas, feeling my heart and lungs labor.

"I wore out," I said.

He glanced sharply at me. "We'll stay here," he said.

He was adding boughs, which formed a sort of thatch, and helped make the hut tight against the wind. There would be little snow filtering through all that. The wavering fire threw heat into it, and I lay comfortably, but too worn to go on. I thought maybe the mountains would claim me after all, but I would make a fight of it.

"Richard, take my journal with you tomorrow. It's all that's left of me."

He turned. "Ben, don't talk like that."

"I quit writing in it a few days ago."

"You and your journal are both coming along with us tomorrow," he said.

The next evening we were delighted to welcome Raphael Proue to our humble camp. Proue was the oldest of the Creoles with Frémont and was clearly worn to the bone backtracking from the main party to our camp.

"I bring this," he said, unloading a heavy burlap sack.

We clustered around and found frozen haunches of meat, cornmeal, and coffee.

"Dis here, it's buffalo the Colonel saves and pork and buffalo fat and some meal, eh?"

"His private stores. I didn't know he had any," Richard said.

We were amazed. Where had this provender come from? I stared at the food as if it were gold. The very sight of it sent a wave of strength and energy through me.

"You're worn out, Raphael. Sit with us," Ned said. He knew Proue from the time they both served together.

"I do dat," Proue said. "I got no strength left, not any."

He dropped heavily onto the rubberized tarpaulin before the fire.

"It's gonna snow," he added. "You got some good hiding place here."

We soon were pumping Proue for news. Had the relief party returned? Were food and mules coming, as everyone hoped?

"They aren't far ahead of us. We can tell, maybe day or two. Dunno what slowed them down, but they aren't doing good."

No relief in sight. That was discouraging.

"The colonel, he's got a place picked out to cache the stuff. Down from here five, six miles. He says we gonna cache everything we can, and then wait. He's gonna take a bunch and head for the settlements himself and leave old Vincenthaler in charge, and after the cache we should maybe keep on going. Good hunting maybe."

I hardly knew Lorenzo Vincenthaler, but I knew he had been with Frémont's California expedition and had served in the army during the Mexican War. He had been so quiet that I scarcely had visited with him, and the only impression I had of him was that he was a stickler for rules and wanted to do everything by the book. Well, I thought, that was an odd choice, but it would be alright.

Proue stayed the night, and we fed him from the fresh provisions he had brought. He looked worn, but so did we all. I was a ghost of the man I had been only weeks before. Captain Cathcart was down to bones, and his clothing flapped on him. My brothers were a little better, but looking gaunt. And the Indian boys were down to ribs. But Proue alarmed me. When he started downriver the next morning, he staggered his way along the trail and staggered his way out of sight.

CHAPTER TWENTY-FOUR

Alexis Godey

When we reached the foothills bordering the San Juan Valley, with the Rio Grande winding through it, Colonel Frémont summoned me.

"We need to cache everything," he said. "There's a cave up La Garita Creek a bit; you probably noticed it. That's where we'll stow our goods."

He smiled amiably.

"Everything, Colonel?"

"Why, yes. My goods are scattered clear up the mountains, and now we'll cache them while we await the relief party."

That was a, how to say it?—formidable—order. There were packs and gear scattered for miles over our downhill route, most of it mule tack and saddles. It made no sense to collect all this useless gear, and I eyed my leader sharply before I surrendered. "Oui, I'll begin at once, Colonel."

"I knew you would," he said. "We'll set up camp under the cliffs there."

He had chosen a sheltered notch on the west edge of the Rio del Norte Valley, a place where there were trees and cliffs to supply some comfort. But to the east, there was nothing but arid plains. Not a tree to stop the wind or supply fuel.

"I'll put the company to it. They're as scattered as the packs."

He smiled, yawned, and walked away.

I corralled various of my best men. "We'll be caching the colonel's equipment in that cave we passed. And that means we'll be heading up the creek, maybe clear to Groundhog Creek, where the Kerns probably are."

They were game but not happy. Every one of them looked worn and ragged. While the colonel and his manservant set about making the new camp, my men and I began the long trek into the mountains again. Fortunately the drainage was wide and the way was easy. But we were trumped by the weather. The warm interlude between Christmas and New Year's Day had passed, and now a bitter wind howled out of the north, weakening and dispiriting all of us. It stung our cheeks, as if our beards weren't even there. Nonetheless, there was a task the colonel wanted done, so we set out to do it. I would do it, as required, but I wondered why. I could not fathom why Frémont had such a grip on me.

We examined the shallow cave in the point of rocks and decided it would do. The colonel had a good eye. But that abandoned gear stretching miles up the trail darkened our mood. I heard no man complain. No one had ever complained about Colonel Frémont, at least in my presence. The question in my mind was whether to obey his command or not. Was the colonel mad? Did he have any grasp of how worn to nothing his men were? I did not give the order I ached to give, by which I would relieve these desperate men of this foolish mission. So we proceeded up the mountain once again.

We hiked up the drainage, step by step. Whenever we found some of the seventy-pound packs, we sent a man or two back with them, while the rest of us continued up the valley. When Preuss and I reached the Kerns' camp we discovered them lying mutely in their blankets, their fire dead. They were in a bad way. Wordlessly, the German and I started their fire going and got some deadwood together and revived their spirits.

"We're collecting the packs," I said. "When you can, work your way down to the colonel's camp. He's on the near edge of the San Juan Valley at the foot of this drainage. Bring what you can."

Ned Kern had revived the most with the fire blazing. "We'll be there. Have you any food?"

I shook my head. What little I had of macaroni and sugar had to go to the men hauling the colonel's instruments and tack and bedding. "You're on your own," I said. "But keep warm. It's the cold that does a man in, not hunger."

Ned nodded. He was the one veteran among them and had been with the colonel in California, but I could see he was the most disheartened.

"Ned, I'm appointing you to keep your brothers and Captain Cathcart warm, and the Indian boys, too. I'll have Micah McGehee keep an eye on you."

The bright fire seemed to pump life into those wretches in Richard Kern's hut, and that was the best I could do. I nodded to my men, and we plodded up again, through deepening snow as we retraced our steps to the mountaintop.

That day we collected fifteen of the packs, but it wore my men to the bone. The north wind was our master, slicing through our frayed defenses and taking the strength straight out of us. We were spread out now, in half a dozen camps up and down the creeks. As January progressed, so did the cold. There was no more cloth or leather to repair boots or make moccasins or fashion into hats or waistcoats or leggins, and we were being frostbitten again—ears, noses, chins, fingers, toes, ankles, lips. Around our miserable fires, which did little to warm any of us because the wind sucked away the heat, we worked thong through our clothing and boots, sewing together what we could, making do with rags and scraps of leather.

Some of my men resented the Kerns because they weren't helping with the hard work of getting the colonel's packs down to the cache. Indeed, they told me that they found Richard playing his flute by the fire one time. Just like some Philadelphians, they said. I was less judgmental, having seen them at death's door. In fact, Ben looked ashen to me, gray of flesh despite weeks of outdoor living, and I knew he wasn't far from his Maker. A man ought to play a flute when he could. A song, a melody, a flute could cleave the living from the dead.

But the men didn't like it, and they didn't like my forbearance. I thought it was best to let well enough alone. On the sixth of January Hubbard shot a prairie goat, or antelope as they are called, and generously divided the precious meat up and down the line. Even the Kerns and Cathcart got a small meal of it, and all were heartened.

We were far enough off the mountain to be among game again, and the very thought inspired every man who was dragging those parfleches and packs through the snow. I lost track of what the colonel was doing down below, but mostly he was simply waiting for relief. It never came. For my part, I camped at the point of rocks and oversaw the cache. The packs had to be dragged into that shallow cave, after we put down some brush and limb bedding to keep the packs dry, and then laid up, one on another, to make use of the small space. And once we finished with it, we would need to seal it and conceal it from the Utes, who roamed these mountains.

The Kerns were boiling up pieces of hide now to make a gluey gruel, but there was some nourishment in it, and I didn't worry much about them. We would soon have relief.

By my calculation we were nearly at the end of the sixteen-day period we had allotted for King's party to return with help.

Then Proue died. The old Creole woodsman had shambled along day by day, getting by until the cold struck, and then he simply began to freeze up. He was dragging packs right to the end, when he tumbled into the snow and said he couldn't go on. His legs were frozen below the knee. Someone wrapped his blanket around his legs, but no one had the strength to help the old man, and so he perished in the snow, the icy wind soon stopping his heart. We had no way to drag him anywhere, so he lay on the trail, frozen to the ice underneath, as man after man passed him by, dragging the colonel's goods down to the cache. That happened on the ninth day of January, and at a time when the cold was the worst I could remember, making us numb and driving us deep into our rags.

I stared at the old man, so cold and still, the snow filtering over his white face, caking his beard.

"Raphael, mon ami, au revoir," I said, watching the crystals collect in his eye sockets. "I'll come for you when I can. I'll let your people know."

If he had any living brothers or sisters, I did not know of them. But I would try to contact relatives in Saint Louis.

Others of us stopped and stared, watching the whirling snow filter through his beard. No one said anything.

That was the fourteenth day since King's party had left the Christmas camp. We were expecting relief within sixteen days at the worst. Proue had missed help by two days. Or was it simply that he had died needlessly dragging the colonel's packs? I refused to think in those terms and set the thought aside. But there was another thought worming through me: Proue's death was the direct result of our effort to drag the useless gear down the mountain. It was a death that Colonel Frémont could have avoided.

I worried about the men, the grunting, laboring men, numb with cold, so cold they could not feel their fingers, skidding the packs past the snow-lost body of Raphael Proue. What were they thinking? Who would be next?

I could not rally them. They were spread out by twos and threes. The company was no longer a single unit but disintegrating before my eyes as men made their own choices and shifted away from their messes. I knew what that foretold and was helpless to stop it. The Frémont company was falling apart.

I paused one last time at the hut the Kern brothers had built and found them huddled within. But the fire was going.

"When you can, make your way down to the colonel's camp," I said. "This wind should quit pretty soon."

"We're out of food," Richard said.

"The relief is due any moment. That's all I can say. Starving won't kill a man. It's cold that kills a man, quick as a knife thrust. Starving men make it through."

"We'll come soon. I'm some better," Ben said.

"Put your packs in the cache at Point of Rocks. You won't miss any of it. Some of the men are camped there. McGehee's there. He's from your mess. You men look after each other."

They nodded but said nothing.

The heat from the fire was welcome. It had warmed my backside. But now I faced my own walk five or six miles down. I was as weary as the rest, but somehow, maybe through sheer willpower, I kept on going. I was dragging two packs, the last we could find. I'd stash them with the rest.

The Kerns stared bleakly at me. They seemed better off than Cathcart, who was a walking scarecrow.

"We'll see you at the colonel's camp," I said. "Help's coming."

I stepped into the murderous wind and felt it burrow through my leather tunic and coat and leggins. But I plucked up the draw-lines and began tugging two parfleches of mess ware behind me, feeling the packs skid, resist, bounce, and sometimes slide ahead of me when I hit a steep grade. I kept my own advice, and when I got too cold, I holed up. There were plenty of refuges from the wind: copses of pine-trees, jagged cliffs, river brush, wind-carved hollows. I set aside my hunger, knowing it would do me no good to cater to it.

I stopped at the cache, where half a dozen men lingered, and stowed the last packs in the cave. These had been concealed with brush as best as my Creoles could manage it. It wouldn't fool an Indian, but we would be back soon enough to recover the goods. The Utes didn't roam far from their lodges in this sort of weather.

Somehow the colonel had gotten us off the mountain. Retreats are chaotic. Retreats are when commands fall apart, and it's every man for himself. But the colonel had held us together, sent for help, gotten most of his goods off the mountain, and so far, except for Raphael, he had kept his men alive. There was something admirable in it.

When I reached the colonel's camp, far below, I reported to Frémont.

"Raphael Proue's dead," I said.

Frémont stared, registering that. "How?" he asked.

"Froze. Lay down and died, dragging a pack."

"What do the men think?"

"He was the oldest of us."

Relief filtered into Frémont's face. "I hoped no one would perish. It reflects badly."

"Sir, it's no one's fault. I'll try to contact his people. I don't know that he had any."

"Yes, do that," he said, absently.

"There's men scattered far upstream; the Kerns are highest up. I've told them to work their way down here as soon as they can."

"Philadelphia people," Frémont said.

I knew what he meant. Yet they were all stouthearted. I thought they would make it.

"Ned is the worst off," I said.

"That's strange," the colonel replied. "He was with us before."

"Ben and Richard seem stronger," I said.

The colonel seemed puzzled. Ben and Richard were the city fellows.

The colonel seemed taut, and as soon as I had reported, he drifted to a place where he had a long view down the Rio del Norte Valley. An observer could see for miles across that barren landscape, where no tree grew and no rise or valley hid a party for long. The vista was so white we soon were squinting and leaking tears.

I joined him. "They're past due. We calculated sixteen days at the absolute worst."

The wind was cutting straight through me in that unprotected valley, and I was more than ready to retreat to the nearest fire.

"They're overdue. Williams misled them again," he said.

"Colonel, it took them four days just to get down that drainage. And they still had eighty miles after that, and they would be hunting, too. I think they're running far behind what we had calculated up on the mountain."

"I never should have trusted him. Kit once told me to watch your back when Williams was around."

"We'll see the relief any day now."

Frémont shook his head. "Something went wrong. They'd be here."

"It takes time to collect mules or burros and blankets and food and men," I said.

"They failed me."

I changed the subject. "Do you have hunters out?"

"Certainly. There's plenty of tracks, but no game in sight. And everyone's so snow-blind that they can't see much."

That was bad news, actually. "I was hoping to see some meat."

"It's an improvement on shoe leather," he replied. He squinted out on the valley once more, with watering, snow-blind eyes ruined by the merciless white everywhere.

"My men are failing me. They're giving up. They don't have stout hearts," he said.

I hoped he would keep such sentiments to himself. They sounded a little like an accusation, but I believed Frémont was too grand a man to permit himself such thoughts.

"I'll warm up and hunt," I said.

"I'm taking a party out at dawn, if relief doesn't come," Frémont said. "I intend to go to Taos, and on to California, one way or another, with or without this company. Of course, you'll come with me, Alex."

CHAPTER TWENTY-FIVE

Tom Breckenridge

Godey joined our relief party for a while when we started from the Christmas camp, but when it was plain that the main party could not descend the drainage we were following, he returned. The four of us, with King in command, and Old Bill Williams as our guide, fought our way down that narrow canyon, struggling every minute. It was choked with snow, for one thing, and we had little understanding where the creek flowed or where its banks were.

We wrestled our way over or under fallen timber and fought through thickets, and once in a while the way was pinched off and there was no goddamn help for it but to doff our nether garments and wade the snowy creek and then put ourselves together on the far bank, numb and wet. The warm weather quit us, too, and the bitter cold bit our flesh, numbed our limbs, and ruined our handgrip so we couldn't hold a thing in our fingers.

When nights fell, we carved a cave out of snow and lit deadwood, which failed to warm us, so we shivered in the thin blankets. Because we were carrying everything on our backs, we had but one blanket apiece. We had three Hawken rifles, a fowling piece, and a pound of powder, enough to shoot game if we should be so lucky. As for food, we had very little: some mule meat, a pack of macaroni, and some sugar. And even the sugar was lost to us when the pack tipped and the white powder vanished.

The distance down the slope to the valley was not great, perhaps eight miles, but we consumed four days fighting our way out, and in the process we ate the last of our food. We consoled ourselves that shortly we would reach the Rio Grande, would find plentiful game along its banks, and would soon stave off the hunger that was even then wrenching at our bellies. Fighting our way down a narrow defile choked with logs and rock and snow and brush made us hungry enough to eat bears and elephants. I'd of welcomed skunk stew.

King was a steady man, a veteran of the California expedition, and had a level head on him. He was heading out there to make a home for himself and his bride and had strong reasons to push on and triumph. Old Bill Williams was a different son of a bitch and soon was grumbling.

"This here gulch, it's not right. I didn't say for him to go this way. I know these hills and this isn't a place to go down. He wouldn't listen. He paid his guide no heed," Williams was saying.

"We'll get out of this gulch and be on our way to the settlements, old man," King replied quietly, while the four of us were roasting our bare feet at the fire, sitting around it like spokes on a wheel. "It's downhill, and that counts."

"What'll we eat, tell me that," Williams said.

"You're the hunter," King replied.

I heard so much whining from the old man I wished he would just plain shut his damn trap while we got some blood moving through our frozen feet. Whining doesn't do a lick of good when you're out in the wilds and there's not a thing you can do but keep on going. He was the guide; the veteran of these mountains; the man who could find his way, turn almost anything into food, keep us warm and healthy. He had been silent the whole trip, clear from Hardscrabble, keeping his own counsel, but now he was belaboring poor King at every opportunity.

Still, Williams was voicing the things that were tormenting us. Up at Christmas Camp, Frémont and Preuss and

Williams himself had calculated that the relief party would reach the settlements a hundred miles distant in four or five days, organize help, and be back up the mountains with food and animals in a dozen days, sixteen at the outside. But we were not yet free of the mountains, which were clawing us every foot of the way. There was something dark in it, the horror of it unspoken as we pulled our thin blankets over and under us and shivered the long night away. The truth of it was that the settlements seemed impossibly far.

Frémont had selected us for our strength. He had pulled me aside and said that he had a mission for me, that he was selecting only the strongest of his men, because the task ahead would test us to our utmost. I was the last bastard he approached, apparently, because he said that King, Creutzfeldt, and Old Bill had all accepted. He had come to realize that the company was in trouble and needed relief. That was the first mention of it to escape his lips, as far as I knew. I accepted at once. I wanted to get off that mountain; I was willing to walk barefoot through snow to get off those peaks.

"I'll go," I had told him, which was stupid of me. And so the party prepared that afternoon, and the next dawn, even as day broke, we began our downward trek, with Godey keeping us company.

I wondered whether we would do better in the next drainage, but so forbidding and high were the walls of the valley, and so thick with snow, that it was a foolish fancy. To add to our troubles, occasionally avalanches tumbled down those slopes, some of them beginning with a crack like a rifle shot and roaring their sinister way, raising a great cloud of powdery snow that choked the valley and stung our faces. It was a horror we spoke nothing of, knowing that any moment one of those snowslides could engulf us and end our worldly lives. And yet we escaped these random menaces and finally reached a point where the miserable creek poured into another branch, and the San Juan Valley stretched ahead, a silent white and naked land that looked like a graveyard.

I had yearned to escape the mountains, thinking that things would improve the moment we reached the great plain. But now, as we absorbed the naked valley ahead, each of us knew the mountains had been our friend; that the bleak plain offered no comfort at all. I stared at my colleagues, wondering if the other poor bastards were thinking what I was thinking. That stretch to the river would be tenfold harder than our descent.

That was the last sheltered camp. We found wood enough to warm us that one last night, and we divided the last of our provisions, the tallow candles that Frémont had given us. Never did anything taste so good as that tallow. We each had a half a candle, the white tallow like a king's feast, and then we dug deep into the snowbank, to put ourselves out of the wind if we could, and huddled miserably.

Worse was to come. No sooner had we emerged from the shelter of the mountains than a bitter north wind engulfed us. If it was cold in the canyon, it was murderous here where not a tree, not a shrub, not a cliff stayed the winds. The winds caught us unprepared. Somehow we had expected the valley to be our sanctuary, with shelter and wood and game and quiet air and sunshine warming our frozen beards. Instead it was a blinding white hell that made our eyes hurt from squinting. Had a band of elk marched slowly before us, none of us would have seen them at all, much less shot any for the solace of our ravenous bellies.

How we continued I don't know. I shot a hawk, which we tore to pieces and devoured raw, but it did nothing to allay our misery. We struggled slowly ahead. Far in the distance a thin band of trees marked the river. But the distance from where we saw it to there seemed impossible to negotiate on our frozen feet. We were stumbling now and could walk only a few yards at a time. No man complained, not even our guide.

It had become impossible to walk. Our frozen feet chafed in our boots, and each step tormented us. We would crawl, just to get off our feet, and when we could crawl through the snow no more, we would clamber to our feet and plunge forward another few yards. We were still following the tributary, and after a mile or so that day we stopped where some cottonwoods grew along the bank and dug a shelter for ourselves and our miserable fire. If we stayed upwind of it we got no heat out of it; if we edged downwind we didn't get much more heat, but we got the bitter smoke of cottonwood in our faces.

And for food we did what we had to do. We removed our tormenting boots, cut strips off of our blankets with which to wrap our swollen feet, and tied these makeshift moccasins tight. Then we sliced leather from our boots and set it to boiling. We stared at those slivers of leather, watched the boiling water percolate through them, extracting a thin yellowish paste and softening the leather itself. It took a long time and a lot of dead cottonwood before we had reduced the boot leather enough to eat it. We devoured it swiftly, and it did nothing at all to alleviate the howl of my innards. But we pronounced it tasty. We tied the boots together by their laces and would carry them with us, for that was the only food we had. That night, the temperature plummeted, and there was no way that our thin and diminished blankets could spare us from the brutal cold. Not even the fire was a solace.

I did not know where my feet were or whether they were connected to my body. They were severed from my senses by cold, and only when the fire had warmed them did they start to hurt and prickle. I sat there, shivering, and wondering whether I would live to see any more dawns.

The next day was much the same. We stumbled ahead, ate more of our boots, fought snow blindness, cut more strips off our blankets to wrap around our feet, and in all we made only a mile or two. We had ceased talking: to speak was to waste energy. At one point Bill Williams sat down and wouldn't budge, but we urged him on, and so we reached another place where a little wood might be found, again dug into the snow to get out of the deadly wind, and again boiled up our boots. We had, in all, managed another mile or two; I could no longer reckon distances, and none of us could see a thing, having been so blinded by snow that all the world was a glinting blur.

That night was, if anything, colder than the previous, or maybe our bodies could no longer generate enough heat to keep us alive. Save for the fire, we might have perished. I surveyed the misery around me, and a great darkness filled me. King was gaunt and drawn, the flesh gone from his face, his eyes sunk in pits. Creutzfeldt was no better off but had a little more energy. Williams had crawled inside of himself. There were great icicles hanging from his beard. And the tears from his ruined eyes had frozen on his cheeks. I began to experience a leaden sensation in my muscles, as if they could function only in the slowest and heaviest manner, and I judged that the others were afflicted in the same way. We boiled more of our boots that night. There were still a few miles between us and the Rio del Norte, and I didn't know if we would ever reach those bottoms or see the game we prayed would be awaiting us.

And so we lived, following the ice-topped bed of the tributary, crawling when we could not walk, leaving pink snow behind us from our bleeding feet. Some nights there was not a tree in sight; we dug a hole in the snow, laid a blanket under us and the remains of the rest over us, and shivered through the darkness. The smallest storm would have destroyed us, but we lived. We boiled the last of our boots when we could; started in on our scabbards; and, when those were gone, boiled our belts. After that we had nothing.

One day we found a rotted and frozen otter, half–picked over by carrion birds. We boiled it and somehow gagged down its foul and gamy flesh. It was food. It kept us alive one day more. The only thing in our favor was that the tributary of the Rio Grande had no snow on it. The wind had scoured the ice. In our weakened estate, that meant much to us. Slogging through snow would have been fatal.

We consumed still more of our blankets, wrapping the strips around our ruined feet, but they wore out swiftly, and the cold ate at our ruined toes and heels. At least we were progressing toward the wooded bottoms of the Rio Grande, making a mile or two each day. The promise of the river bottoms, wood and game, was all that kept us alive.

Then, scarcely a quarter of a mile from the bottoms, King sat down.

"I just can't," he muttered.

"We're almost there, it's just one last hike," Creutzfeldt said.

King shook his head. "You go on. I'll rest, and then catch up."

"You must come with us," I replied sharply.

But he slumped inert, barely bothering to refuse me.

"I'll follow along," he said at last.

No amount of urging could change his mind.

"We'll come back for you," Williams said.

With foreboding, we struggled the last quarter of a mile, which took us three hours of our usual crawling and walking.

We did at least reach the timbered bottoms and found ample wood, and with our last energies got a good fire going. It would need to burn for an hour before it would throw out any heat, but at least it heartened us.

"I'll go back for him," Cruetzfeldt said, but he was plainly not fit for it.

"He's dead," Williams replied. "I saw the birds circling. I can tell when the birds circle. They circle smaller and smaller, and then come in."

It hardly seemed possible. The youngest and strongest of us might be gone.

"I'll go look," Creutzfeldt said.

We watched him struggle into the dusk. When he returned, out of the dark, he was carrying several pounds of meat.

CHAPTER TWENTY-SIX

Micajah McGehee

The colonel tasked us with caching the packs at the rocky landmark at the edge of the great valley, but we were too far gone to do it. The men were strung up the nameless creek. The Kerns and Cathcart were the farthest behind. With the cruel storms of January upon us, every step was misery, and yet we persisted, sliding the heavy packs downslope or dragging them across flats. All because the colonel required it.

But the food had given out. The Kerns's mess was boiling rawhide and parfleches. Doctor Kern was particularly weak, and I thought for sure he was gone from us. But he lingered on, kept alive by warm fires. The Kerns were reluctant to abandon the hut they had built, but I urged them on. We needed to make our way toward the settlements.

The thing that was gnawing at us more and more was the silence. We saw no relief. We awaited each hour the arrival of burros laden with food, blankets, and needful things, but no one arrived. The sixteen days that Colonel Frémont, Godey, and Preuss had calculated to be the maximum required to get relief to us were almost gone, and I heard that Frémont was anxious, pacing about his camp below us, and sending scouts out every little while to try to locate the relief.

Meanwhile the storms returned, and we were not only starved but also newly frostbitten. Men stumbled on bloodied feet, where frost and thaw and frost again had ruined flesh and set it to bleeding. During all this movement, we passed Proue's body, inert and half-covered with snow, and there was nothing we could do about this horror. Then Elijah Andrews gave out. He and I were trying to get down to the river, but he simply quit, lay down in the snow.

"I'm done," he said.

"Elijah, you've got to come along," I said. "Got to."

He shook his head and slumped into the snow. I knew what lay ahead for him and was determined to prevent it. Just up a shallow slope was a cave, and I somehow dragged him there, where at least he was beyond the curse of the winds and out of the whirl of snow. But he was well nigh inert, and I knew time was fleeing me. I struggled up the slope, needing to reach the timber, but the Arctic blast felled me. Atop the ridge, I found what I needed and tumbled dead piñon down that snowy precipice. I had to work in fits and starts, taking advantage of the slightest cessation of the gale, but in time I tumbled a lot of dry pine down to the cave, and there, in the shelter, with a little powder and flint and steel, I started a fire somehow and watched the wary flame slowly lick at the sticks. It gave no heat at all, but I saw that it cheered Andrews and gave him heart. The warmth was a long time coming, but the cave served my purpose, and soon Andrews was resting comfortably. About then Captain Cathcart and Richard Kern found us and tumbled in, hard-pressed by the storm. And thus we staved off trouble, or so we thought.

We had among us one cup of macaroni and one of sugar, and this we prepared to divide with perfect scruple, there being nothing else. But poor Andrews, still numb, with muscles that did not do his bidding, tumbled the pot over, and the flames soon covered the last miserable bit of provender among us all. No one spoke. No one blamed Elijah. We stared sorrowfully in the fire, locked in our own thoughts. In extremity, I don't think with words, but with images. I saw my mother's bread pudding before me, and a pink rib roast, dripping with juices. I saw eggs frying on a skillet, their yellow yolks mingling with their whites. I smelled my mother's yeasty bread, cooling on her counter. What was I doing here, in this place?

I could never manage my hunger. It had become a dull ache, a throb, and worse, an estate fraught with menace. There was something sinister in it, this conjuring of food, not a thing to eat and a thousand miles from succor, or so it seemed. There was slow death in it. There was weakness; I lurched and wobbled when I walked, as if my protesting muscles were at their limits.

Cathcart clambered to his feet and stepped into the blizzard, and then stumbled back into our shelter.

"I thought I heard the relief," he said. "Could have sworn it."

At least we were warm. Elijah Andrews recovered as the heat of the fire bounced off the walls of our rocky abode.

Only two hours earlier, he had stared up at me, surrender in his face. It was cold that murdered; starvation would only weaken us, at least for a few days more.

If only a stray mule would wander by.

The storm never ceased. I discovered a ball of thong in our midst, cut it into strings, and boiled it. I prowled the cliffside and found wolf bones. These we pulverized between stones and added to our thong soup. We knew that others of our company had been caught as well and were harboring in the hollows of that cliff, awaiting whatever fate would bring. There seemed so little we could do; our fates were no longer in our hands.

When the storm lifted two days later we stumbled our way toward the colonel's camp, down in the great valley, seeing no game all the way. If there were animals anywhere near, they had been driven to shelter somewhere. The thing we had hoped for, an abundance of game down in the wide valley of the Rio Grande, was nothing more than a thin dream. I made my body work, one step at a time, step by step on frozen feet, as we staggered toward the colonel's camp. The rest stumbled, too. We helped one another. When someone wanted to quit, we hectored him, made him continue.

By January 9, 1849, we were all out of the mountains, save for old Proue, whose frozen body lay mutely behind us, buried in drifts. A few of us remained at the cache; the rest had collected in Frémont's camp. That day was important. It was the day we should have relief, even if King's company had been greatly slowed. It was sixteen days past the Christmas camp, when the colonel sent King and Williams and Creutzfeldt and Breckenridge off, with our salvation in their hands.

What had happened? No one knew, but the prospects were forbidding. Frémont sent scouts downriver, but they saw only silence and cruel white snow. How we ached for the jingle of harness bells or the crunch of hooves on snow or the shouts or shots that meant our relief was coming. Down there, out of the mountains, the wind was crueler than ever, but we found shelter in the timbered banks along the river, and so endured. The few rations still in the colonel's possession were carefully divided. We got a spoonful of macaroni or a bit of sugar dissolved in warm water. But no one died, and we had ample deadwood and shelter, and since we weren't moving, our tormented feet had a chance to heal. I pulled my boots off and discovered deep cracks between my toes, with raw flesh visible in them. Some leaked blood. Strange white patches pocked my toes and ankles. The terrible truth was that my feet were better off than most.

Then, on the eleventh, the colonel decided that the King party was not going to reach us, and he resolved to form a new relief, consisting of himself; his manservant, Saunders; Alexis Godey; Godey's young nephew, Theodore; and the little scientist, Preuss, who had weathered over several expeditions as a resourceful and tough man.

Frémont gathered us together on his departure. He looked gaunt and hollow eyed and was suffering from snow blindness more than most of us. And his voice had an odd, thin ring to it.

"I'm taking a party with me to get relief. The King party should have been here by now. Take heart; we plan to move fast, make up for lost time. As fast as you can, head for the Rio Grande and follow it toward the Mexican settlements. As fast as you can, bring the baggage to the Rio Grande and meet the relief party at Conejos, Rabbit River, which you can't miss. It's a summer settlement for herders. There will be shelters. Maybe even some stored grains. Look for relief there, eh? You can hunt along the way; we're in game country now. In a day or two, after we collect at Taos, I'll be going to California by the southern route."

I stared at the man, astonished that he was thinking about that leg of the trip, even while we were caught in our extremity far to the north. Had we just heard what we had heard? I saw others staring at Frémont, not believing their ears. But Frémont was oblivious to our disbelief and continued on.

"Now, I'm putting Lorenzo Vincenthaler in command. He's a veteran of my California expedition, and he will see to your safety."

Vincenthaler. I knew so little of him. He was one of the quiet sorts, a part of Frémont's inner circle of veterans, and not one at any of my messes.

I knew he was an Ohio man and a veteran of the war. I saw no difficulty in it and imagined he would be as good as any. And yet one could not help but wonder at the colonel's choice.

The next two days were miserable in the extreme, as we hauled the rest of the colonel's luggage with us and subsisted on boiled parfleche, which produced a repellent, thin gruel. We dragged his barometers and thermometers, spare rifle parts, kettles and spoons, heavy rubberized camp mats, iron rods, canvas, and packsaddles. Then, at last, we set forth along the frozen Rio del Norte, choosing the ice in the middle because it was free of snow and because we could drag the packs more easily. But the farther we pierced into that naked valley, the worse the winds, and soon they were sapping what little energy we possessed. We saw no game and were too snow-blind to kill any.

There was no point in staying. The sooner we headed downriver, the sooner we would meet our relief. Two of the Frenchmen in the company, Vincent Tabeau and Antoine

Morin, decided to go ahead. They were veteran voyageurs. They had been with the colonel on all three of his previous expeditions. They were seasoned and familiar with hardship. Now they were going ahead, perhaps to find game, perhaps to meet up with our relief. Whatever their private intent, they left the day after the colonel, with Vincenthaler's blessing.

Our new commander divided the last of the edibles, doling out exactly one cup of sugar to each man, two tallow candles, and a mismatched supply of parfleche leather and thong to boil down to a foul gruel. That was it. There was nothing more to support life.

The rest of us started down the river the next day, January 13, making our slow progress south. We had resolved to stay together and help one another, but the weaker men soon lagged behind. I was among the weaker. I was in the company of the Kerns and Andrews and Cathcart, whose ragged clothes flapped about him. But I didn't suppose I looked much better. And Ben Kern could barely walk, managing only a few paces at a time before he had to rest. Plainly, it would be a slow, hard trip.

Now the dazzling white world rendered our eyes useless. Our heads ached from squinting; we leaked tears that froze to our cheeks and beards. We pulled hats down over our brows, anything that would spare us that glare.

But if the snow blindness was a torment, our frost-ruined feet were worse. Every step was a torment. Our toes and ankles had frozen and thawed and frozen and whitened and blackened and turned to pulp. Then the California Indian lad, Manuel, surrendered. His feet were black. He begged Vincenthaler to shoot him, and when our commander refused, the young man turned back, intending to die in the camp we had left behind us, and no amount of urging on our part could change his mind. The last I saw of him, he was hobbling back, back, back to a sure death. It was a horror I could scarcely swallow. But that was only the beginning.

Later that very day, Henry Wise, a hardy Missourian, simply sat down in the snow and perished. I watched him sit; I watched him slump. I watched him slowly tumble onto his side and await his fate. None of us could help him. There was only that awful silence that comes from witnessing the things our very eyes were seeing, and then we had to leave him there on the river ice and continue on our way, the dark sight we had witnessed crowding our minds and weighing like stones in our bosoms. Joaquin and Gregorio, the other Indian boys, gently covered Wise's body with brush and snow, and I marveled that they had the energy to do it.

That night, as we sheltered as best we could from the bitter wind, a new horror rose among us. Another veteran, Carver, from Wisconsin, went mad. He rambled through our messes, ranting, saying he would go on and find food. He had a plan. All night we listened to his exhortations, and with the following dawn he drifted away, and we could do nothing to oppose it. It is odd, how well I remember my very last glance, remember the exact expression on Carver's face. And the last on Wise's. These were moments when I was staring into the great void.

The horrors had not passed. The Frenchman, Tabeau, who had rejoined us, began to rave. This, he said, was a visitation from God. His suffering was beyond what any mortal can endure, but somehow he survived the night. When we once again started down the icy river, he stumbled along as best he could for an hour or so, utterly blinded by the glare, and then sat down. His old friend Morin sat beside him, the two choosing to depart from this life together, and that was the last we saw of them. They never caught up with the rest of us again.

After we made camp, the rest of us drifted in one by one each man on his own, all semblance of a company gone. We had gone through the last of our provisions, even the miserable leather.

Vincenthaler had only one thing to say to us as we struck our fires and warmed our tormented feet.

"You're on your own now," he said. "I can do no more."

CHAPTER TWENTY-SEVEN

John Charles Frémont

Ere long, we picked up the trail of King's relief party and followed it. The information it yielded was not good. Preuss noted that the camps were only two or three miles apart and that their progress was so slow that they would not yet have reached the Mexican settlements.

"What do you suppose was the trouble?" I asked him.

He simply shook his head. None of us could know. But it might simply have been the want of food. Now they were somewhere ahead, foraging for food as they went. We had a bit of sugar and macaroni and nothing else to sustain life. But unlike King's company, I had first-rate men with me.

Godey roamed ahead but found no game, and our own position was growing desperate. We examined each of the camps of the relief party, looking for clues, but they yielded nothing. No bones or feathers, no blood, no apparent sickness. Just miserable progress wandering down the middle of the frozen river, camping wherever they could find shelter.

My own party was about to experience the same fate. We ate the last of the macaroni, boiled up the sugar, and prepared to feast on our boots and scabbards, when one of those fateful turns of fortune caught us up. Our own progress was slowed. Theodore, Godey's nephew, could scarcely walk, and I feared for Preuss. There, ahead, was an Indian. I was so snow-blind I could scarcely make him out and thought he might be one of King's party, but as we approached Godey told me this was an old Ute. He was all alone, or so we thought.

I made the peace sign, palm up.

He stood somberly, wrapped in a leather cape, his gray hair falling in two braids. He carried a bow and quiver of arrows, one of which was nocked. His face was seamed copper, and his cheekbones ridged his face. He surveyed us one by one, reading our hunger.

I knew little of the hand language and feared we might have trouble.

He said something in a tongue I could not fathom. I remembered that this people had generations of contact with the Mexicans and tried Spanish.

"Buenos días," I said.

"Hablo un poco de español," he replied.

After that, with much hesitation, we conducted what surely was one of the most critical negotiations in my life. He seemed slow, almost ponderous, all the while weighing us in ways I could not fathom.

I learned that he was with a small Ute hunting party camped nearby. Yes, they had seen the other party and had seen their smokes but had not visited them. The other relief party had spilled much blood in the snow.

"Are they alive?" I asked.

He hesitated, and finally nodded.

"How far ahead?"

It was not a question he could answer, so he remained stone silent.

"Have you food we could trade for?" I asked.

He eyed us, seeing our rifles and powder horns and the bedrolls we carried on our backs.

I told him we needed horses or mules, food, and I wanted a guide who would take us to the closest Mexican settlements on the Chama River. He studied us, uncertain whether we were true friends or somehow dangerous.

"I have blankets, a rifle and powder and shot to trade," I said.

I could not make out his reply, but then he beckoned, and we followed him up a drainage to the south and came suddenly on a small encampment of brush huts with skins thrown over them, with perhaps a dozen men in it, all of them warmly dressed in skins. I did not see a woman. They circled around us, wary but not hostile, and I once again made my wishes known to them. I feared ambush; their numbers were large enough to put arrows into us. But it didn't happen. Instead, they invited us to sit at their council fires.

We received a thin, hot meat broth. As I downed this blessed soup, drinking directly from a pottery bowl that was being passed around, I noticed several bony horses gnawing at bark and sticks in the brush nearby. A sorrier lot of horses I never did see, and how they had survived in this white world I could not imagine, and I thought maybe the horses couldn't imagine it either. But I knew one thing: I wanted those horses. I wanted them so badly I would trade anything and promise anything to get them. They would carry us to safety.

I needed to give them some sort of gift and settled on my camp hatchet, which I laid before the coppery old man. He nodded and examined it with pleasure. Anything of metal was a treasure to a Ute.

That broth was so savory we could have emptied their kettle, and I know every man of us stared hungrily at that soup, but it was time to negotiate our salvation.

I told him my name was Frémont and waited to see whether it brought a response. He said he was known as San Juan, a chieftain of the Utah people. That was a good start.

I told him, fumbling for simple words, that we needed food and horses and a guide to the settlements. We had things to trade. What would he want in return?

He arose, came to me, touched my Hawken rifle, shot pouch, powder horn, and bedroll, which held two blankets in a canvas groundsheet. He pointed to the horses and held up five fingers, and then to a parfleche, which he opened. It was brimming with jerked meat, probably venison. There were twenty or thirty pounds of it as far as I could tell.

"More food?"

He shook his head. That was all he could give us, and it wouldn't sustain us long.

"If you guide us to Abiquiu, I will reward you when we get there," I said.

"How?" he asked.

"I will see to it," I replied, for I had no idea what I might discover there.

He arose, sharply commanded a youth to follow, and then headed into the brush. In the space of a few minutes he and the boy returned with four scrawny nags, so poor I wondered if they would carry us far. He laid the heavy parfleche before me. I slipped my rifle off of my shoulder and handed it to him, along with the powder and balls and patches, and then pulled my bedroll from my back.

He smiled broadly, baring gaps in his browned teeth. It was our moment of triumph, and I felt my burdens slip away. It was my destiny.

But it was not quite as I had thought. The horses would carry us or our baggage but would remain his. We would borrow them. He would come with us to the Mexican settlements, and then he would reclaim his horses. He was being abundantly paid for this service and a little food, but I ignored his extravagant demands. These tribesmen put a larger value on things than they're worth.

I explained my negotiations to Godey and Preuss, who congratulated me.

We started at once, the four bony nags hauling our truck, and San Juan leading the way. We cut across an oxbow of the river and soon picked up the trail of the relief party. Both Godey and Preuss, who had become a keen mountaineer, noted that the camps seemed fresher. We were gaining on King's party. I had become so snow-blind that I could barely see and gladly left the navigation to the old Indian. For the moment, we walked, but there was not a man among us who didn't wish to throw himself over a bony horse and be carried to safety. Either that or eat the horse.

We made good time. The guide was able to bivouac us in drainages where thick brush supplied a little fodder for the starved horses, as well as some shelter from the relentless wind. We boiled up a thin soup of jerky and a few roots the old man dug up from the frozen earth, and so mollified the demands of our stomachs, though we were just as hungry after as we were before.

We rejoined the Rio Grande and were quickly comforted by firewood and the prospect of game. I left it to Godey to hunt, since I no longer had a rifle, and I noticed the old chieftain was walking wide of us, hoping to scare up game. Then, not far from the frozen river, we came upon a disturbance in the snow, some blood frozen to the earth, giving it a pink pallor. But there was no sign of life here or habitation or a camp. Maybe they had killed an animal and dragged it to the river.

"Something live, or newly dead, was butchered here," Godey said. "If there's blood, it was not a frozen animal."

It was a good observation. There were skid marks, so we

pursued them the quarter or third of a mile to the frozen river, and there we found another campsite, fresher than the others, and with some sign that it had been used for several days. There had been two fires, and not all the wood they had collected had been consumed by them. But there was no sign of the animal they had consumed, which led me to believe that they had devoured every scrap of it.

But the German was restless and began a slow circle of the camp, poking and probing the dense river brush. What he was hunting for was quite beyond my imagination until he stopped suddenly.

"Ach!" he exclaimed.

We headed at once through dense willow brush to Preuss, who stood sourly, his lips curled down.

There, at his feet, was King. Without trousers. And without legs. King's open eyes stared upward. The carrion birds had not yet plucked them out. In fact, there was no sign that any animal at all had discovered this frozen corpse caught deep in the tan brush. The man's legs had been crudely severed, perhaps with an axe, and there was no nether part of him in sight.

"So," Preuss said. "They should have put an apple in his mouth and baked him whole."

I knew at once whose work this was.

"Williams! I'd been warned about him. That man's a degenerate. He'd eat the whole party if he had to."

Godey knelt beside what was left of King and attempted to roll him over, but his shirt was frozen to the ground. With some effort, Godey pulled King loose and turned him over. There was no evidence of violence, other than the lost legs.

"Froze to death," Godey said.

"It was Williams. No man of my company would do it," I said.

Preuss grinned at me. He was an oddly cynical man and could annoy me at times.

"I want that body removed from here, far away, buried in brush. I don't want this known," I said. "I want this kept entirely between us and of course request your silence."

I waited. Godey nodded. Preuss grinned and nodded. Young Theodore frowned. The boy was the most likely to talk.

"Theodore, I want your word of honor. Some things must never be mentioned, not ever."

"Yes, sir," he said.

The Indian stood quietly. I knew the more I urged silence from him, the more he would whisper, so I ignored him. No one would believe him anyway. He stared at the body, then at us, a deep curiosity in his seamed face. Then he looked away, into the white skies.

Godey found a canvas and rolled King onto it, and he and Preuss slowly dragged the corpse through brush, into timber, and finally to a frozen swampy spot. They put King out among the cattails, where he would sink as soon as the thaw came. Then they heaped brush over King's body.

I thought it was a good choice.

I did not want Senator Benton to know, nor Jessie. Or my sponsors. I didn't want the army to know, nor the public or the press. I didn't want the rest of the company to know. I did not want it said that there was cannibalism on my expedition or in my command. But if word did leak out, I knew exactly what I would say. Old Bill Williams was the responsible party; men of mine would not do such a thing but would choose to perish before eating the flesh of any other mortal.

It was a good and valid riposte. It was well known that the beaver trappers and mountaineers had sometimes resorted to desperate measures in starving times, and many a man now living in Saint Louis owed his life to the flesh of his companions. So, if whispering began, it would not be about Frémont but about the guide, who had deliberately slowed the party, let it starve, and finally had partaken of the forbidden.

"Are we going to say a word over this man?" Godey asked.

"A word? I've asked you not—oh, you mean a prayer. We'll have a moment of silence," I said, and doffed my fur hat and felt the icy fingers of the north wind filter through my ragged hair.

Later, I wondered how his widow would receive the news.

CHAPTER TWENTY-EIGHT

Tom Breckenridge

I hated Creutzfeldt. I despised Williams. I peered at them through snow-ruined eyes, the tears freezing on my lashes. I had partaken of the meat; I was helpless to stop myself. I swallowed it as soon as it was half-cooked over the wind-blown fire. King ham. Precious little of it, too. What good were two skinny thighs of a half-starved man? There were hardly ten pounds of flesh for the three of us. I have no recollection of the taste; it didn't matter. It could have been chicken or elk or beefsteak. It was poor food, and it went down with my stomach clawing at it, and my revulsion vomiting into my soul.

I could never again walk through the doors of my church. I could never receive the bread and wine of communion into my mouth.

I looked at Creutzfeldt and loathed him. He was the devil. He had tempted me. He had turned into something grotesque, some gargoyle or griffin guarding a dark building.

His cheeks had sunk, his eyes bulged, his matted hair flapped out from his grimy hat. Williams was quieter, and I loathed the man. It was he who had built up the fire, sliced meat from King's hambone, and set it sizzling in the miserable snow pit we occupied. I stared at myself, at fingers that had held the dreadful meat, the devil's fingers. And yet my belly stopped gnawing at me, at least for the moment.

By unspoken agreement, we set the rest aside. We could go two days on it, a pound of King a day for each of us. It would get us a few miles farther toward the northern settlements. Or Taos on the Rio Grande. I didn't care which. If we made it, we would walk into the village and they would know. The mark of Cain would be on our foreheads. We could not hide ourselves.

I looked into the sorry sky, knowing nothing had been hidden. Later, I imagined our conduct might be hidden; life would go on. But there are no secrets; every foul deed is made known, sooner or later. By agreement, the three of us dragged King into some brush, hoping wild animals would obscure our sin, then fled the abattoir and stumbled southward once again, carrying six or eight pounds of King. The snow wounded my eyes; I could see nothing through the frozen tears but followed mutely along. Williams led the way; we stumbled behind, Creutzfeldt and I. And so we passed a day, camped in some sheltering brush that night, hid under the cutbank against the wind, and ate another parcel of King. We had made only a few miles before we had all given out. And then we tackled the next day, crueler than the previous, and made a few more miles. Who knows how many? That eve, Old Bill settled us in a riverside woods, where shelter and firewood were plentiful. And there we demolished the last of King. Our friend had given us only a reprieve. We were still forty miles from the Chama River villages. What had King's flesh bought us but a stone in the bosom for the rest of our days?

The next day, with wind lifting and whipping snow, we set off again, this time aware that no meal would await us at the end of the day. We resolved to hunt; I checked my load. I fantasized. I would find a few deer; I would steady myself, aim, and drop one, and we would be saved. There would be venison enough to see us through. But in my feverish imagination, I saw myself shooting an antlered King and slicing him up. Still, we had put King behind us; we were three days along the river road from that horror. If I could have run, I would have run and run, day and night, run away from that place. And we were seeing signs of game in the snow; hoofprints, tracks, marks of passage everywhere. Surely, surely, I would find a deer, and that would somehow wipe away our shame. We would eat clean, well-cooked venison, and be freed of the stain. I even pushed ahead, weary as I was, so that I might have first crack at any game we found. But the afternoon stretched away in silence, and the winter sun plummeted, and we made camp in a good place where we would be warm—and starving once again.

None of us could see much anymore, and that was why we scarcely knew what was coming upon us until men and horses plunged into our camp. I arose, startled, to see the hazy shapes of horses, some bearing men. Other men were walking. They collected silently around us, peering down.

"Breckenridge? Is that you?"

The voice was Colonel Frémont's.

"Yes, sir," I croaked.

"And Williams? And who is this?"

He was pointing to Creutzfeldt, and indeed, the scarecrow in rags bore no resemblance to the man the colonel knew.

"I'm Creutzfeldt, sir."

"I see now," Frémont said.

He dismounted and peered about, and I suddenly was glad there was no meat in camp and no sign of any cooking.

"I have men with me; we thought you were lost. I'm the relief this time," Frémont said.

I could not tell what men were with him, so terrible were my eyes. There was an Indian among them.

"Have you food?" Williams asked.

Frémont ignored him. "Twenty-two days ago you started out. What happened?"

"We had food only for four," I said. "It took that just to get out of the mountains."

"Rough country, like I say," Williams added. "I been saying it."

"Two or three miles a day?" Frémont asked.

This was accusation, and I didn't care for it. "No one could have done better," I replied.

"Have you chow?" Williams persisted.

"Not up to your tastes?" That was Preuss talking. I still hadn't figured out who all was with Frémont.

"We got a little jerky from the Ute," Godey said. I knew the voice.

I managed to focus long enough to see the whole party. Frémont had the German with him, Preuss, tough little devil. And his manservant, Saunders, and Godey's nephew, Theodore. And an ancient Ute.

"His horses, not ours," Frémont said, to allay any instinct of mine to slice the throat of one of the miserable animals. What those starved beasts fed on, I could not imagine. "He's taking us to the settlements. We'll get help there."

Now I could see that these scarecrow horses were the poorest I had ever seen. They carried packs, except that the strongest carried Frémont. There were four. The rest of the company, along with the Ute, walked. Or maybe they exchanged rides.

Preuss studied our camp, poked around its periphery, as if looking for something, but we had nothing to show him. We had bedrolls, a few tools, and a rifle or two. I thought they would stay, but Frémont had other ideas.

"We're going to put in another hour," he said. "I've got hungry men upriver waiting for relief. We can't dally."

He let the word hang in the air. We had dallied. On the other hand, we had not met any Utes with horses and food to trade, either.

"We have no food," I said.

"I can imagine," Frémont replied. He studied us a moment. "Alex, how much jerky is there?"

Godey dug into a pack on the back of a scrawny horse. "Maybe thirty pounds," he said.

"Give them a third," Frémont ordered.

Godey parceled out a third of the jerky and handed it to Williams. Old Bill instantly handed a piece of jerky to Creutzfeldt and me, and I jammed it between my teeth.

"Follow along. I'll send relief out as soon as I can."

"How do we get to the settlements?"

Frémont stared at Old Bill Williams and me. "Charts show some hills west of the river below here a mile or two. Leave the river there. Circle around the hills and bear southeast across open country. There won't be any running water, and not much wood."

"Our feet have given out," I said, wanting leather or blanket or anything I could get. We were walking on strips of blanket.

"We could use some canvas for our feet," Williams said.

"So could we," Frémont replied.

"You'll send the Mexicans?" I asked.

"I'll send relief as fast as possible. And I'll be outfitting for the California leg while you others come in."

"California?"

"The next leg. We'll head south and then west to the Gila River and across. I'll be buying livestock and stores. I'm going to reorganize, recruit a company, head down the Rio Grande. The place where we head west is near Socorro. That will take us to the Gila drainage. It should be a warm and pleasant trip, that far south."

"California?" I whispered.

"Don't lose heart," Frémont replied. "You'll make it."

With that, he reined his pony and the whole party drifted away, leaving us behind. I watched, hating Frémont and Godey. I hoped the Ute would steal away with his ponies in the middle of the night. I loathed the man. They could have taken us along. Abandoning us was probably a death sentence.

Preuss had looked through me, as if I were transparent. The others were cold. Godey, usually the most affable of men, had stared quietly. Surely we had been found out. But I was beyond caring. I stuffed another stick of jerky in my mouth and tried to make a meal of it, but there is nothing less satisfying. It is nothing but an emergency ration, and not a good one at that. Still, if we resisted the temptation to devour it all, right then and there, we might make it.

"Bill, maybe we should divide up that jerky," I said.

He grinned wolfishly, but then he did arrange the sticks of meat into three piles and beckoned. I grabbed one, the others caught up theirs. It would suffice us or we would die. I ate mine in small crumbs, letting my saliva release the flavor. If I could not really eat, at least I could pretend to and let the juices linger in my mouth.

We stumbled back to our campfire and collapsed in the

small circle of heat it threw out. We ate more jerky than we intended, since none of us could slow down.

There was something gnawing at me: "He didn't ask," I said.

"No, I reckon he didn't," Old Bill said. "Like maybe he had that part of it all figured out."

"They know," I said.

"Anyone coming by, they'd sure enough know," Williams said. "So what? It don't matter none. Happens all the time, and a man can be glad of it."

The unasked question haunted me. They knew. It was in all their faces. It was in the ginger way they talked. It was in their politeness. It was in their silence when I asked for food.

I should have just accepted it, but instead I was enraged.

"They'd have done the same," I snapped.

"Maybe more," Williams said. "There's a lot more to King than a pair of hams."

I stared into the twilight. Not far south the second relief party was cheerfully marching into the dusk, accusations in the minds of them all. Still, maybe none of them would say a word. If I knew Frémont, I knew he would bury it deep.

We started the next morning in a whip of snow. The restless wind would not leave it alone but drove it into drifts and carved hollows in it. Still, we made our way slowly along the route that angled away from the river. It would save us miles by cutting across the oxbow, but we would lack shelter.

In many ways, those legs of our trip were hardest of all. There was no wood for fires, no shelter from the wind, no comforts at night. We could only huddle in our thin blankets, one beneath the three of us, the other rags heaped over us, and endure until the next cruel sun would blind us but offer no heat. We sucked our jerky, gathered our strength, and marched out on another blinding day.

But our feet were failing us. They were frostbitten, bleeding, numb, and painful all at once. We left pink trails behind us. We took to crawling for a hundred yards at a time, just to relieve the pain that was lancing our every step. We exhausted ourselves on our hands and knees; that consumes more energy than walking, but our feet rebelled at every step we took, and we had no leather or cloth to ease our torment.

I raged because Frémont didn't take us with him. They could have carried us. They saw our feet, the ragged bits of blanket, and yet they paused only for an hour and then hurried on.

But we didn't die, and I credit the jerky for it. By the third day we had consumed the last of it and were more starved than ever, but we pushed on. The settlements were nigh, and the reality that we were close to help and comfort was the only food we possessed.

I gazed ahead, with snow-blind eyes, aching to see our rescuers coming toward us, bearing food and blankets, mules and warmth. But we saw nothing at all, nothing but the great, hollow snow-swept valley, and we stumbled on.

CHAPTER TWENTY-NINE

Benjamin Kern, MD

It was only later that I grasped the horror of Frémont's intent. With men starving to death and frozen and weakened, his thought was of his equipment. We spent days ferrying the truck that had been scattered up that creek down to the cache, days spent consuming the last of our energy.

I was too numb to see it, and so were the rest. If the colonel wanted his equipment collected and cached, then it was up to us to do it. I heard in that awful span of time no complaint at all. The colonel had a mesmerizing effect on all of us, and we would have followed his instruction unto death. I do not know where or how he acquired that grip over other mortals, but he had it and used it, his soft polite voice sealing our doom.

His choice of Vincenthaler is instructive to me now. The man was a dutiful sergeant, incapable of doing anything but following the colonel's command no matter what new circumstances arose. I think Frémont intuitively understood that; in Lorenzo Vincenthaler he had the man whose will was a slavish copy of the colonel's own. So without question or cavil, our new commander set us to the task, no matter that his own eyes told him we were all on the brink of collapse and our sole chance lay in leaving the mountains at once, reaching the bottoms of the Rio Grande, and finding game. But he did not abandon the mountains. He didn't send his best hunters ahead to scout for game. He didn't send the strongest of his men to prepare a warm camp that might sustain us for one more night. As the perfect surrogate of the colonel, he required us to drag the last of the colonel's stuff over the snow and stow it in the cache. Then we set out across the valley, in a gale out of the north that began murdering men before we were a mile or two out of the mountains.

Then, with several men down, he chose to abdicate.

He collected those of us who had survived a day of stumbling along with our rifles and blankets and nothing more and announced his decision:

"You're on your own," he said. "Some of us are stronger, some weaker, and I can't let the weaker delay the stronger. So, I'll take the stronger men with me and try to get relief. I can do no more."

It made sense in a way, if you wish to excuse the days we

had spent sliding the colonel's stuff down the mountain. We devoured the last bits of tallow candles that night. The next morning Vincenthaler's chosen party sneaked away before the rest of us were even aware. He took with him the two California Indians, Joaquin and Gregorio, as well as Scott, Martin, Bacon, Hubbard, Ducatel, and Rohrer. There was hardly a man among those of us left behind who could lift a rifle to shoot a passing raven. There was Andrew Cathcart, skin and bones but doughty and alive; Micajah McGehee; Captain Charles Taplin; Joseph Stepperfeldt; Elijah Andrews; my brothers, and I. We were on our own, we who were so worn we could scarcely walk thirty paces to collect firewood. We vowed we would not leave one another, so long as there was breath in us, and so strengthened ourselves in our solidarity.

Still, we were not yet defeated. If we had no flesh on us, we still had heart. I surveyed the creek where ice did not cover it, looking for anything, water bugs, fish, aquatic plants, that might sustain us, but it was a feckless search. I did find some wild rose shrubs and collected some rose hips and shared these with the rest. They are known to allopathic medicine as being therapeutic. It behooved us to be off. The farther ahead the stronger party got, the worse would be our chances. If they might shoot a deer, they would send a fair portion of it back to us if we didn't lag too far, or so I believed. I should have known better.

All that day we proceeded along the river, sometimes a few steps at a time, but never failing to make headway. By dark we were spread out again, but some of us went back for the stragglers whilst the rest got a fire going and made some warmth. I was one of those stragglers and had fallen insensate only to have the rest get me to my feet, and by that means I staggered into the camp and the welcome warmth. There remained only Andrews not accounted for, and soon we heard one hoarse cry and nothing more. We found him a hundred yards back and got him in, but he lay inert, in a stupor that awakened a dread in me. I have seen that sort of stupor all too often in my practice.

Then Rohrer came in, rising out of the dusk, much to our surprise.

"Couldn't keep up," he muttered.

We welcomed him to our campfire, where he collapsed in a heap. Soon he was warming himself, but I eyed him sharply and didn't like what I saw.

We were much too famished to break camp the next morning and resolved to hunt whilst we had strength enough to shoulder a rifle. The whole lot of us were so snow-blind I couldn't imagine we would have much luck, but my friends persisted, and in time, they brought in two prairie hens. Oh, that was a fine moment, even if it meant only one bite apiece for the nine of us. We divided everything, including the entrails, and felt that single morsel slide into our gullets.

One of us, Taplin if memory serves me, found a dead wolf and dragged it in. It was mostly gone, gnawed away by raptors and other hungry creatures, but we got some well-boiled flesh out of it, boiled the hide for more, and ground up the bones and gulped them down, too. That barely sustained life, but in truth we could travel no more. We were worn out.

Elijah Andrews lingered in a stupor, and nothing I could do induced him to live, and so he perished quietly in the night. He was a Saint Louis man and had served long years in the navy, only to meet his Maker out in the middle of the continent. He had struggled to live but had weakened steadily. McGehee had saved him earlier in the mountains, but the span of his life was only a few days more. I wondered what little family in the city would soon be sorrowing.

We found a small gilded bible in his pocket and resolved that if any of us should live, we would deliver it to Andrews's relatives in Saint Louis. It was a most sacred vow: that bible would be carried from one end of the continent to the other, if need be, but it would come home in Saint Louis. We laid Andrews out flat; the cold wasted no time permeating his flesh, and we covered him with brush, for that was all we could do.

My eye was on Henry Rohrer, who was mumbling and ranting and drifting to and from the fire. He was a millwright, making his way to California, where his skills would be greatly valued. I knew the madness as a prelude to what would come next, but I was helpless. I had no remedy but hot water, which I attempted to put into the man and thus warm his innards, but he would not drink it. I could not fathom what he was saying, but the flow of words told me he was off in his own memories, or his own world, and already lost to us. So our camp began another deathwatch, as we waited for the maddened man to quit life. It did not happen at once. By unspoken agreement, we planned to head downriver as soon as Rohrer left us. I don't suppose anyone wanted to remain in camp with two of the dead.

But ere long, his breath stopped. And so we had lost another. We stared at the bodies. That's when my brother Ned, one of Frémont's trusted lieutenants in the conquest, offered the proposition:

"It's a hard thing to say, but that meat's as good as any other," he said.

I wasn't surprised. Or rather, I thought it might be Richard, the weakest among us, who would raise the prospect. Ned had his ways in the wilds and managed to pull bits of food from everything he passed. I once watched him dig up cattail root and mash and eat it. But now he had come to his Rubicon and was proposing that we all cross that river, even as Rohrer's body began its long and fateful cooling.

I had no objections. Men do what they have to do in extremis. My own empty stomach groaned with need. Captain Taplin, who was the strongest among us and had stayed with us to hunt if he could, simply stared. The awful prospect hung among us.

"Do what you must, but out of my sight," Taplin said roughly. "I will not see it."

But McGehee, courageous lad from the Deep South, offered his own plea. "Let us wait. Relief is coming. It might be here tomorrow. We can endure. Give it three days, and then we shall do whatever we must do."

That was a sensible and courageous suggestion. We nodded, feeling the hollowness of our bellies, our tongues and teeth and throats and stomachs rebelling against this great moral act Micajah had proposed. But for the moment, we subsided. I pulled a bit of canvas over Rohrer, the millwright who wanted to live out his life in a sunny, warm land. The canvas cast a veil over him and made a small, redoubtable barrier.

"Who's going to write them?" I asked, thinking of all the newly made widows and orphans, mothers and fathers, brothers and sisters scattered across the country, but most commonly in Saint Louis and Missouri.

"Someone must," McGehee said.

"The colonel, of course," Taplin said. "It's his duty."

It's odd how that thought dispirited me.

Hunger doesn't abate. It's there, down in the gut or under the ribs every waking moment and during sleep as well. It is not only a physical pain but an incompleteness. It feeds a gnawing worry; life isn't right. Now this hunger afflicted us all. The faces in these men, as I watched them in the flickering light, were almost unrecognizable. Something had scooped and shrunk their faces, like a lingering disease. I wondered how well I might read the sign of my own failure, and thought I could well enough.

I forced my mind to other things. Tomorrow, if I had any strength, I'd chop through the river ice and see about fishing. A morsel of fish would go a long way among us. I had nothing to fish with, but the dream of catching one fevered me.

Captain Taplin was a saint. He was hardier than the rest of us but chose to shepherd us and hunt for us instead of joining Vincenthaler's party ahead. If we survived, he would be the rock of our salvation. It was he who collected wood and fed the fire and drove away the misery of the icy night. It was he who helped me up when I fainted away and got me to this place.

My thoughts returned, as I knew they would, to those two departed men and the meat of their shoulders and arms and thighs that might support us for a few days more. Would it be so terrible? It's odd that I debated the moral ground for it, when all I wanted was flesh, any flesh, to eat. And yet my mind persisted in examining the issue, perhaps with a clarity that only a starving man can experience. I thought it would not be so bad; the dead might even have wanted it. And yet, somehow, I was grateful when McGehee suggested we wait for our rescuers. It came to me as a vast relief, a release from my own temptation.

That was a long night, filled with strange phantasms. I thought the Utes had fallen upon us, but that was not the case. By the cold light of dawn I surveyed our number and saw that the living lived; the dead lay just apart. It was plain that we were going no farther. We would either be rescued here or perish here. Most of the men did not bother to sit up but lay in their miserable blankets, staring at the white sky.

I urged upon them the last medical advice I had, which was to drink hot water, as scalding as they could endure, for in the heat was life, and it was cold that would steal in and murder them. Some did. We had a single kettle among us, and Taplin kept it filled and close to the flames. I was worried about Cathcart, who didn't stir, and I managed to get some hot water to him. It was all I could do to get him to sit up and swallow it, but he seemed better for it after he had downed a good hot cup.

That day was the beginning of helplessness. There we were, sensate, aware of our world, and utterly helpless. Our bodies failed us. Taplin, the strongest, tried to hunt, and he managed to walk to a copse a hundred yards distant and sit on a log, awaiting whatever game might wander. Nothing came, and he made his way back to lie down beside the fire.

Helplessness is a strange sensation. I wanted to live, to walk, to eat, to sit up, and all I could manage was to lie close to the flickering fire, turn myself occasionally to warm the front or rear parts of me, and peer half-blindly off to the south, from whence our help must come, if it were to come at all.

The others were in the same case. I was too weak to attempt my plan to fish or find anything aquatic to eat. I could not wield our camp axe enough to breach the ice. And so the helpless day passed, followed by an even more helpless day, and then another, while we slowly wasted the last of our strength.

I had reached the point where I could barely raise my head to look after my brothers. I had tried to doctor them all along, but now I stared into the whiteness until my eyes blurred and smarted, and I waited for whatever fate would bring.

Of the two dead I knew nothing. Whether any among us chose to slice aside the men's shirts and britches and find some meat, I could not say. If it was done, it was done so furtively in the deeps of the night that I had no inkling of it. I supposed it would be someone's deep secret and unknown to me.

Then on the third day, or perhaps it was some other day, for I had lost count in my perpetual twilight, we heard a shout. I could no longer lift my head and don't know what it was about. But I managed to rise a little, by dint of determination, and saw men and horses approaching. Whether our relief party or Utes I did not know.

CHAPTER THIRTY

John Charles Frémont

We reached the Red River settlement late of a winter's day, and no place looked more like heaven. Here, in an arid brown valley off the Rio del Norte, lay a northern outpost of the Mexicans, a scatter of low adobe homes surrounded by snow-ribbed grain fields and pumpkin patches. The usual adobe defense tower guarded these farming people from the sallies of the Utes and other tribes. White smoke drifted from their chimneys, but we saw no other sign of life.

We five stumbled in, guided by our Ute chief. His horses were so poor they barely moved, so it had taken us four more days from the time we encountered Williams and Breckenridge and Creutzfeldt to reach the settlement.

The Mexicans soon herded about us, warm and sympathetic, and swiftly brought us into a heated, if austere, one-room jacal, where they hastened to feed us with a corn gruel and bread. Never did anything taste so elegant. The walls were festooned with strings of dried red peppers, a local delicacy. There, before the hearth fire that cast its thin heat into the adobe room, we found warmth and comfort. Bronzed, jet-haired neighbors wrapped in serapes crowded in, watching us silently as we wolfed our food. The children were shooed away, and perhaps for good reason. We were a shocking sight. I am adequate in their tongue, and Godey spoke it passably, and we made our needs known: we had starving men upriver. We needed men, mules, bread, blankets, and livestock feed, and fast.

The villagers simply shook their heads. There were not food stores and blankets and mules and burros enough in the whole settlement to meet our needs. A man who introduced himself as the alcalde, Juan Solis, said he could spare but three burros, five mules, and a little cornmeal, but maybe more food might be found. A goat or two might be slaughtered. He and his villagers would do all they could. They would also prepare for the next arrivals. A little goat milk would help them.

At Taos, one long day's ride south, they told us, there would be everything a relief party would need, as well as a detachment of American soldiers who had been there since the conquest. The next dawn, well fed and greatly strengthened, I set off for Taos, along with Alexis Godey, my man Saunders, and Godey's nephew, Theodore. The Ute chief, having delivered us, retreated after receiving what remaining gifts we could manage, which were Saunders's and Theodore's rifles and powder flasks and shot. The Mexicans treated the old man kindly, offering him a bowl of the cornmeal, which he ate swiftly before he left. I watched the old chief wander off with his weary nags, two powder horns dangling about his neck and his new rifles slung from his saddles. Preuss, who was unwell, stayed on at the Red River settlement, to gather strength and deal with the survivors as they straggled in.

It was an itch in me to send relief at once, but these things take time, and I could only hope that my men could endure a few days more. The horror of it had descended on me, and I could scarcely look northward without feeling the lances of tragedy stab at me. We four, mounted bareback on borrowed mules now, made our way to Taos in a long day and reached town as an azure twilight, the heavens transparent as stained glass, settled over the village. Snow topped the tawny adobe homes, while the incense of piñon smoke hung over the place, delighting my senses. Off to the east the forbidding Sangre de Cristos caught the red light of the dying sun and threw it back on the settlement like some last benediction from the Creator. It was a hushed moment, all sound blotted up by the lavender heaps of snow.

But at last we rode into the old town, past low adobes with tight-closed shutters, toward the small plaza and merchant buildings hemming it. Taos stood on a plain at a great altitude, and the winter had not treated it kindly. There were dimpled drifts about and footpaths through them. Still, this was the place of our succor.

We were a sorry lot, wild and savage looking, and starved down to nothing, and we wrought a great malaise among the staring villagers who saw us make our way to the heart of town. A black-clad older woman could not bear the sight of us and turned away. I wanted to find Carson at once and sought a certain cantina where he might be at an early evening hour.

"Godey," I said, "begin the relief, and make haste. Take whatever you can find. You and Theodore. I'll be at La Tristeza, if not Carson's house."

He nodded, smiling. Thus commanded, he set off at once looking for the soldiers stationed there. I had done all I could and now looked forward to a needed rest. I wandered into the cantina just off the plaza, adjusted my snow-ruined eyes to the flickering firelight, and spotted Carson, along with Dick Owens and Lucien Maxwell, old stalwarts and friends gathered at a hewn trestle table beside a beehive fireplace enjoying the crackle of piñon logs and some aguardiente

So far was I removed from the man I had been that they didn't recognize me at first.

As I approached, they surveyed me, noting my unkempt manner and hollow cheeks. Then they turned away.

"Kit," I said, tentatively.

He stared a long moment. "Is that you, Captain? You?"

"It is."

Lucien Maxwell sprang up. "My God, man."

"I took bad counsel," I said. "And now I have starving men scattered clear to the San Juans."

"They want relief?"

"Yes. Godey's with me. He'll do it."

"How much time is there?"

"We've lost the first. Frostbite, starvation. There's no time. My topographer, Preuss, is at the Red River settlement organizing them."

"Are you going back with relief?" Owens asked.

"I'll leave that to Alexis."

"Then you'll stay with me," Carson said.

"Major Beall can help. He's commanding here," Owens said.

"Godey's looking for him."

"They've got some men and rations and mules," Maxwell said.

"What needs doing now?" Owens asked.

"It's up to Godey. He plans to leave in the morning with relief."

"Who else is here?" Maxwell asked.

"My man Saunders and Alex's nephew."

"Are they all right?"

"A little sleep and a feast or two will make them new. They're with Godey."

"What happened, Captain?" Carson asked.

"I listened to Old Bill Williams, that's the whole of it. He got lost, bumbled into the wrong drainages, and led us into snowy traps. I kept asking him about his course, but he just ignored me. I think the man's addled. He had no idea where he was."

"What about your mules?" Carson asked.

"Lost every one."

"Didn't you eat them?"

"Buried under drifts almost before we knew they were gone."

"Who's lost?" Owens asked.

"Raphael Proue, for one. Henry King. You know him from the conquest."

"Not King! Proue! I knew him, too."

"These men—some of them weren't made of the same stuff as my battalion. It was a mistake, you know. Men without heart. With more heart, we'd now be over those mountains and on our way to California."

"What is their condition now?" Carson asked.

"I don't know. I put Vincenthaler in charge. Remember him? From California? He's charged with caching my equipment and getting the men down to Rabbit River. He'll do his duty. Wait for the relief there. That's what I directed. But I've men in that company who don't heed me, so there's no telling where they are. I imagine Godey will deal with them."

"The San Juans, Colonel, can be tough. Especially with a winter like this," Owens said.

"If I had better men, they would not have yielded," I retorted. I was feeling testy. The company had thwarted my design, mostly from the lack of manhood, and now I had been forced to retreat. I knew one thing: I'd be off to California in a day or two, and I would take none of the malingerers with me. The Kern brothers would remain here, and so would Old Bill Williams, and maybe some more.

I told them my story, even as the stout proprietress plied me with sugar cakes. But ere long the pleasant heat from those piñon logs wore away my resolve. I knew that in moments, I would tumble to the earthen floor. The warmth and comfort were engulfing me.

"You come with me, Captain. It's not a hundred yards, you know. Josefa will help get you settled."

I knew that. Carson's rambling home, built around a courtyard, lay just to the east.

"You'd better plan on a couple of days in bed," Carson said.

"I'm not going to dawdle here—off to California in a day or two."

Carson remained uncommonly quiet. We pushed through the gated wall into his yard, and soon he and Josefa steered me into a tiny bedroom and laid a bright fire in the adobe fireplace. In my weariness I scarcely had a look at Josefa, Carson's young bride. She seemed more a servant-girl to me, though I did notice she was heavy with child.

I fell into a luxurious sleep, well deserved after my ordeal, confined in a warm room with ample blankets above me and a corn-shuck mattress beneath. I was confident that Saunders and Theodore and Alexis Godey all found a suitable loft.

Well into the morning I was finally awakened by a stirring and realized Josefa was peeking in. She was a pretty young thing. When she saw me stir, she smiled, and brought me a tray bearing a pottery mug of hot chocolate. I had not expected such a delicacy in Taos, but there it was, warming my body with its medicinal powers and making me whole again. I thanked her and sipped while she watched anxiously.

"Bueno," I said.

She fled at once.

I was not yet up when I received a caller, who proved to be Major Beall, commandant of the detachment there. I received him whilst I sipped. He wore his blue winter issue and eyed me with some curiosity.

"Colonel, I'm pleasured to meet you," he said.

"And likewise, Major. Do have a seat."

"I'll get right to it, sir. Your man Godey reached me at supper last eve with news of your distress, and I hastened to supply from my stores whatever is needed. He left at dawn with several mules and muleteers, and my men will follow with more supplies. I've sent along rations and blankets. He's taking several dozen good round loaves of bread, some blankets, and some maize to feed his mules and horses. I'm sending a squad behind him with more food, salt pork and hardtack; some horses we can dispose of; and some manpower to assist."

"Most gracious of you, Major. I will make a point of repaying the army as soon as I reorganize."

"It's a pleasure to meet you, Colonel Frémont. Your reputation as an explorer precedes you, and I take a delight in placing myself at your service, sir."

I nodded, taking the measure of the man. "Even a man in my circumstance?"

He nodded, amiably. "By all accounts, you were caught by conflicting orders, sir."

I was satisfied. "Major, this railroad exploration has come to grief because I didn't have well-trained regular army men with me. Even at that, this guide I was forced to hire against my better judgment turned out to be worthless. Keep it in mind."

"I've heard similar about him."

"I don't mean to be unkind, but I do wish to warn away the army. Use Carson if you need anyone."

"So I've heard, sir. But what's happening up there?"

I told him that my men were giving out and that I had directed them to reach Rabbit River, where they could find shelter and expect relief. But I suspected some were still higher up. Hadn't the first relief party dawdled its way south for twenty-two days now, and had not yet reached the Red River settlements?

Beall nodded, as I briefly apprised him of the ruinous decisions of our guide and the lethargic response of some of our summer soldiers, as I thought to call any who had not hardened themselves, and thought the trip to California would be a lark.

"But of this, say nothing, sir. I wish to deal with the matter privately," I added. "I'll be in touch with Senator Benton, with a full report, and I want it to be the true and accurate account of my travails, so he can deal with the repercussions. I'm afraid that some of those men, who were plainly chafing at my direction, might say things of no substance and thus cast aspersions on the honor of my good veterans and my company."

I ended the interview there, having already grown weary of politics, and begged leave of the major.

Carson saw him out and a moment later joined me.

"What's the word, Kit?" I asked, still abed.

"Godey left at dawn with four muleteers and about ten mules. He said to tell you he'll hurry on ahead, getting bread and blankets to all who are still alive, and he hopes that will include most everyone."

"I could not ask for a better man than Godey," I replied.

"He'll pick up more provisions and mules and blankets at the Red River colony and should be intercepting your men within a day or two," Carson said. "Beall's men will be a day behind with some slaughter colts and will do some camp tending, getting the survivors up to a trip here."

"Tell me candidly, Kit; what do you think of Old Bill Williams?"

Carson pondered it a while. "Well, I've heard it said that in starving times, you'd best not let Old Bill walk behind you," Carson said.

"I think I'll tell that to Jessie," I said. "Have you a pen and ink and paper?"

"Never had much use for those," he replied. "But Lucien Maxwell ought to."

"I want to set down the facts," I replied. "Before anyone else attempts to."

CHAPTER THIRTY-ONE

Alexis Godey

I labored ceaselessly to put a relief mission on the trail. The great-hearted Mexicans were ready and willing to help. I found muleteers willing to travel through the perilous winter. They offered their services with a shrug and a smile. For payment they would soon have gaudy stories to tell their families. Families donated blankets woven from unbleached wool. Others volunteered their mules and horses and saddles. I loaded golden cornmeal into sacks, collected the coarse round loaves of bread that would sustain lives, found some multicolored maize with which to feed our livestock in those snowy wastes, and soon had enough collected for temporary relief.

Major Beall's soldiers would follow with some rank condemned horses, hardtack and other rations, and the manpower to tend fires and feed the desperate until they could be recruited to travel again.

"But are you going back, sir, after your own ordeal?" he asked me.

"I am. My friends are in great peril. I will not stop."

"But look at you. You're worn."

"I've had bowls of cornmeal mush. They call it *tole* here, and it revives me. If I can eat, I will be alright."

"It's a solid meal, that's for sure," he said.

I would do what I had to do. At dawn, my Mexican muleteers and I hastened upriver, through a frosty gloom I can barely describe because it seemed hostile and dark. But my men, mostly wearing heavy wool serapes, hurried the sluggish animals with switches. Their burros and mules were all half-starved. But on their backs was life itself. The day of our departure was January 22. A disastrous four weeks had elapsed since Colonel Frémont had sent the first relief party from the Christmas camp, and we began making our way out of the white mountains.

We reached the Red River settlements late that day. Preuss, who remained weakened and unable to travel, told us that none of our company had come in, which alarmed me, so we didn't tarry except to collect more bread and blankets and shoe leather from worried villagers and hurried north once again. Surely our men could not be far ahead. But they were. It took us four days to cover the first forty miles, and finally we raised the original relief, Breckenridge, Williams, and Creutzfeldt, huddled miserably around a flame, unable to move because their feet were ruined. They had staggered along on strips of blanket until at last they could go no farther and were waiting for help or death in a sheltered arroyo where there was some wood.

I scarcely recognized any of them, but one thing will remain with me. Breckenridge clasped the loaf I gave him and began sobbing, and soon the others wept also, as they tore at the bread.

Creutzfeldt was the weakest, and I wondered whether he could even eat the bread, but he nibbled, gained a little strength, and began tearing at chunks of it, tears leaking from his eyes the whole time.

This was clean and honorable food. They were eating something that evoked no shame. I thought the tears had something to do with that as well as the joy of their salvation.

"The army's on the way with rations. They'll tend camp here until you can be moved," I said. "Eat sparingly."

"What will they think of us?" Breckenridge asked.

"Whatever you think of yourself," I replied. They would have to live with themselves, and if they couldn't, they faced sad days and years.

I left those hand-woven, hand-carded Mexican blankets with them and a little cornmeal to boil up. The muleteers gathered firewood for them and wrapped them in thick blankets and made them comfortable, and that was all we could do for the moment.

"Look for help tomorrow," I said, eyeing those tear-stained, smoke-blackened faces.

"You have saved us," Breckenridge said. "We would be dead."

"Are the others alive?" I asked.

None could answer.

It was snowing again. Never had anyone seen such a winter. But these three, with bread and meal and blankets could endure. Reluctantly, we parted. I was shaken by the encounter. These men were but hours from crossing that bourne from which no mortal returns. If Colonel Frémont had not sent me swiftly back with aid, surely these three would have perished.

We hurried upriver, the snow biting at our faces and driving the heat from us. I marveled that these good-hearted muleteers braved the hardship with such cheer. They had a way of coiling their serapes around them that protected them from the stinging snow. We reached Vincenthaler's camp suddenly, out of the white whirl, men slowly rising out of their snow-covered rags beside an almost-extinguished fire.

"Relief! It's the Colonel!" Vincenthaler cried.

They were so snow-blinded and deaf and devoid of their senses they scarcely knew who had come.

"It's Godey," I said. "The Colonel sent me."

Now these ruined men stirred. I wasted neither time nor words but dug into the sacks and began handing out those brown loaves.

"Bread!" someone cried. I could not make out one man from another, so ruined were their faces, blackened by wood smoke, their dull eyes peering out from the parchment over their skulls.

Two of my muleteers, Carlos and Esquivel, swiftly handed each trembling man a round yeasty loaf. One lacked the strength to pull it apart, and Carlos attempted to help, but the man would not let go. The man finally bit into the side of the loaf and tore bread loose. For the life of me, I could not tell who was who.

"Don't eat fast," I cautioned. But it landed on unheeding ears. They would wolf it down just as fast as they could.

I waited for Vincenthaler to demolish a few pieces before seeking to know how they stood and who was where. I dug into a sack of blankets and wrapped Martin in one, and found another for Bacon and another for Ducatel, who stared numbly at me, looking demented.

"Bread," Ducatel said. "I live. The bread of life, thanks be to God."

It was some sort of communion, and I found myself the priest distributing this sacrament.

I squatted beside Vincenthaler. "Who's here? I scarcely recognize these men."

He took a long time, as if he weren't sure himself. Somehow, most of these men were confused, including their leader. "Hubbard quit us a while ago. He couldn't go another step and sat down."

"We'll go for him. Where's Scott?"

Vincenthaler shrugged. "Left us."

"That's two. Where's Rohrer?"

Vincenthaler didn't seem to know.

"You've got Joaquin and Gregorio. Where's Manuel?"

Vincenthaler shrugged. "They thought they'd be eaten so they came with us."

"Eaten?"

Vincenthaler nodded.

"The Indian boys came to your camp because—they feared for their lives?"

Vincenthaler shrugged.

I saw that my men had fed everyone and had covered the most desperate with blankets.

"The army's coming. Be here tomorrow. They'll tend camp and feed you and then help you out of here."

"Leave a mule."

"No, but some colts are coming, and you can have them. We've some cornmeal we'll give you. Boil it up. It's a sturdy food. It'll satisfy until you get some army rations and meat. You should have horse meat and hardtack in a day or two."

We could do no more except collect ample deadwood and build up their fires and make sure these men had blankets. We also built up their shelters a little. The longer I stayed at each camp, the itchier I got. Maybe, just ahead, would be a man I could save.

The snow lessened, but we had miles to go, and if need be I would wrestle up the river in the dark. If the sky was clear, snowy nights could be quite bright. My muleteers had given the wretched beasts a few ears of maize, but that was all there was for the animals, and I marveled that they moved at all.

But then we plunged into the wintry dusk, a wild hunger to move ahead impelling me.

We stumbled on John Scott, scarcely a hundred yards ahead. It was incredible. He was within shouting distance of the camp. He sat stupidly in the snow, unmoving, and I thought he had perished. But his eyes tracked me. Life flickered.

Swiftly, Esquivel wrapped him in a blanket.

"Scott! We're here. Hang on!"

Scott, a veteran of the California battalion, simply stared. He was bone cold to my touch.

"The Colonel sent me! I've bread for you."

This time Scott's eyes focused a little. Whether he comprehended any of it I could not say.

Esquivel drew a bladder canteen from his bosom, pried open Scott's mouth, and squirted. Scott coughed and sputtered.

"Aguardiente!" the muleteer explained. Taos Lightning, the fiery brandy made locally.

"What?" said Scott.

"Frémont sent relief."

I tore some bread from a heavy loaf; his hands could barely lift even the small piece I gave him, but in a moment he was masticating, swallowing it. I rubbed his shoulders and back, willed life into him. He ate another bite. And another. My muleteers lifted him onto canvas, and we dragged him back to Vincenthaler's fire.

"I'm cold," Scott said.

The sight of Scott alive energized some of the party, and they drew him close, built the fire, and began feeding him.

"Look after him," I said. "This is his loaf."

They would.

My muleteers started out once again in the whirling snow and soon stumbled across Hubbard, sitting upright, like Scott, staring at us as we descended on him. He was a Wisconsin man, used to cold.

"Hubbard! We're relief!"

Hubbard stared stupidly.

I shook him, a deepening dread in me. His body flopped about, but I saw no life in it.

"Hubbard!" I rattled him hard, and he simply sagged over.

Esquivel shot aguardiente into his mouth, and it dribbled away. Hubbard was dead. And he had died so recently warmth lingered in his body.

We stared at one another.

"Ah, Madre," he cried.

These Mexicans had come to share my passion to save lives. Hubbard toppled the rest of the way, lying on his side. I knelt, straightening his limbs, folding his hands over his chest, until he stared sightlessly into the falling snow, which still melted on his face. We had come so close. A half hour, maybe fifteen minutes was all that separated this man from our relief. So close. A terrible melancholy swept through me. If only we had hurried a little more, driven a little harder.

How many had died? I could not say.

We pushed ahead another hour, until a snow-choked dusk caught us and we were in peril of losing our way, and then we huddled through an overcast night. We could go no farther. My own body was rebelling. My sainted muleteers boiled a pail of *tole*, the hot cornmeal mush that did so much for me, and I recovered my own strength as I lay buried under blankets. They fed the bony mules a few ears of maize, but it was not enough, and the plaintive bray of a hungry beast we were abusing sometimes lifted me out of my doze. It was an especially black night, without stars or moon, and I felt almost strangulated by it. I wanted to be up and off. There were men ahead whose lives hung by a thread, if indeed they still lived.

Restlessly, even before dawn, I arose, built up the fire, and boiled up the mush. When first light permitted us to leave, we burdened our mules and horses with packs and set out in dull gray light. A thick ice fog lay over the land, and I knew it could cloak the survivors, making them invisible and muffling our shouts. I would shout every little way, because it was possible we could pass them by. And so we proceeded in a cold and lonely morning, making such noise as we could all the while.

It turned out that we did pass the camp of the Kerns, Cathcart, Taplin, McGehee, and Stepperfeldt, striking a camp of Josiah Ferguson, who had a fire blooming, though the thick fog caught the choking smoke. He was another of Frémont's veterans, an able man in the wilderness, and somehow he had survived.

He smiled broadly. "Thought maybe that was no elk drifting through the fog," he said.

"The Colonel sent me. You alright?"

Ferguson shook his head and gestured toward a dark bulk lying in the snow a few yards distant.

"Ben Beadle," he said. "I thought maybe a pair of Show-Me Missourians could beat the game. He's dead."

I felt something give way in me. Esquivel handed Ferguson a loaf, which he tore apart and began steadily chewing. I pulled out a blanket and wrapped it around the man's shoulders.

"Colonel got through and sent us with relief. The army's coming along behind, with rations."

"You mind if I eat one of them mules?"

"There'll be some horse flesh tomorrow. We've got the bread and some *tole*, good cornmeal mush, that'll put some warmth in you." I nodded toward Beadle. "How long ago?"

"Yesterday. We couldn't keep up, me and Ben, so we made camp. The Kerns, that bunch, are below us."

"Below? We passed them by?"

He nodded. It had been a thick, cloistering fog that muffled sound.

Ferguson quit eating and buried his face in his arms, the blanket wrapped over him to hide himself from us. I knew he was crying. We quietly built up his fire. I looked at Beadle's body. It was intact, though snow had drifted over it. He lay sprawled on his belly. Another of Frémont's hardy veterans from the third expedition gone from this world.

In time, Ferguson recovered some and resumed his meal, while we heated up some cornmeal for him. "Is there anyone above here?" I asked.

"Manuel, but he's dead. He quit first day out of the mountains, froze up, his feet black, that was some days ago, and he headed back to the cache. He said he'd be there. Stay warm there, if he could. All the rest, they're down in the camps below."

Ferguson seemed to rebound a little more than the others with some food in him, and we helped him onto a mule, which shuddered under the weight, and headed downriver through the morning fog, which was composed of tiny, mean ice crystals that bit at us.

Even at that, we almost missed the Kerns' camp.

"Halloo?" someone yelled.

"Relief," I yelled back.

"Who is it? We're all snow-blind."

"It's Godey," I replied.

We rode in and found a few men huddled in misery, too worn to greet us. I stared at Cathcart, wondering who he was. And Taplin. And young McGehee and Stepperfeldt. And the Kerns, all unrecognizable. But soon we would have their story, too. All alive.

CHAPTER THIRTY-TWO

Benjamin Kern, MD

That shout rising from the mists was the most welcome I ever heard. In short order, Godey burst into our midst, along with some Mexican men and mules. They wasted no time. One dug out round loaves and handed one to each of us; another man tugged blankets out of packs and wrapped one over the shoulders of each of us.

"Who's here?" Godey said, as soon as he and his men made us comfortable.

We were too busy tearing at our bread to reply. I could not answer; my belly cried for this bread, and I was jamming it into my aching mouth faster than I could swallow it. All the cautions of my medical training were trumped by the wild taste of something in my mouth.

"I can't tell one from another," Godey added. "But I need an account."

I paused long enough to warn the others to eat slowly, but the words would not form on my lips. Cathcart was the weakest. He hadn't the strength to tear that big loaf open, and I pointed at him. Godey caught my gesture, knelt beside the Scots captain, and gently broke the loaf into small pieces, a great tenderness in this act.

Cathcart nodded. I saw tears swimming in his blue eyes. I felt like weeping myself.

Godey built up the fire, which was almost out, found our camp kettle, and poured a golden meal and water into it and set it to boiling.

"Cornmeal mush, what they call *tole,*" he said. "It's the best we've got to build a man up. I've lived on it the whole way."

I was ready for the cornmeal. I was ready for anything. I lacked the strength even to sit up, so close had I come to perishing. But I knew I would soon gain some command over my helpless body. I felt that bread in my belly. It was amazing. Something real down there, something being transformed into life. My stomach was ready for ten more loaves. I didn't feel stronger, but I knew I soon would.

After helping us all he could, he turned at last to me. "You Kern brothers are here. Captain Cathcart. Stepperfeldt over there. McGehee yonder. We brought Ferguson with us. And Captain Taplin, who seems to be doing alright, over there. Am I missing anyone?"

I did not want him to visit the places just outside our camp where others lay.

I nodded, miserably, the gesture pointing Godey toward the ones who had fallen. I knew what he would see. Some of those bodies were not whole. I had not partaken of any of that flesh, but some had, each furtively cutting his own piece in the deeps of the night. I thought Godey would find us all guilty, and there was naught I could do about it.

Godey left camp and soon enough found Andrews and Rohrer, or what was left of them, and returned wordlessly. I somehow expected recrimination but instead found only silence and the same gentle affection he had given us as he set about feeding the starved. To this day I know not what he really thought. He found legless and armless bodies there and let it pass.

He hunkered beside me, waiting for the mush to heat. "The Indian boy, Manuel. Ferguson says he went back to the cache?"

"He did. He could walk no more on frozen feet. His calves were black from frostbite. Dead flesh. We had gone only a mile or so when he turned back. He'd be gone. There wasn't a scrap of food."

"But warm, at least."

I nodded. That was a good camp, sheltered in a cave, with abundant deadwood. But he had been there a long time.

"I'm going to go. I need to account for every man. And maybe I can bring some of the colonel's equipment."

"Equipment!" I glowered at him. We had died shuttling the colonel's equipment instead of escaping to safety.

The bitterness welled up in me. "You say the Colonel sent you?"

"He did."

"What is he doing?"

"He's outfitting for the next leg."

"He did not come with you."

Godey rebuked me. "He sent me, and it was my honor to come, and his honor to do his best for us all."

"He summoned the army?"

"He asked me to."

"His friends there, Kit Carson and Owens. Did they help?"

"Every way they could. The colonel is Carson's guest. They made him welcome. The colonel needs to reoutfit, you know. He needs credit and contacts, and that's what Owens and Maxwell and Carson have been doing for him."

"What did he tell them about us?"

"He had men stranded on the Rio del Norte and was sending help."

"What happened to the first rescue party?"

"They starved and froze and made no progress, and finally King died."

"Young King? The strongest?"

Godey suddenly drew into himself. "You would not have liked to see them, Ben. I saw the survivors, if you can call them that. The colonel gave them some jerky and headed for the settlements. We had the whole company to relieve and couldn't spare the time to help them much. The colonel did the right thing exactly. I would have done the same."

I nodded, not liking that story and all that was missing from it. "Would you?" I asked.

"An army detail will come here with rations and a few slaughter colts in a day or so. They're dropping men off at each camp."

"Who's below? Who lives, who died?"

Godey tolled the names of the dead.

"With Manuel I count eleven," I said. "A third of us. You spared the rest of us."

"The Colonel did. He sent me."

I wondered why I hated that statement so much.

Godey saw to our comfort, left a muleteer to tend camp along with more *tole*, and headed across open country, going clear to the edge of the San Juan Mountains, another day's travel. I watched him and his remaining Mexican men vanish into the fog and was overwhelmed with an odd sadness I could not explain. That was January 25, a month after our Christmas camp, when we all still lived and enjoyed health.

Alexis Godey was everything a man should be; more man than I could ever be. He was carrying the world on his shoulders.

The army failed to come that day. I was beginning to see the scope of this rescue. It would be several days before any of us could gather the strength to leave. We were the living dead, and nothing anyone could do for us would spring us back to life in one or two days. There we were: hairy, gaunt and ragged, our faces so sunk down and fire blackened that Godey could not recognize us. Cathcart was the worst off, I thought. He was so reduced that he could barely swallow his cornmeal, and we had to break his bread into small pieces he would nibble and drop. Relief had come, but I wondered if Cathcart would yet perish.

I collected Edward and Richard to me. They looked better. Ned was stronger, and Richard had some color in his face at last.

"Colonel Frémont's busy outfitting. Are we going?"

"Not with him," Richard said. "I will not travel with that man. I will not be a part of any company he assembles. I bear him no ill will; I just don't trust his judgment. None of this needed to happen, and that is the hard rock lying in my bosom."

My younger brother spoke for the three of us.

A pair of soldiers hallooed the camp that evening, driving four bony horses. They looked colder than we were, in thin army coats that plainly didn't provide much warmth.

"Corporal Hochshuth here, and this is Private Grubb," one said.

Captain Taplin managed to get to his feet. "You sure are a welcome sight," he said. He introduced himself, leaving his rank unspoken, and then the rest of us.

"We're going to slaughter a colt and use the others to carry you out when you're fit for it," the corporal said. He eyed Cathcart dubiously. "Mister Godey, he's gone ahead?"

"Yes," I replied. "That's the last, up there."

"Alright then," the corporal said. The pair saw to their camp, got firewood, saw to our comfort, and settled in.

"You have any news about the men below? And the colonel? Frémont?" I asked.

Grubb replied. "Played out, sah. We got there in the nick. The explorer, he's in Taos looking after his affairs."

I wondered what those might be.

"Has the colonel said anything about this?"

"I wouldn't know, sah. Well, yes, I know a bit. He's saying it's the guide, Williams, that let him down. I don't suppose I should be repeating it."

"I'm glad for any news I can get, Mister Grubb."

"Most things, they're nobody's fault, sah."

"Sometimes, the wrong man takes the blame," I replied.

The men doled out army rations, hardtack and salt pork. My teeth were loose in their sockets, but I didn't let that stop me from gnawing that food. I got it all down and was ready for more, and so were the rest. I wondered whether this would stop my bowels, but I did not suffer trouble.

I ached for simple comfort: a room, a roof, a fire, but that was still a long ways off. In truth, I didn't see how the army could get us down to the settlements. We were all too weak to walk, and most of us too weak to ride a horse. But somehow, we were going to get there.

Alexis Godey and two muleteers returned the next day, and with them was the California Indian boy, Manuel, clinging to a mule.

"Alive, alive?" I cried. "Let me look at him."

They gently pulled Manuel off his mule, laid him on a tarpaulin, and covered him with blankets. Gingerly I drew back the blankets and stared at those ruined feet and ankles. At least they weren't bleeding. There was dead flesh peppered over those feet, flesh that would slough off in time. I could do nothing at all, lacking my powders and kit, but the several days spent in the warmth of his cave had wrought some improvement.

"I'm glad to see you, boy," I said.

He nodded. He understood enough English to get along with us. Frémont had brought him east with the California Battalion.

"You're going to get well," I said, and I felt sure of it, so long as Godey and the army could get him to the settlements.

"We fed him some," Godey said. "He came right along, with some of that cornmeal and bread in his belly."

"This makes me very glad," I said. "We'd given him up for lost when he turned back."

"He had a regular nest, doctor. He got him into an open-sided cave and got warm, lots of wood, and stayed warm, and waited."

The arrival of Manuel lifted the spirits of the whole camp, and for the first time in many days, I saw men smile.

"There's not much I can do with him. I don't think binding that frostbitten flesh would be a good idea." I turned to Manuel. "You eat up, and stay warm, and keep those feet clean if you can."

"Sí," he said.

I stood slowly. It made me dizzy. "What's the count, Alex?"

"Of the lost? Ten. Until I found Manuel, I was counting eleven."

"It would have been all of us, but for you, sir."

Godey turned away, hiding his face from me.

He and the muleteers and soldiers spent the next day burying our dead. They hacked the two bodies free from the blood-caked snow and ice while we watched in utter silence. The soldiers moved those two lost men to a bushy area, heaped brush over the bodies, and added deadwood to weigh it down and protect the remains from animals.

Which animals? I thought. I suppose the rest of us were thinking the same thing. We had not seen so much as a coyote track. We broke camp the next day, working toward the settlements in easy stages. For most of us it was a grim trip, as desperate and painful as any of the rest of it. There weren't enough horses and mules to carry us all, so the stronger rotated, but some, like Captain Cathcart, clung desperately to manes and saddles all the way and barely lived to reach the settlements, even on horseback.

It took days, and we were well into February when we reached Red River and were greeted by Preuss, who rejoiced to see us and accompanied us the rest of the way. It took more days for us to stumble south to Taos, but eventually we collected in that earthen outpost, the sorriest lot of men imaginable. Godey shepherded us the whole way, gentle and yet insistent that we come along, keeping us fed and warm and comfortable.

Taos, rude and humble, billeted us. Godey saw to it. There we were, bedded under roofs by smiling Mexican people, fed and warmed, in comfort. We did not see Frémont at first but heard he was busy assembling the gear and livestock for the California trip. I wondered about it, why he did not show his face, but in time he did collect us together. I marveled because he looked quite the same as always, his lithe body no worse for wear, his beard trimmed, his gaze benign and secret. I detected in him no great interest in us or our condition and heard no words of comfort.

"We'll be leaving in two days," he said. "Those of you who wish to join me, please make your wishes known to me, and I will take them under advisement. Those who are unable will find good company in Mister Carson and other of our friends. I'll be taking us over the Gila River route, first to Santa Fe and Albuquerque, and thence to the point where we will abandon the Rio del Norte and strike west to the

Gila drainage, which will take us to the Gulf of California and across. It ought to be a mild trip. I'm provisioned, we have stock, and nothing impedes us."

He paused.

"Perhaps you've heard. Gold has been found in California. In great quantities. Even now, people are rushing there. I have heard that some has been found near my own Las Mariposas, which I acquired during the last expedition."

Gold. I had heard something of it while we were being settled in Taos, but now the colonel confirmed it.

I consulted with my brothers and Captain Cathcart. "Are we going with him?" I asked.

"Not for all the gold in the world," Captain Cathcart replied, and my brothers seconded the sentiment.

CHAPTER THIRTY-THREE

John Charles Frémont

It was imperative that I set the record straight. I contemplated what I would put into a letter to Jessie about the troubles I had encountered in the San Juan Mountains and knew what I wanted to say. Only by prompt communication might I head off public criticism drawn from sensational accounts. Jessie had probably departed for California via the isthmus, but I intended to write her at Saint Louis anyway. Maybe I could still catch her. The mail in that direction was fairly prompt, and communication was assured by both army and civil post. I would soon see her in California and could tell her privately the things that I thought should not be put in a letter.

So while I waited for news of Godey's relief operations, I penned a letter to Jessie.

"I have an almost invincible repugnance to going back among scenes where I have endured much suffering," I wrote to introduce her to the worst, "and for all the incidents and circumstances of which I feel a strong aversion. But as clear information is absolutely necessary to you, and to your father more particularly still, I will give you the story now instead of waiting to tell it to you in California."

There was but one thing to convey, and that was the utter incompetence and stupidity of the guide, Old Bill Williams, who took us into country he obviously didn't know, got lost, and gravely endangered my party. He took us into snow-packed defiles, cost us our mules, and cost the life of Raphael Proue, who froze in his tracks. All this I conveyed to Jessie at length, along with my plans to depart for California at the beginning of February. I also planned to write my father-in-law, Senator Benton, a briefer letter that might set the public straight. There was no need to impart any details, but I wished to make it known that the army detachments posted hereabouts had been most cordial to me and had helped with the relief. I thought it might gain some ground for us in the Senate. But I deferred writing that one until such time as I heard from the relief.

There was ample to occupy me in Taos. The stark reality was that I had lost nearly everything save for some instruments and lacked funds to outfit myself. Thanks to Carson and Maxwell, I discovered an old Saint Louis friend, F. X. Aubry, was in town. He had business interests in New Mexico. I welcomed him heartily, and soon we were recollecting good times at the Benton household. I borrowed funds from him against the surety of my cached saddles and tack and other equipment up in the San Juan Mountains and used the thousand dollars of credit to purchase fresh livestock. It was my hope that Godey might return with the materiel, and if so that would spare me much grief.

I obtained further aid from my old friend and California companion Major Beall, who opened army stores to me, offering livestock and rations. I had the distinct pleasure of working with officers who possessed none of the jealousy or animosity that had been poured out on me by those higher in command. For these able men, I was simply one of their own.

I spent a most amiable time in Taos among old friends and new acquaintances but was never far from uneasiness about the relief. Day after day slipped by with no word from Godey or those upriver. I wanted only to put the whole business behind me; it was something to bury and get past, but the delay gnawed at me, until I thought I should saddle up and discover what had become of my party. I was certain that the hardened veterans of my California Battalion would fare better than the easterners who had joined up, thinking the trip would be a lark. I could trust my old soldiers to endure through the worst.

Early on, I had discovered that the Kerns and their friends were slackers, a drag on the whole expedition. What was Richard Kern doing while my veterans sweated? Playing his flute. If they had pulled their weight, we would have topped the San Juans and continued on our way, despite Bill Williams's bungling. The men of my old command were able to deal with the snow, while the newcomers slowed us day by day. More and more, as I waited for news from upriver, I determined to settle the blame for the calamity on the Kerns. I had imagined that an artist like Richard would provide valuable sketches that would augment the railroad survey, and a doctor like Benjamin would serve the injured, but little did I know these pampered Pennsylvanians would slow the entire company to such a degree that precious days were lost high up in the mountains, when haste was our salvation.

In time, the survivors did drift in, by twos and threes,

assisted by muleteers and the army. They were a horror to see, still snow-blind, starved to nothing, weakened by their ordeal. I wished they had stayed in the Red River settlements longer, cleansing themselves, trimming beards, repairing their attire, so they would not be a spectacle to the citizens of Taos. Indeed, some did linger there, unable to travel the last lap. From Vincenthaler I finally received the bad news. Ten had perished: Proue, King, Wise, Carver, Hubbard, Beadle, Tabeau, Morin, Rohrer, and Andrews. Godey was bringing the last and weakest along and would report to me in a few days. I was impatient to be off and waited restlessly for the remaining men to drift in. I thought of leaving without them, knowing they would be weakest, but I stayed on out of a sense of duty.

It was clear that in my absence there had been no effective leadership. I had held them together, and on my departure, their discipline had vanished and they had fallen into small fragments, no one of these wandering groups helping any other. Yet I could not regret leaving them. But for the relief I sent to them, all would have perished. I saved their lives. One thing puzzled me: of the dead, all but two were veterans of my California Battalion. Only Rohrer and Andrews were not with me in California. It made little sense to me that softer men, like the Kerns and Cathcart, had survived while my resourceful veterans had died. I had intended to make a point of it with Jessie and Senator Benton and thought better of it.

We gathered at last on the sunny plaza in Taos, on a particularly pleasant February afternoon, with little sign of the grave winter we had endured. Banks of rotting snow persisted, but the earthen town was shaking loose from the worst. I looked them over, not liking what I saw. Some of them were too diminished to stand while I addressed them. Curious villagers, including heavy-boned women in black shawls, and urchins had collected and watched me quietly in the amiable sunlight. I doubted that any could understand English, for which I was grateful.

"Gentlemen," I began, "tomorrow at dawn we leave for California. It's clear to me that some of you are not able to travel and will stay here to heal. I'm adding several new people to my company. Now, I regret not being able to take all of you with me, but my first choice rests with those seasoned men who were with me during the third expedition and others, old friends and veterans of past campaigns. Those who I've decided should, for their own sake, remain here until they are better able to travel include the Kern brothers, all three; Captain Taplin, Captain Cathcart, and Mister Stepperfeldt. As for Mister Williams, I no longer require his services. I wish to thank all members of this company for engaging in this enterprise and offer my heartiest best wishes to those I will be leaving behind here."

That wrought silence, at first, and then smiles. These doughty veterans would actually gather strength with regular meals, warm weather, and horseback travel. We would enjoy a mild climate the rest of the trip. Altogether, it seemed a good choice. I saw no one objecting. Those whom I had excluded gazed silently from within a little knot.

But Doctor Kern did speak up.

"Colonel, have you notified the families of the departed?"

The question caught me utterly off guard. This wasn't an army command, and it really wasn't my duty to do anything of the sort. But I understood his sentiment.

"Why, Doctor, I shall attempt to do so when we reach California," I said. "This is neither the time nor place, and I have no information about them."

"I'm sure you will look after it," Ben Kern said.

Was there something in his tone that offended me?

That was an oddly disturbing moment, as if Kern wanted

to revive memories of what we had all just been through, instead of burying them and getting on with life.

"I will," Taplin said.

"That would be most appreciated, Captain," I replied.

Everyone seemed well satisfied with that.

I caught Ben Kern and Charles Taplin afterward, and privately offered them a mission. "I've a great deal of equipment cached up in the mountains. It's worth several thousands. If you gentlemen could quietly retrieve it when the weather is more favorable and turn it over to my creditor here, Mister Aubry, you would do me a great service and one I would reward. I fear the cache will be plundered by the Utes if no one gets to it soon. You'll need to employ some men with mules here to haul it all to Taos."

"I'll make the effort when I am able," Kern said.

"I know I can count on you."

I spent the evening at Carson's house, absorbing what I could of the southern route from charts and from his recollections. He had been over it several times. At an hour before dawn, February 13, I collected my men on the south edge of town, in gloomy moonlight near a big adobe church, and by first light we were off. I had with me Kit's brother Lindsay Carson, who would serve as guide, as well as Tom Boggs, the former Missouri governor's son. I even had Charles Preuss with me. My topographer had recovered his health in the Red River settlement and arrived just in time to join us—tough little fellow, and I had forgiven him his derelictions. We were in fine fettle and glad to put our trials behind us. Just as I had hoped, the trip down the Rio Grande was easy, and the weather remained perfect for traveling. The nightmare of the mountains swiftly vanished from all our minds.

At Albuquerque, another little mud town without the grace of Santa Fe, I did more outfitting, and soon we were en route through the arid river valley, an empty stretch not fit for human occupation. A man could only wonder why the United States wasted its energies on such country. It was infested with hostile Indians, was worthless for crops other than what might be produced in a melon patch, and added nothing to the United States.

That first sunny afternoon south of Albuquerque, I invited Preuss to ride with me. We were, actually, at the rear, where we could talk peacefully. The reliable Godey was at the van.

"Ah, Charles, it's good to be on our way again," I began. "I should like to talk about California. You have a position with me, if you want it."

"Doing what, Colonel?"

"The Las Mariposas, which Larkin bought for me. It will need some topographic mapping. It lies in the gold country, and if there's gold on my property, I'll need metes and bounds. The boundaries were rather vague. I'll need to lay out wagon roads and locate villages and camps."

He simply grunted.

"The gold stretches along the western flanks of the Sierra. My grant's right there. Taos is buzzing with stories about the gold. With your geology and topographic skills, you could be a most valuable employee, and a well-paid one."

"I have my own plans, sir. I'm sorry."

That was a disappointment to me. I did not inquire into his plans but ventured some other business. "Alright. I have other business to transact. I plan to complete the railroad survey and intend that your topographic data should be completed as well. As soon as I'm settled out there, I'll plan the rest of it. We'll approach from the west, and connect where we left off."

Again, he said nothing.

"We were so close," I said, showing him two fingers a fraction of an inch apart. "If Williams had followed my instructions and taken us north, up the Saguache River, we would have topped the San Juan Mountains, descended into the drainage of the Grand, and continued west. That close," I said.

"I'm very sure of it," he replied.

"Well, I intend to finish it up."

"In winter?"

"No, I've proved whatever needed proving. We'll complete the link, and I'll report to Senator Benton and his business friends."

"I don't think so, sir."

I wasn't sure whether he was turning down my employment or was simply skeptical about the route. "There might be a better route still farther north," I said. "We can survey it."

"No, sir. In California, I will be pursuing other matters. It is a territory that remains unmapped and little known."

"I see. Well, I still plan to engage your services once we arrive."

"I am honored by your attention, sir."

The German seemed as amiable as ever, and yet something had changed. We had been colleagues all this while, in previous expeditions and this, but now he was clearly separating himself from me.

"I suppose you'll be making your journal public," I said.

"I keep an account for my own reference, Colonel Frémont."

"I plan to write about this expedition at length. What especially pleases me is the strength and courage of my veterans, the ones like yourself who were with me in the conquest."

He didn't respond, and we rode some while through the

mild day before we arrived at Socorro. Plainly, this Preuss was not the Preuss who had measured every mountain and valley we had crossed together and shared his every measurement with me.

At Socorro, the southernmost town in the area, I enjoyed the hospitality of Captain Buford, who commanded a detachment there and helped me complete my outfitting. While at his quarters I penned a brief letter to Senator Benton, wanting my father-in-law to be well apprised of all events. I made reference to the calamity of January but did not dwell on it beyond a bare account. There was no reason to dwell on it.

CHAPTER THIRTY-FOUR

Jessie Benton Frémont

Mr. Frémont's letter reached me while I was the guest of Senora Arcé y Zimena, in Panama City. It was dated January 27, 1849, and was mailed from Taos, where my husband was a guest of our friend Kit Carson.

I read it and trembled. Before my eyes was an account of deprivation, cold, starvation, and death. And yet Mr. Frémont had escaped except for frostbite, and at this writing was recovering among friends. How close he had come, and he was only a third of the way to California. The letter had found its way to Saint Louis and had been forwarded downriver, ultimately arriving in Panama, where postal authorities diligently tracked me down. Mr. Frémont and I had known Senora Arcé's nephew when he was his country's ambassador to Washington.

I was most grateful for her hospitality. Panama City bulged with Americans and others from all over the world, waiting for transportation to the goldfields of California. They were camped throughout the old town, and many were sickened or dying from mysterious tropical ailments. I was fortunate to have the connection. The flies and biting bugs were terrible, but at least Lily and I had our own room, with a blue couch, hempen hammocks to sleep in, and a bit of privacy. It was a paradise compared with the steaming cauldron of the rest of the city.

We were all waiting for the mail steamer to California, which didn't come week after week, while we hung on desperately, most of us without funds and no way to go forward or return to our homes. Somehow Lily and I had eluded the awful diseases that caught and killed the flood of immigrants. We had been transported across the isthmus, first by river canoe, and then on foot over the mountains, following a path overarched by jungle. Through the courtesy of so many of our countrymen, we made the trip unscathed, though I was certain I would never attempt such a venture again.

It was gold that changed everything. Mr. Frémont and I had planned all this before its discovery; we had no inkling of what was about to happen. I read and reread the letter, concealing it from Lily for the time being, looking for signs that he was past the worst of it. He seemed eager to put it behind him, and it was clear to me that he bore no guilt or responsibility in it; the fault lay in the incompetent guide he had been compelled to employ. It was Mr. Williams who had almost felled my husband and wrought the deaths of a third of his company. It was this Old Bill at whose doorstep this tragedy must be laid.

But that did not allay the tremor that shook me when I considered how close my beloved husband had come. I was stricken with anxiety, because he had yet to travel the main part of the trip and was gravely weakened. In time, once I could choose my words carefully, I did summon Lily and explained to her that the Frémont family had narrowly escaped disaster.

"Your father is safe and on his way overland, but on a different route, milder in wintertime," I told her.

"He likes trouble," she replied.

I almost reprimanded her for expressing such sentiment, but for some reason didn't.

I ached to travel north, but all I could do was wait helplessly, like the teeming thousands living on the grubby old streets and filling the cemeteries. Street vendors sold monkey meat and fly-specked chickens and filthy fruit, and on these things my countrymen survived or sickened.

I was among them. A newspaper account of Mr. Frémont's disaster in the mountains reached Panama City and greatly disturbed me. I fear the shock of Mr. Frémont's catastrophe unhinged me, for next I knew I was gravely sick with brain fever, which also afflicted my lungs, and both a Panamanian and an American doctor attended me. I ceased to think or care, and scarcely knew where I was. There were no leeches to bleed me, but some croton oil from a ship at anchor blistered my chest and wrought a healing. I remained greatly enfeebled, and my condition worried Senora Arcé and others who knew me.

But one May day the Pacific mail steamboat did appear, with great fanfare, and a welcoming shot from the shore battery. A virtual brawl ensued as to who would occupy its few berths. The ship could accommodate eighty in its cabins and finally embarked with hundreds more deck passengers, so jammed on board that each man's bedding ground was a chalked-off rectangle. I was given a narrow cabin, but in that small, dank chamber my lung fever returned, and I arranged to live in a tent hung over a mast on the quarterdeck, which I shared with Lily and another proper woman.

I felt better in the fresh sea air. I even came to enjoy the company of all those men as we sailed north, filled with hope and adventure. Actually, they all treated me with respect.

Still, those days were wrought with anxiety as well as hardship. There was not food enough on board to feed that mob, and the steward was lining his pockets by selling the ship's tinned food at exorbitant prices, so many on board sickened just as they had been in Panama. It was rumored, too, that the steamer hadn't enough coal to make San Francisco and might be set adrift or forced to use its spindly masts and pull out its canvas. Indeed, it was true. The ship reached San Francisco only by burning its deck planking.

Our first California stop was at the Pueblo de San Diego, and I so dreaded it and the news I might receive of Mr. Frémont that I reclaimed my old room and barricaded myself within, unable to face what I dreaded. But in time a knocking summoned me to the door, and with dread I received the news from the ship's purser, who had been asked to convey it from someone on shore. Mr. Frémont had arrived in California safely, though his frostbitten leg troubled him, and was even then making his way north to rendezvous with me in Yerba Buena on the bay of San Francisco. I accepted the news with a flood of relief that left me unable to stay upright for a while.

We reached San Francisco, as it was being called, June 4, 1849, steaming through the strait my husband had named Golden Gate, into a vast inland sea. A cold fog swirled over the scabrous little village on our right. Before me stretched a graveyard of bobbing sailing ships, their rocking masts a forest beside the shore. Their crews had decamped for the goldfields. There was no pier, and our sole recourse was the lighters that took us to the shore. Scores of little boats swarmed us, and I peered anxiously into the cold mist, hoping to discover Mr. Frémont among them. But I was soon disheartened. Men everywhere, scarcely a woman in sight, but the colonel was not there.

The city climbed into hills just beyond, but all its vitality seemed to collect close to the water's edge, where mountains of supplies, wagons, tents of all descriptions, and hundreds of males were congregated. If Mr. Frémont should not be present, I scarcely knew what I might do; Lily and I would be at the mercy of a lawless and savage lot of people. The mail steamer suddenly seemed a safer and better place than this cold, wretched camp along the inner shore.

Then a stranger, in one of those bobbing lighters below, hailed me, pointed directly at me until I was sure he was addressing me.

"I'm here to get you settled, Mrs. Frémont. Your husband saw to it. William Howard's my name, and I've a room for you at Leidesdorff House. It's up that hill, and it's all there is for you."

He helped us into his boat and took us to shore, where his hesitant and embarrassed sailors lifted us over the surf and settled us on the strand because there was no pier.

Mr. Howard did settle us in a single, well-furnished room in the private home. There was no wood for its parlor stove, and it was as cold and dank as any place I have ever been. I drew my shawl tight about me. But it had walls and a roof and was some distance from that fierce crowd below, and I accepted gratefully, thinking that Mr. Frémont had looked after his wife and daughter, even while some distance away. I was curious about the delay, how he could be elsewhere. Mr. Howard soon enlightened me.

"He went directly to Las Mariposas, madam. He needed to have a look at once, assess its value, and determine what to do if gold should be upon it. He'll be along soon."

I thanked the man, who immediately hurried off. The

mail steamer was unloading cargo, and he needed to claim his own.

I learned that food was scarce, services impossible to find, firewood and lamp oil nonexistent, and I would have to fend for myself. Still, we were fortunate: in a canvas city, we had an adobe room and a roof over us, and I would see what I could see about food.

So Mr. Frémont was nearby. I did not yet understand the size of California and didn't know that the grant he had purchased through the consul, Thomas Larkin, was far distant and not easily reached. He had told me it was seventy square miles, a size beyond my fathoming. How could one person hold so much of the earth?

"Well, Lily, we're here; our trunks are here; we'll look for food if you wish."

"All those men," she said.

"All those men," I said. We had scarcely seen a woman.

Fearfully, we ventured out into a maelstrom of life, knowing there was no law to protect us from whatever savagery might exist. We would depend entirely on the civility of those around us. Plainly, gold fever had created the frenzy we walked through. Men stared but never paused as we passed by. We found canvas gambling halls, and I hurried Lily past them, and there were drinking stalls and hardware stalls, all open-air or canvas, where things might be purchased at outlandish prices. There were thousands of males arriving and nothing to sustain them. We found at last a vendor who had a little rice, which he was parceling out to eager buyers at a breathtaking five dollars a pound. Reluctantly, I bought some and tumbled it in my reticule for want of a sack. It looked like we would be eating rice, if we could find enough wood to boil it. On our way home I salvaged some wood from packing crates to cook our dinner.

Thus did we occupy our first day with the sheer necessities. I had only a small sum and dreaded that I might run out. Later, gentlemen callers arrived in great numbers, to my relief. The colonel had not been forgotten here, and many of them brought precious gifts of food, hoarded or garnered from somewhere. I swiftly learned that there was scarcely a young man in California tending herds, butchering meat, hoeing gardens, hauling produce to market, gathering eggs, feeding poultry, milling wheat, baking bread, cutting firewood, or milking cows. They had fled to the goldfields, leaving these tasks to old men and women, who were somehow carrying on and getting amazing prices for whatever foodstuffs they were able to deliver.

I learned to accept gratefully whatever was presented to us. We were soon entertaining army officers, diplomats, businessmen acquainted with Colonel Frémont, politicians, and strangers, some of them brandishing heavy leather sacks burdened with nuggets.

We endured day by day, in what surely was the coldest place I had ever lived, its fogs and skimpy sun laying an icy chill over the whole place, which was rapidly affecting my lungs, until I feared I would contract the lung fever once again unless I could escape.

Then one blessed day he appeared. I saw him walk quietly up the slope, survey the Leidesdorff House, and approach the door. My heart leapt. I wrapped a shawl about me and hastened to the door, admitting him into the house, into my arms, and into the quiet circle of my embrace.

Lily found us embraced, and I hastily retreated, my instincts always decorous. He paused, smiled at Lily, and clasped her hands in his own.

"You're a young woman now," he said.

She stared uncertainly at this father she had not seen for almost a year.

As I examined this husband of mine, I discovered the

marks of his suffering. He was gaunt; his cheekbones seemed to protrude under parchment flesh. There were great pits below his eyes. His gray-shot brown beard, without a shred of gray before, now bore the streaks of hardship. He walked with a visible limp.

"I've heard you suffered greatly in Panama," he said, his glance taking in the darkness that lingered under my eyes.

"She almost died," Lily volunteered. "They blistered her chest. She's still sick, and this cold air isn't doing her any good."

"Then we'll move at once to Monterey," the colonel replied. "This is not a proper place for my family."

We three trailed into our icy room, and my cough told me that this place was a menace to me.

There was so much catching up to do. "You went to Las Mariposas?" I asked.

"I did. I know this much. There's gold there. I hired some experienced men, Mexicans who know about these things, to prospect. And even while I was looking over this holding, they found gold everywhere."

"Gold, gold?"

"Mrs. Frémont, I am going to be very rich." He dug into his old coat and pulled out a small sack, and poured nuggets into my hand. Heavy, glimmering rounded bits of gold, cold to my touch. "This is from my land," he said.

And that is how the news came to me.

I ached to hear his story, everything he could tell me about his harrowing journey across the continent. I ached to tell him my story, that odd, sinister trip from Chagres to Panama City, surrounded by parrots and monkeys and buzzing insects and serpents and a world I could scarcely fathom, in which we traveled in canoes propelled by near-naked men.

But within the hour, he was out the door. He said he

needed to see people, make arrangements, hire miners, talk to lawyers.

I buried my yearnings in my heart and let myself bask in the joy of our reunion. But somehow I grasped that things were different. That this man, my husband, was not the man I had left in Missouri, but I didn't know how or why.

Over the next days, I felt more than the chill of San Francisco Bay. I felt a growing chill that had settled around my heart. Mr. Frémont would gaze at me, smile as he often did, and yet he was not seeing me, not hearing me. His own gaze had turned inward, and I no longer knew what his thoughts might be, and he no longer shared his deepest yearnings.

We would sit at table, just the three of us, and he would say all the right things, thank me for the rice pudding, comment on the fog and cold, and yet nothing was the same. There were only two of us at the table, Lily and I. I did not know where he had gone. Was this the man I had eloped with? Was this the man who once lay beside me, talking through half the night? Was this the man whose journals I had transcribed day by day, sharing every moment? Was this my beloved?

I wondered if I would ever know this other Mr. Frémont, or whether he would ever love me as he once did. And I wondered what had happened in the San Juan Mountains that had taken him away from me.

AN AFTERWORD

The character of John Charles Frémont has fascinated me for years. Although I have read a great deal about him, he remains a mystery to me. He was a man of considerable courage and ability who nonetheless was constantly getting into grave trouble, often from lack of judgment.

His early biographer, Allan Nevins, did not look deeply into the causes of the Pathfinder's checkered career. But later biographers took a harder look at the man. Andrew Rolle, in his study of Frémont, concludes that Frémont was a narcissist. David Roberts describes a ruinous recklessness in the man. Pamela Herr, Jessie Benton Frémont's biographer, notes Frémont's inability to live within ordinary social boundaries, including those of marriage.

Frémont seemed indifferent to the needs and hopes of others, and yet his soldiers greatly admired him. He ultimately treated his wife badly, and yet she adored him. He could not bring himself to obey the commands of his superior officer in California and was court-martialed and convicted for it, and yet he became a national hero. He was involved in the shadiest sort of business dealings, and yet he was a reformist presidential candidate. He led his fourth expedition into desperate circumstances for no good reason, and yet most of those who went with him supported his leadership unconditionally.

In this novelization of Frémont's disastrous fourth expedition, I have attempted to draw Frémont as a man with all these conflicting traits at work in him. He remains, however, an enigma. Since he had failed to locate a suitable railroad passage over the Wet and the Sangre de Cristo Mountains of central Colorado in the vicinity of the 38th parallel, why did he plunge into the far more formidable San Juan Mountains in the dead of winter? One thing is certain: he was not pursuing a railroad right of way, no matter that he continued to talk about it and use that as his rationale for crossing the mountains in winter.

But his fourth expedition makes no sense. I was tempted to look for other motives, such as his wish to acquire a reputation as someone who could do most anything or to show the army, which had disgraced him, what he was made of or even to enter politics. But at bottom all these rationales for his conduct fall short, and I remain as mystified by his reckless assault on the San Juans as I was when I first looked into the strange fourth expedition. He led ten members of his company to their doom, yet we find in him little sympathy for them or their families, virtually no regret, in any of his writings or utterances. He was somehow disconnected from everyone else, including Jessie.

For some reason, he could not fathom boundaries, no matter whether they were imposed by society or nature. These were impediments to his will, things to be surmounted. When the Bentons resisted his courtship of a very young Jessie, he eloped with her. When he commanded early topographic expeditions, he grossly exceeded or ignored his orders. When General Kearny arrived in California late in the conquest period and required the subordination of Lieutenant Colonel Frémont to his command, Frémont resisted. When Frémont was warned not to cross the Sierra Nevada in winter, he ignored the warnings and imperiled is entire command. And even though he had lost ten men nd a hundred and thirty mules in the calamitous fourth expedition, he attempted the same perilous winter trek over nuch the same territory in the fifth expedition, losing another man and escaping disaster only because some Mornon villagers rescued him. He was made wealthy by the old on his huge California estate and yet managed to quander his fortune through mismanagement.

One trait that ran through his life was his remoteness. He lways seemed distant, and to be surrounded by invisible valls, which deepened as he aged. He was private and even ecretive, largely keeping his feelings to himself. His real urts, angers, bitterness, delights, and satisfactions were oarded—kept on the private shelves of his mind—and vere not in public view.

His remoteness was ironclad. The exception was Jessie, he only person he admitted to the privacy of his heart, but s the years went by, he distanced himself even from her. t times he seemed to be scarcely aware of the needs or the uffering or the joys of others, and he did not share his own. uring his campaign for the presidency he was ineffectual, emote, and formal, so surrogates did his campaigning for im. The paradox is that many loved him and devoted themelves to him. People reached out to him, even if he did not eturn their affections, or maybe because he didn't.

I cannot explain this man. But neither can I explain Jesie, who knew about his failings, his philandering, and his ubious ethics and yet devoted her life to making him into national hero. She was his enabler, to use modern parlance.

Virtually all the primary source material written in Enlish that deals with the disastrous fourth expedition has een collected, annotated, organized, and introduced in a ingle volume by Leroy and Ann Hafen. *Frémont's Fourth xpedition: A Documentary Account of the Disaster of*

1848–1849 with Diaries, Letters, and Reports by Partici pants in the Tragedy is the bedrock source for most of wha happened during the expedition. Patricia Joy Richmond' *Trail to Disaster* is a valuable resource. She located all bu one of Frémont's camps in the San Juan mountains, and pro vides a powerful narrative of the unfolding tragedy, alon with maps and illustrations. Dale L. Walker's *Bear Flag Ris ing* is a superb history of the conquest of California an offers a shrewd and balanced evaluation of Frémont's char acter.

The sources are so contradictory and self-serving that i is impossible to sort everything out, and my novel is base on educated guesses instead of well-anchored facts. Som scholarship noting the contradictions, evasions, and self serving interpretations of events by those in the Hafe collection would be welcome, but this is not the place for it Suffice it to say that another novelist could portray thes events in quite a different light and be just as grounded b primary source material as I believe I am.

—RICHARD S. WHEELE

ECLIPSE

For my friend and editor Dale L. Walker,
eminent historian, Jack London scholar, biographer,
critic, journalist, teacher, and bookman

PART

I

1. LEWIS

I knew myself to be the most luminous man on earth. The sun was at its zenith, and so was I, but like the setting sun, my light would lessen soon. At this moment, surely, I shone more brightly than Napoleon or Wellesley or the king of England, and maybe even my friend Thomas Jefferson.

Was I immodest? I allowed myself to be this fateful Tuesday, September 23, 1806. Will Clark and I took the corps all the way to the western sea—I tasted its brine with my own tongue and then stared at China—and back safely, a journey of eight thousand miles across an unknown land. And without loss, save for poor Floyd. Forgive me my exaltation; I have done the impossible.

Those people rushing to the St. Louis levee would never know, could not even imagine, how it was. They would hear my words but not fathom the dangers, the heat and cold, the starvation, the exhaustion, the *glory.*

My men paddled steadily toward the gathering crowd, their hewn paddles drawing us through the glittering Father of Waters in our dugout canoes and the remaining pirogue toward that slippery black bank that carried the effluent of St. Louis into the river. We would return to civilization in a noisome place.

I shall not forget the moment. The air as clear as my mind; the hosannas of that crowd swelling across the lapping and thumping waters as we rounded toward that golden strand. They were cheering *us*. The rude city jostled itself along the levee, a chaos of rain-stained squared timber structures, whitewashed plank mercantiles, fieldstone warehouses, all hemmed by a low bluff, upon which stood the mossy stone mansions of the French traders and prominent men, islands of elegance in a barbarous outpost. No doubt Clark and I would stay in one of those.

The men paddling the pirogue paused, marveling at our reception, which struck them like a double gill of spirits. Word of our imminent landing had arrived ahead of us, perhaps by horse from General Wilkinson's Cantonment Bellefontaine on the Missouri, where we had spent our final night. I saw Sergeant Ordway settle his dripping paddle at his feet, and lift his Harper's Ferry rifle. The others did likewise. There would be a salute.

He checked the priming and aimed his piece skyward to shoot at God; the men did likewise, and at Ordway's shout they fired a salute, the scattered reports sharp and joyous, the popping of triumph. Men in the canoes fired as well, a ragged volley that announced our triumph to the whole world, and startled crows to flight.

Our salute occasioned a new round of cheers from the flocking crowd. I scanned the seething mass of people not for dignitaries, or people I knew, but for women. How we starved for women. How much we needed the sight of nankeen skirts and ivory lace, and cotton-covered bosoms, and porcelain faces, and glossy hair in ringlets or curls, women's hair in blue bonnets. How the sight of them there, gathered on the black and muddy bank, swelled our hearts and loins. There was no mistaking what was racing through the minds of my men. I knew them all. I could recite their private thoughts to them though they had not shared a word. They wanted women, and if need be they would spend their entire back pay to have one or a dozen.

I feared an incident.

"Sergeant Ordway, look after the men and equipment. Take them to the government house, the old Spanish stronghouse where we ran up the Stars and Stripes on the parade ground that day. That will be the armory for our rifles and gear. Give the men leave when all is secure. Tell them I'll try to get some cash for them. Be patient."

Ordway nodded. There could be no better sergeant.

"And Sergeant; look after the papers, diaries, specimens, bones—the whole collection. Especially those. The president's collection."

"In the government's house, sir?"

"General Wilkinson's, yes. It's empty now, they tell me."

I needed to say no more. My good sergeants would see to my good men, and in due course they would be paroled. It would be a merry night for them, though I doubted they would remember any of it by dawn.

I turned to the men in the pirogue with me. "I'll look after you; you can count on it. The nation owes you more than it can pay."

They paddled again, steering the small fleet toward the clamorous bank. I saw friends now; several dark-haired Chouteaus, who had been so helpful during the outfitting.

We pushed for shore as eager boys steadied our barks and caught our elkskin ropes. They swarmed us now, excited, crazed even, and I remember only one refrain: we thought you were long dead. We thought you had met your Fate. We had given up hope . . .

I clambered out, the wound in my buttocks paining me viciously, and skidded as I set foot on that vile muck. Other craft lined Leclede's landing just north; flatboats headed for New Orleans, keelboats destined for Pittsburgh.

"Ah, messieurs," Auguste Chouteau proclaimed, a vast and Gallic sweep of the arms drawing Clark and me up to dry ground. "It is a blessed miracle. You, alive! *Mon Dieu!* We starve for the news."

We pumped hands and clapped backs, and bathed ourselves in the excitement and tasted nectar. Questions flew, and we could not answer.

The mad crowd swarmed around the men and canoes, and I saw that Ordway would not succeed in executing my plans, at least not for a while.

"Has the post left?" I cried.

"This morning, for Cahokia."

"When does the post rider leave from there?"

"*Après-midi,*" Chouteau said.

"Send a messenger to hold the post. A letter to the president of the United States must go with it," I cried in a voice that brooked no quarrel.

Chouteau was no man to dither. He wheeled toward one of his servants, instructed him in short volleys of French, and I saw the man race to a bankside canoe, board it, and paddle furiously toward Cahokia, two or three miles away on the far shore of the Mississippi, in the Illinois country.

"I must write," I insisted. "I have urgent news to send my president."

I wished I hadn't used that expression. Jefferson was the president of all these people in this vast territory of Louisiana, newly purchased from Bonaparte. But I had been his secretary; he was certainly my very own president in a way that set me above the hoi polloi.

"I ache for your news, Monsieur Chouteau, but that must wait. I abjure you, sir, show me to a quiet corner where I may draft my message."

"*Bien*, monsieur, my warehouse will answer."

But it was not to be; not just yet. There were sweaty hands to shake, fulsome greetings to absorb, compliments to blot up lasciviously, honor to be paid, and I would have to hold off with the quill for a time. The town's great men had pressed around. Will Clark had his own circle to deal with, though after a few minutes I saw him slip free and attempt to put things in order with a wave of his hand and a laconic command or two: the Harper's Ferry rifles and black cook-pots and powder to the Government House, my leather-clad men breaking free of the crowd, the sweet pouty girls, and gimlet-eyed matrons hoping to discover breaches of decorum to condemn, the twitchy boys trying to be important, the silent sloe-eyed Indians, to settle our meager stores in safety.

I saw Will help Big White, She-He-Ke, the Mandan chief we had brought downriver to treat with the president, and his wife and son, out of the pirogue, and guard them. The savages stared. They had never seen a white man's city.

Leave it to Will Clark to put things right. Without him, I would not have succeeded. He deserved a reward exactly equal to my own: a captain's rank, though he was but a lieutenant; pay, bonuses, land warrants identical to what would come to me. I would see to it, fight for it.

I needed to write, not only to the president, but to my mother and family. I needed a suit of clothes. For two years, I imagine, my body had been clad in animal skins, which formed our moccasins, our pantaloons, our hunting shirts, our capotes, our gloves. They had some advantages over cloth, being proof against wind, but they captured our salts and sweats and oils in them until they rotted off our backs.

I knew I smelled as vile as the slime of the levee, and hoped soon to have fresh smallclothes and a broadcloth suit of clothes made up by a tailor. But all in good time. We all looked like scarecrows, stank, needed to tend to our hair and bodies, and needed our wounds, and boils, and rashes attended. We looked like brigands instead of a corps of the United States Army.

I discovered myself still clutching my rifle, the instrument of my salvation; we had learned never to be without our well-cleaned, loaded piece, and our caution had saved our lives more times than I could remember.

"Will, take this," I said to Clark. "Won't need it."

Clark handed my oiled, primed, well-tended rifle to Sergeant Gass. I felt naked without it.

"*Mes amis,* what did you find? What of the beaver?" asked Jean-Pierre Chouteau.

"Beaver aplenty, a fortune in beaver."

"Ah, beaver! And Indian trouble?"

I paused. "Later, my friend," I said.

"Minerals?"

"A few, but no mountain of salt." President Jefferson had asked me to look for one.

A winsome flirty-eyed girl with brown ringlets was pressing a jug of wine upon two of my men, the Field brothers.

"Ordway," I yelled.

My sergeant broke it up. If my men imbibed spirits just then, there would be no stopping a debauch, and all the matrons of St. Louis would be nodding their heads. I did not know whether St. Louis would dose my men with the clap, or whether my men would dose St. Louis.

I headed in a determined fashion for Chouteau's grimy warehouse, determined to announce our triumph to the world.

"Gentlemen," I said, "bear with me for but an hour: I must impart my news to the president of the United States."

They opened a path. Chouteau settled me at his own desk, fetched a quill and paper and inkpot, and I began the letter that would transform the world, secure me the gratitude of the nation, and offer indelible proof of my contributions to botany and zoology. It was high noon.

2. CLARK

Meriwether excused himself to write letters, retreating with elaborate courtesy from the crowd. I knew it was painful for him to tear himself away; he was drinking in the adulation like a man craving for spirits. But I could see that familiar taut compression of his lips that told me he was enduring delays he could scarcely bear; that reporting to Tom Jefferson came above all else, and his sole passion was to scrape his quill across foolscap and wing the great news east. He had stood there as long as he could, hearing the music of the Creoles while chafing to send the letter that would burst upon a world that had supposed us all dead.

I knew I must write some letters, too, but first there was the matter of She-He-Ke, Big White, his squaw, Yellow Corn, his boy, and the interpreter, René Jessaume, his Mandan wife and family. The Mandan chief was ill at ease, trying his stone-faced best not to show it, glancing dumfounded at the white men's structures, the whispering mob, the enameled carriages, the parasoled grandes dames in black.

The Creoles crowded around me, sharp with greed, as I oversaw the last of our debarkation. Ordway and Gass had marched the men toward Government House, freeing me to meet these calculating merchants, none of whom I knew well, for it had been Meriwether who had dealt with them all before the expedition while I erected Camp Wood across the river.

"Monsieur, Chouteau here. *Bien,* what a grand day, *oui*? It is a day always to remember!"

"Pierre Chouteau, I remember."

"Ah, Capitaine, tell me every grand thing."

I laughed. "Well, first of all, I want you to meet a friend of ours, Chief Big White of the Mandans." I spotted the translator. "Jessaume, come help us out, and bring the chief."

"It is so? This is a Mandan *sauvage*?"

"We're taking him to meet the president, and maybe put together an alliance."

"Ah! A concord."

Jessaume arrived with the chief and his family, and the translation proceeded in French, which let me out. But that was fine. I had things to do.

A short swart Spaniard I knew slightly, who had been hovering about like a bumblebee, saw his chance and approached.

"Manuel Lisa, Captain. It was a formidable journey, and we are pleased. Have you a moment?"

I nodded, reluctantly.

"Are there perhaps beaver up the Missouri?"

I laughed; that was answer enough.

"And what are the little impediments to reaching them?"

I could see where this was heading. "The Sioux," I said. "They block the river."

"Could they be pacified, or stupefied, with gifts?"

"We weren't able to, sir."

"How many would it take to break through?"

"More than you can hire, and I doubt that the government would let you."

"Are the British trading up there?"

"They certainly are. Nor'westers, mainly."

"Do they have the tribes in their possession?"

"Yes, mostly they do."

He was stroking his small jet-haired beard. "And have you a map showing the beaver streams?"

"Mister Lisa! I haven't been on shore but half an hour!"

"I shall await your instruction," he said.

I turned, discovering half a dozen men lusting after our words. St. Louis was a city built on furs; these were entrepreneurs, fur men, blotting up my every word, concupiscent for beaver that could earn them a bonanza. I grinned, perhaps cynically. I knew the sort. St. Louis was not so much celebrating our safe return as it was celebrating the opening of a Golconda. About our survival, about our reaching the Pacific, about a river route to the Pacific, about our charting an uncharted continent, they were indifferent; about the streams habited by *Castor canadensis,* they were ardent students.

"More later, gents," I said, seeing their disappointment. Fortunes, empires, monopolies, rivalries, lives of ease hung on every word I breathed, but I had no time for that. We had a guest and his family, half awed, half afraid, stiff as a plank, and needful of my comforts.

"Jessaume, tell brother Big White we're going to take them to the big chief's house and get them settled," I said.

The translator repeated that in Mandan, and soon the somber Mandan, a big, lumbering man gotten up for the occasion in his finest ceremonial leathers, and his entourage were trailing me, along with half of St. Louis, as I hiked upslope, past warehouses and then mercantile firms along the Rue Principale, on up to the decaying Spanish military post.

I found our men stacking their arms in stands, in an orderly's quarters under the supervision of Patrick Gass.

"Good," I said. "Who's in command here?"

"Don't know, Captain. They're all down to the water thinking up ways to get rich."

I took matters into my own hands, surveyed the old seat of government in Upper Louisiana erected by the Spanish, studied a dusty barracks that appeared unused, and rejected the idea of putting the Mandans in there. These savages were tribal royalty. Big White was a king. I would give my coppery brother a king's billet.

I found General Wilkinson's chambers, but no Wilkinson, made a swift decision, and put Big White and his family in them, explaining to Jessaume, who barely grasped English, that this place was the very home of the American big chief, and Big White would be his guest for now. This was high diplomacy; the navigation of the Missouri River was at stake, and the friendly Mandans would be our passport.

I liked Big White. He had a powderhorn full of courage to come down the river with us to meet his new Father, past his enemies the Arikaras, and the truculent Sioux, and there had been wailing aplenty when he stepped into our canoe. Most of his people thought they would never see him again.

Big White nodded. I hoped it would do.

"Tell him we'll feed him just as soon as we can," I said to Jessaume. "Settle yourself and stay with him."

The interpreter nodded. I didn't much trust him, and never had, since meeting him on the way out to the Pacific.

And then, for the first time since debarking, I had a moment to reflect. Where was that damned York? Never in sight when I needed him. Where would I billet myself? Probably in a tent somewhere, in my buffalo robe. What about the men? Turn them all loose?

I found Sergeant Ordway posting the corps to that empty barracks. He approached me.

"Don't know what you intend, sir. Some signed on for the trip, and should be released. Most are still regulars, and still under command," he said.

I seconded that. "Look to their mess, and let 'em loose tonight. You, too. All the sergeants, all the corps, so long as there's a guard here tonight. I'll find out who's command ing here." I grinned. "Whether or not Captain Lewis comes up with some back pay, I don't imagine you'll suffer for the want of spirits."

He nodded wryly. We understood each other. For three years we had been understanding each other.

I stepped into sunlight and found myself strangely alone, even though we had scarcely arrived. It was over. We were safe, but plentifully embroidered with boils and rashes and wounds. I had seen feet so lacerated I wondered how a man could put weight on them; men so ravaged I wondered how they could step one more time through hip-high snow. I had seen Meriwether vomit every last shred of camas root he had eaten, turn so sick I thought he'd expire; and most of the men, too. I'd been fevered and bilious more times than I could remember. I don't know how we survived, though I credit Meriwether, who learnt something from Doctor Rush, and plenty more from his mother.

Upper St. Louis was deserted and hushed. I hiked back toward the crowded levee, absorbing the city's foul stench, fetid air, the cess in the mucky lanes, the stone structures with real glass in the windows, the temporary squared log ones. Not a brick had been set to mortar in St. Louis, yet stone mansions rose upslope, and shacks jostled one another everywhere.

I wouldn't stay here long. I knew exactly where I was headed. Miss Judith required my attention. As soon as we could put matters in order here, Meriwether and I would head east, stopping at Mulberry Hill, our family home near Louisville, en route.

I remembered how she looked the last time I saw her, this cousin of mine, Judith Hancock. She was trying to deal with a disobedient horse. She was twelve, not yet a woman, a pretty thing, flat chested, in a girl's brown skirts, bright-eyed. She captured me then. I named a river for her, Judith's

River, high up the Missouri. I had the same design then as now; when I got back—*if* I got back—I would head for Fincastle, Virginia, where Colonel Hancock resided, and put my designs forward.

They were affluent people, the Hancocks, landed and comfortable, but I didn't suppose I'd long be poor or unequal to their measure. Jefferson had promised me much: the captaincy had been turned down by the War Department, much to Meriwether's disgust, but as for the rest, land warrants, back pay, bonus, I'd be comfortable . . . if Judy would have me. It had been a long time, and I hadn't the faintest idea of her circumstance. I knew only my own condition, which was to make haste and claim her whilst I could. For nigh three years I had been thinking on it.

Meriwether and I had talked much of what we would do: we needed first to see the president and present him with the fruits of our labors; not merely an account of our journey, but my maps, of which I am proud because I know they are true. And the specimens, pressed and skinned and pickled by the hundreds. We plucked them up. We shot them, skinned them, preserved them, and packed their bones. We had boxes and barrels full of them, diligently described by Meriwether, less by me, though I copied out many of his pages to give ourselves a duplicate record. All of that we would soon deliver to the President's House in Washington City, or Monticello if Tom Jefferson so desired, for we had been faithful to his command, and except that our diplomacy with the tribes has to some degree failed, we had met his every objective.

But first, I would put a letter in that post bag being delayed for us at Cahokia; and soon we will be rowing and poling up the Ohio to my family home on Mulberry Hill where my older brothers George Rogers and Jonathan will be waiting.

3. LEWIS

Pierre Chouteau took Will Clark and me into his home until we could find lodging. But today we rented a room from a tavernkeeper from Kentucky to store our baggage, of which we had considerable.

I had scribbled furiously at my letter to Mr. Jefferson, and sent it off with discontent, knowing I had barely touched upon what needed saying. Ah, the impotence of words! But I took special pride in announcing that "in obedience to your orders we have penetrated the continent of North America to the Pacific Ocean, and sufficiently explored the interior of the country to affirm with confidence that we have discovered the most practicable route which does exist across the continent by means of navigable branches of the Missouri and Columbia Rivers."

I wanted the world to grasp the implications. So I emphasized the riches in furs, the commercial potential of Louisiana for the republic, and prated a little about our botanical and zoological collections and Indian vocabularies. And I did not neglect my co-commander, urging the president to make certain that Will received an equal measure of the rewards and emoluments of our perilous journey.

I had an eye to publication, and wrote not only for the president but for the whole nation, not neglecting to tell the world what perils and hardships we had endured, and what progress we had made in charting the unknown continent upon which the republic had seated itself along one shore.

I intended to pen a reprise of our experiences, and achieved that, though I knew I could not tarry long, for I was holding the government post. I drafted a letter for Will as well, which he copied in his own hand, and we sent George Drouillard canoeing across the Mississippi with our missives. And so it was that the news winged eastward, officially proclaimed by my own hand. I knew what the effect would be. Washington City would celebrate. But I much more wanted to hear what the sage of Monticello would say when I stood at his door. Well done, good and faithful friend.

There was much to do that day, and the next days. Will and I found a half-deaf tailor who had several bolts of suitable black broadcloth, and had ourselves measured for suits of clothes and smallclothes as well, having nothing between our flesh and the public eye but the animal skins we had been reduced to wearing, and a few borrowed rags we were fitted out in until we could have some garments made up. We were both scarecrows.

I for one regretted every moment I was clad in elkskin and doeskin, though the woodsman's costume did have its effect upon the imaginations of those who beheld me, for my attire was a mark of my passage through a barbarous land. Still, I wanted my blue and white uniform, my gold thread epaulets, my lace, my well-blacked boots, my emblems of rank and honor, and felt naked without these proper ensigns of rank and position.

Will grinned at me, but he had no proper care for his person, and often it showed in his mode of dress.

"Try wooing in buckskins, and see whether you go nose to nose with your fair Judy," I said by way of retort.

He had no reply to that.

I turned that day to other matters: the men needed cash and I had to provide it. By employing my power to sign warrants upon the government, I was able to get them some coin, though little of that existed in this rude city of St. Louis; and none of it in dollars. I got them two-bit pieces, dimes, doubloons, ducats, pieces of eight, shillings, francs, and all manner of coin that the city's merchants provided by digging deep into their private hoards. Enough to help my doughty men buy what they needed, mainly pantaloons, shirts, ale, and women, for they were as reduced as I, and without means.

I turned next to a matter most delicate and private. Prior to our departure, I was greatly assisted in medical matters by the Parisian doctor Antoine François Saugrain, a royalist refugee who had settled in St. Louis and brought within his mind the most advanced knowledge of medicine available anywhere, and a mastery of science unknown outside of Philadelphia. He had provisioned me with medical supplies and also shared his medical knowledge prior to the expedition. Now I turned to him for help.

Several of my men suffered gravely from certain diseases of the flesh gotten from the savage women we had encountered along the way. This matter was so private that I made little mention of it in my public journals, but confined myself to reporting certain symptoms in some of my men, in particular Goodrich, Gibson, and MacNeal. What the enlisted men did was one matter; what the commanders did was quite another, and so I had chosen to write nothing, though in fact a certain disease had ravaged me in the autumn of 1805, and so severely that Will despaired of my health.

Thus, this twenty-fourth day of September, I excused myself from the warm ministrations of my hosts, and set out to see the eminent Doctor Saugrain with the intent of seeing to the health of the men returned from the Pacific. I did not wish to make my visit known, and thus loitered about the Rue L'Eglise until no one was watching, and then I burst into his chambers.

He welcomed me at once, this diminutive gentleman of four feet and six inches, and heard me out.

"In short, sir, we are suffering from various venereal infections gotten from the savage women, and I wish to have you consult with my men. I will write the president and ask him to appoint you as an army surgeon, thus securing your pay and achieving a desirable privacy for the corps."

Saugrain eyed me sardonically, his pointed black beard bobbing as he weighed the matter.

"My capitaine, step behind that screen and disrobe. Everything. Even the stockings. The bottoms of your feet will tell me much," he said. "And your hands, *oui,* the palms."

"Ah, I'm talking about the men. Not the officers."

His response was a small ivory finger pointed at the screen.

I surrendered. I had dreaded this moment, the shame of it, the revelation in it that I had lain with a savage woman long before. All the way up the Missouri I had ruthlessly resisted the opportunities thrown my way by eager chiefs and their eager women; but I imagined one lonely night when I was ahead of the corps, there in the Bitterroot Mountains, isolated from the world, that the Shoshones would be well insulated from this New World disease and that the chances of catching what Columbus's crew brought to Europe would escape me. I would avoid the mortification and pain that attends the discovery of such congress by friends and family and even strangers. Was I not the explorer who had been the first to reach the Pacific? I could not endure the thought that a secret vice might sicken me and ultimately expose my folly to the world.

How I rue that single night with the Shoshone woman when I and three of my men had found Cameahwaite and his people, far in advance of Clark and the rest, who were toiling up the headwater streams east of the divide. The chief had given me a good buffalo-skin lodge and I had surrendered to my voluptuary passion, thinking myself safe enough. I was not. If I could but live my life over, I would excise that night from it. I have reproached myself a thousand times, aching with remorse and shame, but I cannot undo the bitter truth of that bitter night in the Bitterroot Mountains.

I had treated numerous of our corps with the purgative calomel, mercurous chloride mixed into a salve, directing them to apply it to any chancres on their private parts or elsewhere, and directing them to ingest my pills in considerable quantities to alleviate the burning when they passed water, and to quell the outbreaks of chancres and rashes and infections on their flesh. And I had quietly taken the same courses myself, though I made no note of it in the journal, and for some while not even Will was aware of it, though he soon figured it out.

What interested Saugrain at first was the fresh wound through my buttocks, wrought by Cruzatte's ball, which had been slow to heal and troubled me greatly, suppurating for weeks and healing improperly, so even now I could barely sit.

"Now, sit yourself on the table there, and let me see the bottoms of your feet, Capitaine."

I raised a foot, then the other.

"*Bien*. Were they sore?"

"Yes. Blisters, about the time I was so sick in the fall of eighteen and five. I had to ride a horse. I couldn't walk."

"*Bien*. Show me your hands, palms up. Those too?"

"Yes, hard liverish lumps. They went away."

"I see. That is to be expected."

From within his gloomy office, stuffed with steel instruments of torture and morocco-bound books, I could see no part of the world; his examinations were well screened from prying eyes. And yet I felt a thousand eyes upon me as he studied the evidence of my folly, the healed-over chancre on my member; the scarce-healed pus holes of a ruined flesh. He hummed, sucked breath, touched no part of me, but bade me turn this way or that, and thus he took my entire measure, his small, delicate face creasing into frowns, his small lips pursed. He spent an amazing amount of time examining my skin, the inside of my mouth, my nostrils, and the rest of me as well, often with a magnifying lens.

"*Bien*," he said, which I took as a sign that I might restore my clothing.

"The rest, they are like this?"

"A few: I could not help Gibson; I fear for him."

"And yourself, *mon ami*."

The way he said it shot a chill through me.

"It is far advanced, the stage *deuxième*," he said. "You are perhaps entering the benign stage when it lurks out of sight, but the disease does not sleep, it crouches and waits. When did you, ah, acquire this badge of honor?"

I thought back to that joyous moment when we had finally found the Shoshones in the folds of the Bitterroots, and the relief I felt when I learned we might obtain horses from them; and the joy they expressed when we gave them meat that Drewyer (as I've always spelled Drouillard's name) had shot, for they were starved and intent upon going on a buffalo hunt. Oh, I remember those days and that sole night, when Will wasn't around and the main body of the corps was far below, dragging the canoes over endless shallows, and I felt free and my secret would be safe.

"Over a year past," I said. "It was the middle of August of eighteen and five."

My diminutive physician paced about, his hands decorously clasped behind his back, his black beard thrust forward like a bayonet. "You soon will enter the third and final stage, which does widespread damage to your organs. The heart and arteries especially, the brain, the system of the nerves that carry the messages of the mind to muscles."

I blanched.

"But we will try to arrest it. Monsieur le capitaine, the salt of mercury slows and arrests, but only for a while, and then the disorder gains ground again, becomes puissant, dangerous. Ah, how a man regrets his impulses then! Ah, Capitaine, what this infirmity does to the soul!"

A cold fear crawled through me.

"But there is much hope," he continued. "Many times, the disease diminishes, disappears, and it is as if nothing had ever afflicted the sufferer. I have found that perhaps a third of those who suffer it escape its effects entirely and many more are only mildly afflicted. And oftentimes years, decades, go by and nothing at all happens, as if the pox lies dead within you. I believe half of those who suffer this disorder survive it."

That heartened me. There was ample reason to hope. "Well, what shall I do?"

"We will begin a course of treatment, Capitaine. It will take some little while."

"But I *must* go to Washington! The president is expecting me. The whole world is expecting me. It's not possible."

Saugrain shrugged, a Gallic gesture that contained within it an entire argument. "Your condition prevents it. In a few weeks you will be sufficiently improved to go. You must avoid all spirits whatsoever; they accelerate the affliction. Here now, I shall mix the first batch of pills, *oui*?"

And so I knew I must tarry in St. Louis, even though I itched to head up the rivers to Philadelphia where a great reception would await me, for I had learned that I had been elected to the membership of the American Philosophical Society; to Washington and Monticello; to Locust Hill, and my family.

I paid Dr. Saugrain with a chit, for I hadn't a shilling, and arranged for him to examine my corps discreetly. I would put out the word for those suffering from the venereal, and I would charge my men with secrecy. We were heroes, and there would be no public sign of pestilence.

"I will do what I can, which is much," Saugrain said, as we parted. "Send them to me."

I stepped into the afternoon, looking both ways to see if anyone might see me emerge from the French doctor's chambers. I saw a few people down the street and a cart hitched to a mule, but no one was looking, so I slipped into the middle of the street. Not a soul in St. Louis knew where I had been, not even Will. There were things a man needed to keep entirely to himself.

Will and I would be the honored guests at a banquet at Christie's Tavern given by the leading men of St. Louis the next evening, and our great journey would be toasted and celebrated the entire night. And even before Doctor Saugrain's courses began their work, I would be violating his advice. But a man being toasted would have no choice. I would raise a glass, too.

4. CLARK

I have taken my leisure this late October Sabbath, enjoying the fine autumnal weather. I don't have much else to do. I thought we would be off for Washington City long since, but Meriwether tarries, I know not why. The president awaits us, and so does the whole republic, eager to give us the approbation that we have no doubt earned.

When I broached the matter to Meriwether, reminding him that winter is closing in swiftly, he grew short with me.

"I'm not ready. Don't press so hard, Will. I'm outfitting the whole entourage, you know. We're taking Big White and his family, and several of our men, too. The merchants don't have half of what we need. Just getting the men some money took me days. I've not gotten them a quarter of what they're owed. And not just my party, either. I've agreed to outfit Pierre Chouteau, so he can get his Osages to Washington. I'm going to auction off some of the rifles and gear, and raise something that way for the men."

It wasn't what he said that seemed testy to me but the way he said it, impatiently and shrill. I couldn't remember that metallic tone during our days on the trail.

He has been in a peculiar humor for weeks, at once drinking in draughts of acclaim along with the endless draughts of wine, but melancholic.

And so he tarries here in St. Louis. I wondered whether he wanted the word of our safe return to spread before us, thus making our passage east a sort of triumphal progress. But Meriwether is not so vain as all that. He is simply in a peculiar mood that I have not ever seen in him.

A few days ago an elderly butcher in a soiled bib approached us and shook Meriwether's hand. "I want to touch the hand of the man who walked to the Pacific," he said. "Walked to the western sea, tasted the brine, and walked back again. Now, sir, having taken that very hand in mine, I am content."

Meriwether smiled, and then reminded the old man that over twenty more had done the same thing. He is eager to share his accomplishments, and I count it a virtue in him.

But I never doubted that the command was really his, not mine, and in those cases in which I disagreed, especially about the Indians, I held my peace and found ways to be agreeable, preferring to modify his thoughts by degrees. He consulted with me frequently, usually in the confines of our tent when we still had one, or at least apart from the men, and always heard me out. But tacitly, we both knew the decisions were his to make, and he made them, and still makes them. He really gives me more credit than is due me.

He has written generous letters to the president, urging a reward for me equal to his own, including a captain's pay, and likewise he has written a commendation for almost every man in the corps, and has singled out a few for special compensation; he always was good with his men; reserved and distant, but a man to follow without question. I did follow his lead and still do, marveling in so grand a vision and keen a mind and withal, an eager quest for every scrap of knowledge that might advance science.

Time drags. I proposed a fortnight ago that I leave at once, visiting my brothers and family at Mulberry Hill until he might arrive, but he forbade it. I know exactly what I wish to do: hasten to Fincastle, Virginia, just as swiftly as foot and horse and sail can transport me, and lay siege to the castle of my dreams.

She for whom I named a crystal virgin stream.

Judy is much on my mind. She is of marriageable age now; if she will have me I intend to wed her. The vision of her sustained me during our long progress, and stayed me in moments when I might have plucked the ripe fruits being offered by tribal women. And now I am prepared to win her. My battery will consist of telling her that I named a beautiful stream for her, one that pours out of mountains and is as clear as pond ice. What woman can resist so tender an assault as that?

I think of little else. I will not be an impoverished suitor, not with three years of double back pay owing and land warrants promised me. I have already resigned my commission, having served my country well, and will begin a family, fashion a comfortable plantation in Kentucky not far from my brothers at Mulberry Hill across the Ohio, and prosper for as long as health permits. Assuming, of course, that Mr. Jefferson and the Congress keep their commitments.

Not that one can trust any government to honor its commitments. My brother is painfully aware of it. It mattered to no one, apparently, that George Rogers Clark secured the whole northwestern territory clear to the Mississippi for the republic, beating the British regulars and their savages out of it with little more than an undisciplined militia. When it came time for the commonwealth of Virginia to make good the warrants by which he equipped and provisioned his ragtag militia, the commonwealth's clerks reneged, found excuses, reproached him for the loss of receipts, and tossed him to the creditors, and so my brother was ruined save for a small amount of almost worthless land. I wonder whether that will be my fate as well. Let it be a Clark motto: put no trust in the government!

And that is why I found myself, this warm and sunny October 26, strolling the riverbank, my eyes peering across the rolling river to the east, where my heart is tugged. I am a prisoner here. I am weary of the banquets. We have been to several at Christie's Tavern where I now abide; the businessmen toast us, celebrate us—but I do not delude myself. They pump us for every scrap of knowledge about the high Missouri they can glean, knowing that their fortunes swell with such information.

The wily Spaniard Manuel Lisa makes it his business to learn everything we have to teach, and I am wary of him. Meriwether, who was almost abstemious during the expedition, has taken much to drink and at the end of such evenings needs a steadying friend to get him safely to his bed, which consists of a buffalo robe he spreads on the floor, for he cannot find sleep lying upon straw or feathers or stuffed cotton.

I strolled hard by the blue Mississippi this bright chill morn, and an hour out of town I spotted the solitary figure of a familiar and esteemed man before me, also stretching his legs. Drouillard, our Shawnee-French guide, interpreter, and hunter was the most valuable of all our men, supplying our hungry bellies with meat where none among us could find anything to shoot at. He is a dark, heavy-boned, and solitary man, preferring to roam apart from us, keeping much to himself, and yet he always had a kind word for me, and I mark him among my favorite of all those in the Corps of Discovery.

He saw me and paused.

"George, taking the air, I suppose?"

"Yes, Captain."

"How is your circumstance? Were you released?"

"Yes, sir. Captain Lewis paid me my twenty-five a month, which he got out of the merchants, and my service is over."

"You linger here, though."

"It is a place to make money, Captain. Half a dozen merchants have approached me about going upriver. Lisa, Chouteau, all of them. I may do so. I've been where they want to go, so it seems I am a man of some value."

"Along with most of the others," I said.

"A few. Most are indisposed."

"And the regulars are still under command. Who's indisposed?"

"Captain Lewis could tell you better than I."

"I thought by now most of the corps would have recovered. Better food, plenty of rest, warmth, and comfort."

Drouillard grunted.

"But maybe too much to drink, is that it?"

"There's a parade of them visiting Doctor Saugrain, Captain."

I knew of it, and knew why. "Poxed, are they? Captain Lewis told me he had appointed Saugrain an army surgeon; it would be cheaper than paying for every visit."

"Poxed, yes. Half the corps."

"But not you. You were lucky."

"No, Captain, it was not luck. I do not live by luck, but by calculation. I did not like the chances."

I thought back to all those evenings among the Mandans, Hidatsas, Shoshones, Nez Percés, Clatsops, and all the others, when men slipped away into the darkness with the laughing women. Meriwether and I had to guard our stores to keep the men from stealing a hank of ribbon or an awl or a mirror to give to the squaws. I could not remember Drouillard indulging himself. Maybe he was, like me, a careful man. We could no more stop our men than we could stop a waterfall.

That put me in mind of York. The squaws had fallen all over him, and yet he was unscathed by pox, though he had lain, I reckoned, with more Indian women than anyone else in the corps. How he fascinated them! I could not fathom it, though I would have been much vexed if he had sickened and lost his value to me. He bothers me now; the expedition taught him too much independence, and he looks at me now with a gaze I don't like, and intend to do something about.

I had Judy to think of, and a dream of a good life, and that was enough to teach me prudence. I thought it would suffice for Captain Lewis, also. Meriwether had several belles in mind, and a physician's knowledge in his head, garnered from his mother, Doctor Rush of Philadelphia, and Saugrain as well before we started. No doubt he was aware of the venereal, but maybe thought to avoid it or heal it.

He didn't. He was poxed like the rest and was dosing himself with the calomel, though no word of it entered our journals. I do not know whether he suffered the drip, or worse. I cannot name the time or place, though it was plain he was suffering by the time we descended from the Bitterroots into the Columbia drainage. I myself treated those festering eruptions on his legs and arms when we were among the Nez Percés, though he bade me do so privately in our tent, fearing discovery by our men. I kept his secret.

Though Drouillard had said nothing specific, I realized suddenly why Meriwether had not headed for Washington earlier. He would not go until Doctor Saugrain was done with him. That put a new light on things, and I pitied my co-commander. Were Drouillard and I the only two of the corps who had kept our senses—and our health?

He fell silent as we blotted up sun. Then he paused.

"You will excuse me, I trust, Captain," he said, and turned off the path. That was the way of him, to vanish from our midst after the briefest encounter.

I hiked well north of the town that day, restless and itching to get on with life, but actually still under orders. We managed to go clear to the Pacific while maintaining the fiction that we were co-commanders; but that was solely because I, Lieutenant Clark, did not press the issue when we differed. I would not press it here. It was Lewis's expedition, and he was admirably suited to the task, and to my dying day, I will view him with unbounded admiration and affection.

I returned to St. Louis with a breeze at my back.

I supped this evening with Meriwether at Christie's Tavern, as we usually do, now that the city's merchants had at last wearied of our tales of great brown bears, buffalo beyond number, tribes that subsist on salmon, and the presence of sea trader's items far up the Columbia.

I examined him with some care, it having been revealed

me why he tarries so long in St. Louis. He looked well nough; certainly better than when we had arrived. Dr. augrain has done him some good. As if to confirm it, he nnounced that we would leave for Washington City in a eek or so.

He ordered porter, and then another goblet of it.

"I've had to outfit quite a party, you know. The Osages nd Mandans. Chouteau's people. Several of our corps. But imagine in a few days, Will, you'll be in the bosom of your mily."

"And then Fincastle," I said, smiling.

"Ah! You are a lucky man. I have never had much luck ith women, though I plan to change that," he said lightly. Miss Randolph, for one. Miss Wood, for another. But y burdens have been so heavy, I haven't given it much ought . . . until now. Wish me luck, eh?"

There was something in the way he said it that sadened me.

I truly wished him luck.

. LEWIS

My joy upon arriving at my Virginia home, Locust Hill, was unalloyed. I discovered my mother, Lucy Marks, my brother, Reuben, my half-brother, John Marks, and y half-sister, Mary, all present and in good health.

My mother met me on the lawn that sixteenth day of ecember, for word of our arrival preceded us. When I dis- ounted, she clasped me to her, her hands telling me how lad and grateful she was, and how proud, too.

"My very own Meriwether," she whispered. "At last m fears are behind me. And now I have a mother's pride. Ah my son, alive and honored . . ."

I laughed, told her we would have a long visit in which promised to reveal to her every wonder, every success, ever danger. Her fingers lingered on my arm, touching the so she had thought she would never see again.

I had Big White and his family and our translators wit me, and Private Frazier, who served as my aide; but Ser geants Ordway and Gass and Private Labiche, who had lef St. Louis with us, had gone their separate ways. At Frank fort, on November 13, we had split up: Will had taken th trace to Fincastle, Virginia, Pierre Chouteau headed fo Washington City with his Osages, and I took my party t Ivy, in Albemarle County. Ultimately I would progress t the City of Washington.

It had been a triumphant progress, and we were greatl slowed because every hamlet along the Ohio River wishe to banquet us and celebrate with grand oratory, toasts and bonfires. Most of all they wanted to hear our storie and we had obliged them as best we could. I am sure the were disappointed that we did not encounter mountains c rubies, fields of gold, giraffes, elephants, and pygmies.

Little girls in dimity met us with bouquets tied with yel low ribbons; raggedy barefoot boys wanted to inspect ou Harper's Ferry rifles. Clerks and butchers and harness makers wanted to shake hands, and memorize maps, an learn if the soil out west was fertile. They all wanted sou venirs, anything at all, even a patch of cloth, that had bee to the far Pacific. And everywhere, towns spread their bun ting, the red, white, and blue, and hoorahed us, and told u we were as bright as the circle of stars in the flag, and me of destiny.

But at last I was home in sweet hazy Virginia; we settle

Big White and his family in a spare bedroom. We were at once beset by convivial neighbors, for word of our arrival had preceded us, and in the hubbub I discovered that we would be honored at a great banquet in Charlottesville two days hence, with all the leading lights of that part of Virginia attending us.

"You look splendid," my mother said, when at last we had a moment. "I would have supposed to find you worn to a skeleton."

"That aptly describes our circumstance on more than one occasion," I replied. "We had moments so desperate I despaired of feeding my men. But somehow we survived, and we had learned the woodsman's art so well that we made meals of things civilized people scorn."

My mother, small and thin and discerning, with eyes that probed me, drew me to her and examined me, somewhat to my discomfort, for it was as if I could have no secrets from her. She was not a physician, but was much called upon for her medical knowledge, and put stock in a number of simples that were famous in the county, herbs and barks and roots she gathered in the fields each year which she decocted into teas. They said she was better than any doctor in Virginia.

"Are you well, Meriwether?" she asked velvetly, her fragile hands resting in mine.

"See for yourself," I replied. "I endured everything that harsh nature could devise for us, and yet we all got home, except for Sergeant Floyd."

I was in the very bloom of health, having benefited from the efficacy of Doctor Saugrain's courses, and I was certain that *lues venerea* was a thing of the past, and gave it no more thought.

She touched my cheek, stubbled from the neglect wrought by travel, and I was grateful that I was unshaven, for the skin eruptions of 1805 had left the faintest brand on my cheeks, small circles of obscure scar I fervently hoped she would not discover. Doctor Saugrain told me that the disease scarcely yields scar tissue, and that the healing of the skin is complete, but in my case a sharp eye might see the track of my tribulations. Under her scrutiny I had to nerve myself into the appearance of calm.

"I hope that it is so," she said softly, and I felt a great uneasiness. I did not wish for my mother to learn the nature of the vile disease that had afflicted me, and that I now had conquered; the plague of scoundrels, vagabonds, and loose women.

How swiftly our house filled. Here were laced and perfumed cousins and aunts and uncles: Lewises and Meriwethers, including my uncle Nicholas Meriwether, who had been my guardian after my father died.

And they had questions. What was it like out there? A desert worse than the Gobi? What lies beyond the Mississippi? An aching void? Did you see no white men at all for three years? Is it all barren and naked, unfit for any but savages?

For me there was no longer a mystery in it, but for them I had undertaken a journey as exotic as an exploration of darkest Africa. I may as well have been describing a probe up the Amazon, or a marooning at Juan Fernández Island.

"Louisiana," I said, "is a land so great, so rich, so filled with natural treasures, so fertile, that when it is finally settled we shall be the largest and most populous and most powerful nation on earth."

"But what of the tribes?"

"They will become our friends; I made great progress with them, except for those fiends, the Sioux, which know no fear of anything but force."

Even as I spoke, I was watching Big White and his squaw,

Yellow Corn, who were wandering in sheer bewilderment through our home, marveling especially at the mounds of food hastily brought by our slaves to the dining table, along with our splendid sterling silver and Wedgwood china. Civilized life was beyond their fathoming and I was glad they were being introduced to it, because once they returned to the Mandans with their stories, the power of the American eagle would be understood within the minds of all the Missouri River savages.

Using the good offices of my translator, René Jessaume, whose own Mandan squaw was quite as dumfounded as the chief, I urged my family and neighbors to converse with this wild specimen of Louisiana mankind, which they did with great relish, along with much finger-wiggling, evoking solemn responses from the chief.

Ah, that was fun. Chouteau was on his way to Washington with the Osages, and the purpose was the same: we would overawe them all, they would return to their huts and tell the others what they had witnessed, and that would establish permanent peace and prosperity in the unsettled country.

"Well, Meriwether," said my uncle Nicholas, "you have done a grand thing. Your fame has spread far beyond the county, and I have no doubt that your name will be celebrated even in Vermont, and Georgia."

I relished the compliment and am not shy about taking credit for the successful expedition, which I knew to be the greatest in history.

But I was keenly aware that others had contributed to our success, and was fervent in my wish to give credit where it was due. "Will Clark was my equal in all respects, sir. And we had doughty men who, after certain disciplinary troubles at the start, welded themselves into an unmatchable corps, so devoted to duty and mutual protection that it was scarcely necessary for me to drill or order them about, or even instruct by the time we began our second year. But Will Clark, with his boating and mapping skills, sir, that is what made us a match and a team."

"You share the glory generously, Meriwether."

"That is my exact purpose."

After an interval I looked after my aide, Private Frazier. He had never been in so fine a house, and he gaped his way through our white-enameled parlors, studying the oil portraits, the Hepplewhite and Sheraton pieces, and ended at last at our lengthy dining table, where cold pink beef and a succulent sugar-cured Virginia ham rested, with orange yams, brown breads, creamy sauces, and sundry other items, including an ample stock of whiskey and porter. I ate my fill, and urged him to do so also.

"This man," I explained, "has been to the Pacific Ocean with me; has seen its dashing waves and tasted its salt. We have eaten the white blubber of a whale beached there. We have subsisted on elk and buffalo, ducks, beaver, dog, salmon and bear fat. And now we go to Washington to tell Mr. Jefferson what we have seen."

I was very proud, the cynosure of much attention that hour, and I saw no reason not to enjoy it. I had done what no other mortal had done. I told them of the great humped grizzly, larger and more terrible than other bears, so great that sometimes half a dozen balls did not stop them. I told them of bearded buffalo beyond number, of the rivers we named for Mr. Gallatin, Mr. Madison, and Mr. Jefferson; of the streams Will and I named for Maria Wood and Judy Hancock; of Charbonneau's little girlsquaw, who led us toward our fateful meeting with the Shoshones and their horses.

Of many things did I speak, wonders all to these Virginia gentry for whom the great continent rolling westward was a deep mystery full of deserts and terrors. And from the bright gaze in some women's eyes, I knew myself to be an unexplored continent also.

And then I paused, addressing my mother. "And where is our cousin Maria?" I asked.

"Maria Wood? She married some while ago, Meriwether, a most blessed match, and we are pleased."

"Ah," I said, "ah . . . I named a river for her, you know. I should like to tell her. I was looking forward to it."

"I'm sure you'll soon have a chance," my mother said.

It had been fanciful of me to think she might still be available these three years. I had admired her from afar, but never had encouraged her interest before the expedition. And yet the vision of her had always sustained me. Now she was taken. I breathed deeply, eyed the clamorous horde, and knew there would be others.

Two days later they banqueted us at the Stone Tavern in Charlottesville, and there we were feted with toast after toast, and there I took pains to tell these Virginians that I had indeed succeeded: "I have discharged my duty to my country," I said. And I dwelled at length upon what Will and I had achieved on behalf of botany and zoology, for I wanted them to know that we recorded innumerable new species of plants, birds such as the magpie, and animals such as the dog of the prairie, dutifully described, sketched, pressed between pages, skinned, boned, and in some cases even returned live to Monticello.

I drank too much. Saugrain had warned me, in the severest language he could summon, against all spirits. But that was quite impossible given the hospitality I was experiencing and the fetes prepared in my honor. Should I refuse a toast? In any case, I was in fine fettle, my health was splendid, save for the endless pain wrought by the wound in my buttocks done by Cruzatte's ball high up the Missouri.

And for that I had a comforting remedy: a few drops of laudanum always sufficed to ease my pain, and balm the aches of all my muscles.

They were even penning odes about us, and proposing that rivers and territories be named after me. I would not oppose the idea, for I had done what Columbus had done: what Amerigo Vespucci had done, and he had gotten his name on two continents out of it. But I count myself a seemly man, and later was relieved when Congress did not take up those suggestions.

I relished the adulation but was eager to go to Washington, and on to the nation's true capital, Philadelphia, for the acclaim I thirsted the most for would come from my president, and then from those erudite periwigged savants in the Quaker City, who had formed themselves into the premier New World organization devoted to the advancement of all branches of learning, and especially science.

The American Philosophical Society had elected me a member—I who lacked a formal education! I planned to repay them the honor, by offering them the sum total of my hard-won knowledge of the continent, including the incomparable map that Will had fashioned day by day, out of our ceaseless measurements of latitude and longitude as we ascended the great Missouri. I give him the credit for it; my own cartographic skills are no match for his.

And so, with Christmas looming, and the most remarkable Yuletide of my young life awaiting, I set off from Albemarle County for the capital, and the President's House, half-unfurnished still, to report to Mr. Jefferson, and to arrange as best I could to give Congress reason to reward all of my bold men with all the generosity a grateful nation could afford.

What better Christmas than to report my success to the governors of our new republic? And to show them my successes at diplomacy in the form of my Mandan guests? I had received word that Mr. Jefferson pined to meet Big White, even as he had rejoiced when Chouteau brought him the Osages, and the president had greeted them warmly, given them gifts and medals, and cemented relations with the savages who barred our way west.

Sometimes, in my rare moments of solitude, I was disquieted.

I was playing a new part, but I ill understood the role.

6. CLARK

I beheld the altar of my dreams, Fincastle, from a considerable distance because it lay below my vantage from the trace over Brush Mountain. Fincastle had been much on my mind, not only recently but all the way to the Pacific and back, and now my heart quickened at the knowledge that it rested in the broad valley down the long slope ahead, lost in the familiar haze of the blue ridges of Virginia. I had come a long way, and Fincastle was my lodestar.

It was the address of George Hancock's plantation, and the home of Julia, or Judy to me, his daughter and the woman of my fancies. Courting her was foremost on my mind. Let Meriwether reap the acclaim of Washington and all the leading men; all I needed was the promise I would seek from those soft lips. She would be fifteen now; the age my mother was married to my father. If Congress did its duty and ratified the promises given me, I would be eligible and with means.

We had miles to go, York and I. York walked through the

December chill and led our two packhorses, while I rode along the trace we had been following across Kentucky and western Virginia, pausing at inns along the way as was the custom.

I was no longer a lieutenant, having made haste to resign my commission as soon as I reached St. Louis, desiring not to keep the subaltern commission a day longer than necessary. I wrote Secretary Dearborn a resignation letter that made it clear what I thought of the rank. I do not trust the promises of government; my brother George Rogers Clark did, and was ruined by that trust. I would not succumb to such sentiment.

"Almost there, York," I said. "Hurry now."

He nodded. York had been lost in deep silence ever since we had returned from the expedition, and I hadn't liked it.

"I will freshen up at the next stand," I said. "You will cut my hair."

"Yassuh."

"Are you sick, York?"

"Nosuh."

"Well, then answer me with respect."

I had not been barbered since St. Louis, and I would have York do it, as he often did. I had kept my auburn hair short in accordance with our republican principles. So did Meriwether. Mr. Jefferson had decreed that all army officers must abandon their queues and wear short hair, because the officer's queue was a mark of aristocracy, improper in a republican government and a citizen army. Most had. A few officers had refused and were finally pressured into cutting off their hair or resigning. Since the army's officers were largely Federalists, the change came slowly, reluctantly, and with smoldering rage. One was finally court-martialed.

But I certainly didn't mind. My queue, when I wore it, was an annoyance, needing my attention, easily dirtied. But

I had known plenty of commissioned officers who wore their queues as a lordly prerogative; their mark of rank, as plain as epaulets and gold braid.

I fumed my way down the long slope, with York trailing barefoot behind me. He had been silent for weeks, a virtual stranger in my house. It had been a mistake to tender him a certain measure of liberty on the expedition; even worse a mistake to equip him with a rifle and teach him some marksmanship. But Meriwether and I knew that every man counted, and if we could conjure a rifleman and hunter out of York, we would be that much more secure.

But now I could see that it went to his woolly head. My thoughts turned severe: he would come around or be whipped. And if he didn't, I would lend him to a master who used slaves hard, and then he would learn his lesson.

We stopped that last night at a public house at New Castle, though I was tempted to push on the last fifteen miles and awaken Judy and her family in the small hours. But I checked my impulse. At the public house I would order some hot water brought to me, freshen my suit of clothes, and make myself presentable. We would be at Fincastle by noon, a good time to discover the shine in the eyes of my beloved.

The suit the tailor had stitched up in St. Louis was ordinary black broadcloth, there being no other fabric in town. That distressed Meriwether, but I am indifferent to clothing. So long as it comforts me I care little about it.

I got an entire room at that public house but could not preserve my privacy because I was instantly recognized. Post and express riders had proclaimed my progress in every hamlet along my route.

"Captain Clark, sir, we are honored to welcome so illustrious a figure to our inn," announced the rotund proprietor, one Barteau.

"It's Mr. Clark. I'm out of the army, sir, and want no part of it."

"Captain you are, though, and a captain's billet we'll give you."

"That's fine; put me up, put my slave in your hayloft if that's suitable, and fetch me plenty of hot water. What's the tariff for three horses, myself, and the darkie?"

"For you, my esteemed sir, nothing; for the horses and the black man, a shilling apiece, including hay and feed."

"Feed them all well. I can't afford to let them sicken."

He nodded.

I had little cash; only a small purse that Meriwether had gotten from St. Louis merchants against my back pay. But it had sufficed.

We were the only guests, but I little doubted that in minutes we would not be. That was how it had been: the whole neighborhood had to poke and prod Captain Clark, wherever we stayed.

York hauled my chest and saddlebags into my upstairs room, and stared at me questioningly.

"Hay the nags, eat, and then come back and cut my hair," I said.

"Us beasts o' burden gets fed," he said insolently.

I laughed, even though I had resolved to deal sternly with him. We were old friends, York and I.

The missus arrived with a leaky oaken bucket of hot water, not much but I didn't need much. I poured it into a porcelain basin on a commode and began to scrub myself, wanting to unskunk myself sufficient not to scare off young ladies. I started with my hair, which was begrimed from days on the trail, and the application of a little lye soap restored the coppery shine to it soon enough.

By the time York was done outdoors, I was ready for him,

sitting bare-chested on a homemade bench next to the candle.

My straightedge sufficed for both my beard and my hair, and York set to work with some skill, reducing the mop of wet red hair to something that might pass muster on a parade ground.

"Make it good this time," I growled. "It's going to get looked at by female eyes."

York didn't reply.

"What's bothering you, dammit?"

York sawed off some more coppery hair. I could feel his heat. You don't live with a slave from childhood without sensing everything that passes through his mind.

"You gonna let me see my woman?"

There it was. He wanted time off to see his wife, who was owned by a tobacco man outside of Louisville.

"No, I can't spare you," I said.

"Sometime, mastuh?"

"You just mind your business and let me decide. Maybe. In a few years."

"Rest of them, on the big trip, they got pay and go fetch them a woman and catch the crabs."

"You catch yourself any crabs, and I'll put the lash to you."

He irritated me, wanting his liberty like that. I probably shouldn't have taken him west. He spent those years as free as any of the soldiers, and now I had a surly servant. Half the squaws on the Missouri had sampled his black pecker, and I didn't doubt that many a lodge contained a dusky little papoose.

No sooner had I completed my toilet than the local burghers arrived, wanting to toast me and hear the stories about grizzlies, mountains with snow on them year around, wild

Indians, little prairie wolves, unknown birds, and the buffalo. I obliged them; didn't mind a bit. They raised their cups of porter, just as others had done along the route, and I accepted their homage. Why not? I would have my day in the sun, and then retreat to Kentucky with my bride, lay waste to some hardwood forest, and put in some tobacco.

The next day, Sunday the fourteenth of December, was a blustery one reminding me of how narrowly I had avoided winter travel. I dressed up in my black suit, stock, capote, and set off with York for the last lap. I hoped it would suffice. If it had been Meriwether, he would have gotten himself up in a new blue uniform with a good black tricorne hat, gold braid dripping from the shoulders, new-blacked boots, and a clanking dress sword. But I had nothing to turn the eye except maybe some land warrants and some back pay, and a reputation.

The Hancocks knew I was coming and they knew why. I had written from St. Louis. They would have heard from a hundred other sources. So I would be expected. But as I trotted my chestnut down the muddy post road, I began to rue my haste.

What if all this turned into some sort of fiasco? What if my brown-haired Judy, whose vision kept me going through cold and heat and hunger, didn't care about me, or worse, what if she wasn't anything like what I had remembered? What if she brayed instead of laughed, tittered and whickered instead of smiled, belched instead of lifting a white hand to her lips, displayed rotten yellow teeth . . .

I tormented myself clear to the portals of that imposing home erected on fertile tobacco cropland. Behind it stood several whitewashed outbuildings, a squat barn, slave quarters, summer kitchen, and sheds. One look at George Hancock's rambling house nearly did me in: my distant relative had prospered. He was a country squire, one of the first citizens of Fincastle, and here I was, an adventurer.

I gathered whatever wits I had left to me, dismounted, left my horses to York, and stiffly assaulted the front door.

She opened, and I stared at a vision of white silk, and the world stood still.

7. LEWIS

Mr. Jefferson himself welcomed me at the door of the President's House late in the evening of December 28, having heard of my arrival in Washington, and never was a mortal so gladdened as I to see my friend and mentor and commander in chief.

I had paused long enough to find lodging for my royal Mandan guests, She-He-Ke, his wife, and our interpreters. And then I hurried to that unfinished white manse to find the lanterns lit, every window lighted with tapers, and the president at the door in his slippers, gotten into a faded blue robe, his yawning stewards standing about behind him.

We shook hands heartily, Mr. Jefferson not being the sort to embrace, while the stewards saw to my chattel, especially those trunks that bore the journals and the few botanical specimens I had not earlier sent east.

"At long last!" he exclaimed, and I nodded ruefully, knowing I had been negligent about keeping him apprised of my progress and safety.

"Are you well? Hungry? Shall we talk?"

"Mr. Jefferson, let's talk if you're up to it."

"I'm certainly up to it, but are you?"

I assured him I was in the very bloom of health, and that settled the matter. I was in fact weary, but who could surrender to Morpheus at such a momentous time? I fairly seethed with delight. I was bursting with news and observations, and at the same time aware that my arrival had caused great jubilation in Washington City; they were calling me the great explorer, celebrating our safe return, writing treatises about me.

It took but a little time for the excellent stewards to settle me upstairs in a capacious four-poster room next to one occupied by Mr. Jefferson's son-in-law, Thomas Randolph, and then escort me to the president's private chambers, where he, still in his robe and slippers, his gray-shot red hair in disarray, received me with heartfelt delight, and beckoned me to a feast of cold beef, creamy rice pudding, chocolates, and ample amounts of fine French wines, which delighted my palate.

I poured some ruby Bordeaux and plunged in, aware that my auditor was acutely absorbed, hanging on to my every word, and processing everything I had to say in that phenomenal brain of his. Mr. Jefferson was more than my president; he was a sentry patrolling the lusty frontiers of botany, zoology, commerce, art, literature, philosophy, mechanics, astronomy, architecture, ethnology, cartography, and a dozen other fields.

He did not take notes, though he was an avid note-maker, but listened so intently that I was sure he could repeat back to me, word for word, everything I told him about the course of the great Missouri, the fierce tribes along it, the falls, the headwaters, the passage across those terrible white peaks, and the descent of the Columbia to the brine of the western sea.

We talked until two, when I began to nod, and he urged me to rest myself in the bosom of the nation's gratitude, and we would pursue other matters in the morning. He stood, began extinguishing the beeswax candles with a silver snuffer until a yawning servant rushed in to complete the task, and I retreated at once.

I did meet him for breakfast, having as usual slept on my bearskin, finding beds too soft after my years of sleeping on hard ground. That grand day we examined everything in my trunks; plants he had never seen, such as the wild flax I had discovered near the great falls of the Missouri; birds, such as the sage grouse I had spotted near Maria's River and the black-billed magpies I had recorded; skins of animals new to him, such as the prairie dog; and he paused long at Will's superb map of the Missouri River, which I knew to be a masterpiece of the cartographer's art, anchored by the innumerable soundings of latitude and longitude I had taken.

When at last we had examined my specimens, he straightened up, placed a hand on my shoulder, and searched a moment for words. "Meriwether," he said at last, "you are the very embodiment of the best in this new nation. You have proven yourself in the most trying conditions, found courage when you needed it, advanced science and knowledge, acted with humane and affectionate regard for our Indian neighbors, and have shown yourself to be more than worthy of the trust I vested in you. I am proud of you; I am more proud of what you've achieved than anything else I've accomplished. You, my son, are worthy of the esteem of every citizen, and I will say so to the world."

He said it so gently and firmly and kindly that I stood transfixed. The president of the republic was saying these things of me.

"Thank you, sir," I said, fumbling for something more suited to this occasion. "I will always try to live up to your expectations for me, and give myself to a life unsullied and honorable and fruitful."

And therein had I sealed my fate.

He smiled, breaking the solemnity of the moment.

"Now, Meriwether, you must see to the publication of your journals. In fact, they belong to the government; you recorded them in pursuit of your duty. But they shall be yours. My son, they will be profitable to you, and the true reward for your courage and perseverance and fortitude. Prepare them, and swiftly, for half the naturalists in Europe, and all of them in this country, are crying to me for word of the publication, and until now I've had little to tell them."

"I will directly, sir," I replied fervently, for I would crawl a hundred miles on my knees to please this man. "I will set upon that task at once, saving only the business of looking after my men. I hope that Congress will be generous, and that my men will receive what was promised; back pay, a grant of three hundred twenty acres, and if the War Department is willing, improvements in their rank according to my commendations."

"Consider me your ally in all that," said Mr. Jefferson. "Congress meets in a few days, and we shall commence our assault upon their purse."

Ah, it was grand to be at the President's House, three and a half years after I had last seen him, my mission fulfilled and successful in every respect, for I had succeeded in every part of my instructions, save perhaps my pacification of the Sioux, which was deeply disappointing to me because they controlled that mighty river of the plains. I had not failed him.

"I fear I am keeping you all too much to myself," the president said at last. "Let your Mandan chief know that we will have a reception here for him tomorrow, along with the Osages Chouteau brought us. You know, there's a play tonight. I imagine the red men might marvel at our theater, and get the drift of the show even if your translator—Jessaume is it?—has to interpret."

That sounded like a grand idea, and I told the president I would make the arrangements.

"Stay here as long as you wish, of course, Meriwether. We're having the usual New Year's Day open house, with many a fair lady in attendance, and I imagine half of Washington, eager to hear your stories. Have you seen the *National Intelligencer*? You will discover you are somewhere between canonization and sainthood."

I laughed, though I preferred not to.

That fine evening we loaded our savage king and queen into a carriage and made for the theater, and there before much of Washington and the diplomatic corps, we entertained the Mandans and Chouteau's Osages, who gaped and stared and giggled at the thespians, and then returned the favor by performing a frenzied pipe dance on stage, with ululating howls and horrifying screams, much to the shivering delight of the leading lights of Washington.

I sat there benignly: let them all be aware of the savage wilderness that I had penetrated, I thought. Let the howling savages, almost naked in their breechclouts, remind the civilized world where the Corps of Discovery had truly been. We had brought the menacing wilderness to Washington.

I spent the next hours preparing material to give to Benjamin Smith Barton and the American Philosophical Society in Philadelphia, my next port of call, where a banquet awaited me, and my work would be received and reviewed. That would be the crowning glory, and it would be mine alone, for I alone in the Corps of Discovery had been adequately prepared to reap the botanical and zoological harvest. I looked forward to it as keenly as I looked forward to counseling the president about Louisiana and all our western dominions.

New Year's Day, 1807, turned out to be my chance to meet the cream of Washington, who flocked in great numbers to the annual open house given by Mr. Jefferson. They came to examine my Mandans, to examine me, to discover what gaudy stories about grizzlies and savages and strange animals they could memorize to decorate their own conversations. I did not disappoint them. Most of Congress had already arrived, and I wanted to make myself available to answer their questions and at least implicitly, though it was a social occasion, to speak in behalf of my men and the awards they so richly deserved.

Ah, the women! Mr. Jefferson had mentioned them. I yearned for them. And here they all were, flocking about me with eyes aflutter. My dear cousin Maria Wood had not waited for her wandering admirer, but married. And so I had no one, but I supposed that a young man as favored by fortune as I would not find it difficult to pluck the sweetest fruit.

So it was that I found myself in the company of a fabulously eligible Miss Cecelia, daughter of a New England senator, enjoying those glowing brown eyes, alabaster cheeks, so lovely after my long years among dusky savages, and chestnut hair in ringlets.

I smiled, but not too openly, for fear of revealing the blue-tinted gums that Dr. Saugrain's courses of mercury had given me, gums that would tell all too much to the knowing eye. That was the sole remaining evidence of my former disposition, and I hoped that the blue gums would soon vanish, just as the illness had.

"Would you favor me with an account of your trip?" she asked, over a crystal glass of Mr. Jefferson's silky red Burgundy.

"I would be honored," I replied, fending off a dozen others who wished also to glean whatever pearls of wisdom dropped from the lips of the explorer. There was but little privacy, but I steered her to a corner of that familiar manse, where I had been the president's aide for so many months, and there told her of my adventures, the great white bears, as we first called the grizzlies, the savages, the treacherous river, the dizzying mountains, now a litany so well rehearsed that it spilled easily from my tongue.

"And now I have it all in the journals and must prepare them for publication," I said. "The advancement of science and the fate of nations depends on it."

"Do you like my frock? I got it just for the occasion."

"Your gown?" I gazed at a lemon yellow silk affair, with ruffles of white lace, which sheathed a perfect young form.

"Yes, for Mr. Jefferson's open house. Father didn't approve, you know. He's a Federalist, and saw no reason to spend so many shillings on a dress to wear for an odd republican president who wanders about in his bedroom slippers."

"I see. A nice dress."

I spotted Mr. Dearborn, the secretary of war, and thought I might profitably spend a while with him. I had numerous accounts to settle, and meeting him in these auspicious beginnings of a new year might prove useful, not only to me but to my corps.

"Forgive me, Miss Cecelia, but I must say a word to Secretary Dearborn," I said.

She curtsied and turned to explore the party for other amusements, and I retreated, a little melancholic, for as usual, I had my troubles with women. I am a serious man, and have no stomach for twitter. Still, she had enchanted me with a form that had been turned on the lathe by a master, and I reflected bitterly on my endless bachelorhood, and my frustrated plans to warm my domestic hearth.

But there would be others. I, of all men on earth, had my pick.

8. CLARK

I suppose I should thank the harsh weather for my betrothal. It kept us bound to the hearth. Give me a better clime, and I would be outside, as is my wont. I would have gotten us a picnic lunch in a hamper from the mammy and some saddle horses from the grooms and headed for the nearest green bower where I might woo that bundle of joy while slapping mosquitoes and fending off red ants.

But Julia is distracted by insects, and my ardor might well have been defeated by crawling bugs on her limbs, wasps, hornets, black horseflies, green-bellied flies, bumblebees, inchworms, caterpillars, and the whine of bloodthirsty mosquitoes for whom flesh is food and blood is drink.

So I ascribe the weather to my successful assault upon the citadel of my desire. The Hancocks left us to our own devices in a stove-warmed parlor, but there were servants hovering about, not always out of earshot, and plainly at hand to protect Julia's virtue. I take some pleasure in the discovery that she didn't entirely relish being protected, or being virtuous, for that matter. For her gaze began to swim when she surveyed me, and I saw the blush rise to her smooth cheeks, and I knew the train of her innermost thoughts.

We were not entirely decorous, for the mistletoe hung from the chandelier, a dangling invitation perhaps the sly work of old George Hancock himself, who was scarce a decade older than I and knew well the ferment of the loins. I steered Julia under it whenever the occasion permitted, and thus discovered that she was as enthused by its magical powers as I, and for a few moments, at any rate, I wrapped that bundle in my arms and blunderbussed her, or that is the word I chose for it, being an inept man with women.

The colonel accepted my assault upon his daughter well enough; he even set aside his ardent Federalist passions to be hospitable to me. And trouble him as it might, he found the means to praise Mr. Jefferson for sending me out into the unknown.

"Cost too much, though," he said. "An engaging folly, this scheme, but you got back in one piece and I suppose the government can afford a little nonsense."

I smiled benignly. If my future father-in-law could summon a compliment for Mr. Jefferson, the courtship would not go badly. He was a great oddity in Virginia. The bastion of the Federalists was New England, and rare was the Virginian who would make common cause with the Adams family, or the late Hamilton.

"What are the western lands like?" she asked me one day, as we sipped mulled cider before the hearth.

"The air's so clear you can't imagine it, and the prairies run off to the horizon, and you can see a hundred miles, and see the future. It's a place so big it doesn't know you're walking over it."

She shuddered, and touched me. I thought to make her shudder more, and touch me more.

"Most of the savages are friendly sorts, but there's some with a look in their eye that's like a tomahawk blade, and it's pretty easy to see what's boiling inside their skulls. The proud mean ones maybe keep quiet because the chiefs make 'em, but you know what's itching them, and what they want to do."

"I don't think I would care for that!" she said, this time shuddering right up tight, and drawing her fingers over my sleeve.

I thought maybe I could shudder her into just the right mood, and get the assault over with.

"And if it isn't the savages, it's the big brown bears, so big they tower up on their hind legs and stare down at you from the treetops, almost, with their little pig eyes, and claws as long as kitchen knives, thinking how they maybe will claw you to pieces and have you for supper because you stumbled into their lair."

"Oh!" she exclaimed, this time wrapping a fastidious arm around my neck. "I hope we never go there!"

I realized the moment had come, and cleared my throat.

"Miss Julia . . . you would find Kentucky much to your liking."

"Captain Clark, I am not sure I would care for Kentucky, with all its savages."

"They're just as subdued as all the servants here, and you needn't worry about them."

She laughed.

"I am a tad older than you, but you will find that much to your advantage," I said.

"Why?"

"You will know later." That was all I could manage. "Now, it is my design to lay the proposition before your father, if you are so inclined."

She pouted a little, and I realized I had not made any declaration. Somehow I found the matter most difficult, and while I normally am plainspoken and forward, this time I was tongue-tied and flummoxed.

"Ah, my little Julia, I have had you in my mind all these years."

She frowned. "Well, I never knew it. After all, you are being presumptuous." She sipped the steaming mulled cider and eyed me levelly, being far better at the game than I. I thought hotly that I would abandon this place and head for

Vashington. I would be too late for Christmas but my re-
eption there would be warmer than the chilly one here.

Then she laughed.

"Ah, Julia, the truth is, I have had naught but the vision
f you in my bosom all this while; it was upon me at the
ery shore of the western sea. I am not a young man, being
nore than twice your years, and yet in all my days I never
vas drawn to any but you, and so I declare myself."

It was awkward, but my plain tongue had deserted me.

"I have not heard the word," she said.

"Ah, ah, it is you I love."

She smiled, and touched me again, with such gentleness
hat I turned to wax. "I should rather like an older man,"
he said, and I kissed her, servants be damned.

So it was, that Yuletide, that I formed my alliance, but
irst I had to take the case to her father. Since my purposes
vere known from the beginning, I didn't surprise him, and
no doubt had helped that the Clarks and Hancocks were
vell intertwined over several generations.

The colonel received me in those office chambers from
vhich he counted his tobacco receipts and totted up the
osts of the plantation. I supposed that this was a transac-
ion like any other. He received me the afternoon of Christ-
nas Eve, his square ruddy face surveying me with a sardonic
ilence. He wore his dark hair in a queue, a sign of his Fed-
ralist leanings.

"Sir, I should like Julia's hand," I said.

He smiled thinly. "And she approves?" he asked, in that
hick, hoarse voice that suggested too intimate experience
vith the fine-leaved product of his fields.

"You might ask her," I replied cheerfully.

He gazed out upon the barren fields, half exhausted be-
ause tobacco depleted the soil. "And your age is no impedi-
nent to her?"

I shook my head. "She rather prefers a man to a boy."

"It's an impediment to me. She's barely upon her wom anhood."

"My mother married at fifteen."

He nodded. "She has grown up in pleasant surroundings, he said. "Can you assure me that it will be so in the future?

"I am expecting considerable back pay and a land gra of some size."

"In Kentucky."

"Yes, federal lands in the west."

He opened the snuffbox and inhaled a pinch, wheezin a moment. "I never imagined she would end up with one c Jefferson's radicals," he said. "I don't suppose you'll b heading for France to lop off the heads of a few noblemen– and women."

I laughed. "I believe simply in an aristocracy of meri not heredity."

"And not in the leadership of good families?"

"Good men, yes, that is close to my republican principle sir. Let them elect good men."

"There are no impediments? Your health is good?"

"Excellent, sir. I know of no impediments at all."

"A soldier's life is hard." There was a question in his ob servation.

"I am no longer a soldier. I resigned my commission, an for good. I have no disability."

He grunted, his brown eyes glowing brightly. "Your ir tentions have been plain, Will, and that has given me tim to ponder the matter, and discuss it as well with my wife. W are close, our families, and I am pleased by the connectio but we think it would be desirable to wait a year. She is b half a woman still, at least to us, and knows you little enoug If you should agree to that, and would postpone until Januar of eighteen and eight, we would welcome you most hearti into our family, and into our bosoms." He smiled. "Even if your politics are impossible."

We laughed. I shall always remember the moment, Colonel Hancock wheezing his delight; rising up and clapping me on the back, and leading me back into the great house to inform the mistress, and receive her congratulations, and then to the parlor where Miss Julia sat doing crewelwork for the seat of a dining chair.

She peered up at her parents and at me, and set aside her yarns.

"It is a very special Christmas, Julia," her father said. "Happy for us, happy for the Clarks, happy for you, I trust."

Julia smiled, uncertainly.

"If you can manage to wait a year, settle into womanhood a while, make sure of your heart, then you have our blessings to marry this big redheaded son of our kin John Clark."

Julia cried, and I took her hand and lifted her up from her chair, and we had the most sweet and sacred of Christmases.

9. LEWIS

The deplorable sergeant Patrick Gass is forcing my hand. He has announced the forthcoming publication of his journal, even though I have expressly forbidden it. I gave permission only to Private Frazier to publish his account, but Gass has proceeded anyway, much to my annoyance.

These are unlettered men, not versed in any branch of arts or science, and likely to spread a great deal of misinformation. They have the advantage of me, hastening their small journals into print while I labor at larger tasks, not least of which has been securing the back pay of all the men in the corps, including Sergeant Gass.

This Thursday morning, the twelfth of March, 1807, I stormed into the president's office with the Gass prospectus in hand, and insisted that something be done to stop it. Gass would ruin everything.

Mr. Jefferson eyed me through those gold-rimmed spectacles of his. "It's not among my principles to stop publication of anything," he said quietly, after studying the publisher's brochure. He stared out upon the lawn. "But I do think it's going to be damaging to us. I'd suggest a warning to the public that it and any other diaries are not authorized by you, the commander, and also that they are likely to be unreliable." He smiled at me. "You wouldn't be fretting about your profit, would you?"

"Certainly not, sir. I want only for the truth to reach the public."

Jefferson laughed, which irritated me. Why couldn't the man be serious? I am not after the money; I'm concerned with the *truth,* and worried that half those note-takers among my corps will publish undisciplined, uneducated versions of events and permanently twist what Will and I so assiduously recorded.

But even the president thinks I want the bootleg journals suppressed so that I can make an additional dollar. I flatter myself that my conduct is grounded upon the highest motives of patriotism and truth, and that such base motives as private gain have no hold upon me.

We agreed that I would write the letter and he would vet it, and maybe put a stop to this bootleg publication of journals. And by afternoon that was accomplished. I wrote the *National Intelligencer* condemning these spurious publications by persons unknown to me, and cautioning readers to beware and to hold out for the true goods, the first of which I would bring out by year's end. I mentioned as well that I had authorized the publication only of Frazier's journals, but took pains to point out that the man is only a private, unlettered, unacquainted with science, and that his work must not be taken seriously. I sent it off today, and expect it to run tomorrow.

I cannot stop these pirate editions, in part because I have resigned my commission in the army and have accepted Mr. Jefferson's appointment of me as the governor of Upper Louisiana, which was affirmed by the Senate March 2. I suppose I shall have to bear the burden of these inferior tracts. Will and I ordered the sergeants to keep journals; the more of them, the safer the record of discovery. Some of them merely copied what we had written. And now these unlettered men want to cash in, and their greed disgusts me.

I face the complex task of reducing the official journals to a coherent narrative, excising those entries not intended for the public eye, and organizing the scientific discoveries, and producing the maps we completed, and not until then will the public receive an accurate and sound depiction of all that we experienced.

Gass's brochure has put me into a funk from which I will not recover for some while. What makes it all the worse is that from the dawn of this year, Mr. Jefferson and I have been doing our utmost to extract from the public purse worthy rewards for my Corps of Discovery. We proposed to Mr. Alston of North Carolina, who chairs a special committee of the House to see into our compensation, that all my men, including those who returned from Fort Mandan with the keelboat, be given double pay and a land grant of three hundred twenty acres. And that Will Clark receive a compensation equal to my own, a recognition he richly deserves.

Alas, the War Department, in the annoying person of Mr. Dearborn, recommended less for Will Clark, a thousand acres for him as opposed to sixteen hundred for me, and a lieutenant's pay for him, and a captain's for me. But the president and I got Alston's ear, and the chairman was able to even things out somewhat: Will and I each will get sixteen hundred acres.

The president submitted my appointment as governor of the Upper Louisiana territory, and also asked Congress to raise Will Clark to a lieutenant colonel, but again the secretary of war managed to foil Mr. Jefferson, and Congress eventually agreed with him, it being the wish of the members to abide by seniority and not jump Clark over the heads of other deserving men. But I was heartened by the news that they would gladly confirm Clark in any other office within their power, and thus, at the president's behest, he will be our superintendent of Indian Affairs in St. Louis, and a brigadier of militia.

All this business consumed my days and nights this winter. It took a month of heated debate before the representatives passed even a scaled-down version of what I had asked for my doughty corps, but at least the Senate nodded it through in a trice, and I am gratified that my courageous men will benefit from a grateful republic.

Meanwhile I am the cynosure at one banquet after another. It seems all of Washington must have me at its table. The city welcomed me with a great affair January 14, in which I was the honored guest, along with Chouteau and Big White. I vaguely remember seventeen toasts. (*Vaguely* is the exact word for it.) It was at that time that Joel Barlow, powdered, periwigged, and bedizened in scarlet and periwinkle silks, first intoned his new ode, "On the Discoveries of Lewis," and I was greatly smitten by some of the bard's orotund verses:

With the same soaring genius thy Lewis descends,
And, seizing the oars of the sun,
O'er the sky-propping hills and the high waters he
bends
And gives the proud earth a new zone . . .

Then hear the loud voice of the Nation proclaim,
And all ages resound the decree:
Let our Occident stream bear the young hero's name
Who taught him his path to the sea.

I fancied teaching the Columbia which way to go. And I wondered what Big White thought of all that.

There have been balls to attend, and the social life is heady. I am finding feminine company abounding, and little doubt that I shall make a proper match. I require a serious woman to match my own seriousness, and that is no simple matter, especially in Washington. There seem plenty of the fair sex making themselves pleasant to me, but I have no stomach for the twittering things.

In January Will Clark wrote me that his assault upon the fair citadel of Fincastle pulchritude was successful, and that he would capture his prize in January of next year. I rejoiced at his success, and have regretted being so busy with the President and Congress that I scarcely have found a moment to pursue the lovely and fragile beauty that appears at every prospect.

I expect him momentarily. He will head for St. Louis at once, with Private Frazier, bearing back pay for my men. He will also take our Mandan royalty, She-He-Ke, and his entourage, back to St. Louis and begin the preparations to take the chief upriver, past the hostile Arikaras, which will be a delicate business but one Will Clark can well manage.

I am glad he has delayed his journey to the capital because the President's House has been a hospital for several days. First Tom Randolph caught the catarrh; then I, and finally Mr. Jefferson. I bled the president's son-in-law considerably, and he recovers slowly.

Doctor Saugrain in St. Louis opposes bleeding, saying it weakens the patient, but he is isolated. I prefer the counsel of the eminent Benjamin Rush of Philadelphia, the finest of all physicians this side of the Atlantic, who instructed me in medical matters before I headed west. He, of course, believes with all progressive physicians that it is necessary to purge the blood of whatever bad humors evoke the disease and the way to do it is to drain away the tainted blood and let the body generate healthier blood.

As for me, I examined myself with some concern upon taking sick, studying my mouth, my gums, my eyes, my skin, and found nothing amiss but a bilious fever, and for that I had Rush's excellent Thunderclappers, specially compounded to abate fevers, which I took to good effect, and upon this very day I am back to my usual bloom of health and so is Mr. Jefferson, though Randolph lingers abed. I make no public or private mention of Saugrain; it is as if I have never met the man, though of course I am privately grateful to him.

I expect to wind up my business here by the end of the month and head for Philadelphia, where I will join the savants of the American Philosophical Society, and negotiate with a printer to begin work on the journals. Mr. Jefferson has been conversing with me about Upper Louisiana. We will need to pacify the tribes on the Missouri, arrange free passage of our traders, license them to deal with the tribes, keep the British out, and encourage settlement sufficient to anchor that vast territory firmly to the union of states.

Ah, Philadelphia! My pleasure in presenting the most

learned men of America a bounty of new plants and animals, all carefully observed and recorded, along with accurate maps, and a firsthand account of the passage through that great mystery, the interior of North America, will, I imagine, be unparalleled and perhaps will exceed even my pleasure in reporting to Mr. Jefferson that I had fulfilled his mission in all respects.

I expect to be in Philadelphia some little while preparing the journals and discovering just what the printer needs. I am in no hurry to head for St. Louis; not with Will Clark on hand to handle our Indian diplomacy, and not with an old acquaintance, the experienced public servant Frederick Bates, brother of my old friend Tarleton Bates, heading there to be secretary, my lieutenant. I rather expect the two of them will govern excellently while I see to the maps and papers, and to that sacred duty to transmit what I have learned of the world to these men of science.

I reflect, when I am alone in my room in the President's House, how fortune has smiled upon me. It was not long ago, writing on the occasion of my thirty-first birthday in the Bitterroot Mountains—just after that moment of weakness—that I wondered whether I had given the world anything worthwhile or done anything notable during my life. Now I know I have.

But I have no desire to dwell upon memories; the future beckons. I am torn between my wish to become a man of science and a man of public affairs, and I will have to resolve the matter eventually. I am in a rare position to choose my course in life. For the moment I must set science aside and focus on the western reaches of the republic, and if I am blessed in this endeavor, perhaps I will be invited to fill larger offices, perhaps even the office held by the resident of this very house.

My public purpose, then, is to draft a paper informing

Mr. Jefferson and his successors what lies to the west, an
how to subdue it, and how to encourage commerce in it
and how to treat the tribes that live upon it. I will make it
first order of business to provide the government with my
insights, and if my perceptions find favor, so will I.

I should like to be regarded as the new Sage of the West
publish my thoughts regularly in some news sheet, and stan
up and be counted. If all that occurs as I hope, then some
day my confreres in the Democratic-Republican rank
might find me worthy of higher office. And I would accep
it gladly.

I have come into myself; for this was I set upon the earth
That vast Louisiana territory is mine; etched indelibly o
my mind, though the world knows little of it, and won't un
til I publish my journals. How odd it is, during these reflec
tive moments, that I sometimes find myself reluctant t
share all that wealth of information with the public. I hav
little desire to publish. I would rather confide my secrets pri
vately to men like Benjamin Smith Barton, of the philo
sophical society, than cast my pearls before the swine.

The Missouri country is a comely land, well watered
hilly, forested, verdant, and fertile, and I will make it my
home. I am especially fond of it because it windows th
world that I recently conquered. I see myself rooted i
the West, settled upon a great green estate, my happy brid
beside me, our children blooming. I should like to settle ou
there in the virgin land, my eyes upon the horizons. I shoul
like to be a country squire, rather like Tom Jefferson, holdin
office, improving knowledge, and devising better ways t
prosper. Every door is open.

10. LEWIS

I arrived in the City of Brotherly Love on April 10, and after settling into a room on Cherry Street rented by a Mrs. Wood, I began at once to tackle the business before me. The chestnuts were in new leaf and so was I, so happy was I to be there in that seat of learning.

I have been paid by Congress at last and am in comfortable circumstances, and can indulge my every whim if I choose. But I am a serious man, and do not indulge myself. I did, however, lay in a stock of porter, ale, and Madeira, with which to entertain guests at my lodging.

Those journals weigh heavily on my mind, along with the hundreds of specimens and drawings and pressings of plants that I have with me; not only what I had brought from the Pacific, but much that the president had kept for me, sent to him from Mandan villages in 1805.

Upon good recommendation, I chose John Conrad as my publisher and found him at his chambers at 30 Chestnut Street. I liked the man at once; a dusty, gray, scholarly gent who took his tasks seriously. His seriousness recommended him to me.

I had taken but one of the journals, and this I showed to him after we had exchanged greetings.

"I have in mind the publication of the journals in one volume, and the scientific findings, maps, and so forth, in another," I said.

He pulled on his wire-rimmed spectacles and examined what I regarded as my treasure; the daily records, mostly done by Clark, that supplied a day-by-day progress of our journey.

"Ah, I see the captain was a little loose with his spelling," Conrad said, "but that is easily remedied. I suppose you mean to condense these items, and perhaps improve them?"

"Yes . . ."

"I would recommend it. Now, what about the illustrations?"

"Well, I know little about publishing, Mr. Conrad, and perhaps you can advise me."

"What have you?"

"Field notes, including drawings; pressed plants; some feathers, pelts, bones, seeds . . . and of course the maps. Clark has some gifts, and he put them to good use. The maps are most important to all, I suppose."

"We can have them copied and I can make a plate. The drawings, Captain, are up to you. It is your project. Bring us an edited version of your journals—I'm sure a man of your experience can reduce them quite nicely. You'll need to prepare the drawings, maps, all of it, just as you wish us to produce your books."

"Have you good artists here?"

"You have come to the very place," Conrad said.

"We are in a great hurry," I said. "Mr. Jefferson is fairly demanding publication as soon as it can be arranged."

Conrad smiled for the first time. "We are honored to attend to such a project, Captain, and I assure you of our utmost cooperation. You need not complete the work before submitting it to us; in fact, the sooner you begin submitting your material, the better; I will have typesetters upon it instantly."

"Up to me, then."

"Yes, it is, sir."

"I suppose we should discuss costs."

I gave him the particulars, and he told me he would get back to me as soon as he could do the calculations.

I lost no time in contacting my old friend Doctor Benjamin Rush, from whom I had outfitted the expedition with a fine closet of medicines. He was a member of the American Philosophical Society, a signer of the Declaration of Independence, and most important for me, the nation's preeminent physician. He had charged me to make certain medical observations of the savages during the trip: time of puberty, the menses, condition of teeth and eyes, diseases of old age, and the like, and now, with utmost joy, I had the answers for him. Eagerly did I make for his home on Chestnut Street.

"Ah! The conquering captain!" the jowly old man exclaimed upon descrying my ingress into his musty brown library in the wake of a pale servant. We shook hands warmly, and the doctor promptly ordered a glass of port apiece so we might progress through our business in ample humor. "Tell me, tell me. Everything!"

"Ah, it is a joy to be back, and the pills, sir, Rush's pills, so prevailed over all manner of dispositions that I count them a universal salvation. The men, sir, called them Thunderclappers, and indeed, Doctor, they were the sovereign of all maladies. I only wish I had more with me, but I ran out of everything."

The Thunderclappers were mighty doses of calomel, which consisted of six parts of mercury to one part of chlorine, and the Mexican cathartic jalap, the pair of them a purgative that brooked no argument from any mortal bowels. I dispensed them freely, not only for bowel troubles, but as a general cathartic to purge the blood and intestine.

"I received constant petitions from them; buffalo meat especially bound them up, and I was able to end their distress with great success!"

Rush laughed. "And did you collect answers to my questions?"

"I did, sir. The customs and practices varied so much from tribe to tribe that I can scarcely recount them now, but I plan to include my entire observations in a final volume. I've engaged Conrad to do the journals, and am already at work."

Rush listened to my practiced tales of grizzly bears, the great falls of the Missouri, the sicknesses of the men, and all the rest, nodding as I spoke.

"I shall arrange a banquet directly," he said. "There are men in the society aching to hear what you have accomplished, and aching, my young friend, to pay you appropriate tribute."

Again I was awash in pleasure, and our visit proceeded with utmost joy. I could see, after the better part of an afternoon, that the grand old man was tiring, so I made haste to wind up my discourse. But one matter stayed me.

"Before I take my leave, sir, I have a matter of medicine to discuss, a delicate matter. It involves my corps, sir. Many are in St. Louis, still soldiers. During the expedition they came into intimate contact with various dusky women of the tribes, and to put matters plainly, contracted various maladies which I endeavored to heal by liberal application of mercury ointment and calomel."

"What diseases, Captain?"

"Why, they are ordinary soldiers, sir, and as one might expect they took little care. The tribes are oddly wanton and at the same time strict; a husband might offer a guest the favors of his wife, and yet if the wife engaged in such conduct on her own account, she might be severely chastised or beaten."

"Yes, yes?"

"Well, sir, I applied your remedies for what they vulgarly called 'the clap,' and of course for *lues venerea,* which many of them caught, and then caught again and again. Now, upon returning to St. Louis I contracted for their care with a French physician, a most estimable man, but of course he's isolated from the advances of science.

"I'll be returning to St. Louis soon, and thought to ask you whether there might be new remedies opened to science, known to you but not known to a physician so isolated. I have always looked after my men, sir, and continue to take their part even after the corps has been disbanded."

"Something for the men of the corps, you say?" There was a question in Rush's eyes.

"Yes, sir. For them. The captains, of course, were above such things—at least I have every right to believe that Captain Clark stayed carefully aloof. He brims with health."

Rush nodded. "Mercury is all we have," he said. "But in many cases the disease simply vanishes. Mercury in steady courses usually inhibits the disorder. Salts of arsenic or bismuth are sometimes employed, but they are dangerous and without proven effect."

"Then the St. Louis physician, Doctor Saugrain, has followed the right course?"

"I imagine," Rush said tersely.

"I am comforted that all is being done that can be. Some of them, Private Gibson especially, are sick."

I left with a new supply of Rush's Thunderclappers, and turned to other business.

But awaiting me at Mrs. Wood's boardinghouse was an issue of the *National Intelligencer* that had been forwarded to me by Mr. Jefferson himself. I made haste to discover what within its columns had occasioned the delivery to me, and found a letter from one McKeehan, of Pittsburgh, Sergeant Gass's publisher, slandering me in every sentence; declaring that my real purpose in suppressing the publication of other journals was my own profit; and much more of that bilious sort of thing. He even took the liberty of recording my very thoughts, or so he imagined!

"I'll squeeze the nation first, and then raise a heavy contribution on the citizens individually; I'll cry down those one-volume journals and frighten publishers and no man, woman or child shall read a word about *my* tour unless they enter their names on *my* lists, and pay what price I shall afterwards fix on my three volumes and map."

I was enraged, and for a while thought to challenge the man on the field of honor. My motives are as lofty as I can manage them, and I wish to produce a sound, educated, and thoroughly accurate account of the voyage of discovery, including every plant and animal we revealed to mankind, and every feature of the land we traversed. Profit doesn't even enter into it.

But the more I thought on it, the more I decided to forgo the satisfaction of honor. I contain, within my mind, a vast body of knowledge, which I alone possess, which my field notes only hint of, and not even Will Clark can imagine. The possibility that a ball from a dueling pistol might forever darken my mind, and deprive the world of the greatest body of information since the discoveries of Columbus, stayed me from that course. In the end I chose to ignore the scurrilous assault on my integrity, and proceed.

I returned to my printer, Conrad, who supplied me with an estimate: four thousand five hundred dollars to publish the journals and the scientific material and maps, and the supplement dealing with Indian glossaries and ethnographic observations. That was far more than I could afford, but Conrad had worked out some costs, and recommended that we offer subscriptions to the complete set, three volumes, published octavo, running four or five hundred pages each; the price to be thirty-one dollars. I agreed.

Worse, the entire burden of preparing drawings, engravings, the map, reducing the astronomy observations to longitude, and finally the editing, would be borne by William Clark and me, and was not included in Conrad's services. I feared we would go heavily into debt, and Will Clark would be worse off because he had been paid less.

I hired a promotions man and commenced work on a prospectus advertising "Lewis and Clark's Tour to the Pacific Ocean Through the Interior of the Continent of North America," and soon placed it in the *National Intelligencer,* where it occasioned much interest.

11. LEWIS

I must head back to Washington to settle the accounts. The clerks keep pestering me to provide receipts for the drafts levied on the treasury; I keep telling them that they traveled all the way across a wilderness to the Pacific and back, and some got lost. But that doesn't seem to faze officials: they want paper, or else to lay the bills upon me. I am growing testy about it.

I did not suppose I would ever weary of Philadelphia, the most civilized precinct of North America, and yet I am, and want to retreat to Locust Hill and begin work on my papers. They banqueted and toasted me here through the spring and summer, so much that my head would be turned by it all were it not for the steadiness of purpose and good character instilled in me by my mother.

I've attended three meetings of the American Philosophical Society, and in each case was besieged by members wanting to know about the West. I am flattered by such attention, and have promised them numerous notes and papers. In May I visited the eminent Benjamin Smith Barton, head of the society, and returned to him a book about Louisiana I had carried all the way to the western sea and back. He was most delighted.

Nor was that the least of it. Charles Willson Peale, the eminent painter, sculptor, and museum director, has sketched me and done a facial mask. The sketch will become an oil portrait, and the mask a waxworks image of me. C. B. J. Fevret de Saint-Menim, the French artist, has done a fine likeness of me in native attire, especially the ermine coat given me by Cameahwaite. Here am I, at age thirty-three, greatly celebrated by savants and artists and poets. Peale's museum will be the repository of many of my artifacts. I have employed him as well to illustrate the journals with drawings of the animals we discovered.

I hired a fine German botanist named Frederick Pursh to plant my seeds, illustrate my books with renderings of my fieldwork, and classify my discoveries, so I have that aspect of publication well in hand. He was commended to me by a local nurseryman and botanist named McMahon, who has tenderly cultivated numerous of the Western species I managed to bring back, though so many were lost in the cache at the Great Falls of the Missouri that I am able to offer only a modest improvement in the knowledge of North American botany.

I hired the engraver James Barralet to portray the falls of the Missouri and Columbia, and employed Alexander Wilson to portray the birds. And for a hundred dollars I hired the Swiss mathematician Ferdinand Hassler to reduce my field observations to accurate longitude. Will and I had agreed to split the cost of preparing the journals but now I find myself suffering a want of funds, having laid out so much, so fast, to launch our journals.

So I have been very busy, but not so much that I could not enjoy many a night out with my old friend Mahlon Dickerson, a lawyer of great distinction and as much a man about town as a rural Virginian like me would want to know. He lightens my serious disposition, bantering about frivolous things, which I accept because he is at heart as serious as I am, and not given to triviality, which is the perdition of many a life. We have made a fine bachelor pair, roaming this venerable city, meeting the ladies at various levees, balls, musicales, and lectures, and sometimes escaping town to test our firearms against assorted stumps and toads.

It was upon one of those social evenings that I encountered the dazzling Elizabeth Burden, a young lady of such grace and fair beauty that I was instantly entranced. There she stood, in a green cotton frock, its waist gathered just under her bosom, with puffed sleeves, all of it summery and cool. I had no difficulty arranging an introduction: that occurred following an ethnology lecture at Carpenters Hall. She was in the company of her eminent father, a widowed ancient history professor at the university, and I sensed at once that here at last was the woman who combined the magnificence of form I cherished with the accomplishments that I considered absolutely essential.

I was particularly glad I had finally completed my new wardrobe. I had nothing to wear after returning from the West, and Washington was scarcely the place for a gentleman to be outfitted. So within a day of my arrival in the Quaker City, I engaged some tailors and put them to work. I certainly wanted appropriate clothing for my new and prominent life, and took pleasure in looking my finest.

This Wednesday evening, July 22, 1807, I was splendidly accoutered in cream silk knee-britches, a royal blue coat with brass buttons, white cotton stock, and a fine black bicorne, though it was perhaps too hot for such attire. I kept my coat open so that I might not sweat too much at the armpits.

I invited the Burdens to a nearby tavern and they gladly accepted, eager to meet the explorer. I used my status shamelessly, and why not? What better entrée into the lives of strangers? I bought a round of Madeira and cheese and other sundries for the gentlemen, while Professor Burden ordered lemonade with pond ice for his daughter, and I got down to the business of exploring this fair lady as if she were an unknown continent, whose rivers I was gradually ascending to their source.

"Ah, what beauteous company we share this evening. Tell me, Miss Elizabeth, about your accomplishments, quite apart from being the cynosure of all eyes."

She eyed me levelly, and I wondered whether it had been the wrong approach.

"I mean, you are here attending a lecture on Ohio River tribal ethnology."

She smiled at last, and like a sunburst. "It was my father's wish."

"I imagine you profited from it."

"I imagine," she said.

"You have been reared among books. Have you a library?"

"Governor, my particular joy lies in keeping a good house for my father, so that he may pursue his vocation. I bring him a tea tray every afternoon at four. I have a good hand. Sometimes he permits me to copy things he needs, or to prepare a draft he will be sending to a printer."

"Oh? A copyist you say, familiar with unusual terms and all?"

"We have Doctor Johnson's dictionary. It doesn't always suffice."

I began to grow excited. A copyist! And I, with an enormous project looming over me. Not just a copyist, but one who could correct errors and spellings and put things right.

"I think you perform a most valuable labor," I said, and turned to the florid-faced professor, who wore his gray hair in a long queue. "You have a great asset, sir, in this fair maid."

"I've never thought of her as an asset, Governor." There was a certain asperity in his tone, and I retreated.

"A helpmeet, then. A daughter who is there, upon your service, doing all that is required to advance knowledge and scholarship."

He smiled. "I am the beneficiary, that is true, but I worry about my Elizabeth and her future. She is twenty-three."

Ah, I thought, the fine old gentleman is playing Cupid. He's aware of what a match I would make, and what I can offer a woman. Twenty-three is older than the usual nuptial age, and she had been withering on the vine, and that only improved my chances.

Once I had properly inventoried her charms, I began at once to spin stories of my adventures.

"Mahlon has heard all these, but I always have some additional thing to tell about, and so he'll just have to listen," I said.

She smiled at Dickerson, and I began anew to relive those crucial moments in my existence when I was walking across a wilderness populated by unruly savages, dangerous beasts, hunger and cold and sickness . . . Thus I entranced her for the evening, and managed to meet several more times, always during the bright June afternoons, to take tea in the company of her aunt.

I thought surely she would succumb, but then one afternoon she declined my attentions, saying she had a headache, and after that it became more and more taxing to see her, though I found out what lectures her father was attending and sometimes caught a bright glimpse of her in those moments. She was always the soul of courtesy, but I knew that she had rejected my suit. Ah, this business of being a perpetual bachelor is woeful at times, though of course I cherish the liberty it affords me.

I knew that once again, domestic joy had eluded me, though I could not quite see how I had failed or what I had said that turned her away. St. Louis, probably. A woman so civilized and accomplished might not relish life in a raw town west of the Alleghenies. I could not find anything to fault in my own conduct, save perhaps that quality of which I am most proud, that I am a serious man and take life as a matter of much gravity.

I made light of it to my boon companion, Dickerson, and made ready to return to Washington to deal with those pesky accountants who could not grasp why I did not have duplicate or triplicate copies of every draft upon the treasury I signed during my preparation and after the corps had returned.

During this whole period I had not penned a word for Conrad. He was impatient, beseeching me to send him material so he could begin the great project, but I did not feel like doing it, and wanted to do it in a proper manner, with quiet exactitude, and not in Mrs. Wood's rooming house in a strange city. Mr. Jefferson had been beseeching me as well, saying that the scientific world awaits my journals, and he pressed me so much to begin them that I began turning aside his letters. I had scarcely gotten accustomed to life in civilization, and now I am facing impossible demands. So I am off to Washington to settle accounts, and then Virginia.

It is terribly hot. Jefferson is at Monticello, where he prefers to while away the moist summers, and I will visit Locust Hill to say goodbye to my family, and see the president there.

We have business to discuss. The Aaron Burr conspiracy trial has started, and I know he wants to brief me. I know little about the ambitious former vice president's grand scheme, having been on my great journey, but it is affecting politics in Upper Louisiana, and I will be forced to deal with the clamors of ambitious men whom Burr had recruited to sever the western territories from the republic. And the president will want to know how the publication of my journals was progressing. I could heartily assure him that work was advancing on all fronts, and I would soon begin the editing.

The heat has been troubling me; the damp air, soggy post roads, rainy weather, enervating warmth that leaves me sticky and uncomfortable and yearning for the dry high plains. And I am not feeling very well. I had some chills and diagnosed the ague and began taking an extract of cinchona bark, but the biliousness does not go away.

12. CLARK

My return to St. Louis this April of 1807 was not nearly so arduous as the eastbound trip, because I employed gravity to good effect, taking my party on a sturdy flatboat down the Ohio River. It was painful to leave Julia behind, but I was buoyed by the knowledge that soon I would return to claim my bride. And meanwhile, I had urgent business to attend.

I was charged by Mr. Jefferson to pursue several matters with utmost vigor. First would be the difficult task of returning the Mandan chief, Big White, and his party to his home, no easy matter with the hostile Arikaras blocking the Missouri River, and the Sioux sullen and questionable.

Another would be to reorganize the militia. And that would cause turmoil because I would need to purge it of numerous officers who had conspired with Aaron Burr to separate the whole territory from the republic. As brigadier, I would have to rebuild the weakened militia and prepare it for whatever might come, including war with the British, who are behaving in a deliberately provocative manner.

And finally, I would as superintendent of Indian Affairs need to effect Mr. Jefferson's policy of pacification and trade, a most arduous undertaking that would mean repealing some of the licenses General Wilkinson, the former governor, had awarded to friends, and at the same time build up government-operated trading posts, what Mr. Jefferson calls "factories," where each tribe could obtain reliable goods and pay in furs, under the watchful eye of the government.

But en route for St. Louis, I made one last stop at Fincastle to see my beloved Julia. Ah, what an occasion that was, for I had no sooner won my beloved than I must leave her.

I think back now on a moment I will not soon forget, at table with the Hancocks, the colonel at the head, ruddy and square-faced; Julia's fluttering mother at the other, and various family and guests in between, including their future son-in-law. Julia sat beside me, slim and girlish and done up in bottle green velvet for the occasion, so handsome I could scarce stop my hands from straying.

I waited until the servants had cleared off the platters and lit some fresh beeswax candles, and a pause enveloped us. I had in my brown waistcoat a small packet wrapped in tissue, and this I removed and placed before me on the white linen.

"Julia," I said, "when I was late in Washington to get instructions from Mr. Jefferson, I made known to him our attachment and received his heartiest congratulations. The very next day, though he was sick abed, he sent me this. It is a presidential gift to you, upon our betrothal."

I opened that mysterious packet, which had become the cynosure of many a Hancock gaze, and withdrew from it some jewelry, including a necklace, two bracelets, earrings, and a ring, all fashioned from pearls and topaz, a gift so astonishing that I marveled at it.

"Oh, oh!" she exclaimed.

I handed them to her, and she fingered them lovingly while the family craned to see. Then I stood, and slid the necklace about her, taking some liberty, I imagine, as I swept her hair aside, and clasped the necklace. Then I slid the bracelets over her wrists, and tried the ring, which didn't fit.

"I am quite without words," Julia's mother breathed.

"A fine thing, a fine thing," the colonel muttered. "Topaz, is it? Pearls from the Orient. Mr. Jefferson has outdone himself."

That was quite a concession from so ardent a Federalist, and I smiled. I liked the gentleman despite the chasm between us, for I am and always will be an ardent Democratic-Republican, like my president.

I could see on Julia's face that she was transfixed, not only by the grand gift, but also by the occasion. Her bosom and wrists bore the gracious gift of a president upon them.

"Oh, Mr. Clark, my good sir, thank him for me, and thank you for these things. I shall write him myself to say it."

It pleased me that Julia could write.

Colonel Hancock addressed me. "General, your plans have changed. When last you visited us, it was my understanding that you would be settling in Kentucky or the

Indiana Territory not so far that we might not see Julia, yet here you are with a new agenda."

That was George Hancock's way of asking what had happened.

"Well, sir, Mr. Jefferson proposed first of all that I be made a lieutenant colonel of infantry as a reward for our voyage, but the War Department and Congress thought better of it, and Mr. Jefferson proposed these offices instead. I had some misgivings about the regular army anyway, but none at all about these new offices."

"But St. Louis?" Mrs. Hancock exclaimed. "Such a vile place, I hear!"

I chuckled. "Not as fine as Virginia or Louisville, but Julia will be at ease."

"But it's all French! And Catholic!"

I had found the French a rascally lot and didn't want to praise them, but neither did I wish to alarm my future in-laws about Julia's safety and happiness.

"They are much like the rest of us."

"It's a turbulent city, filled with schemers and cutthroats," Hancock said. "General Wilkinson let it happen! He was a part of the Burr conspiracy until he backed out. Everyone knows it! There isn't a tawdry scheme that General Wilkinson doesn't want a piece of so long as he sniffs a profit. Imagine a city seething with traitors, eager to saw off the territory and start a new nation, and there you'll be, general of militia, the sole armed commander representing Washington against all your fellow republicans and riffraff. I fear for your safety, sir."

I smiled. It wasn't long ago that every Federalist in sight was denouncing Mr. Jefferson for buying that worthless desert called Louisiana. "I imagine I can look to my own defense, Colonel. I managed to do so for eight thousand miles."

"It is a dangerous place, and I will worry about you both."

Julia's attention had followed this exchange closely. She knew little of politics, which is the way I wanted it. I addressed her: "You shall be the queen of the city, my lovely Julia, celebrated at every ball and levee, at home in the parlors of our friends."

Her eyes thanked me, and I saw Colonel Hancock subsiding. The man had heard all the stories bursting from St. Louis; that Aaron Burr had fled to Spanish Florida but was arrested in Alabama, and now was being brought to trial before Mr. Jefferson's cousin, Chief Justice John Marshall. And there was I, taking Julia into the maelstrom. No wonder George was concerned.

"Colonel," I said, "I was not born red-haired for nothing. If anyone in St. Louis, whether its French citizens of dubious loyalty or dissident Yankees, mounts a threat to me, or my government, or my president, you will see what a Clark can do."

That mollified him, and I knew there would be little further objection to taking Julia so far from home.

I started for the trace over the Alleghenies at once. On my parting Julia wet my coat with her tears.

"I will be back in a few months, my fair lady. Be patient, and plan the matrimonial day, and you will see me before the snow flies," I said, hugging her one last time, disciplining my heart and body and hands though I never felt less disciplined in all my years. I wondered how I could wait for so long. Then I mounted up, while York held the reins, and that was the last I saw of her.

I had sent my reliable Private Frazier ahead with an important burden: he was to circulate freely in St. Louis, gather intelligence for me and for Mr. Jefferson, and report to me in private, if need be at my brother's home in Clarksville, opposite Louisville. I stopped there, of course, to see my older brother General George Rogers Clark, who was gouty and taking too much whiskey to curb his pain. They were calling him things behind his back that I didn't like; assailing the character of a great hero of the revolution, a man reduced to poverty because the government wouldn't repay him for his drafts supporting the army.

We rode the river to Mulberry Hill, in the Indiana Territory, and all the while York grew more and more agitated. He had been annoying me ever since the expedition, sometimes turning sulky, sometimes defiant.

The request came as we approached Louisville, as I knew it would. He caught me in a private moment on the flatboat, at dusk, and put it directly to me:

"Mastuh, could you be letting me see my wife a little? Get me some papers saying I can be wid her?"

His wife was owned by some Kentucky friends of my brother, who used her on their tobacco plantation near Louisville.

"No, I need you."

"I was thinking I sure do miss my woman."

"York, I said no! You will come west with me."

"I could maybe work for hire and be wid her."

"No!" I roared, and his black face crumpled. It was common enough to lease a slave and collect the proceeds of the lease, but I wouldn't allow it. I would need him in St. Louis. I had a house to buy, an office to fill, an army to raise, Big White to care for and return up the river, all on an austere budget of fifteen hundred a year, and I couldn't afford to lose a manservant, not for a moment.

He stared at me in pain, but I could do nothing about it. Maybe someday I'd give him some papers and let him visit his woman for a while. Not now.

He mumbled his way aft, and stood beside the Mandans,

watching the darkly glimmering water slide by. Big White, Yellow Corn, and their son had come all this distance, absorbed the civilized wonders of the white men's world and even wore its clothing, and now were returning to their own savage society—if I could get them there.

13. CLARK

I took up quarters in the old Government House, a sorry place but it would do until I could find a home for Julia and me. It was also a military barracks, which proved to be handy for a new brigadier of militia.

Even before paying a social call on the leading lights of St. Louis, I summoned Private Frazier, my shrewd old friend from the expedition, who had been working assiduously to find out what he could about the Burr plot. It turned out he had found plenty:

"Ah, Captain, it's a pleasure to see you, sir. I guess I should call you 'general' now, eh? A general you are, and please forgive me."

I laughed. "Whatever rank suits you, my friend," I said, clasping his hand. "Now, tell me what you've found."

What he had found was that the Louisiana militia had been riddled with minor officers ready to act on Burr's behalf, merely waiting for the word that never came but might still. Traitors to the republic, the whole lot, self-aggrandizing wretches.

"I got a list, Captain. Me, I just sat in a grog shop and palavered like a Burr man, and next I knew, I had me a wee little list."

He handed me a list of militia officers, ranging from sergeants to lieutenants and one captain.

"Is that most of the militia?"

He laughed. "What militia? It's a paper army. These are border men, Captain, and not happy about being called to serve, not now, not ever, unless six thousand cutthroat redskins are descending on them. But yes, I reckon it's most of the sunshine officers. I mean them that won't show up if it rains."

I nodded. It was an old refrain. My brother George Rogers Clark had welded an effective militia and staved off the British with it, but only with harsh measures combined with generous rewards. He had shot deserters.

"What about the French?"

"Don't rely on a one of 'em. Sure, there's some loyal French, they fancy the Yank republic, but they were here before we set eyes on Louisiana, and they just want to be left alone."

"Burrists?"

"A few, them that think maybe they'll do better in the purse under Spain or even England."

"English involved?"

"With the Indians. That's how they work, lining up the Indians, buying scalps."

"The businessmen?"

"Now there's something." Frazier peered into the rosy dawn light seeping through the window. "Actually, I think the ones in the fur business like the new government; they worry more about the British snatching all the beaver than they do about what flag they serve. They may be Frogs, but they like the liberties we give 'em."

That made sense, too. Frazier had done a fine job. We conferred a while more there in the barracks, I clapped him on the shoulder and commended him, and he slid out unseen into a peach-tinted St. Louis dawn, with moisture on every leaf. Intelligence was the first priority. I needed to know who was for the government, and who wasn't.

Those of us in the old Corps of Discovery had forged bonds of steel. I would trust any of them with my life, and they would trust me. I had cash in hand, and intended to trace them all and give them their back pay and federal land warrants. Congress had awarded each of them three hundred and twenty acres of virgin land. They had dispersed, and it would not be easy to track them down.

The turbulent territory seethed with troubles, and I wasted no time putting a bayonet to the problems. At once I paid a call on the territory's secretary, and acting governor in Meriwether's absence, Frederick Bates. I thought he might be just the right man, being a Virginian, a lawyer, a Democratic-Republican like Mr. Jefferson, and a holder of numerous public offices back East.

I found an odd puffy man at the helm, his pale brow furrowed, his expression pleading, his generous brown lips pursed, and his humor rancid. He was sallow, as if the outdoors was a foreign nation to him, and his eyes were bagged with furrows that told me he did not profit from his nocturnal rest. He exuded so much dignity that I itched to step on his toe.

"Mr. Jefferson commends you, and urges upon you the importance of curbing the Burr conspiracy," I said affably as soon as we had poured ourselves a dark glass of amontillado from a decanter on his desk. "Is there still talk of a filibuster against New Orleans?"

"It's pandemonium, General," he said. "This place! You can't imagine the skulking schemers and what they want! I will be so *glad* when the governor arrives, for these matters are beyond my jurisdiction and authority, but I wish to declare, my good general, that I have proceeded resolutely anyway, in a most judicious manner, with due *prudence* and rectitude, to ameliorate these clamorous and Machiavellian uproars."

That was a mouthful.

"Mr. Bates," I said, settling back and propping my muddy boots upon his desk, which horrified him, "you just begin right at the beginning and tell me what you've done and what needs doing."

Not much, it seemed. The man had a way of papering over inaction with rhetoric, but it wasn't so much what he said as how he said it that gave me the measure of him. He put stock in words, the longer the better, and had a way with them that might spell trouble for Meriwether. Bates's brother Tarleton was an old friend of the governor, Virginians all, and that spoke well for the future.

And yet I worried. I imagined Bates loyal enough to Tom Jefferson, but doubts nagged me. His conversion to Jefferson's principles had been recent, and looked just plain opportunistic. Well, I would not confide in him, not yet anyway, but would set about putting the new command in place until I could show some strength.

My next call was to Pierre Chouteau, prominent Creole merchant in St. Louis, supplier of many goods to the expedition, trusted friend, and the man who had gone to great effort and expense to bring the Osage chiefs to Washington to meet the president, and then got them safely back to Upper Louisiana. I counted him among my best allies, sterling in his faithfulness, reliable, and eager to serve the republic.

He received me in his spacious home, a suitable domain for a young merchant prince. He had taught himself adequate English, and in that alien tongue welcomed me into his enameled green parlor during a meridian time of day when most Creoles lay dozing.

"Pierre," I said, enjoying the firm clasp of his hand. He had dark French features, and lively eyes and a mouth that suggested amusement, though he was a serious man.

I am a plainspoken man and wasted no time telling him of my mission, after we had sipped a ritual goblet of red wine from his glass decanter.

"Mr. Jefferson's commissioned me to begin certain things, and I think there might be opportunity in it for you," I began.

His eyes lit up. The Chouteaus were never known to scorn opportunity to fatten their purse.

"We are most anxious to return She-He-Ke, Big White, to his people, along with his party, and not delay his homeward journey any more. He's been away from the Mandans a long time. My first business here is to mount an expedition to take him up the river."

Chouteau listened intently, and I knew I had him well and properly hooked.

"I've detached Ensign Pryor—he was a sergeant when we recruited him for the Corps of Discovery—and will put him in command of a small detachment of troops. I've already talked to another of our corps men, George Shannon, who will go along. They've been up that mighty river, know the ropes, and have great ability."

Chouteau listened, saying nothing.

"Captain Lewis and I found that the tribes were much more tractable when goods were available, and we expended much of what we brought with us as gifts to pave our way. And that is where you come in. We want you to join the party with a trading expedition of your own; your traders and boatmen would enhance the strength of the party. The government will provide your entire party with rifles, powder, and shot, and we'll include four hundred dollars of presents. You and your fur trading party can continue upriver, trading for pelts at your leisure, once we return the Mandans to their people."

"Ah, it is formidable," he said. "Formidable."

"We had some trouble with the Sioux, who are a danger, and you might have some difficulty getting past the Arikaras because of the presence of Big White on your keelboats. But we think some gifts will smooth that over. With your group of traders, and our soldiers, you will be as large and as well armed as our Corps of Discovery. What do you say?"

"My general, we do not hesitate for one moment. I myself will go."

"Good. We're going to open up that river and license the traders and make the fur business profitable and safe. And you'll be in a good position to profit from it."

He nodded, happily. How could he refuse? I didn't doubt he would corral a small fortune from the expedition, and he would enjoy the safety of our troops as well.

I turned to other matters. "Mr. Chouteau, this territory is torn by rivalries. I am a plain man and will ask a plain question and hope for a plain answer. Are the Creoles happy with us, indifferent, unhappy, hostile?"

Chouteau did not hesitate, and as far as I could tell, he did not hedge.

"General, in the bosom of every Frenchman is the hope that the tricolor of France will fly here. But if the choice is between Spain and the new American republic, there is no choice at all. We are Americans. The Spanish, you see, have a peculiar attitude toward business. They seek to make business as difficult as possible, and at the same time, extract every possible centime for the crown. For as long as they held New Orleans, we could barely win a profit out of furs.

We like your liberty. We like your equality." He shrugged, an expressive, Gallic shrug that spoke more than words ever could.

I knew then I need not worry about the French of St. Louis, and could turn to more urgent matters, including the scheming of the British, who wanted to pluck the territory from us without wasting a shot, by using the tribes as their proxies.

14. LEWIS

My struggles with the War Department exhausted me. They want receipts for everything, and I cannot provide them. I wrote numerous drafts on the treasury, every one of them to purchase essentials, wasting not a penny, and yet I was treated as if it had been my intent to skin the government. En route, I traded my officer's coat to some Indians for a canoe and wish to be reimbursed; how shall I receipt that?

I left Washington as soon as I could to escape the steamy heat, intending to improve my health at Locust Hill. The air of Albemarle County is better. It is November now but the ague still afflicts me, and just when I feel I am past it I am besieged once again with the usual chills, shakes, fever, and sweats. As soon as I arrived here, much to my delight, my mother began administering the cinchona bark extract that abates the intermittent fever, and supplemented with those simples for which she is so renowned in Albemarle County. I have in addition the services of my brother Reuben, who in my absence had completed his medical training. They have steadily nursed me back to some sort of health, though I remain oddly indisposed and afflicted with a melancholy.

She doses me every two hours with a tea decocted from the bark of yellow birch, sweet flag, thoroughwort, and tansy, boiled and then mixed with sweet wine. Her other remedy is distilled from burdock, narrow dock, yarrow, knotgrass, cleavers, bloodroot, Jacob's ladder, and wormwood, boiled in rainwater. Of this I am to take all that my stomach will bear.

When I was able, I rode to Monticello and discussed Upper Louisiana with Mr. Jefferson. I promised him a paper detailing my observations about the economic potential of the territory and the nature of the tribes inhabiting it. I work on it desultorily, every word wrenched from my brain.

Mr. Bates, the territorial secretary serving as governor until I should arrive in St. Louis, writes flattering and alarming letters, urging me to hasten west to my post because, he explains, the turbulent territory needs a governor's authority which he cannot provide. I will go when I can; but now I must enhance my health and vigor, and where better than in the hands of my two physicians?

Mr. Conrad petitions me for the edited journal pages, so he can begin work. I have not yet started, and do not quite know why I keep putting off the task. Mr. Jefferson presses me on every occasion, reminding me how important the publication of the journals is to several branches of science. And to the nation, and I might add, to his administration. He regards the expedition as the crown jewel of his two terms, but it will require the publication of our journals to persuade his adversaries, the Federalists, that there was much good gotten from the trip.

I have looked over Captain Clark's entries, and mine, and they bring back a host of memories, struggles and triumphs, matters that only he and I know about, things barely hinted at in the pages. I dread to touch any of it. The whole task of editing those journals is so formidable it seems worse than the trip itself. Shall I correct our field notes or leave them intact? How much should I alter the original? What should be cut out? What is not for the public eye?

All these matters swim in my head. I have tried twenty times to begin; to take the first of the bound journals and simply begin copying in an orderly manner, dates, places, times, observations, men, equipment, miles traveled, solar and weather data, plants discovered, sickness, equipment failures. All of it. I spread some foolscap before me, dip the nib of my pen into the inkpot, and then do nothing. I cannot explain it. I wish this task might be lifted from me, but the thought of that afflicts me because then I could not control what is used, what is not, and decide whether some things might best be rewritten.

At first I supposed I was troubled simply by the fierce desire to make the journals perfect; that I was simply paralyzed by the cry of soul that insists that my task must be to make the flawed flawless, the insipid fascinating, the obscure clear, the language precise and accurate. Now, after numerous attempts to start the great work, I simply don't know, and with each effort, I find myself less willing to proceed. I am disappointing Mr. Jefferson, Will Clark, the publishers, and everyone at the American Philosophical Society.

And the more I sense their disappointment, as time drags by, the worse I suffer. Captain Clark expects half the profit. The society expects a treasury of new information. The government expects maps and an understanding of the tribes and a substantiated claim upon unexplored lands.

And here I am, with more burdens pressing me than I can endure, sinking deeper into melancholia each day. I do not know what to do. Time has slowed to a halt. I am the governor of a territory several hundred miles distant, but here I languish.

Maybe in St. Louis I will do better.

My mother keeps a shrewd eye on me, but stays apart because I am not in the mood for company. She is the model of all womanhood, and I despair of finding a mate who can even approach her graces and learning and ability. I am constantly invited to balls and banquets all over Virginia, and I accept some, though my heart is not in the social life. I have been toasted and honored too many times, if such a thing is possible. I attend these affairs, so that the world might see the explorer in the flesh, and drink their toasts, and return to Locust Hill all the more melancholic.

At Captain Clark's behest, I traveled to Fincastle, near Roanoke, to visit Julia Hancock and to meet some of the young women he thought I might find attractive. I have met more women in the past months than I can count, but they all fall short one way or another. I am fussy. If an eligible young woman is not serious, and cannot address me on the terms of my own thinking, then I find little of interest in her, and she drifts into the arms of someone else.

At Fincastle, while a guest of Colonel Hancock, I finally discovered a young woman who filled the bill, so far as I could see. Certainly Letitia Breckenridge is a comely damsel, of exceptional beauty and quickness. I met her and her sister Elizabeth by design, for Will had paved the way. They are daughters of General James Breckenridge, and thus well suited to my social requirements.

I well remember when we met; the nankeen dress, the subdued intelligent gaze from hazel eyes, the seriousness she displayed, unlike her more boisterous sister. She did not then know that I would court her; the whole had been artfully arranged by Colonel Hancock so as to appear to be a Sabbath stroll, taking the air while the weather held.

By then they were calling me "your excellency," or "governor," and all that, so I had the advantage, and made haste to pace beside her on a stroll along a shady lane that led into the hazy hills, and thus engaged, made inquiry into her nature. She did not measure up in terms of education, but no woman does, and I assumed that she would be too busy rearing a family to pursue scholarship further. She had a sublime form, which the shifting gold muslin, a lovely autumnal color that complemented her bold beauty, sometimes revealed to me as we strolled.

"Your Excellency, when you are quit of St. Louis, what will you do?" she asked.

"I am thinking of high office," I replied. "Often I ask myself the same thing. Just now, I wrestle with a paper that distills everything I have learned of the Western country for the edification of Mr. Jefferson and future presidents. But that's just the beginning, you know. Here I am, at thirty-five, and known from top to bottom. I am thinking that the Democratic-Republicans may call upon me, and so I regard my tenure in office as a sampler, Miss Letitia."

"Call upon you?"

"I am a simple man, much given to philosophy, and my predilection is to return and look after my mother, and care for Locust Hill. But if duty calls, I will be ready."

"I see," she said.

I inquired of course into her political views, and found them appropriately republican, at least as someone in her female estate might grasp the term. I discerned that she was exploring me, as well, inquiring into my plans, how long I should reside in distant St. Louis, and whether I had slaves. I confessed that I had none as personal property, but I oversaw the estate of my mother, who possessed many, and was therefore familiar with the handling of them.

I found myself coming to life at last, after so long a hibernation, and when we returned to the Hancock home I raised a toast to her and the happy future, and then several more. She flushed, and this time her gaze was averted. I could not tell how I was affecting her, but knew that I would pursue her.

I had seen a President's House devoid of its mistress, and while the vivacious Dolley Madison, wife of dapper James Madison, served admirably for Mr. Jefferson, the president's society wanted that domestic touch. I eyed the lady beside me with that in mind, and I fancied that Letitia understood the matter.

Her father collected her in time to drive his carriage home after an afternoon's repast, and I raised a last toast to her, her sister, and her illustrious father before settling them in their carriage. I spent the next days in a reverie. Here was a woman I might propose to; in most respects suitable, and one to stir my blood. I had been smitten many times since returning from the West, but in the end, all of those damsels were unsuitable. Letitia was suitable. I proposed to call on her in a day or two.

But Fate intervened. When I did ride to the Breckenridge estate, some miles distant, I discovered that Miss Letitia had gone to Richmond with her father and would be away for some while. I grieved, and then put it out of mind. I never should have confided my ambition to her. But I am too serious a man to waste feeling on a disappointment of the heart. I considered Elizabeth, but set it aside. She was not adequately serious.

I languished unwell in Ivy this autumn, uncertain what was eroding my health. My discerning mother eyed me sharply from time to time, and once even inquired if I was well. I assured her I was, and yet I was much fatigued and in a distemper. I resolved to see my friend and companion of the trail General Clark married in Fincastle in January, and then be on my way west, though I would be traveling in winter. The general would honeymoon and then join me in St. Louis, where by arrangement I would board with them.

I completed my lengthy treatise on the West, which I presumed would form the foundation of Indian and fur-trade policy for the next twenty years, and fell into one of my moods again. I do not know why I was able to write ten thousand words with fierce discipline, yet am stymied every time I open my journals. Is it because the journals are mostly Will's? Or is it because the whole world awaits their publication?

It was then, nearing the end of November, that Mrs. Marks, the legendary healer of Albemarle County, called me into her drawing room, and into the aura of the tile-clad stove.

"You are still unwell," she said. "Indisposed. Fevers."

"It is only the ague."

"Yes, the ague," she said. "But the weather has turned."

"I am in perfect health; just a little of the intermittent fever now and then."

"You wander the plantation, doing nothing, writing nothing. Are you troubled, Meriwether?"

"Not a bit!"

"Thirty-five and a bachelor."

Her candor shocked me. "I simply am unlucky," I replied testily. I did not want her sympathy. Letitia Breckenridge had fled, for whatever reason, and I hadn't met another I cared about more than a day or two.

"When are you going to St. Louis?" she asked.

"When I am ready!"

"You were appointed in March; now the year has passed."

"I have things to do here."

She asked me to draw close, and ran her experienced hand over my face and neck, discovered some gummy thickening of the flesh on my forehead, and along the jawline lumps so subtle I had not been aware of them myself until her fingers found them.

"Let me see your arms and hands, Meriwether."

I undid my sleeves, and pushed them up. She examined my arms, her gaze pausing at the arciform red-stained scars there.

"Your hands?"

I extended them to her, filled with a nameless and terrible dread, a pit of horror whose jaws were opening wider and wider as the minutes fled by.

She studied the palms, turned them over and examined the backs. I saw nothing amiss with them. But she traced her finger over a discolored area.

"There, you see? I am fit as a fiddle."

"Meriwether," she said, "I am here only to help, not judge a son whose life has taken him so far from the comforts of civilization and religion. It is necessary to begin a course of mercury immediately, and I have some simples, my wandering Meriwether, that will relieve you. The venereal is far advanced."

15. CLARK

Tomorrow, January 8, 1808, will be my wedding day. I await that holy event with scarce-concealed anticipation. Tomorrow, before the Episcopalian parson from Roanoke, the Reverend Mr. Smith, my Julia and I will recite the vows. The colonel has turned his spacious home into a virtual hostelry, so many are the guests.

I arrived here in Fincastle, Virginia, from St. Louis in ample time for the Yuletide, and spent a most joyous Christmas at the hearth of my in-laws, who have treated me with grace and affection. There is merriment in their eyes. They permit me a while alone each day with Julia, and make much reference to the mistletoe once again hanging from the cut-glass chandelier in the parlor.

She has met me each day, her face flushed and bright, her lips soft and welcoming. She has been full of questions about St. Louis, and wild Indians, and the ruffians of the border, and the army. I assure her things will be terrible; we will live in a dirt-floor log cabin, she will slave at the hearth and garden and spinning wheel, I will shoot marauding redskins through the loopholes of our fortress house every hour or so, and we will lack beds, tables, chairs, windows, and privacy, and sleep on bearskin robes.

She laughs, but uneasily. I tell her that I am a general of the militia, and command an entire army of bedbugs. She thinks that is very merry, and I see panic in her eyes and kiss it away, enjoying the moment.

Guests are arriving at every hour; my brothers and sister and assorted relatives are staying with friends in the area. Colonel Hancock has put me in one of the bedrooms, and

York out with the darkies, and that offends him. I will let him taste the whip if he remains in such a mood for long.

Ah, tomorrow! For too long have I dreamed of this. I will sweep my bride away to a bower that is prepared for us, and there we shall know each other in tenderness and joy. It is for this heaven that I have returned from St. Louis; it was for this heaven that I sustained my courage and resolution on that long journey into the unknown West. A wedding is a little like a voyage of exploration. We do not know what land we are piercing, or what we may find there; but I do not doubt it will be full of wonders and sunshine.

Soon after my arrival I met with Meriwether about the condition of the territory he governs, and found him in a peculiar mood, taut and irritable but papering it over with vast bonhomie. Something is troubling him.

He ventured here from Ivy a few days after I had arrived, knowing how much I wished to be with Julia. I greeted him, noted that he seemed unsettled as we exchanged news, and then we closeted ourselves in the front room to discuss affairs of state.

"Secretary Bates begs for you," I said. "You are certainly needed."

"What sort of man is he?"

"An able one, I think, but a handwringer."

Meriwether laughed, a brittle, strange cackle that was entirely new to me. "Not used to command, I take it."

"No, and brimming with anxieties."

"That is not a kind assessment."

I sighed. "I am a plainspoken man," I replied, and let it stand. Frederick Bates had rubbed me wrong, and I could not fathom why Thomas Jefferson had entrusted him with so weighty a position.

"What about the militia? And Burr?"

There I was on better ground. "I inherited a paper militia that could not muster a hundred true men. It was shot through with Burrite officers, too. Frazier got me a list of them. I did some interviewing and cashiered most of 'em. Now I'm rebuilding. It's hard to turn border men into a force, and the only hold I have on 'em is Indian dangers. I've been working with some loyal noncoms, good stouthearted men, and building around them rather than the officers, who are mostly sunshine soldiers. When I get a militia I can trust, we'll have a grip on the territory."

Lewis nodded. "You got Big White back to the Mandans?"

"What? I thought you knew!" I said.

He shook his head. I had sent the news by post, but that was a slow and unreliable means, often two months between St. Louis and Washington this time of year.

I told him about Ensign Pryor's trip up the Missouri to take the Mandan chief home, in the company of Pierre Chouteau and twenty-two trappers. It had come a cropper at the Arikara villages, where the tribe we supposed to be our friends savagely assaulted the party on September ninth, killing three of Chouteau's traders, wounding ten men including our old friend from the Corps of Discovery, Private Shannon, whose leg had to be amputated. Pryor had fled down the river, reaching St. Louis not long before I headed east. She-He-Ke, Big White, and his family remained in St. Louis, his way home barred by the suddenly ferocious Rees.

Meriwether absorbed that, his gaze darting about, his brow furrowed. "We will have to try again with a stronger party. The president will be distressed. He takes it as an obligation of honor to get Big White safely back . . . and now this."

"We'll try again," I said. "A stronger party. Meriwether,

I can't properly govern, and Secretary Bates is, well, ineffectual, and Upper Louisiana can't be governed from Virginia. We need you."

He glared at me, as if I had affronted him. "I will come when I am ready. I am pursuing important matters here."

"The editing?"

"The work is proceeding. Pursh is drawing the plants. Hassler's astronomy calculations are almost done. Peale is sketching the animals. I have an artist on the birds."

"Soon, then. You promised the first edition by year's end."

He looked horrified. "Well, not so immediately."

"I would welcome the profit, Meriwether. The burdens of marriage and office tax me and the salary of an Indian superintendent doesn't cover."

"Well, I can help you. When are you returning to St. Louis?"

"We will honeymoon a few weeks in Virginia, visiting relatives. I hope to be in St. Louis early in the spring."

"Count on the army," Lewis said. "I will move you."

That sounded like a good offer, and I chuckled. "I think you ought to find some lady and follow suit."

He laughed almost boisterously. "I'm just an old bachelor, too fusty and musty for 'em," he said.

"No, Meriwether, you are the most eligible man in the United States."

He cackled happily. "Then they'll give me a good chase," he said. "I will let one catch me."

His laugh was as brittle as old parchment. He was hiding his sorrows, and I knew at once that his disappointment at the hands of Letitia Breckenridge had afflicted his spirits.

"Governor, let me tell you, in St. Louis the belles will flock to the balls, and if you know a few words of French, such as *oui, oui, oui,* you will captivate more hearts than you'll ever know."

He wheezed out a laugh, and it was like hearing old paper crumple.

"You look to be in good health, Meriwether."

"I'm in perfect health, brimming with life, ready to advance my fortunes in St. Louis. But I've been wrestling with the ague. It comes and goes, you know, but as soon as my dear mother gives the word, I'll head down the river."

That sounded fine to me. We spent an hour talking about the politics of the territory, the innumerable trading licenses General Wilkinson had granted to cronies before he departed, the smoldering embers of the Burr conspiracy to peel the whole area away from the republic and build a new nation out of scoundrels and traitors. Lewis brought me up to date on a myriad of things; the Burr trial and acquittal in Richmond, Jefferson's struggles with the British, who were boldly provoking war by pressing American seamen and engaging in other calculated affronts. That worried me.

"Meriwether, if there is war, I command a hopeless rabble. Half don't have rifles. We need some steel—cannon, rifles, everything—and I'll count on you to apply for it from Congress."

He nodded, unhappily. Again I had the deepening impression that Lewis was a troubled man, insecure, in pain of some sort.

That was the last I saw of him until today. He arrived for the wedding, looking fit and strong, and acting more like his old self, gorgeously accoutred in his gold braid and blue. I had little time other than to greet him and see to his quarters.

York greeted the old captain effusively. "Massah Lewis, Captain, is mighty nice you come to this heah wedding," he exclaimed.

But Meriwether ignored the darkie, as if York had not traveled with us clear to the western sea. I watched York closely, worried that the man's insolence would get the better of him, but York held his peace.

Lewis is much the center of attention today; men, women, children all press him to spin his anecdotes once again, but he does so reluctantly and by rote. He's worn down by the attention. There is a banquet tonight, and a ball tomorrow, and Colonel Hancock has kept the punch bowl filled for days.

Meriwether hangs about the punch, downing cup after cup along with port and porter and whatever other spirits the Hancocks provide.

It has been a long while since we returned from the West, and yet that expedition affects us both even now, and Lewis especially. I see it in the face of everyone I talk to; they see the explorer, and not the Clark. I am eager to turn a new leaf.

Tonight they will hide Julia from me and I will not see her until the sacred rites, when she will be an angel on the arm of her father. I will be waiting there, in the green parlor, when she waltzes down the stairs in rustling white silk and ivory lace, her hair aglow, her lips ruby, her eyes shining upon me like little suns . . . or slides down the banister with a whoop, if I know my Julia. I will be there, and so will the preacher, and so will a hundred guests, my brothers and their spouses, my sister and hers, assorted cousins and friends. And I will take my beloved to my bosom there, pledge myself to her there, hear her pledge herself to me there, and that will be the beginning, as well as an end.

16. LEWIS

I tarried this January of 1808 in the frail warmth of Locust Hill, but my heart is cold. Many were the dreams that had sustained me during my eventful life. I had dreamed of honor. I had dreamed of love. I had dreamed of devotion to our infant republic, that we might prove to the whole world that men may live free and equal. I had dreamed of accomplishment. I had wanted to make my widowed mother proud. I wanted the name Lewis to shine for a thousand years. I had hoped for children. I had hoped for an illustrious name that would echo through the generations, a name unstained and blameless.

Now, by terrible mischance—or was it my own folly?—everything that I dreamed of, everything that I was, everything that I might still be, lay in ruin, blackened by a shameful disease that evoked the loathing of the world, a disease whose name was not uttered.

I could not talk to my mother about it; not Lucy Marks, who had borne me, raised me up, educated me, and quietly nurtured me through the vicissitudes of youth. I could barely talk to my physician brother Reuben, either, but held it all in, mortified, desolated by the scourge that rotted my parts as well as my very soul. I told Reuben very little; only a date: August of 1805. He had remarked the speed at which the disorder had devastated my body, faster than usual. I had no reply other than that we were famished, eating poorly, and suffering the want of many necessaries in our diet, and maybe that had advanced the plague within me, which rolled like a black tide through my flesh and blood.

He held out a little hope, and I clung to it.

"Meriwether, often the pox passes by, and leaves the victim unscathed. It is the common thing," he told me.

"But what of the others? Half the corps has it."

"We'll never know how they fare. It's a disease that mimics several others. It attacks different parts in different people, choosing the weakest portion. In some, it savages the heart and veins and arteries. In others it assaults the mind and nerves. In others it aggrieves the flesh, muscle, bone. I see none of that in you."

He was holding out hope to a mortified, mortifying man, and I clung to it desperately. He put me on mercury courses while Lucy Marks boiled her simples, and fed me this or that extract or broth. She brewed a tea of cuckold (or beggarticks as it is sometimes named), especially sovereign against venereal complaints, but also ginseng, fitroot, slippery elm, and burdock, which purifies the blood. She favors blue flag steeped in gin, which is also effective against venereals. She did not probe, but Reuben sometimes did. He wanted to know everything, as if my telling of those August nights in 1805 would somehow be my catharsis. But I knew he was merely curious.

I will always keep those nights to myself. No one on earth knows of them, not even Drouillard, Shields, and MacNeal, the only men with me as we probed the east flanks of the Bitterroots looking for the Shoshones. Clark and the rest of the Corps of Discovery were far behind, toiling up the Jefferson River.

We spotted a native boy; then some women, all of them shy as bats in daylight. But finally we did connect with the chief, Cameahwaite, and his band, and we rejoiced. They were starving and we got them meat. They promised to sell us horses. We went through tense times waiting for Clark to show up with what few items we had left to trade them for horses. But thanks to the sign-talker, Drouillard, we parleyed with the young chieftain, assured him of our friendship and demonstrated that we wished no ill upon them.

By the firelight they danced for us in those mountain meadows, and got my two privates and Drouillard dancing, and persuaded me to dance as well. Their women were sinuous and comely and honey-fleshed, and their eyes glowed in the firelight. The chieftain offered us our choice; it being a great honor among their women to embrace an honored guest. It took little effort to persuade the soldiers, but I designed to tarry long after they had vanished into the buffalo-hide lodges that soft autumnal evening.

I wrestled long with my own temptation: both Will Clark and I had steadfastly refused the offers of other tribes along the Missouri, though the men partook of all that savage hospitality, and paid a price for it in the drips and other venereals, all of which I treated with mercury salve and calomel. Sometimes the chiefs had taken great offense at our reluctance, thinking that we were disdainful of them and their women. I can't speak for Will Clark, but I was merely being prudent. And he had his Judy to think of.

I feared that Cameahwaite might take similar offense; he who could provide us with horses and spare the whole discovery expedition from disaster. And so I reasoned my way forward.

This one time, far from the corps, far even from the eyes of my three companions, far from civilization, far from white men's diseases in this remote corner of the mountains, far out upon a sea of wilderness, I might quickly enjoy the great embrace.

I had, indeed, my eye upon a glowing young woman with come-hither eyes, lithe and sinuous, with strong cheekbones and smooth, tawny flesh; a woman with a bold assessing glance that spoke to me in ancient ways, beyond what words could convey.

I smiled at her; she returned the compliment tenfold. We drifted off into the pine-scented darkness, far beyond the campfire and its dancing light, into a starlit void, and finally into an arbor paved with thick robes. And there I threw my life away, all unwitting, all with the purpose of avoiding offense to these savage people.

Or so I tell myself. At other times, I am more honest. She had awakened in me a lust that had slept restlessly in my loins for more months than I could remember.

Oh, if only that night had never happened! I have cursed my fate ever since, choked on my own desolation and shame. I prowl the hills, thinking of nothing else. I meet young women, and shy from them: can they see? Do they know? Has word about me filtered out insidiously, whispered from lip to ear, a blackening pool of horror about the explorer?

I walk the lonely paths beyond the barren fields, thinking of Letitia, of the others, of the women I cannot have. If I am an honorable man I must not even taste the pleasures of an unsuspecting wanton, much less a woman of virtue. But all that is dead in me except for the dread of being discovered. It maddens me, the thought of whispers, the pursed lips, the side glance, the turned head. Did Letitia Breckenridge flee because she read something in me, something that I did not yet know about myself? Ah, God, what is left of my dwindling life? And how long will it run before my vile secret is made public?

I tried to rejoice at Will's wedding, but my heart was all ash. I bantered with him about women. I told him I would find mine. I made great sport of the chase and the conquest. And all the while my soul was shriveling inside of my parched and fevered body. I made a great show of merriment at the punch bowls, but I did not feel it, and any close observer of Meriwether Lewis must have seen my dissimulation and wondered at it. What did Will think? Or was he too much absorbed in his own good fortune to notice?

My mother and brother have improved my health, and my indisposition wanes, and as it does my hopes prosper. Most survive! In many the plague vanishes! And yet I cannot put the horror of my condition out of mind. It is there, stalking me, my very shadow, whenever I take some porter at the public house and talk to my neighbors; whenever there is a quadrille or minuet or a hunt.

Reuben warns me to avoid spirits; but if I were suddenly to stop, the world would study me too closely and wonder why. I cannot change my conduct in the slightest for fear of discovery. They may not know, but I do, and I cannot walk the lane without this grim ghost stalking behind me, my bleak shadow, my shame waiting to ruin me.

I have not written a word. My journals are untouched. A thousand times I have opened the morocco covers, and plucked up a quill, only to slump in my chair, watch the rain drip from the eaves, and close the journal.

My publisher, Conrad, presses me for pages. The president of the United States sends me letters in that fine hand of his, courteous, affectionate, but between the words is an edge, and I see it, and he means for me to see it. The unpublished journals reflect on his administration. I had promised the first volume before year's end. It is not even begun. This is maddening. For the life of me I do not know why I avoid that great task.

I hear from Secretary Bates, who says the territory is in an uproar and he is dealing with scoundrels, and that his word lacks the authority that mine must have. But his excellency Governor Lewis does not come, and Bates is growing desperate. I draw a governor's salary from the federal treasury, but I languish a thousand miles from the seat of government.

I cannot go. Not until my brother and mother finish the courses with which they treat me. I probably slow their progress, sipping as much as I do, and yet I will not stop. Reuben warned me; Dr. Saugrain warned me. My mother didn't, but I see the disapproval in her eyes every time I sip some port.

I tell them nothing of the laudanum I sometimes use for sleep, when my worries lie too heavy upon me and I can get no rest. Six drops in a tumbler of water puts me into a peaceful sleep, and I awaken refreshed, unlike so many nights when I lie abed swimming in my bitter fate.

Reuben tells me I am much better and can leave in a fortnight if the weather permits. That would put me in St. Louis in March. I am eager to go. At moments a heady optimism lifts my spirits; I shall be one of those who has conquered the venereal! I shall put all this behind me, govern that unruly province with a firm and fair hand, deal sternly with traitors and opportunists.

I will treat with the Indians, assuring them of the items they need, such as kettles and iron implements, in exchange for their good conduct. I will restore order to the fur business, get my Mandan chief, who still languishes there, back to his people, deal with those treacherous Rees, subdue the haughty Sioux, and return after a few years in triumph. Never let it be said that I lack determination.

PART II

17. LEWIS

I arrived in this raw, secretive, scheming city of St. Louis on the eighth of March, 1808, after an overland journey in which I paused in Kentucky to make sure the family's land claims, some of them won by my father for service in the Revolution, were in good order. That meant examining the tracts for encroachment, checking the stakes, making sure of the records. Reuben accompanied me that far and then sailed with my equipage down the Ohio and up the Mississippi, while I continued by land. He reached St. Louis a fortnight ahead of me.

I am in robust health, never felt better, and am eager to begin governing this unruly province. For months I have been receiving a dire correspondence from Territorial Secretary Frederick Bates, describing the anarchy prevailing here, especially as regards Indian policy. I will deal with all that soon—if it really exists. St. Louis is tranquil, greening, and brimming with spring warmth.

I paid a courtesy call at once upon Bates, who greeted me effusively, apparently relieved not to have to cope with the ambitions of various factions who want the government to stay out of Indian affairs altogether so that ruthless traders may have their dubious way with the tribes, virtually ruling them with their trinkets. I will see about that.

Mr. Bates is a sallow and bag-eyed sort of man, mellifluent with words, an attorney given to much rhetoric but also bending with the wind. I very nearly drowned in his compliments. He was telling me all at once what villainous parties roam the territory; how treacherous are the Indians, British, Spanish, French, and other dubious sorts; how wisely he has governed, with shrewd appointments and policies intended to quiet the clamor and placate the cutthroat traders. I listened much, said little, and took the measure of the secretary. I sympathized: he had been the sole federal official for many months, with General Clark getting married and I at Locust Hill.

"Now, Your Excellency," he said, "General Wilkinson issued the trading licenses promiscuously, the *congés* as the Creoles call them, and to the benefit of his own pocket. I suffered great opposition when I attempted to repeal them, it being my design to limit the licenses one to a tribe, so that rivals wouldn't demoralize the savages . . ."

"That's not our policy. Mr. Jefferson and I believe that the government should establish forts with trading stores in them, open to all tribes equally, to keep the peace and win their allegiance, and license traders only above the Mandan villages."

"Very good, Your Excellency, but you would be advised to consider the weight of my experience here, and consult me about the difficulties you will encounter among these avaricious Frenchmen, and other rascals. I will, Your Most Esteemed Excellency, save you infinite grief. I am, of course, at your service."

I saw at once that he was unhappy. "I am grateful for your counsel, Mr. Bates."

"You must grasp, sir, that this is a territory rife with anarchy. Trading parties head up the river without the slightest approbation of the government, much less a proper trading license. They bargain for furs with whatever tribes they encounter, and set the savages against their rivals. I cannot stop the scoundrels. They buy a load of trade goods and are off."

"I'll be putting a stop to it. General Clark and I plan some fortified posts commanding the river."

"Command the river? With what? Your Excellency, General Clark has done wonders with the militia, but take it from an experienced man, sir; the Creoles cannot be trusted. Their loyalties are highly suspect. My instinct is to show them some muscle, and compel them to serve, and if they don't, deny them licenses . . ."

"I have found the French to be eager to cooperate with us, Mr. Bates. Mr. Chouteau brought the Osages clear to Washington to meet Mr. Jefferson, and then took them safely back here. We have good militia officers in Lorimier and Delaunay."

He paused, as if to regroup. "Yes, of course, Your Excellency, some small fraction of them will cooperate, but I recommend, upon long observation, that they bend with the wind. You would wisely exclude them from command—"

I refused to let him impugn loyal Creoles. "Mr. Bates, they are good men. What have you done about the land titles? The lead mines especially?"

"Why, sir, it is a very cauldron of troubles. First Spanish, then French, and now American grants of title. And is the measure in arpents or acres? The older settlers show dubious title to the mines; little was recorded, you know. So I have encouraged the American claimants. They stake their claims, and we describe them in acres. It is good business, Your Excellency. The government has collected numerous patent fees from the mining claims, and I count it one of my small but shining triumphs."

"But what of the Creoles? Does any one of them think his title is secure? Mr. Bates, I want you to affirm the original titles at once. It is not the policy of the Jefferson administration to dispossess any of the original owners."

"But Governor! Ah, yes." He smiled suddenly, with a great contortion of his facial muscles. "That involves a radical change from settled practice, but if it is your wish, count me your loyal and obedient underling."

"What of the Spanish, Mr. Bates?"

"They connive to peel the tribes away from us; the Osages in particular, Your Excellency. My recommendation, sir, is that you employ agents along our southwest frontiers, and keep ever vigilant, even as I have done these months when duty devolved upon me in Your Excellency's absence. I believe you will find my labors on that account most satisfactory."

"Yes, General Clark and I have something like that in mind."

"I fear you trust too much. General Wilkinson, sir, might be the commander of our armies, but he is a treacherous and unscrupled man, and up to his elbows in Colonel Burr's schemes, Your Excellency. The trouble is, there's no *proof.* He covers his tracks." He leaned forward to add a note, sotto voce. "But I can tell you, a ring of his cohorts flourishes in St. Louis, meaning to weaken your regime until all of Louisiana can be tied to England or Spain."

"And how do you know this?"

"Spies, sir. Men come and whisper in my ear, and I take heed. You and the president and the secretary of war have all been apprised by my correspondence, you know."

"Who are they?"

"Why, sir, I hesitate to *name names.*"

"Who, Mr. Bates?"

"I will prepare a list of suspects, sir."

I nodded.

It was an odd interview, with Bates acting, in turn, obsequious, welcoming, delighted at my arrival, but at the same time resentful of my presence, secretive, distressed by the slightest change from his practice, and eager to charge me with how little I knew of territorial politics and strife. The message was clear: let him continue to govern and propose and issue permits, and I would put the official seal upon his policies, and take my leisure. He wanted me to be a figurehead, he the éminence grise employing my legitimate authority, and he must have supposed that my limited experience fitted me to be nothing more.

"What a beneficent moment this is, sir," he said. "At last! We shall elevate the government to its proper majesty, and you may count me your trusted advisor and the *executor* of your design."

"Very good," I said. "I'll get settled and assume my responsibilities directly. I am grateful for your professions of allegiance."

Oddly, he grimaced.

I sensed that I would run into the classic bureaucratic obstructionist, resisting me whenever he felt my policies didn't agree with him. Perhaps it was a family matter. His brother, Tarleton, had hoped to become the president's personal secretary, and when the president appointed me instead, I fear the seeds of bitterness may have been sown.

I would be patient with Mr. Bates, and magnanimous, and complimentary, and hope I might yet fashion a good relationship with my second in command.

I spent the next days hunting down a home. Rents were appalling in that burgeoning city. Most suitable houses went for five hundred a year. Will Clark agreed to let me board with him, the bachelor at their table, and toward that end I hunted an establishment adequate for us all.

I finally found one on South Main and Spruce Streets for two hundred fifty a year, four rooms, a summer kitchen, and an attic for slaves, and hastened to engage the place from the landlord, who fawned over me as if I had the blood of kings in me. It was substantial for St. Louis, but nothing compared to the great, comfortable stone mansions erected by the Creole gentry, stuffed with fine furniture, the best imported wallpapers, and fireplaces in every room.

I sent a card to my friend Moses Austin, thus announcing my arrival, and joined with Reuben on a tour of St. Louis. It was, by any measure, a gray, filthy, and disgusting city, teeming with new arrivals, dangerous to life and health, raw and gross, except for those heights well above the reeking waterfront where the Creole merchants lived in spacious mansions, sipping the finest coffee brought up from New Orleans, attending each others' soirees and balls in imported silks and satins. But that is not where we headed.

I showed my brother the levee, swarming with rough rivermen and slaves unloading keelboats and flatboats, swart odorous men who spoke strange tongues. I showed Reuben the sprawl of Creole buildings, their squared timbers set vertically in the French manner, that served for dwellings; the mucky streets that bred mosquitoes in every puddle, the flats along the river suffocating in fetid air, redolent with sweat and other, ranker, odors.

"Here is where the furs arrive from high up the Mississippi, in that vast wild around Prairie du Chien," I said. "Here is where the boats are outfitted, and the crews hired, and brave men push and pole and pull these keelboats up the Missouri, day after day, far beyond the world of white men, into a lonely land of savages, seas of grass, countless buffalo, and innumerable beaver."

"I want to go up there," he said.

I feared I had talked too much, too enticingly, of the voyage of discovery. "I need you here," I said.

"No, Meriwether, you need your very own brother in

whatever fur company you invest in, to keep an eye on your investment and keep the crew in good health."

I could not object to that. But I had hoped he would remain in St. Louis as my aide and confidential assistant . . . and private physician. But he was a free man, not bound by any promise or agreement, and I could only wish him his heart's desire. He had healed me of that unspeakable disease, but I wanted him close in case the ague or other indispositions might arise in this moist and unhealthy place.

We had talked much of investing in the fur business. I had acquired some experience with it, and knew who was competent and who wasn't. I imagined I could triple my investment in a year. I certainly wished to profit from it, and from the rising prices of land about St. Louis, where happy investors doubled their money in a year. I would see about that, too, if I could borrow enough to purchase some tracts. I wanted a share of everything: the mines, the land, but especially the fur trade, the one field I understood perfectly.

Reuben agreed to stay with me until the Clarks should arrive, and together we settled the house on Main Street, the Rue Principale, and moved in.

A youth found us there, unpacking crates, and handed me an envelope. Within it was an invitation from Pierre Chouteau to sup with him that very evening, and to let the boy know.

"Yes, tell him we'll be there, with great pleasure," I said.

The boy nodded and hurried upslope. This evening would mark the beginning of many things, including the landholdings and fortunes of Meriwether Lewis.

18. CLARK

We arrived in St. Louis yesterday, June 30, by keelboat, having made good time from Louisville because Meriwether had detached Ensign Pryor and a squad from the regular army and sent them to our assistance. I had, aboard, an entire household in one keelboat, and in the other, trade goods, a grist mill, blacksmithing equipment, and other items for the government Indian posts we intended to establish along the lower Missouri River.

Meriwether met us at the levee, having gotten word of our slow progress up the Mississippi. Even as the boatmen were securing our keelboats, he was pacing the muddy bank, bursting with energy, handsome in his royal blue coat and white silk stock, which he wore even on this steamiest day of the summer when it was so close it was hard to draw breath.

"Ah! How good to see you at last! How beauteous is the new Mrs. Clark! How ravishing is Miss Anderson," he exclaimed gallantly, barely after we had set foot on the mud. Alice Anderson is my sister's daughter, a comely and marriageable young lady who will be a part of my household for a while. "Why, Miss Anderson, every bachelor in St. Louis will toast you, and rejoice at your presence, and I expect there will be duels and jousts among the bachelors. You will slay the whole unmarried class of males with that smile."

My chestnut-haired niece colored up at all that, but only smiled at such effusive greetings. She was not accustomed to such gallantry in the Clark household.

We all greeted Meriwether warmly. Even York trumpeted

is pleasure, though I thought it was unseemly. Julia curt-
ied shyly in her white cotton frock. She wasn't much used
o being in the company of governors; she wasn't even used
o being in the company of generals, though I have been giv-
ng her lessons. I have so far persuaded her that a general is
ess formidable than a lieutenant, but when she met my
rother George a few weeks ago, a respectful silence fell
ver her. George Rogers Clark is an old man, but with a cer-
ain august presence, and she has yet to celebrate seventeen
ears. I fear she might be ill at ease in a household that in-
ludes the governor.

"Come, let me show you your house," Lewis said, clap-
ing an arm around my shoulder. "I put some effort into
inding just the right place. You'll like it."

I nodded to York and the two black women, Julia's house-
naids and cooks, to follow, and we proceeded through a
orpid afternoon when sensible people should be under
oof, to Main and Spruce Streets, not far from the riverfront.
There indeed stood a comfortable, mortared stone house
vith a rain-stained verandah on its east and south façades.

"I hope you like it; I've reserved a bedroom for myself,
ut if that should not be convenient, I'll board elsewhere.
The Chouteaus have already offered me a room. But you're
ny old tent mate and it seemed so natural just to con-
inue being messmates," he said. "Together, we'll bring good
rder here."

I glanced at Julia, who was looking less than happy, and
viping her brow where sweat had already accumulated from
ur brief passage from the steaming levee. I had my doubts
bout such an arrangement but thought to say nothing for
he time being.

Julia kept glancing at the governor who was suddenly
ntruding upon our happy lives, a stranger in our first home,
nd I could almost hear the objections forming in her mind.

The house proved to be a suitable one for my purposes; it had four rooms downstairs, two bedrooms, a parlor that opened on a dining room; a pair of rude attic rooms suitable for the slaves; a detached kitchen with good stone fireplaces; a carriage barn; but only a noisome, small outhouse that fouled the air of the rear yard, and would be inadequate for our purposes. I would need to do something about that, and would set York to work.

"How is this? Perfect, I'll wager," the governor said. "See, everything's right. Room for the slaves up there."

I studied the two attic rooms: the women would go on one side; York on the other. The rafters were exposed, there were small grimy windows at either gable, and a narrow precipitous stair wound down to the back of the first floor, They would have to sleep on the planks, but I had a few old buffalo robes for them. I understood slaves. If they were tired from lack of sleep they wouldn't work as hard, so it paid to offer some comforts.

The governor had taken the sunlit corner bedroom for himself; that left one for Julia and me, and none for my niece. However, we could convert the dining room, and eat at the commodious table in the detached kitchen. It was far from a perfect place for us as long as the governor was present.

"This will serve, Meriwether," I said, not very certain that it would. But I did not wish to spoil the moment of our reunion.

Julia looked downcast. Ever since leaving Virginia, she had been discovering the hardships of the frontier, and I had bolstered her spirits daily with reports that St. Louis was the very cradle of civilization. She had not been assured by the rough-timbered buildings, boatmen's shacks, foul muck on the streets, or the hard men who watched us pass by with calculating stares. My promises weren't worth much just then.

"All right, York," I said. "Sergeant—ah, Ensign Pryor is getting drays, and you'll move our household goods here. You'll move in upstairs, and so will the women. I want supper by six."

"Yas, mastuh," York said dismissively. Damn him! He was becoming less and less valuable to me, and I glared at him. Sweat had beaded on his sooty brow, and collected under his armpits, staining his loose blue shirt.

He herded the slaves back toward the waterfront. The women as well as the men would be toting and hauling for two or three days. But I wanted that kitchen functioning in time for supper.

Lewis was addressing the ladies: "You'll enjoy St. Louis. The Creoles throw a ball for every occasion. There's a fiddle in every household. Wait until you see the great homes, the finery that rivals anything in Paris, the pianofortes, the harps, the libraries, the Paris wallpapers, the fruit trees, the spacious grounds. Ah, you'll see the real St. Louis soon!"

I wiped beads of sweat off my brow and lips. "I think the ladies may wish to retire and freshen," I said, responding to the pleading in Julia's eyes.

"Use my room; there's a commode," the governor said.

Julia nodded, curtsied, and led my niece to that haven. The door to the governor's bedroom closed firmly.

"What a lovely beauty your niece is," Lewis said. "A Grecian beauty! Alabaster flesh! She'll drive the bachelors mad. Ah, youth! I've lost it. I'm such a fusty old man that I won't even make my bid, but of course I'm busy with this territory. But I wager you won't be lacking suitors at our door."

"I'd thought maybe my niece might be a good match for you, Meriwether."

"Ah, Will, my heart's not in it. Letitia's gone! Married. And a good match, too. Maria gone, married. No, my friend,

I know my fate. I'm doomed to bachelorhood by a broken heart."

"Meriwether, you old gallant, you could beckon to any damsel in St. Louis with your pinky and end up with a wife."

He sighed unhappily. "No, no, they'd just turn me down, like Letitia. That's how it is with me, Will. I'll dance a few waltzes, dance a few quadrilles, and sigh a few sighs."

That struck me as a sharp retreat from his gallantry of the past. I had the strangest sense that something was amiss. What was that undertone in his voice? Was this the Meriwether I remembered? Maybe it was. Which startled me.

"Alice wanted to sample St. Louis life," I said, "but I don't know how long she'll stay. Perhaps you'll give her a reason." He grinned at me crookedly, so I changed the subject. "Well, now, old friend. Is there news?"

"Yes, always, and I am having my difficulties, mostly Indian troubles, the Great Osage and Little Osage, and the problem of Big White. He's here, put up by the Chouteaus. How will we get him back? It will take an army! His presence is embarrassing the president. How is it that a big nation of white men has been stymied by a handful of dusky savages? That's one problem. But my main problem is Bates. How did you find him?"

I smiled, and then proceeded recklessly. "A man on every side of every issue. A pessimist, who thought my every effort was futile."

"That's my impression also. Ah, Will, it is so good to see you. There's so much to discuss. We're cocaptains again! This place will make us rich! I've already bought land, two farms from the Chouteaus, over a thousand arpents, they're eighty-five hundredths of an acre, and I plan to buy much more. I'm in over a thousand dollars. I've already leased my farms out, and I'm a dairy farmer now. It's all going up.

"That's just the beginning. I'll buy shares of companies

in the fur business. You can't help but prosper, Will, and half the French in St. Louis are eager to put us properly into business. This is the best place in the country to gain wealth, for any man with money or slaves."

I grunted. Meriwether had always been the plunger, sometimes acting rashly, and now he was at it again. A thousand dollars! On a modest governor's salary. Tom Jefferson had cautioned him before the expedition about that trait of his, and as long as we were in the field he contained it, but now I could see that Meriwether was losing the discipline he had imposed on himself, and it worried me.

I could see that this was not the day to begin boarding Meriwether, as I had agreed to do, so I suggested that he dine for a day or two at a tavern until we could put the house together. He agreed instantly, having a sensitive regard for my wife and household. He said he would return only to sleep, and if that bothered us, he would find other quarters. And with that he strode into the lowering and motionless air, which plastered our clothing on us like soaked rags and made every move miserable.

Julia emerged from the bedroom, peered about, and relaxed.

"He's gone?"

"Until this evening."

"General Clark? I fear to trouble you. I . . . know I am being selfish. But please . . . would you do something for me?" She looked at me so plaintively that I knew her mind.

"If you mean evict him, no. He's my friend, my cocaptain, my commander, and now my governor. I also owe my success to him."

But Julia had a steely will and a mind of her own, as I soon found out after we had exchanged vows. "I know that," she said. "But this house is too small. It wants comforts. I have no proper closet to bathe. The slaves are right above us and can hear our every word. *Everything we do.* There's no room for Alice. It would all work out if the governor would leave this house to us."

On principle, I couldn't let a wife whittle at me like that, substituting her will for mine, so I shook my head. A man has to resist women and slaves and come to his own judgments, or he's not a man. But I thought the world of her, loved her, knew she had started a child in her womb, and I didn't like disappointing her, and truth be known, she had a valid point.

"Give it two months," I said, wanting Meriwether to see the difficulty himself.

She smiled resolutely, and then the first furniture arrived, and she was herself commanding the sweating army.

19. LEWIS

I opened the confidential letter from the president eagerly, knowing the great esteem he held for me. It had been some while since I had heard from him, so I relished the wax-sealed missive that arrived in the posts this day, Friday, August 19, and unfolded the thick vellum.

It was dated July 17.

"Since I parted with you in Albemarle in September last, I have never had a line from you," it began.

I paused, my brain swarming with objections. How could I write him before I had sorted things out?

The president went on to say that perhaps a letter from me was en route, that he would have written sooner but for his belief that something from me was coming.

It wasn't. In truth, I didn't really want to have him or Secretary of War Dearborn looking over my shoulder overly much, especially during my first months when I was making crucial decisions. They were seven hundred miles away, and could not easily be consulted. They had delegated power to me to govern in St. Louis, and I was doing just that.

Mr. Jefferson, always courteous, said he was writing to put aside this mutual silence, and to ask for a report.

He went on to say that it was not until February that he had learned of Ensign Pryor's defeat by the Arikaras and his flight down the river. He stressed again the necessity of returning the chief of the Mandans, Big White, to his home. "We consider the good faith and the reputation of the nation as pledged to accomplish this." He added that he wanted Big White returned, at whatever reasonable expense.

Well, that was an authorization to spend, and I would have to do just that to get the Mandan home.

There was more. He told me of a great company being formed by John Jacob Astor to harvest furs in the West. He wrote about the deteriorating relationship with the British, and how badly he wanted to avoid war even in the face of deliberate British provocations at sea.

And he ended with a sentence that evoked such a conflagration of feelings in me that I have no words for them:

"We have no tidings yet of the forwardness of your printer. I hope the first part will not be delayed much longer."

I read the letter again, in a sinking mood. It was as close to a rebuke as President Jefferson ever came. The publisher and I had promised the first volume would appear in November last, but I had not prepared one line for typesetting. The president was so eager to see the journals in print that I knew he was containing himself, teaching himself patience. And I was failing him, failing my president.

I set the letter aside, my mind in turmoil. I could not

fathom my own conduct. The stark reality is that I wishe
to be left alone with my projects, without officialdom look
ing over my shoulder and questioning my every move
Someday soon I would write Secretary Dearborn and tel
him the Territory of Upper Louisiana was secure. I ha
penned three detailed letters to him since I arrived; was tha
not enough?

I had worked in a perfect fury ever since I landed here
and now Will Clark and I were succeeding. For one thing, w
had brought the dangerous Osage tribes under control
The Osages live no great distance west of St. Louis, alon
the Osage River, and are the source of constant friction wit
settlers. They are an unruly and sullen lot, horse thieves an
raiders. Will Clark promised them a mill, blacksmith shop
and trading post in exchange for a treaty, and he has bee
delivering on his promise.

We will end up treating with two bands separately, th
Great Osage and Little Osage, but we will have our treaties
with a line demarcating the settled country from Osag
lands. I sent Pierre Chouteau, who has great influence wit
them, to get the terms I want. When I have a satisfactor
treaty I can submit to Congress for ratification, and settler
there are safe, I will inform the president about it. But nov
I fear I will have to report it prematurely, and there will b
backbiting. I've had Will Clark appoint Reuben subager
for the Osages, which will not only profit my brother, bu
help me keep an eye on those obstreperous savages.

Secretary Dearborn has already rebuked me for my si
lence. His letters irritate me with their petty complaints
How can I tell them that I have barely begun? They have n
idea just what I face here, and how governing so immens
a territory consumes all my energy.

I will write him in response to his rebukes, saying that

s my utmost concern to administer the territory in accord vith United States policy, and I will be more diligent in my correspondence, but I will also ask him to take into account he six weeks it takes for a letter to travel between us.

I am glad Will Clark is on hand. He is a man of such soidity that I trust everything he does. Already, he is hard at vork on a new fort overlooking the Missouri River, named Osage, which will have some cannon with which to command the Missouri, and will bring illicit traffic to a halt. He s also building trading posts and government forts at other points, to pacify the savages and supply them with the neans to become yeoman farmers and acquire civilized vays.

It took the counsel of a wise friend, Moses Austin, to help ne make sense of the strife in St. Louis and I have privately lined or sipped porter with him numerous times. Austin nows men, and knows who is loyal and who isn't. There are those who want licenses to trade upriver because they ave none; others who have trading licenses and want to exclude competition so they can enjoy a monopoly.

There are agents of the British, seeking licenses to trade upriver even while undermining the tribes' allegiance to the epublic. They succeeded in gulling Frederick Bates, who granted them trading privileges on United States territory even while swallowing their pious protestations. The British trader Robert Dickson is such a man, a soft-talking provocateur whose lullabies lulled Secretary Bates. The Scot ames Aird is another, both of them bent upon ruining our grip on Louisiana and fomenting Indians against us.

Austin has steered me well. He has given me the measure of several troublesome men, most of them Bates appointees, and I have removed one from office and am vatching others. But the most troublesome of all is Secretary

Bates himself who spreads his discontents across St. Louis
I resolved this day to confront the man and if possible wi
his cooperation, for without my secretary I am ineffectual.

This afternoon I approached him in his Governmen
House office. He keeps regular hours, and is actually punc
tilious about his duties, and I knew I would find him there
in the brown and tan rooms vacated by General Wilkinson

He glanced up as I entered, a bland mask dropping ove
those puffy features.

“What is it, Mr. Bates, that troubles you?” I aske
abruptly, for I wanted to catch him unprepared.

“Why!” He started up from his chair, and stood acros
the waxed desk, exhaling much air. “Why, Your Excellency
it is true that perhaps I don’t always agree with your deci
sions, but you may count me among your most admirin
colleagues.”

“I hear otherwise, Mr. Bates. I hear that you can barel
mention my name without casting aspersions upon it.”

“I’m sure the gossipers are giving you spurious informa
tion, Your Excellency.”

“I hear that you oppose my appointments.”

“Well, now I concede that now and then, without the ex
perience that only long residency can bring to you, som
unfortunate appointments—”

“Who? Daniel Boone?”

“Why, sir, I would not wish to delve into names.”

“Word comes to me that you find my decisions unsa
isfactory. Now is your chance to tell me to my face.”

To my face. All of it had been behind my back. Fortunatel
I have friends, like Moses Austin, who listen carefully, an
make note.

“You are a most admirable man, sir, and a great explore
and the territory is honored by your august presence. On oc

casion your behavior is a bit, ah, uninformed. If you would call on me to instruct you before you act precipitously, you might thereby save yourself the inevitable grief of a mistake, as well as spare the government a great sum of money." He continued, peaceably. "I know that Secretary Dearborn is much vexed, sir, at your inability to convey to him on a *regular basis* the state of affairs here, and I know that this silence is something that needs your close attention."

Bates always spoke like that to me, often in windy tropes. But I wanted particulars this time, and intended to press him.

"Mr. Bates, I have it on good authority that you are telling people my public approbation here has waned. Have you said it?"

"Why, I cannot recollect it. You see, this is a treacherous place where words are twisted—"

"Is it perhaps because I proclaimed the land to the west of us an Indian Territory in April, and informed those settlers west of the line, who were squatting on Indian lands to which we have no title, to abandon their homesteads?"

"Well, Your Excellency, I hear much anger about it. You are siding with the savages against our own white settlers."

"I'm favoring the fur trade as well as the tribes. And now the paradox, Mr. Bates. Have you also told people that my Indian policies are too harsh and that I will bring down war upon St. Louis?"

He shook his head sadly, even as his eyes blinked and blinked.

"That my celebrity as an explorer has gone to my head? That I have been spoiled, as you put it, by the flattery and caresses of the high and the mighty?"

"I have not publicly said anything of that sort, Your Excellency; only that you want experience."

"Then privately, if not publicly?"

"I can't imagine where such gossip rises from, sir. This is a city of wagging tongues."

"And does yours wag?"

"I try always to be the soul of discretion, Governor."

"I am told that you feel I have no ability to govern and that my military habits make me inflexible, that I don't take advice, and that my acts are harsh. That you resent my partnership with General Clark, and that you feel left out."

Bates blanched. "Really, Your Excellency, this is scarcely the time or place to hash out such matters—"

"What better time, Mr. Bates? Let us put matters on the table. If you have aught against me, tell me first. If you oppose my policies, tell me first. You are a conscientious public servant. You've organized and published the legal codes of the territory, and been of great service to me, and I will make a point of thanking you for your attentions to duty. If you are unhappy and want to hold this office, say so to our superiors, and to me. If you are not content as secretary, then make the proper decision based on your circumstances. I am offering you the hand of friendship now."

I extended my hand. He grasped it and pumped vigorously. I hoped it might lead to peace, but my instincts told me it wouldn't.

20. CLARK

Julia has been pressing me for relief from the crowded conditions here. She braced me in our bedroom the other night, just before we snuffed the candle, saying that she needed more space and privacy. The baby is due in the spring and she wants room to lave and cradle it. My niece lives a half-public life in the makeshift bedroom we have supplied her and is talking of returning to Kentucky. I would rather she stayed to make company for Julia.

I could see the fear in Julia when she asked me the question she had obviously been working toward for weeks: would I ask Meriwether to find other quarters? I listened carefully, keeping my own wishes hidden, and reluctantly agreed. In fact, the governor's presence in our household allows us to proceed seamlessly in public affairs, because we hash things through at supper each evening, and come to a meeting of minds.

But Julia has a point, and as loath as I am to change the arrangement, I know I must.

There is something more about this that has concerned me. My young bride does not like Meriwether. She has not told me so and never will, but it is plain to me. She curtsies when he enters the house, addresses him stiffly, turns from an effusive and chattering young woman into a starchy one at the table, and avoids him whenever possible, pleading the press of household duties.

I have watched this odd behavior for months and last night, when she again broached the subject of evicting our boarder, I questioned her gently about it.

"Is there something about Meriwether that troubles you, Julia?" I asked.

"General, he is a most esteemed man."

I laughed, spotting the evasion. I took her hands and clasped them. "I think you are not at ease with him."

She stared at me a moment, like a doe caught in lamplight. "The very opposite, General. He is not at ease with me. His voice rises, and he becomes, well, very strange and polite. So I am not at ease with him. He is not comfortable with anyone of my sex, sir."

"You don't say!"

She wouldn't say more, just shook her head, even though I probed further. I did not want discord in my household and knew I would be forced to act.

"Very well, Julia, I'll ask the governor to find other quarters. But I will urge him to partake of our suppers, as always, because we have much to discuss. It is an arrangement very satisfactory to me."

"Oh, would you?" She beamed at me as if I had conferred a great honor upon her. "Alice will be so happy! And once we have the bedroom back, I'll . . ."

I chuckled heartily. I enjoy pleasing her whenever I can.

"Oh! I'll have a place to wash the baby and change the diapers," she said. "Oh, General!" She clasped me to her bosom and gave me a great hug, so tenderly that the clocks stopped.

She was so ecstatic over that small change in our lives that I marveled. And yet I should not have marveled at all.

Julia's conduct affirmed something that was becoming more and more obvious to me: Meriwether has an oddly negative effect on women. Alice Anderson flees him just as much as Julia does, and he has made no headway with her. Something about him falters at the doorstep of the fair sex. I am too dumb in that department to fathom why. But it is plain to me. I have watched it at balls and banquets. I have seen it in his banter: he rattles on about women almost obsessively, as if he was trying to make a point. Of his manhood I have no doubt at all, but his defeats have disarrayed him and women flee from him.

"You will need another laundress, maybe two," I said, alluding to the burden of diapers, in addition to the bed and table linens and towels and clothing the household dirtied in abundance.

"Yes, General, I will."

"I will send to Kentucky for some of my slaves," I said. "I need one myself. How about Khaki, Truman, and Mousy? I've leased them to my brother, and I can get them back. This is October fourth; we should have them before Christmas."

"Oh! I'd feel pampered!"

"Consider it done."

I had not seen Julia so happy since we arrived here. She beamed, pressed her hands to her stomach, and sighed.

I will have my slaves shipped from Kentucky. I need another houseboy. Public service requires every moment of my time and I cannot devote it to the mundane management of my dwelling. I am beset by impending war with Great Britain, and war with the Sauks, Fox, Potawatomis, Sioux, Osages, and maybe other tribes, and I've a half-trained, half-armed militia.

So I will put them all under York's supervision, and make space in the attic. It will be crowded up there, but they should be grateful to be out of the cold. The alternative would be to build a slave shack in the back lot, next to the slaves' privy.

This evening I will tell Meriwether our family is growing and we need the space. He will understand, being a sensitive man and affectionate friend. He has already told me that he can have a room with Chouteau until he finds rooms.

I hunted for York, and found him carrying stove wood into the parlor, his black muscles rippling.

"You lookin' for me, mastuh?"

"I'm bringing three more slaves into this household, and placing them under you. Two laundresses and a houseboy."

He settled the wood carefully, unsmiling. I had thought he might enjoy having more of the darkies around.

"You gonna stick them up the attic, too?" he asked.

"There's room enough."

"Room enough, yassuh, so there is, lying side by side."

"You have objections?"

He fidgeted a moment, his yellow eyes peering at the floor. "I've been meaning to ask, boss. You maybe hire me out in Louisville for some little while? You gets the money for me workin'?"

"Why?"

"Ah sure wanna see my wife, mastuh."

"No, I need you here," I said.

He looked so crestfallen that I regretted my tone. "Maybe a visit. I can send you back there for a few weeks, but not now. Next year."

His cheerfulness deserted him entirely. "You mind if I ask something? You let me speak some?"

I nodded. He was my old friend. We had grown up together from childhood and he had been my personal servant for as long as I could remember.

"I goes out on that big trip, and I's as good as any man you got there. I cooks the food just as good, and I hunts good, and I lifts and totes just as good, and I paddles hard, and I guards you like a soldier. I gets just as hungry as them white men, and I gets colder because I's the last to get some skins to wear. But I never do no complaining, not like some white men. You nevah hear a word of anger out of me all them days. You pay them, but you don't pay me because you own me."

He was raising my bile but I pushed it back. I knew where this was heading and didn't like it. He was virtually a free man out West, welcomed into the company of my men. He had the same liberty as they; wooed the dusky maidens as they did. Carried a rifle and hunted, dressed the meat, cooked and walked and paddled and starved. It was like schooling. Once they learn their ABCs, they're ruined. You can't make a slave out of them if they get their learning, and the only use is to sell them for field hands and let them taste the whip. Now, suddenly, York is remembering how it was, and he's little good around here anymore.

"Get it out of your head, and don't ever let me hear it again," I said. "I'm not going to let you go. I'm not going to let you buy your way out, either. You're worth fifteen hundred dollars, and I can't afford to replace you. You are going to keep on right here, and do it cheerfully, or I'll sell you to someone who's a lot harsher than I am. Count yourself lucky."

He seemed to pull deep into himself.

"You can see your woman next spring," I said, intending to soften the decision a little.

He said nothing, but he lifted his gaze from the floor, and stared directly into my face, and I could see those yellow-brown eyes examine me, as if I was on trial. He radiated pain, a hurt so strong and dark that I almost recoiled.

"Yes, General," was all he said.

I stalked away, itching to whip him for his insolence. But I am a man of slow temper and I checked myself. I do not fathom why he irked me almost beyond my limits.

This evening, while Meriwether and I sipped some New Orleans amontillado while we waited for the mammies to finish cooking the supper, I braced him.

"We've a child coming, Meriwether, and my wife would like to commandeer the rest of the house." I smiled. "She is a woman of great determination, and has taken to ordering the general of militia around."

"A child! I might have guessed! Congratulations, old friend!" Lewis exclaimed, the brittleness of it odd in him. I had never heard this tone during the whole expedition.

"I shall be the gallant and remove myself forthwith," he said.

"Meriwether, I salvaged a little from her onslaught: we hope you'll continue to sup with us."

"General, how can I resist, with so fair a young lady as Miss Anderson to grace our table?"

There it was again, this banter about women. "We always have certain matters to discuss, and it seems a very good time to do it," I said.

"I fear we just bore your beauteous niece with our business," he said.

I had no answer to that.

21. LEWIS

Almost every day I open the journals and read them. Most entries are in Will's hand, and are brief. He was faithful to the task, and recorded the day's events without fail, save only for a brief hunting trip, and even then summarized what had happened during that one lapse.

I planned to keep a full journal myself, but found myself otherwise occupied, so that I did not live up to my good intentions. I wish to excel in everything I do. But it had been a matter of indifference to me whether the events of a dull day were recorded. I always had a higher task in mind, which was to record anything of *importance:* plants, animals, geographical features, oddities, weather, and always, the savages. This I did as faithfully as steady old Will kept the daily accounts of mundane matters.

It is a matter of temperament, that's all. I am inclined to scribble endlessly about a *new species;* he is content in his phlegmatic way to record the miles we traveled, the latitude and longitude, and the condition of the troops.

I room now with Pierre Chouteau in a spacious, sunny manse delicately appointed in all the latest fashion, with fabrics and furniture sometimes brought clear from Paris or England. The place suits me, though I will not abide here long for fear of their hospitality wearing thin. I am looking for rooms. I have rented an office not far from Will's house, to which I still repair after a day's toil to sup with him and his blossoming Julia. She seems more at ease now that I no longer intrude upon her nest.

The journals cast a spell over me and I cannot escape it. They seem heavy in my hand, like pigs of lead, crushing my fingers under their weight. And yet it is all illusion. The cold weight, really, is the expectations of the world and the growing impatience of Thomas Jefferson and the eagerness with which my colleagues in the American Philosophical Society await the detailed account of our great voyage. Here it is, mid-October of 1808, and I have not yet started.

Each day I open them intending to begin an edited version for my publisher, Conrad. Each day I read the entries and they release a flood of memories in me. Here Will describes the time Charbonneau almost sank the pirogue. There I describe the magical moment when I beheld the falls of the Missouri. And here is where we finally found the

Shoshones, shy as mice, and with them and their horses, our *salvation* . . .

I page through them: Will's hand is as familiar to me as my own. His want of learning shows; my schooling shows whenever I put nib to paper. His entries are strong, honest, and prosaic; mine extend beyond the ordinary realm, soaring into feeling, speculation, observation—especially observation, for I pride myself on a keen eye, and with that eye I discovered more new species of plant and bird and beast than I can name.

It is an odd thing, opening those journals and swiftly returning to that bright sweet land, never before seen by white men, the shining sun-baked prairies, the gloomy snow-mantled mountains, the wary savages thinking unfathomable thoughts, the rolling river, the salt-scented breeze off the western sea. This flood of images trumps my best intentions. Why do I pen letters and long treatises on policy, but never put nib to paper when it comes to these journals? It is maddening.

I don't suppose mere words can adequately describe our great journey, the sight of men toiling up the river, the fear and pleasure as we set ashore at the Sioux or Arikara or Mandan villages, the dread with which I first sliced a gray morsel of roast dog and put it in my mouth, the rejoicing when we tasted the brine of the western sea. No, these are too private, too vivid, to convey to the world.

But my president grows restless. And underlying that restlessness is the simple fact that these journals are not really mine or Will's; they belong to the government. We recorded events as officers in the army, as a part of our public mission, expressly for the government.

Mr. Jefferson has graciously given us the priceless opportunity to profit from them, a gift so much larger than anything else he or Congress did for us that it chastens me.

There is a large profit to be had from it. Will and I have invested most of what we received in back pay from the voyage of discovery in the project, but after publication there will be money enough to keep us in fine style for years to come. And yet I have not begun. And daily, Tom Jefferson's disappointment in me deepens.

I tax myself with it. Why have I delayed? It is now two years since we set foot in St. Louis. I am stopped! My mind recoils! In the East I proceeded at once toward publication, getting an education in the printer's arts in the process. I hired various artists, even Charles Willson Peale; put a fine mathematician to work on our celestial observations, put draftsmen to work on the maps, got out an attractive prospectus, and all the rest. They have all been busy working with my drawings and specimens: Frederick Pursh, the botanist, has rendered the plants exquisitely. Everything progresses except me.

I offer myself excuses. I was ill and privately closeted at Locust Hill, I'm pressured by the chaotic territory with its catalogues of troubles, I am in great demand as a speaker and guest and civic leader, which consumes most every evening. My Masonic lodge consumes my time. But they all seem lame to me. I know only that each day I fail to write, I feel further squeezed by a terrible vise, and now I contemplate these journals with quiet desperation.

I have been fitful this autumn, suffering the ague twice, and conquering it with the familiar extract of cinchona bark called quinine that is commonly available here for the malady, as well as some calomel. My body aches; I believe the privations of our long overland journey taxed it and I have been slow to recover. I am increasingly excitable, a humor I ascribe to the pressures I labor under.

To curb my restlessness I sip spirits during the day, porter, wine, and sometimes whiskey. In the evenings, I sample whatever my hosts and hostesses place in hand, and am calmed. My sleep has been restless, but I have found a good remedy in the drops of laudanum I drink before bed.

Pierre Chouteau is the soul of hospitality, and includes me in the bright evening society of the Creoles. I take breakfast with him, and for all this he scarcely charges me anything, which is just as well because my accounts are strained to the utmost.

I have made progress on all but one matter: our Mandan guest, Big White, remains in St. Louis, and I am charged with getting him home. Indeed, Mr. Jefferson considers it the highest of my priorities, believing rightly that our entire Indian diplomacy in the West depends on our success.

She-He-Ke, his wife and son, and the interpreter Jessaume, had been settled at Cantonment Bellefontaine, under the watchful eye of the army, but the chief grew restless and insisted on coming here. Chouteau is good with Indians and I have put our guests in Chouteau's care.

Big White has gotten but a few English words, and I cannot communicate with him, but I gather from Jessaume that he regards himself as a brother of the president, that is, a chief of state very like Mr. Jefferson, and wants to be wined and dined as such. And so we do, at the expense of the territory.

Jessaume and his Mandan wife and son have been cooperative. I've taken a liking to the boy, and see some potential in him and have offered to school the boy if Jessaume wishes it. I have in mind making him a factor in the fur trade someday; maybe putting him in charge of one of the government posts we are erecting. In all this I am borrowing a leaf from Will, who offered to settle our interpreter Charbonneau and his Shoshone squaw hereabouts and raise and educate their son, Pomp. It's my fancy to do much the same.

Meanwhile our savage guest has gotten himself up in a fine broadcloth outfit, along with his wife, and they parade through St. Louis daily, delighting the citizens with their affable greetings, their wonderment at all the devices of white civilization, and their prodigious appetites, for no plate is large enough to placate She-He-Ke's appetite.

Meanwhile I brood about the task before me. With the Arikaras so violently opposed to our passage because of an imagined insult, the whole might of the United States is checked, and the British are playing havoc. The Rees, as most men call them, suppose one of their sachems was murdered by us while visiting here, though in fact disease took him off, and on that misunderstanding rest our difficulties.

The regular army cannot help me. I made application to them and was rebuffed. They are understaffed and desperately trying to prepare for war with England. It's going to be up to our militia to do the job, but I have been thinking there might be ways to engage enough men to get past the Arikaras.

Thanks to the good offices of Chouteau, we are well advanced on a plan. The idea now is to form a company, the St. Louis Missouri Fur Company, subscribed by leading men here, to equip a formidable force that can return our guests to their home. Chouteau has lined up Will Clark as a partner, along with my brother Reuben, though I will not participate because this is to be a mixed government and private enterprise.

The partners will include Auguste Chouteau, the wily Spaniard Manuel Lisa, that knowledgeable Creole merchant Sylvestre Labbadie, Pierre Menard, William Morrison, and the merchant Benjamin Wilkinson, who is a brother of the conniving general, which worries me. Most of these are merchants. Reuben brings medicine and youth to the enterprise, and preserves our family interest in the venture.

They are working on articles of agreement now, though I have carefully stayed out of it. But my plan is to pay them a considerable sum of public money to take Big White home; a sum that will, with their own capital added, permit them to raise a formidable army of trappers and traders. I shall, of course, impose strict conditions, and require their departure as early next spring as possible.

It seems the best way to get Big White back, given our lack of resources. I can only hope that Secretary Dearborn cooperates and approves. It is a matter most vexing to have to explain the realities of life on the far western borders to men back East; and the secretary has often proven to be obtuse. He will raise stern objections to my proposal to arm these private citizens, and supply them with trading goods with which to ease their way past the numerous tribes along the river.

Shall the government endow a favored few who are thus enabled to make a great profit? Actually, it saves the government great expense. Persuading him of the merit of this plan is crucial, and failure to explain the necessity will be the death of me, I suspect.

22. CLARK

I fear I will end up in debtor's prison unless the new company earns me a good return. For some reason beyond my ken, Meriwether had done nothing about the journals, and with each passing day my hope of gain for the heavy investment I have shouldered to prepare them for publication seems to retreat.

I had put my back pay into them; my stipend as superintendent of Indian Affairs and as a brigadier doesn't stretch far enough to cover my large household, much less get me out of financial peril. I have land in Kentucky, but could scarcely give it away just now. I have household slaves but they don't earn their keep, unlike field slaves who produce marketable crops. Here it is December, over a year after publication was promised, but I have said nothing to Meriwether about the endless delay. Whatever is bothering him, it is afflicting my purse.

Meriwether must be even worse off, because he continually borrows small sums from me, an incontinence that surprises me, but that I indulge. He is spending considerable in taverns and seems to be arrayed with medicines, but I don't ascribe his straits to that but to his speculations in land. He is purchasing thousands of arpents of farmland, most of it from the Chouteaus, almost entirely on credit. I privately question his wisdom. He had not been so injudicious on the expedition, and now his conduct puzzles me.

The new fur company revives my hope of gain. The principal merchants of St. Louis have been gathering regularly in Pierre Chouteau's parlor to contrive an agreement. Meriwether was on hand at every meeting, and in fact we could not launch the St. Louis Missouri Fur Company without his support.

We have a sense of possibility and optimism. Manuel Lisa and his partners returned from the upper Missouri with a fine harvest of beaver pelts and buffalo robes. They had gotten past the Arikaras. Now the three of them, Lisa, Menard, and Morrison, are forming the core of the new outfit. They want me in the organization for several reasons, in part because I can license them, in part because of my knowledge of the upper Missouri, and in part because I have been involved in marketing the government's pelts acquired through our factory trading system, and know how to get the best prices.

So we gathered this chill evening to fashion an agreement, after much discussion. Chouteau had a fine blaze going in his fireplace, and treated us to black cheroots and a lusty red port. The Cuban cigars wrought a pungent haze in the candlelight, and put us all in a good humor.

The governor, who had plainly done some thinking, offered us his terms, pacing the parlor with an energy that startled me, as if he contained within something that would burst him wide open unless he released it.

"The government places utmost importance upon returning Big White to the Mandans. Mr. Jefferson requires it of me and has authorized any reasonable expenditure. We lack the armed strength to do it, and must rely on you. I will pay you seven thousand dollars for the safe delivery of Big White. With this money you will equip your own militia of at least a hundred twenty-five men, and will supply them with rifles and powder and lead, as well as other necessaries.

"I will supply a departure date in the spring; you will need to leave before then or forfeit. I'll put that in the contract. We will provide you with trading licenses and whatever other assistance you require."

Meriwether spelled out a great many details, almost as if they were rolling out of some articles of agreement already fashioned in his mind, while the partners—I should say future partners because no such articles of agreement have been completed—listened and smoked.

I knew they would agree to it, without a murmur.

There were men sitting in that parlor I did not trust. Lisa for one, the crafty Spaniard who had overcharged Captain Lewis for the goods he got us on the eve of the expedition. And Benjamin Wilkinson, brother of the conniving general.

But such was my fever to conquer the upper Missouri that I resolved to stomach the opportunists.

The British are up there, flagrantly and openly trading with the Mandans, Sioux, and Hidatsas, and other tribes in Upper Louisiana, and setting them against us. It is a part of their undeclared war, this nibbling at our sovereignty and our commerce.

If war does break out, we might well face a massive Indian uprising, orchestrated by the North West Company in Canada and intended to sever the whole territory from our grasp. To stop that, I would make alliance with the devil. The very word Briton is enough to put me in a bilious humor.

But these merchants are not devils, merely opportunists, and one way to secure their loyalty, and procure the allegiance of the tribes, is to let them profit.

"Mes amis," said Pierre Chouteau, "we have heard the governor. Are we to form the company or not?"

We agreed to form one, a partnership in which we all would put in an equal share, as we had already discussed at length. I didn't know where I'd find the means, but I would, somehow. I had land to trade. Andrew Henry was as strapped as I, but had made enough from his lead mines to invest. About Reuben Lewis I didn't know, but he seemed as ready as the rest.

We spent the remainder of that evening hammering out the articles, while Meriwether sat silently by. Quite possibly he was a silent partner, with Reuben as his proxy, but none of us would ever know. Given his position, he was judiciously staying apart. Most of the partners would go up the river themselves; I was exempted because of my office. They made me the accountant and offered me a small salary to handle all the receipts, expenditures, and disbursements. Given what I knew of the fur markets, I thought I could do a good job of it.

The agreement had still to be drafted, copies made and signed, but we walked out of that meeting with a capitalized company. My fortunes would ride on its success. The government's Indian diplomacy would ride on our ability to restore She-He-Ke and his family to his people. If we did that, and showed our muscle, we would hold the Missouri River.

I started downslope that night with my cape drawn tightly about me, my mood as blustery as the wind. I rather hoped to encounter a pair of footpads, just so I could bang their skulls together. But no one molested me.

I knew what was roiling me: I ached to go upriver. The talk in Chouteau's parlor had unleashed a flood of memories, of breezy prairies under an infinite sky, of the river dancing in sunlight, of iridescent black-and-white magpies darting ahead of us and making as much commotion as they could, of standing on a bluff overlooking the sweet land, the sea of wilderness, seeing the bright snowy mountains on the farthest horizon, the backbone of the continent, and feeling more at home than at any hearth back in civilization. I wanted to go. The westering itch had nipped me. But I had a bride now, and a child on the way, and an army at my command, and a president looking over my shoulder.

An icy gale banged me into my house, and I pulled off my cloak and stood a moment in the darkness. York materialized out of the gloom, but the candles were out.

"You have a good meeting, mastuh?" he asked, taking my cloak and hanging it.

"The partners are saying yes," I replied.

"Goin' up de river?"

"Beaver pelts and robes and maybe chasing the British back to Canada."

"Lots of men goin' upriver, get past them Rees?"

"Two hundred anyway, including a hundred twenty-five armed." I grinned. "We'll get Big White home this time."

"They leaving in the spring?"

"May at the latest."

"You want anything, mastuh?"

"No, York, I'll go to bed."

"The mistress, she done gone an hour ago."

I nodded.

"You mind I ask a question, mastuh?"

I stood, waiting.

"I's wanting to go up the river. You sell my services, you make plenty money, and I go work my way with them that goes to the mountains."

I stared at him. He stood in the shadows, his hands wringing, his cat-eyes soft upon me.

"Mastuh? I been up that river. I knows the ropes. I's experienced. I's good with a gun. I's a good cook. I's a man can skin a hide off any critter. I's a man been there and back . . ."

He wanted to go up there plenty. I could see it in him. I could sell his labor, profit from him, two hundred dollars in my pocket and I wouldn't have to feed or clothe him. He'd be an asset to them. He'd be one of a handful who had been over every inch, who knew every trick.

"No, and don't ask me again," I said, a steely tone in my voice.

"Mastuh?"

"I said no! No! You've got an eye for those savage women, and you can just forget that."

"That ain't it, mastuh."

I knew that wasn't it. Up in the mountains he would be a free man for a few months. He would do better than most of the whites, especially the greenhorns.

"York, go to bed. You will do as I say, when I say, and without objection."

I heard a moan, an exhalation, a collapsing of his lungs, and watched him shuffle off through bleak shadows.

"York! You can go to Louisville and see your woman for a few weeks."

"Thank you, mastuh."

I heard him shuffle up the narrow stairs.

Anger percolated through me. The trip west had sabotaged a good slave. But I pitied him, too, old York. I knew exactly what he was hoping for. Just before the wind blew me into my house, I was thinking of the shining mountains, and longing for the boundless land. York was longing for it, too, but for different reasons.

Well, damn him. I'd whip him if he asked me again, damn his black hide. Old York, my friend from childhood.

23. LEWIS

A great weariness afflicts me. The more I achieve, the more rebuff I encounter. Now it is Bates again. Let me decide on a course of action or appoint a man to any office, and he will take the opposite tack or complain that I have selected the wrong man.

I gave him some advice, hoping to slow down the galloping gossip floating around St. Louis: "When we meet in public, let us at least address each other with cordiality," I said.

He seemed to accept the prescription.

I thought I had patched things up. He promised to bring his objections to me privately, where we could discuss them frankly, but that scarcely lasted a week. He fumes and fulminates and complains and imagines rebuffs and insults in such number that I am baffled. The effect of all this is to make my burdens heavier and impede my progress.

And now about the ball. It is the December social season, and these affairs occur almost nightly and will continue until well into the new year. It is de rigueur to invite the governor, and I go to as many as I can, enjoying the company, and the belles.

But there Bates was, self-important and dour, at the punch bowl, discussing affairs of state with a guest, and staring daggers at me as I approached. I had no wish to offend, nor did I wish to speak or suffer yet another altercation so I simply sat nearby and began conversing with a Creole dowager who knew a little English.

Ah, that was my mistake! I had ventured in public too close to his person!

A great quiet settled over the hall. Bates had proclaimed far and wide in Missouri that he would meet me only officially, and never socially, and here we were, only a few yards apart. The gossips were watching.

With an affronted mien, the secretary of the territory abandoned the punch bowl and walked as far from me as he could, an obvious and blatant insult.

That offended me more than any other of Bates's malicious acts. The ball was over, at least for me, and I stalked into the cold night, boiling at the man, thinking to meet him on the field of honor, outraged at his infinite capacity to cause trouble. I have never been so angry.

This time, I sent my new mulatto manservant, John Pernia, to Clark, thinking I needed a second. Clark hastened to my office, where I met him in the cold darkness, without lighting a lamp, and there I told him I had had my fill of the obnoxious secretary, and that his conduct was intolerable, and I would seek redress. I would not let it pass.

The general calmed me down. "I'll talk to him, Meriwether, and see whether I can win an apology."

"Do it now."

"No, not now. I'm going to let him cool down."

"He gave deadly insult. I'm ready for what comes!"

Will eyed me quietly. "One Aaron Burr is too many."

I thought of Tom Jefferson's embarrassments and how I might add to them out of rashness, and subsided. Vice President Burr had fallen into disgrace after killing Alexander Hamilton in a duel; he had dabbled with empire building out here, inviting the British and then the Spanish to help him detach Louisiana from the republic.

He had been acquitted of treason for want of firm evidence, and had fled to Europe in voluntary exile. His lovely daughter, Theodosia Burr Alston, wife of a Carolina governor, was an acquaintance of mine. The gossips had linked us, but there never was a thing to it. I had watched the Burr trial in Richmond as the president's observer, and that was as close as I ever wanted to get to Aaron Burr.

The image of that hollow-eyed, haunted, and bitter man, sitting in the dock, flooded through me, and I realized that my old friend Will was steering me away from the dock in his own gentle way. It was not the first time I felt a flood of gratitude toward my old comrade.

But Will was not done with me. "Governor, it behooves you to consider what you have said or done that maddens Frederick Bates," he said.

The heat boiled up in me. "Are you accusing me?"

Will grinned. "Just that sometimes we don't see what we do to others."

"I have treated him with perfect civility."

"And so you have, old friend. Why then, do you set him off?"

"I haven't the faintest idea," I said sharply, my tone telling Clark I had no wish to pursue the matter further.

"Do you seek his opinions? Counsel with him?"

"His views aren't worth my attention."

Will started to say something, and then obviously checked himself. "I get along with him all right," he said at last.

"You're not the governor! He was the acting governor until I arrived, and he can't forget it."

Clark clapped me on the back. "Guess he can't," he said cheerfully. "Guess you can't, either."

That last lanced through me, and it was all I could do to stop the black mood that surged through me. Was he telling me the fault was mine? What *was* he telling me? Was he my friend, or had he turned on me, too?

"Let's go home," he said gently.

I parted with him in the dark street, my thoughts riding furiously in all directions. Will was settled and happy; a baby was coming soon. He enjoyed St. Louis. I had never heard a whisper of malice directed toward him. What had Fate given him that Fate denied me? I watched him vanish into the closeness of a starless foggy night, and turned toward my rooms, my mind still churning.

Would anyone ever honor me for all that I had accomplished in Louisiana? Not even Will knew what I had done. As I walked, I took refuge in my accomplishments.

I had made great progress, started a road to Ste. Genevieve and New Madrid, published the territorial codes, proclaimed an Indian territory, promulgated a law allowing villages to incorporate, curbed promiscuous licensing of traders, put up forts on the Osage and Des Moines Rivers that helped check the British, appointed good men to various offices, put out a spy network to keep an eye on the Spanish along our southwest border, put Nicholas Boilvin, my best man with the Indians, to work dealing with the Sauk and Fox tribes up north, and bringing to justice some murderers they were harboring.

And with Will's help I had dealt with the Osages and submitted a treaty to the Senate, cashiered the disloyal and lazy elements from the militia and put good men in command, settled some of the bold stakery, or the claim disputes, over the Ste. Genevieve lead mines, started work on a shot tower, won over the wary Creoles to the republic, and now, at long last, was closing in on the hardest and most urgent of all tasks, getting Big White back to the Mandan villages.

I should have been proud. Instead, I was weary in a strange way that seemed to rise from my very bones. Secretary Dearborn had become more and more abrupt and demanding, and also more obtuse about the dangers here; and Mr. Jefferson, a man I regarded as my father, had written sharply to me about my failure to correspond, and to put the journals in order.

And as great as my accomplishments were, the combined dissatisfaction of the president, Secretary Dearborn, and the territorial secretary, who loathed my very presence, weighed more on me than everything I had achieved. They were hovering over my shoulder like ghosts, wanting to undo my decisions.

Governing was harder than I had ever imagined. I had expected to make enemies as well as friends; I hadn't expected the backbiting, gossip, malice, and secret machinations intended to undo my every act, and drive me from office.

I am feeling indisposed again, and fear another bout of ague is coming. But these come and go, and I am in the pink of health, except for an odd and inexplicable malaise, like a crouched wolf within me. I do not call on Reuben for treatment, and have not seen a physician on my own account since I arrived here. Such remedies as I need for the ague, such as cinchona bark extract called quinine, I can get easily enough from the Creole apothecaries in town.

There is a bright spot. Through my solicitation, I have gotten a newspaper into the territory, the Missouri *Gazette*, and by it I am broadcasting my ideas and publishing my laws and regulations. Though I am consumed by territorial business, I still find time to pen my thoughts, which are duly published under the nom de plume Clatsop. What better means could there be to shape the opinions of my citizens? I much prefer penning my thoughts for publication than writing to all those in Washington who demand things of me. My own father died when I was a boy; it is painful for me to correspond with those who presume to govern my conduct.

I have not neglected my own fortunes, either. I have written my mother to tell her that I am putting the family estate at Ivy up for sale to finance my purchases here. It is my intent to bring her and the rest of my family here and settle them on the generous and fruitful farmlands I have acquired from the Chouteaus. I have already paid three thousand for these lands, and owe two more large payments next May and the following May. And then the Lewis and Marks families will be handsomely established here in the West.

But until I effect that sale in Virginia, I will be pressed to the limit. Just the other day, I borrowed $49.50 from Will for two barrels of whiskey. I have had to borrow from him, from the Chouteaus, and others, mostly for ordinary medicines and spirits, and the care of my manservant, Pernia. I have a few dozen small notes about town, which I will redeem as soon as I can.

There is no margin of error: I have put every cent into real estate and fur trade interests, which should profit me handsomely and secure a comfortable income for my family. But such is the rising value of land here that I can scarcely go astray, and I am deeply indebted to the Chouteaus who have made such rich farmland available to me.

I live in great expectation, sensing that everything for which I was put upon the earth is coming to fulfillment.

24. CLARK

This Wednesday, December 7, 1808, I shipped York to Louisville on a keelboat and gave him four dollars to feed himself. I told him to be back here before the end of May. I supplied him with papers and had him carry a letter to my brother in which I said that if York should prove refractory, he should be sent to the auction in New Orleans and sold.

I am glad to have him out of the house. He was a sullen presence here, full of the notion that he should be freed because of his service during the expedition. He's not fit to be a free man, though he thinks he is. He will visit his wife while hiring out for her master, and if that doesn't cure him I will ship him south to the slave auction myself.

This aggravates me. He was a faithful friend and servant until he got back from the West. Now he is hardly worth the auction price of an aged male. Let him find out what life as a field hand is like, if he continues to spread his malcontent in my household. I blame myself: I never should have taken him with me. He got notions out there that will never go away.

I am having a bad time with the slaves. They don't like their attic quarters, and I am growing impatient with them.

Maybe a taste of the whip will cure them. Meriwether tells me to contain myself. I think he has an eye to the national acclaim we share, and doesn't want my dealings with York to intrude upon our celebrity. He is kind to York, but that is only because he doesn't own York or face his daily insolence.

The holidays are upon us, and my household is greatly improved by the absence of discord. My niece, Alice, left a fortnight ago, having had her fill of St. Louis. Suddenly we have room and privacy. Julia has not yet closeted herself, but will soon. She is suffering from a variety of ailments, including nausea in the mornings. She is feeling ungainly but when she thinks of the child she brightens, and her eyes glow. She takes my hand and presses it to her swollen middle, and I marvel at the life that is blossoming there.

We still have Meriwether for supper each night, and he joins us in our dining room to discuss the state of the territory. He is a gifted man, and yet I worry about him. Why does he provoke Frederick Bates almost beyond reason? I have no trouble with Bates, apart from considering him a windbag and a vain man. But Meriwether turns Bates into a rabid dog.

I visited Bates in his office a week or two after the great public contretemps, and told the secretary that I was acting as an intermediary and peacemaker, and I regarded him a friend.

"Frederick, maybe it is time to reconcile with the governor," I said, after we had gingerly visited a bit. "You might find him eager to accommodate you if you were to stop by and see him."

Bates would have none of it. He sprang to his feet, in a huff, and began shouting.

"No! The governor has *injured* me and he must *undo* the injury or I shall succeed in fixing the stigma where it ought to rest. You come as *my* friend, but I cannot separate you from Governor Lewis. You have trodden the ups and downs of life with him and it appears to me that these proposals are made solely for his convenience."

I nodded, for there was nothing more to say, and retreated.

Once out the door of that meticulously disciplined office, where not a pin is out of place and every paper is nested in its proper folder, I smiled. The secretary evokes that in me.

But Bates's conduct opened certain avenues of thought that perplexed me deeply. The man has trouble getting along with anyone, and routinely ruptures relations with men all over the territory. And yet, and *yet* . . . why is he doubly venomous toward Meriwether? And is there blame on both parts? Mr. Jefferson and Secretary of War Henry Dearborn have confidence in Bates, and that says something.

If Bates has succumbed to an excess of feeling, so has Meriwether, and this new quality in my old friend puzzles me. If it had existed on the expedition, he had checked it so thoroughly that I never imagined him to be turbulent. But Meriwether is increasingly troubled here, just when he should be quiet of heart.

I took Bates's obdurate response back to the governor, who simply shook his head. His heat about Bates has left him, and he queried me about other things, not least the health of my expectant bride.

"She's aglow, Governor. But she's wallowing about like a walrus and wishing it was over. I will tell you something. If it is a boy, we will name him Meriwether Lewis Clark."

The governor paused, his blue gaze gentle upon me, registering that. "I wish I could do the same for you," he said. Then he brightened. "Why, what a thing to do! I hope the little rascal is bright as a button!"

He beamed at me, and I saw a flash of the old Meriwether shining for a moment.

But then he clouded again, and I saw something haunted in his face. "I'm just a musty old bachelor," he said. "I'll never have children, though it has been my deepest desire for as long as I can remember. I'm getting old and set in my ways, and there's not a woman who would want such a man."

I meant to put a stop to such melancholia, but instead it seemed to drive him deeper into gloom.

"Governor, every time I see you at a party, half the women have eyes for you, and the other half wish they weren't married," I said.

He turned to me with such seriousness, with such pain in those blue eyes, that I supposed I had accidentally stepped on his most tender humor, and I pulled back at once.

"Old friend," I said, "the right woman will come along and then you'll know the bliss of marriage, an estate that I find suitable to my temperament."

He brightened. "I have an eye for the ladies, and maybe I'll go wooing," he said, but with that odd brittleness in his voice again.

I sensed he wouldn't. I sensed that woman was an unscalable alp for Meriwether, but I am dumb about such matters, and didn't even hazard a guess why.

"Thank you anyway," he said softly. "I never have had a child named for me. Ah, Will . . ." He sighed.

I do not know why I worry so about the governor.

The new year approaches. We have just received word that Mr. Madison probably will be our next president, though they were still counting rural precincts and nothing was official. He is an intelligent bantam with a bright new wife named Dolley, a Virginian like Thomas Jefferson, but not a quarter the man. I worry about whether he grasps how close we are to war with England and what the Canadians are regularly doing across our western frontier.

I would like to travel to Washington to take the measure of the man, and also to brief him about our parlous defenses here. I could use a few tons of powder, a thousand muskets, and a few dozen artillery pieces, not to mention a shipment of uniforms, boots, gloves, hats, and mess kits, but that won't happen unless James Madison's secretary of war is a man of vision. The new president's appointments will tell the tale.

My ears have already picked up a scandalous rumor, spread by Bates of course, that Meriwether will be replaced shortly. I don't doubt that the secretary of the territory is doing everything in his power to cause it to happen. He is a veteran letter-writer, and a facile one, and I cannot help but believe that the man whom Mr. Jefferson regarded virtually as a son will be the target of abundant criticism now that Meriwether's patron is leaving office. I would not want to be in the governor's shoes.

His future is bleak. He was orphaned during the revolution, and now he may be orphaned again, in a different but equally grave manner. But he is a grown man, inured to hardship, and surely he will ride any storms. The new men in Washington will honor him as an explorer, but whether they will honor him as a governor remains to be seen. He scarcely knows any of them. They don't know me, either, and I intend to go east next year to make sure that there is some acquaintance among us.

This evening at supper with Julia, I quite unwittingly provoked in Meriwether the first petulance he has ever directed toward me. It came so suddenly I scarcely was girded for it, and came on the wings of a question so innocent of malice that I had to take stock a moment.

I said, simply, "How are the journals coming?"

He shook his head and swallowed some of the pureed potatoes before him.

"I suppose you're about finished," I said.

He flared up. "I will write at my leisure, and do a proper job, and correct the innumerable errors, and if that doesn't suit you . . ." He left the rest unsaid.

I sat, astonished. Not in all the three years we toiled side by side on the expedition had he raised his voice to me.

I did not quite let go of the subject.

"We have a lot invested in it. The artwork is done; the astronomical calculations are done; the maps are complete. I would like to see the first edition. Money has become a pressing matter with me."

Meriwether glowered. "You have no idea the work that goes into the task," he said. "It requires education and intelligence and abundant time."

I still had no answer. I did not know whether one page or a thousand had been organized and transcribed for Mr. Conrad.

"You could hire it done. I imagine five hundred dollars would pay for an editor."

He continued upon his biliousness, first dabbing his face with a napkin.

"First of all, I don't have five hundred. Secondly, I am the only one who can do it. I alone have been there, know what we saw, and have the schooling to set it down properly."

I grinned at him, and the governor reddened, and we mopped up our gravy in silence.

25. LEWIS

I have been sick abed this entire wassail season and am uncommonly slow to recover. It is the ague again. I have dosed myself with the extract of cinchona bark over and over, but it has little effect. The chills were not present this time, either. Usually, a few hours of chills and shakes precede my fevers, and I am puzzled by the lack this time.

I purged myself with one of Doctor Rush's Thunderclappers, and that seemed to avail me somewhat, but the remedy cramps my belly.

I have second-floor rooms on the Rue L'Eglise now, a parlor and chambers for myself and my manservant. This Monday morning, the second day of January, 1809, Pierre Chouteau stopped in to greet me and found me abed.

"Ah, it is the *maladie*. Shall I summon Reuben, my friend?"

"No, no, I know as much as he does," I said. "We're a medical family."

"*Bien,* if you need a physician, let me know, then, *mon ami.*"

"I have not only the proper remedy but a knowledge of my mother's simples, which I used effectively during the entire expedition. I have just taken some ginseng and goldenseal."

He pursed his lips a moment. "I know of an excellent physician, a royalist refugee from Paris, who practices the most advanced medicine anywhere—"

"Doctor Saugrain," I said. "I know him."

"Your Excellency, he is the man to consult."

"Yes. I've had dealings with him. I engaged him as an

army surgeon to look after my men when we came back from the West. Some were sick, others wounded, and all half starved. He did an excellent job."

"Ah! Then you know of his prowess. A great treasure in St. Louis! I can send a boy and have him here in no time."

"No!" I said sharply.

Chouteau shrugged, that Gallic signal of resignation. "Very well, *mon ami.* I keep account of your men; their health matters to me. We wish to employ them to go up the river with the new company. Ah, the experience they have! They would be invaluable, knowing every mile, every danger. And so I keep track. They are all well, save one."

"Who is that, Pierre?"

"The private called John Shields."

"He's sick? I hadn't heard."

"*Oui,* yes, *très malade*, very sick. The good doctor Saugrain cares for him."

"I am tired. Thank you for your concern," I said abruptly.

I must have addressed him brusquely because he apologized and hastened out the door. I did not mean to be so abrupt with my friend, who was only trying to help. I must curb this uncivil habit; too often I have seen people retreat from me after an exchange. I am under pressure, and sometimes that rules me.

The news of Shields's sickness troubled me. He was one of those who accompanied me in search of the Shoshones that summer of 1805. Shields, MacNeal, and Drouillard and I had gone ahead of the corps to find the Shoshones and their horses.

Poor Drouillard. He went to work for Lisa, was sent to find a deserter named Antoine Bissonnette and bring him back dead or alive, and he brought him back lifeless. The man's relatives demanded that Drouillard be tried for murder. He was acquitted, but the stain is upon him and he has fled upriver. My best man, who saved the whole corps with his brilliant hunting, being tried for murder. It puts me in the bleakest humor.

Shields in poor health, Shannon a cripple after having a leg amputated; who of the old corps will be next? I am most worried about Shields and think I might go to Antoine Saugrain and inquire privately about the matter when I am up again. I want to know the nature of his illness, just for my own information.

So I lie here, in my rented upper rooms on the Rue L'Eglise, with a view overlooking the levee and the great gray river, mending while the business of the territory languishes. Will has come by regularly, and on him rather than Secretary Bates the good order of the territory depends.

Will tells me the baby is coming soon; that Julia is strong and healthy but so burdened with child that she barely can navigate. She depends now on the slaves to bring her meals to her. Even before she was well along, she preferred to retire to her room for her supper, leaving the dining table to Will and me.

My manservant John Pernia attends me daily even though I have little use for him during my illness, and this time I had a request for him apart from fetching my meals, which I purchase at the Old Tavern.

"Bring me Doctor Saugrain," I said.

Pernia, a capable man, nodded and left, and I waited but a short while for the little Frenchman to make his appearance at my chambers.

He bustled in, eyed me, and pulled up a walnut chair beside my bed. Even as he perched on that chair, his slender face rose barely above my head. He had changed none at all since I had engaged him to look after my corps. The black suit, ivory face, pince-nez, coal eyes, spade beard that jutted cockily outward, the flowing salt-and-pepper hair that was gathered at the nape of his neck with a purple ribbon, all comforted me somehow.

"Ah, monsieur, Your Excellency, the governor," he said with a lavish and Gallic sweep of the hand. "You are indisposed?"

"No, I'm getting well, a bit of ague, but it is almost behind me now."

"Ah, the ague, an intermittent fever that torments its victims. We shall look at it."

"No, no, I just want to ask you about my old Corps of Discovery private, John Shields. He is under your care, I believe."

"I cannot talk about the ailments of others in my care, Your Excellency, so forgive me a thousand times—"

"I think you can talk to the governor," I said, "and to the commander who arranged with you for the medical care of my men."

He considered a moment, all the while reconnoitering me with his practiced eye. At last he sighed, frowned, and proceeded.

"*Monsieur le capitaine,*" he said, thus revealing the military grounds by which he would breach a confidence, "it is so. The private Fields suffers from *lues venerea* in the third stage, afflicting his heart and arteries, and my treatments no longer avail. I would give him maybe a few months at the most."

It could not be! "But Doctor, so short a time!"

He shrugged amply, his small arms spread Christ-like upon a phantom cross. "The disease takes its own form in each victim," he said. "In some it advances slowly; in others it is like a rampage of evil and consumes the victim in a few years. In some it disappears and does not emerge until many years later, and then it is often fatal."

"Are you sure?"

"A classic case, Your Excellency. Fast, yes, but as you yourself pointed out to me, your men were weakened by starvation and hardship and the gates of the body were wide open. It was not hard for a disease to enter the door and conquer."

"But the disease mimics several others! You might be mistaken!"

"I might. There is always that."

"What are Shields's symptoms?"

"The disease assaults his heart and arteries. Already there have been hemorrhages. His pulse is erratic. He may fail from an aneurysm. His nerves fail him. He walks on feet that flop about, as if severed from his brain."

I felt a great weight lift from me. I laughed. "What other symptoms of the third stage do you observe?"

"Why, my capitaine, unexplained intermittent fevers, the gummas, or thickenings, especially around the face, destruction of the throat, usually with craters in the middle of them, scars from lesions, copper-colored nodules, hoarseness, an aortic murmur, the femoral pistol-shot sound and double murmur known as Duroziez's sign, aneurysm, strokes, advancing paraplegia . . ."

"When do these appear?"

"Usually it takes a few years. Who knows exactly?"

I laughed again. His brows shot up.

"It depends, my capitaine. The *lues venerea* attacks the weakest system in the victim. So each case is different. In the most tragic cases, it attacks the system of nerves and the brain, and in time induces paresis, or madness, or deterioration of the mind, of thought, of rationality, of feeling, and the worst of it is that the victim knows exactly why his mind is failing and why his feelings are tempestuous; the unspeakable disease is rendering him into a blundering idiot.

"He can read the signs. He remains mostly rational until

the last. There may be seizures. Loss of short- and long-term memory. Flawed judgment, loss of language ability and vocabulary, strange moods, irritability, anger, delusion, hallucination, apathy, weakness of muscles . . .

"He can share his grief with no one. He hides it from the world. He closets himself. He prays, in his saner moments, that no one will ever discover that his madness was caused by a moment of illicit pleasure and that he got from it the most shameful of all sicknesses. Ah, monsieur, that is the worst case."

I laughed, for none of that had anything to do with me.

"Is there any cure?" I asked.

"None. The salt of mercury, it is less and less sovereign as time goes by, and by the third stage, it does little good at all, and only briefly. It might delay, but it cannot conquer."

"My mother has simples for everything."

He lifted those little ivory hands again. "Then I shall gladly learn from her," he said gallantly.

"You'll have the chance. I plan to bring her and my family here shortly."

"Now that I am here, do you wish an examination, Your Excellency?"

"No, I'm recovering from the ague, and have dosed myself."

"Ah, I see. The bark, oui?"

"Yes, and some calomel."

"Ah, I see. Shall I listen to your chest?"

I had no wish to be examined, but as long as he was here, I supposed it might not be a bad idea.

He was already opening his bag and extracting his black lacquered listening horn, so I lay back and waited, knowing I shouldn't submit because I have no way to pay him in the immediate future.

"Ah, now, Your Excellency, we shall see," he said.

26. LEWIS

In this disquieting manner did the year eighteen and nine begin for me. The Lilliputian poked and probed my anatomy, including the bottoms of my feet, employing his listening horn to hear the rumble of my vitals, and his magnifying glass to examine assorted skin rashes. I was amused, though too feverish to enjoy it all.

"Extract of cinchona bark five times daily," I said. "Five drops of laudanum in water, as needed."

He harrumphed and smiled.

A hard sun low in the heavens bit brightly into the room. At last he ceased, and carefully placed his horn and magnifier into his black bag. He turned to the window, his jutty beard poking at the sun, his small body arched to make it an inch taller than it usually was.

I awaited his verdict with rare humor.

"Have you been irritable, my governor?" he asked.

"Uncommonly."

"Impatient?"

"Of course. If you had to deal with what I deal with—"

"What is my baptismal name?"

"Ah . . ." I paused, trying to dredge up a name I had not used in years.

"It is Antoine François."

I was embarrassed. "Why do you ask?"

"Medical reasons."

That seemed most peculiar. I grunted.

"When you posted me as an army surgeon in 1806 to treat your men, you recollected it readily enough after three years in the West, without prompting, Your Excellency."

"I am sorry I am not measuring up to your expectations," I said tartly. "It's been a while. Send me your bill."

He raised a tiny alabaster hand. "It is not about your social aptitude that I am concerned."

"Well? I have the ague. A fevered mind doesn't serve as well as a healthier one."

He paced sternly about the small bright room. "Are you living within your salary?"

"That is not a matter I wish to discuss. I will pay you for your services as soon as possible. Now, if you are done—"

He smiled brightly for the smallest moment.

"*Ah, non, mon ami.* There is more. I have subscribed to your journals, thirty-five dollars to the publisher, Conrad. For this I apply myself to the English. How soon may I expect them?"

"Ah . . . I've been busy."

He peered at me with those black marble eyes. "I am a great admirer of yours. To make that unspeakable journey into the unknown. Ah! What a grand feat! Your Excellency, I await with the great, ah, great eagerness to read of the voyage, and your gifts to science, the new species of the plants and the animals."

He was making me miserable. "It will be some while," I said.

He turned again, frowning. "Is it that the work seems formidable, ah, difficult?"

I nodded.

"Is it that the words don't come?"

"No, I've just been busy."

"Is it that you are, ah, uncertain? How shall I attack this beast and conquer it?"

I smiled. "I suppose you want to help me. You have a background in science. But I alone am qualified. No one can help me."

"Ah, no, monsieur, it is all part of my diagnosis."

I was weary, feeling out of sorts and feverish. I didn't have the energy for social banter. "I am tired, Doctor, and—"

He perched on the edge of my bed, his miniature body birdlike above me.

"It is the venereal," he said.

I smiled. "You have that on your mind. It is an intermittent fever, common to southern latitudes."

He shook his head. "*Lues venerea* lurks like a vampire in the body, silently eating the parts it attacks, invisible to all but the experienced eye, such as mine."

"No, my friend, it isn't." I knew medicine and I knew that I had an intermittent fever, not the venereal. I brightened, making a joke of it. "You Frenchmen, that is all you think of."

He allowed himself the slightest smile. "A little bit of mercury, not a lot. And avoid spirits. That is what I will prescribe. Too much mercury chloride ruins you faster than the venereal. It poisons the brain and ruins the bowels."

"Ah, so now you think I am mad." I glared at him. "Too many of Doctor Rush's Thunderclappers. That's what you're driving at."

He hesitated. "No, not now," he said. I knew there was more he intended to say, even if he wasn't saying it just then.

He stood, his dignity towering much higher than his small frame, his mien grave and sad.

"In some people the disease arrests naturally. In others it progresses, furtively, a secret enemy, an insidious mole tunneling through the body, fouling it. In some, it attacks the heart and arteries, and in others, it commits its sacrilege upon the brain—"

"Doctor Saugrain, that's a fine description of the venereal, but I haven't a sign of it. You are inflicting pain upon me for no good reason."

"I am sorry. I do not wish to inflict pain upon anyone. My oath and dedication are to relieve pain, not inflict it, Your Excellency. A bleak diagnosis is painful. Perhaps some other time, when you are ready to talk to me, I will be found in my chambers."

He pulled his thick black cape about him, and lifted a shining beaver hat to his head, which increased his height dramatically.

"I am sorry," he said, and left. I heard some indistinct commotion as Pernia saw the doctor to the door.

Fevered or not, I sprang up in my nightshirt and examined myself before the looking glass. Was I not Meriwether Lewis, conqueror of a continent, celebrated explorer and naturalist and soldier and governor? Was I not a man of intelligence and learning, a quick study, a man of many parts? Was I not a man of great repute, admired across the whole republic, friend and secretary of a president, and a man with high office in his own future?

I saw all that in the mirror, and something else. I was fevered, and my face was drawn and flushed with heat.

I had had many of these bouts. The ague strikes mostly in warm weather, when the miasmas rise from the swamps, but it recurs anytime, and that was my trouble.

Venereal, indeed! Those French think of nothing else.

I had a bottle of the quinine on my commode, and from this I poured a generous dose into a tumbler of water. I would dose myself more rigorously with the extract of the miraculous bark from South America until I was past this misery, and then return to my tasks.

I gulped down the bitter stuff; nothing is quite so sharp on the tongue as quinine. Immediately I felt better. I would be up and about in a day or two. I regretted engaging Saugrain; I could afford neither his bill nor his misdiagnosis.

I ached, so I uncorked the blue bottle of laudanum and

poured a few drops into the tumbler. Actually, eight or ten drops, more than I had intended. But the tincture of opium always put me at peace; it was a stalwart friend in a shifting world, a remedy I could always count on. I drank it, and then crawled under the gray coverlet, waiting for its beneficial effects to steal through me.

It was not always available in St. Louis, because every drop of it had to be shipped up from New Orleans, and I lived in constant dread of running out of it. I have often abjured the apothecaries to hold back some for me, the governor, no matter what the case, but sometimes they lacked a supply. If worse came to worse, there was always Dover's powder. My injuries, especially the shot through the buttocks when we were near the confluence of the Missouri and Yellowstone, pain me and require relief.

Within a few minutes I began to feel just fine. Maybe this very hour I would rise and set to work on my journals. It was a simple task, transcribing and correcting them. All I had to do was dip the quill and begin. The sun seemed terribly bright, and I thought to ask Pernia to close the draperies, but instead I rolled away from the blinding light and closed my eyes.

There was so much to do, but I didn't feel like doing it. There would be a new president in a few days, and I intended to write James Madison, as well as the new secretary of war, and let them know what I am about. I intended to write Thomas Jefferson and explain why I had not been a good correspondent. But I decided not to do that; he would only inquire once again about the journals, and I wouldn't want to stir up that line of thought.

My indisposition slows me, and loosens my mind, so that it is hard to collect thoughts and send them to the new men. I am going to have to concentrate my mind. I have met Mr. Madison many times; he has been a part of the Jefferson administration. I never cared much for him. He is not a bright man; I fear I will have to explain things to him that Mr. Jefferson grasped instantly. Nor have I seen in the new man the slightest interest in science, and only a minimal interest in commerce. It will be up to me to school him, and his new war secretary, whoever that may be.

I lay back on my pillow and thought of the little Frenchman, Saugrain, fussing about his governor and finding overly much wrong with him. I smiled. He is an eminent physician, and thus always on his mettle, looking for the unseen, spotting the disease that eludes all else. But he missed the obvious in me: malarial fever, and nothing worse.

Tomorrow I would be up and about, and I would return to my tasks.

27. CLARK

The midwives banished me from my own bedroom a few days ago. I sat helplessly in the parlor while servants bustled in and out of there carrying towels and hot water. I didn't like the sound of it, the groaning that pierced even closed doors, the low murmur of worry, the grim looks of the black women who filtered in and out on mysterious errands. But at last, after waiting through a day and half a night, I heard a new sound, a wail, coughing, outrage at being alive, and quiet sobbing. A half hour later they let me in.

The tapers were all lit. It was much too hot even though a March wind howled outside, thundering against the sides of the house and driving tentacles of air through every crack.

They had cleaned everything up. Julia lay abed, pale and sweaty in a fresh white nightdress, her hair matted, her features gaunt, her eyes huge. But she was aglow, and on her bosom lay a little boy wrapped in swaddling clothes, my firstborn, my son.

"He is perfect," she whispered, as if to answer one question.

I stood beside the bed, my hands clumsy.

"It was hard," she said, answering the other question. This was her first child, pushing his way through untraveled country, little explorer that he was.

I beheld a son, with downy blond hair glinting redly in the wavering light of the beeswax candles. The infant was asleep upon the damp cotton over her bosom.

"I am glad," I said. "For you, for the son. I am blessed."

She smiled wanly, and I knew she wanted only to fall into slumber, a sweet oblivion that would begin the healing.

The midwife, Mrs. Perrigault, stood quietly nearby, candlelight glinting from a great silver crucifix upon her black dress. "Is Julia all right?" I asked.

"She is torn."

"Badly?"

"I will need to watch closely. And so will you."

I ran a hand through my coppery hair, and nodded.

Julia opened her eyes again. "Meriwether Lewis Clark," she said, and closed them.

It had been a disappointment to her. She wanted Hancock in the boy's name.

Her hands fondled the child. I studied its tiny mouth and mottled pink face and thought it was the plainest son ever born, plainer even than I am. I shouldn't have named it after handsome Meriwether.

"*Bien,*" said the midwife, gesturing me out. I knew who

was the real commander in that room. In that company, I was the private.

But I would gladly leave all that to the women. I had supplied Julia with enough house servants to keep the baby in diapers, to take care of the infant, a wet nurse to suckle it if need be, to guard it and clean it and to ease every burden of motherhood. I was glad I had the household slaves to do it.

A son! Like little Jean Baptiste, or Pomp as I called him, born of Charbonneau and the squaw Sacajewea way back in 1805. I had taken a shine to that little lad, and now I had one of my own, named Meriwether, too. Maybe Pomp and my boy would meet someday. Long ago I had invited Charbonneau and the squaw to settle here, and promised I would look after Pomp's schooling. But I had not heard a word filtering down the river. Somewhere, Pomp would be growing into a fine boy. Like Meriwether Lewis Clark.

I notified Meriwether and invited him to see his namesake, but for some reason he delayed, at least until this Wednesday, the Ides of March. He promised to be here for supper, and we would visit Julia together. My wife remains mostly abed, having exhausted herself in this hard labor.

Meriwether is taut as a bowstring these days, and I ascribe it to the burdens of office. He walks catlike, as if afraid to put down a foot; a strange conduct after walking across a continent. He has often pleaded illness and no longer sups with us and I miss his lively company.

This evening he arrived in his blue uniform, gold braid shining, boots freshly blacked. He has often worn it since resigning his commission. He looks dashing in it, though it hangs loosely around him.

I greeted him in the parlor upon being notified of his arrival by my houseboy.

"Ah! Meriwether!"

"I've come to see the little gentleman," he said.

"High time," I replied. "You are got up for the occasion."

He eyed me. "Let my namesake see a captain, not a governor. Let him follow the beat of drums, not the beat of politics."

That puzzled me, but so did a lot of things about Meriwether in recent months.

I excused myself to see whether Julia was up and about.

She greeted me in her pink wrapper, sitting in her oak rocking chair.

"The governor's here to see the boy," I said.

"Oh, pray wait until I make myself ready."

Some lengthy time later—I cannot fathom why women consume the better part of an hour to make themselves ready—I ushered Meriwether into our chamber, where Julia held the infant in her lap.

"Ah, madame, it is so good to see you up and well!" he said.

She nodded demurely. "The same might be said of you, Your Excellency."

"And here's the tyke!"

Meriwether circled about, as if he were examining an eaglet in its nest. "Like the sire, like the sire," he said. "Yes, a Clark clear through."

"Would you like to hold him?" Julia asked.

Meriwether fell back at once. "No, no, I would drop him," he said, discovering that ten feet was safe enough distance from the ogre in Julia's lap. "Babies and captains have different humors."

I laughed, but I didn't fail to note Meriwether's edginess.

"You are a lucky man," he said. "I am just a musty old bachelor, and will never have a child of my own."

"Why, of course you will, Meriwether. A woman is easier to conquer than the Bitterroot Mountains, and you conquered the snowy Bitterroots twice."

He didn't laugh as I thought he might. He just shook his head and then smiled brightly, his lips crooked. Then he remembered the graces: "I'm honored to have this boy named for me. May he be blessed. May he grow up strong and true."

He bowed grandly before the boy and his mother.

Julia's face softened. She had not lost her reserve around the governor.

We repaired to the parlor for a glass of amontillado, and Meriwether hastily downed three before he settled into the horsehair settee opposite.

"A fine boy, a compliment to you and your mistress," he said grandly.

I had not heard of an infant described as a compliment before. But then, Meriwether was acting in a most peculiar manner. I poured him a fourth drink from the cut glass decanter, but this time he only sipped.

"Will," he said, "I'm pressed. Mostly medical bills. This ague, you know. Could you spare a few dollars again? It'll all be returned with the next voucher from Washington."

"How much, Meriwether?"

"Twenty? I need to apply ten to the doctor, and my manservant needs something . . ." His voice trailed off.

I nodded, and dug into my purse for some national bank notes, Hamilton's work. I was hurting badly myself, but I would refuse my colleague and captain nothing. He had borrowed other small sums, still unpaid, but no mortal was more honest and I knew it would all be settled eventually. I only hoped I could hang on, myself.

He nodded and tucked it into his pocket. "It won't be long; I promise," he said.

"I can wait. How is the editing coming?"

I had asked the wrong question. He looked like a rat

trapped on a sinking ship, and shook his head. "No time," he said.

There had been time aplenty. I remembered the balls and card parties and Masonic lodge meetings he had attended. Reluctantly, I put aside all hope of seeing any immediate gain from the journals, or my investment in their preparation. I checked a tide of irritation that sloshed through me unbidden.

He must have sensed my distress. "My investments are going well. Three farms, over four thousand arpents. I have them rented out. Some city lots, too. I've put the family estate at Ivy up for sale, and I'll move my mother out here just as soon as I can. We'll be together here. But it's been a struggle, finding the means. I owe Chouteau another sixteen hundred in May, and a like sum in May of 1810. And then . . ." He left the rest unsaid, his mind elsewhere.

He was leaving much unsaid these days. I had noticed it, the incomplete thoughts. He either supposed his auditors knew what he would say, or else he was groping for words. I never imagined I would see the day when Meriwether groped for words.

I nodded, not wishing to express my true feelings. What was the governor doing, borrowing small sums from me, from the Chouteaus, and others, while engaging in grandiose land schemes to ride what might be merely a bubble?

Was this the competent, prudent man who had governed his mother's estate at Ivy for so many years?

Would those farms really appreciate? We were on the brink of war with England. Mr. Jefferson's embargo had bottled up the traffic in furs to Europe. The economy of St. Louis was faltering because peltries were heaping up in warehouses. He knew all that, and yet had plunged every shred of income into Missouri farmland.

We were soon at supper. The servants brought Meriwether's favorite dish, curried lamb, and he beamed brightly as they set the plate before him.

"Ah!" he exclaimed, all starchy blue and gold braid, across from me. He dug into his tunic, extracted a small phial, and poured several drops of something into his tumbler of water. This he downed before corking the phial and returning it to its nest upon his bosom.

His countenance changed dramatically in the next moments.

"Now," he said peacefully, "tell me about the fur company. Are you gentlemen going to get Big White home at long last?"

Opium, I thought. Opium has got him.

28. LEWIS

Bates again. He stormed into my office in a fit, ruining a spring morning. He had in hand a fair copy of the contract I executed with the St. Louis Missouri Fur Company. He glared down at me, his woolly eyebrows arching and falling, his milky eyes bulging with antagonism for whatever reason I soon would know.

"Yes, Mr. Bates?"

"This contract, sir, is an abomination!"

I settled back to receive the rodomontade, knowing I would not be spared by this uncivil man.

"You have named General Clark as your agent in your absence. But I am your second. When you are absent, I am the acting governor. That is the law. You had no business violating the law of the land—"

I raised a hand. "Mr. Secretary, this contract governs Indian affairs entirely. Will Clark is our Indian superintendent. He's a partner in the company, fully aware of its difficulties. Who better to appoint than the one public official who is empowered to deal with Indian matters?"

Bates didn't subside. "You have offended me once again, sir. You and your coterie of *privileged* men. But things will change. There's a new administration, and you're no longer in the same position. You grasp that, sir? You are no longer *protected* by Mr. Jefferson. He's retired from office, and a good thing if I may say so."

"I'm well aware of it, Mr. Bates."

"And I've written Secretary Eustis about your expenditures, and this abominable contract, which puts public funds into the hands of your cronies. Yes! Your cronies. You are mulcting the government."

"It's the only way, Mr. Bates. The army can't spare the troops to take Big White safely home. It is a matter of highest concern to the government to do just that."

"Hah! No one cares about that savage, save for you and those profiteers who will pillage the public treasury to do it. I shall, sir, let the entire world know. I will see you put out of office, sir, like a cur put out on the streets to starve."

I rose swiftly.

That was a dismissal, but he ignored it. "This contract creates a monopoly. Who but your cronies will profit? No one! You will gouge the treasury, feed on public funds."

I stood, not feeling well, and motioned him toward the door.

"Just remember, you no longer have Jefferson to bail you out of trouble!" he snapped.

I quieted myself. "Mr. Bates, though you array yourself against me, let us at least maintain some civility in public. Pray you, confine your disputes to these private meetings."

He nodded curtly, which I took to be agreement.

I watched the wretched man stalk away, marveled that he could work up such a temper about so little, but I counted him a danger to everything I had worked for so long and hard.

I knew also I could not placate him. I could grant his every wish, cave in to his every demand, flatter him, publicly praise him, and that would only excite him to further assaults upon my person. I was puzzled. I had no idea what I had done or failed to do that excited such a violent passion in him.

I knew for certain that his letters, which he had been mailing to Washington at the rate of one or two a week, would have their effect, and that I would be forced to return to that seat of government ere long to deal with the accusations. He had been bragging about town of his correspondence with two or three secretaries and Mr. Madison. I would have to go back there, as much as I dreaded it.

I wanted to meet William Eustis, Madison's new pinchpenny war secretary. I thought I could allay the suspicion and Bates's wild accusations if we could but meet and if I could sit down with the secretary and the president and explain matters. Some things can't be resolved through correspondence.

It would take an armed force to deliver the Mandan chief to his village, past the hostile Arikaras. I offered the St. Louis Missouri Fur Company seven thousand dollars to do it, thirty-five hundred payable at the start, when they were properly organized and ready to go. But my terms were strict and if they failed to be properly prepared and off by May tenth they should forfeit three thousand dollars. The risk was all theirs.

My contract with them required a hundred twenty-five armed Americans in their entourage, including forty riflemen, all in addition to the trappers and traders they wished to take along. They would be traveling in an armada that would carry over two hundred armed men, a force strong enough to compel the respect of the Arikaras.

How better to do it, as long as the army was unable to help me? The public funds were indeed the foundation for the whole business, but all of the partners were risking most of what they owned in the hope of reward. The company would have a monopoly on the fur business only above the Mandan villages; the government would show the Plains tribes that it could overwhelm any of them, and was not to be obstructed in its purposes. Out of it would come commerce and peace, and the firm hand of the republic ruling the new territory.

Lisa and Chouteau had been working furiously to put the venture together, hire the entire company of men, supply the expedition, and obtain the keelboats to take them up the Missouri. Every partner was busy preparing. Reuben was collecting his medicines; Ben Wilkinson was purchasing supplies or providing them from his store; Will Clark was looking after the finances, along with Auguste Chouteau. Lisa was out on the levee, hiring the best rivermen, trappers, riflemen, cooks, translators, and traders in St. Louis, and finding more takers than anyone had imagined.

I was busy, especially because I had lost so much time to my sickbed. I authorized payment of the translation of a court record into French, knowing Bates would object on narrow legal grounds, and sent the voucher off to Washington. He was objecting to everything, and perhaps that was all to the good. They would see him for the embittered man he was.

Lisa visited me this afternoon.

"Yes, Manuel?"

"Ah, Your Excellency, I am glad to see you up and about. You look the very picture of health."

The man was prevaricating, but I ignored that. "How are you coming? Will you be off by May tenth?"

He shook his head. "It is a worrisome thing, Governor. I come to talk about the diplomacy, yes?"

"With the tribes?"

"Since this is a government expedition, we think you should provide the gifts, the little items of honor, to give to the headmen and chiefs, to win their undying allegiance to the government of the republic, yes?"

"That should come out of your funds."

He shook his head. "Every cent is committed. We will not have enough, even with the payment you have promised us."

"I've written Washington that I've committed seven thousand to this. I can't go further."

He shrugged. "Then we go without the gifts. We have nothing to trade for food, for canoes, for what is necessary."

I remembered how valuable our small stock of trade items was during the great trip west and how I yearned for just a few more blue beads, or hatchets, or iron arrow points, to win the perfidious chiefs. Time after time, en route home, we had come to the brink of disaster because we lacked things to trade for food. Even so, I was reluctant.

"You are going to have to provide those yourselves. The contract we signed is generous."

He shrugged. "And the risks are generous, too!"

I rose and paced my office. With Bates howling about every cent, I couldn't help much. And yet, I felt that I had to. I could not fail to return Big White to his people. That was Tom Jefferson's mandate and it was written in a tone that brooked no failure.

"What is the absolute minimum you need?" I asked.

"Two thousand dollars for the purchase of gifts, beads, metal items, knives, awls."

"Two thousand dollars!"

He nodded. But I knew the crafty Spaniard. He probably wanted five hundred and knew how to turn the screws.

I was weary of being importuned for money. Half the people entering my office begged money from the government.

"What exactly would you spend it on?" I asked.

Lisa shrugged. "You have told us many times what the Corps of Discovery needed and lacked. I would follow your wisdom, Your Excellency."

Blue beads.

I nodded. At my desk I lifted a quill, sharpened the point with my blade, and dipped it into the inkpot. I scratched out a voucher on the United States Treasury, on the account of the secretary of war, for one thousand five hundred dollars, payable to Pierre Chouteau because I didn't trust Lisa, to be employed in the purchase of public gifts to be given to the tribes as needed to insure their allegiance. I spilled ink on two occasions, my hand being unruly these days for some reason, blotted up the ink spots, and handed it to Lisa.

"Wait," I said. "I want to inform Will Clark of this."

I penned a second note for Will, letting him know I was adding trade items from the public purse to foster amity and help preserve the company's passage.

"Give this to the general, please."

Lisa took the note, nodded, and smiled. Was it slyly? Had he gulled me? Was this the crafty Spaniard's way of enlarging the profit at the expense of the public purse?

I exhaled, and watched him go. He didn't linger about for social amenities, and I wondered if the Spaniard was a friend of anyone, or loyal to anything other than himself.

I made a notation to put the draft on record. Bates would cause more trouble. I felt unwell, and settled into my chair, my mind climbing the skies like a hawk.

Oh, to go with them! Oh, to walk those golden prairies, and see the eagles own the sky! Oh, to be young and strong and filled with life again! Oh, to dream great dreams!

29. CLARK

Secretary Bates sprang upon me moments after I arrived at my office, and he was in a wrathy mood. I had scarcely hung my cape over the antler coatrack in the corner and opened the casements to let in some April breezes when he burst in, fires glittering in those milkstone eyes.

"General, sir, I have come for a *confidential* talk about certain matters pertaining to the lawful governance of the territory!" he exclaimed.

I said nothing and made no assurances about confidentiality. I have made it a lifetime habit to listen attentively, and keep my counsel, by which means I get along with all manner of men, and even a man so fiddle-strung as Secretary Bates.

I could tell at a glance that he had rehearsed this moment all night, and perhaps for days.

I gestured him to a seat, but he declined, preferring to pace about like an advocate before the bar, making his case with a multitude of theatrical gestures and postures.

"I know, General, that you are a *close* companion of the governor, the partner in a long journey, and therefore my views are likely to be instantly dismissed. But I am compelled by the *law* and *justice* and *propriety* to make the case before the only other official in the territory whose conduct *influences* the affairs of Upper Louisiana."

I nodded. This was going to take some time. Bates often talked like that, using twice the words he needed to. He paced again, his hands clasped behind him, his kinked dark hair drawn tight into a disciplined queue without a strand out of place. I wondered how a man of such unruly feeling could rule his hair with such total sovereignty.

"By appointing you his agent in his absence, in the matter of the St. Louis Missouri Fur Company, General, he violates the law. The code is explicit. The territorial secretary shall act as governor in the absence of the governor. He is *wilfully and wantonly* offending the government, offending me, and insulting me by demonstrating his lack of confidence in me."

I thought it would be this. I had hoped he would let it pass.

I said nothing, as was my wont, but nodded.

"This is a dangerous and unlawful precedent," he said. "I have written Secretary Eustis about it, intending that the authorities should know at once. I fear, General, that the tides that will wash over the governor will wash against your shore, also."

"I see," I said.

He took that for encouragement. "The man is behaving in a most improper manner. He signs warrants for any *small* expense, expecting Washington to pay. Why, sir, without any authority he had a public notice translated into the French and printed in French, though there is no provision for it. I sent it along to the treasury secretary as directed, but *over my protest*."

I wanted to tell Bates that if some official matter is made public in Louisiana it must be made so in two tongues and the government must shoulder the cost. But I get more from listening than I do from debating, so I simply nodded.

Bates stopped pacing suddenly, and faced me. "All this will come down upon his head. I will make sure of it. He cannot govern improperly without the eyes of *responsible* men observing his misconduct and taking the necessary steps."

He was proclaiming he was the tattletale, which interested me. I nodded.

"He borrows money right and left, General. From you, I know, from Chouteau, even from *me.* Why, he had the audacity to press me for twenty dollars a day or two ago, knowing that a mere *servant* and *underling* cannot refuse his governor, and so I lent it. I have eyes and ears in this town, sir, and I get wind of how he spends all this money. It is upon draughts and pills."

He leaned close, his air confidential. "I happen to know that he consumes large numbers of one-gram pills of opium. One gram! Several times daily. It is a frightful habit. Where will it end? In madness? Do you know what that does to his judgment? He is falling into grievous error, General, because his mind is clouded by *opium.*"

I hadn't known it was so bad, but I suspected it was true. Bates had an amazing intelligence network feeding him dirt. I wondered what he knew about me, or thought he knew.

I nodded.

He liked my attentiveness; it encouraged him. "And that's not all, General. He doses himself with cinchona, calomel, and other powders. But it is not for the ague or intermittent fever. Not for bilious fever. Not for consumption. Have you seen his gums, General? Blue! The *Mark of Cain.*"

I knew what he was talking about.

I hadn't noticed, and the accusation worried me. Perhaps I had been too close to Meriwether to see him clearly. Then again, maybe Bates was merely imagining things. I had not seen any such mark of mercury poisoning upon the governor. But it was possible. He had borrowed, he said, to pay medical bills.

"Mark my words, General. The time of protection, when our heroic governor was *untouchable* because he was harbored in the esteem of a president, has passed. Now he will be scrutinized with care and integrity, and by men who are less impressed with Meriwether Lewis than he is impressed with himself."

That was the unkindest cut but I wanted to let Bates run with his indictment. I was learning fast.

He continued in that vein a while more, and when he finally wound down I knew that Lewis had a genuine enemy in Bates, a man who itched to depose the governor and rule the territory himself. I felt certain also that Bates could do considerable damage to Lewis with those letters; that Bates did have a certain punctilio about the law on his side, and that his sort of songs would find receptive ears among a certain class of lesser clerks in the warrens of the government.

"Well?" said Bates, having emptied himself.

"Mr. Bates, I would like to offer my good offices toward reconciling you and the governor," I said.

"No, you will only take the governor's part," he retorted.

"I will follow my own counsel, I assure you. It is an offer set before you. Perhaps I can help you work out some common ground."

"I do not wish to share any ground with that cur, that dog," Bates said. "Look at me! I am here *complaining*! Yes, *complaining* about another mortal, and thus demeaning myself before your very eyes. You know what the world thinks of complainers! But I have no recourse, sir. I must complain because that is the only avenue open to me, even though it besmirches me to speak so ill of another."

"What do you want of me?" I asked.

"I came to warn you that you are under scrutiny as well, sir. And that you might properly distance yourself from the governor."

I grinned. "Mr. Lewis is my friend and I hope you can be also, Mr. Bates. You are a skillful man and needed here."

He puffed up. "I should hope so," he said. "I mean no man harm who has done me none."

That's how it ended. Like a steam kettle breathing its last vapor into the atmosphere. I saw him off, and settled into my chair, running over the accusations and threats, and finding little in them but wind. Still, a man wrapped in such passion could be nettlesome, and I resolved to brace Meriwether about Bates, as I had several times in the past.

The danger lay in Bates's objections to various expenditures, including those for the St. Louis Missouri Fur Company for the delivery of Big White safely home. I resolved then and there that I must head for Washington before the travel season ended, and talk to Eustis and the president myself. If money was the bone of contention, then I would contend about it.

I settled back in my desk chair, remembering Captain Lewis of the Corps of Discovery. He had been occasionally severe, especially in the way he meted out punishment for military infractions. And yet, no man of the corps, not the lowest private, had grounds to loathe Lewis, and in fact he inspired in them a great devotion and a yearning to excel.

Without Meriwether's skills in dealing with our men the corps might have faltered; might even have died, to the last man. They loved him, love him still. They admired him in the field, and admire him still. He has seen to their back pay, their pensions, their honors, their retirement, their medical needs. He nursed them through desperate times and brought them safely home, as only a great man will.

He preferred to walk the banks of the rivers while the rest of us poled or rowed or pulled ourselves upstream. He walked in perfect grace, his lithe footsteps keeping pace with us, even though he took the time to examine every plant and animal that caught his eye. His great mind is what mesmerized us all. There was something grand in everything he did, as if he could see over horizons, anticipate the next crisis or triumph. He had no Frederick Bates along to whittle him down.

I have little stomach for politics, for backbiting, for the snares some men lay to trip others. I debated there, in the April sun, while breezes wafted across my desk and rattled my papers, whether even to bring this latest bout of Bates distemper to Meriwether.

Blue gums. I didn't believe it. The Mark of Cain was not upon Governor Lewis. But next time I saw him, I would see for myself. It was something I had to know.

30. LEWIS

Dover's powder helps. I take one-gram tablets and find they clarify the mind and help me to see keenly into the mysteries of the world. The powder not only sweeps away confusions so that I see all of life with burning clarity, but produces a fine sweat that keeps my occasional fever under control. In spite of the great burdens of office, I find I can proceed calmly and even with some degree of equanimity. I am able even to cope with Frederick Bates day by day.

I have a standing order with the apothecary, Marcel Rolland, to fill my phial once a fortnight, and I require him to keep some back so that the governor might be supplied as needed. The supply of Dover's powder from New Orleans is tenuous and seasonal. He is admirable in his eagerness to serve me. The powder has an unfortunate tendency to bind me, but Rush's Thunderclappers never fail to relieve my distress, and I count the calomel in them as a good weapon against the fevers that afflict me more and more. My ague is more severe than most, and often leaves me weak and dehydrated.

The St. Louis Missouri Fur Company is engaged in a last-minute frenzy to set off for the high Missouri, and I have turned most of my energies to making sure the partners are well equipped and ready for anything. Big White at last is going home, and the Mandan chief's eyes light up at the prospect. He struts the levee, a dandy now in black frock coat, red shirt, beaver hat, blackened boots, and white breeches, along with his bedizened wife and son, his shrewd savage eye upon the river men loading the keelboats for the great haul into the wilds. I shall be relieved to get him back to his home; nothing burdens me more.

I would love to be present when he regales his brethren in the Mandan villages about what he saw here and in Virginia and in Washington. I hope he is up to it; if not, I fear they will think him a big liar. Toward the end of making him credible to his people, I have showered gifts upon him, all of them calculated to display the magic of the white man. He grins broadly at each item; the compass, the book, the various weapons, the silks, and all the rest.

Some advance elements of the company have already

started up the river; most of the rest must be under way this Wednesday, May 17, 1809, or forfeit three thousand dollars to the government. My contract sets severe penalties for nonperformance, which is one reason I am mystified at the criticism of it by know-nothings. Lisa will follow with the last of the supplies.

Pierre Chouteau came to me recently and asked for more cash for trade goods; there simply were not enough wares to meet the British competition's generous disbursements. Nor enough powder. Word has come downriver that the Sioux and Arikara are determined to stop the company.

Reluctantly, I have offered him an additional draft for five hundred dollars payable on the account of the secretary of war, and another for four hundred fifty, with which to purchase additional powder and lead. I have no choice. The allegiance of the Plains tribes will tilt one way or another, depending on the success of this venture.

I have given Pierre explicit instructions regarding the conduct of the venture, but I have left the field commanders room enough to use their own judgment. I toiled long over this set of instructions, wanting it to be a paternal guide from the seat of government yet not so binding as to defeat the purposes and judgments of the officers, including my brother Reuben.

I see them inviting Big White and his entourage to board the second keelboat, so I know the moment has arrived. It is a fine, breezy morning that promises to make the rowing and poling cool and easy for the horde of boatmen and riflemen and trappers crowding the keelboats.

A great crowd has gathered. St. Louis loves mighty events, and nothing mightier than this army has ever pushed off from its levee. What a sight! Thirteen keelboats and barges in all will head upriver, and seven of them leave to day. One last boat, carrying Lisa, will leave in a few days after he has completed some last-minute purchases.

I have already said my goodbyes to Reuben; he is on the riverbank, in charge of two keelboats, directing the last flow of materiel. He has, on one of those boats, a formidable medical chest and I do not doubt that the ailments and wounds of so large a force will tax his supply of powders and his skills to the utmost. I am rather glad he is not my physician; he does not approve of the courses I choose for myself.

What a city this is! Ebony carriages have drawn up to the levee, and ivory-skinned Frenchwomen in silks watch events from behind their folding fans, while sooty slaves hoist the last of the casks and crates aboard. Rough men in tan buckskins jostle powdered men in black beaver hats, and riflemen in blue chambray shirts and slouch hats stand aboard the planked hulls of the keelboats. Many of them are Delawares.

Oarsmen have settled on the cross benches, preparing to flex their muscles against the mighty flow of the Father of Waters, while other Creole water men hold poles in readiness. Red men, white men, blacks, French, Spanish, Yanks, gentlemen and ruffians have all congregated on this mucky bank, not only to see the armada off but to pray for its success, because all of St. Louis will profit—or suffer—from what is starting on this day.

I find Will standing beside me. He and one or two other partners are not going; his duties are in St. Louis. Lisa and Menard are below, at water's edge, directing the stream of casks to the keelboats. Sweating Creole boatmen are balancing the loads in the holds, shouting in volleys of explosive French.

Sunlight glints from brass swivel guns mounted on the

bows of some of the keelboats. There is muscle here, lead an
gunpowder, lance and staff. Snugged into the holds are thou
sands of pounds of Missouri lead and many barrels of goo
Missouri gunpowder, the finest that the partners could buy

In spite of all the hubbub, there is no cacophony, just
quiet hum of activity, and the low murmur of the specta
tors. Every shop has emptied; every parlor and kitchen i
St. Louis is vacant. I see, standing back a way, my name
sake, Meriwether Lewis Clark, and his lovely mother, an
half a dozen servants attending her and the baby.

It is so bedazzling, so clear, so bright to the eye, that
marvel at the sight that burns into my head.

Then, suddenly, everything is ready, and a pregnant hus
settles over the crowd.

"*Au revoir, mes amis,*" Chouteau cries.

Lisa waves from the shore. A river man touches a fuse t
a brass swivel gun. The explosion startles us all, violenc
in a peaceful moment. Then the hoarse cries erupt from ev
ery quarter, the shouts of the Creoles whip across the win
and the first of the keelboats lumbers painfully away fro
the levee, jabbed forward upon the poles of the river me
while the oars bite the brown water.

Now there is a great cheer, and hats sail. Another bo
sucks free of the levee and lumbers outward, the men strai
ing every muscle against the current. And another and an
other, until at last this formidable force, close to thre
hundred men, is loosed from the nurture of St. Louis and i
toiling northward to the confluence, and then into the might
wilds a thousand eagle flights from this last outpost of civ
ilization.

I watch the Mandan, standing like a statue on the secon
boat, all the mysterious forces of national power and pres
tige gathered about his person like some halo. Yes, truly
halo. A great yellow glow radiates from him.

It is a sight so brilliant that I close my eyes against it.

I shake hands with Auguste, and then with Will.

"Gentlemen, luck," I say.

"Luck is the last thing to count on," Auguste says somberly.

"Powder and lead, then!"

"Ah! Now you talk business," Chouteau says amiably.

"I hope She-He-Ke has the gift of gab," Will says.

"Who?" I ask. The name puzzles me.

"Big White."

"Oh, yes," I say. "Big White." Somehow, I had forgotten the Mandan version of his name.

Will is staring at me. I smile. He is looking at my mouth, so I wipe my lips. What a bright world, everything etched so sharply in the clear air. The crowd lingers, watching the keelboats grow small and finally vanish into pinpricks on the blue water.

I need to escape from the sun. I am feeling feverish again.

I see Bates; he turns to avoid me.

The Chouteaus excuse themselves; they and Lisa must fill one more boat and set out within a day or two. It bobs there below, a forlorn remnant of the flotilla.

I catch up with Will, who has joined his wife and child.

"Ah! There's my namesake!" I say cheerfully. "And how are you, Maria?" I ask.

She eyes me oddly.

"Maria! Did I call you Maria? Forgive me. Julia, how do you fare this May day? I must have been thinking of my old sweetheart."

She edges apart from me.

In truth, I have been thinking much about Maria Wood, for whom I named Maria's River far up the Missouri. I don't know why. By the time I returned she had married, and there went my hopes and dreams, and that is why I am a musty old bachelor now. I never courted her in the first place, though I thought of it long before the expedition. She didn't know I cared. She had been a dreamy, peach-fleshed young thing who caught my eye before the trip, and I kept her virgin image before me, like an icon. Now she is an excuse I use to explain everything.

Never was woman more pure and virtuous than Maria Wood, and that is what I said in my journal. I am quite sure I said it, anyway. I would have to go back and look at the entry for that day in 1805 when we were advancing toward the mountains. I have an altar in my heart, and it is dedicated to her, the bride I shall never have.

I look at the journals these days and marvel at them; that Meriwether and this Meriwether are different people. Someday, I will figure them out and send my material to Conrad, and they will be published. But now I need a pill.

31. CLARK

York returned this Saturday, May 20, in the nick of time. A day or two more, and I would have posted runaway notices and a reward. But he appeared at my office door one afternoon, and I let him in.

"You're late," I said.

"Got took here by a keelboat," he said. "They stopped lot of places on the way."

"You have a letter for me?"

He dug into his duffel and produced a battered envelope. It contained his travel papers and a letter from my brother Jonathan, saying that he was sending York to me on the

Charles Brothers boat, passage for his hire. He enclosed a draft for $36.50, York's hire in Louisville while visiting his wife, minus one dollar for food on his return. He had been hired out to his wife's owners, the Chartres family, for $2.50 a week plus subsistence. My brother said that York had performed his service in the tobacco fields faithfully, but his mind seemed elsewhere and his attention was not on his work.

"I earn you some money, mastuh?"

"A little. Did you have a good visit?"

He smiled for the first time. "Emily, she wasn't so happy to see me. She tired of babies."

"You make one?"

"I sho' try."

"How is my brother?"

"Mastuh Jonathan? He looking good to me."

"And the general?"

"I don't see the general. They don't take me there. They tell me he got the gout."

"Do you bring any news?"

He shrugged. "Not much rain in Louisville. That tobacca not coming up proper."

"Did you see my sister?"

"No, boss. I be taken right to the Chartres place and they put a hoe in my hand before I even get to see Emily." He smiled a little. "They gave me next day off, and her, too. We go out into the woods and have us a picnic."

"All right, York. You go on to my house and report to your mistress. Then I want you to find Manuel Lisa on the levee and help him. He's still loading supplies in the last keelboat."

"Last keelboat, mastuh?"

"A company's gone up the river. They're taking Big White home."

"Big White!" York grinned. "Taking the old chief back. Ah wish you'd hired me out."

"I need you here," I said.

Immediately a curtain fell and he was a stranger again. I knew that he had changed in some unfathomable way. We had been boyhood companions, protective of each other, and now that was gone. The bond could not survive childhood, but until the trip west there had been some old and continuing understandings.

"Yes, suh," he said, as if talking to a stranger.

"York, the letter from my brother says you were not attentive to your work."

"I work hard in them fields, hoeing all them weeds." There was heat in his response.

"But your work was not satisfactory."

He retreated deep into himself again.

"York, you do my bidding. And be quick about it." I didn't like disciplining the man who had been my servant from birth, and so I softened. "I'm glad you're back safely. And in good health."

"Yes, suh, you get nothing outa no sick slave," he retorted.

Before the Corps of Discovery, he never would have said that to me. I let it pass. He probably would settle into routine. But if not, I would not hesitate to auction him at the New Orleans market, and then he would find out what defiance would bring to his unmarked black back.

I knew somehow that soon he would beg again for his liberty, and I knew I would again turn him down. I could not afford to release a fifteen-hundred-dollar slave; not with my finances in precarious condition. And in any case, I had too few hands for my household. Julia and her baby required four, and I needed two, so that I might escape such sundries as getting stove wood.

I knew, right down to my bones, that York was not fit for

freedom; that without the succor I provided him he would careen from one crisis to another and starve himself. He was not competent to handle his affairs or run a business. He was not able to do sums or read and could be gulled by any white man who wanted his labor and didn't feel like paying for it.

I intended to tell him so when his petition came, as I knew it would just as soon as he had gotten back into his daily routine. I again rued the day I had taken him with me; it had put ideas in his head I could never rout out. I hated the idea of auctioning him. I hated the idea of freeing him. I hated his increasing uselessness. He was aggravating me, and my thoughts ran from whipping to manumission. Let the wretch go and just see how he fares in a mean and tricky world.

Had I discovered a cockiness in him? I sprang to the window, hoping to see his sauntering figure in the street, but he was gone. I intended to ask Lisa about him after York had put in a few days loading the boat.

It wasn't too late to send York up the river on Lisa's keelboat. He was an experienced mountaineer and river man, and would be valuable. It certainly would have pleased York, and I could hire him out to the St. Louis Missouri Fur Company for twenty a month. That would be less than it was paying freemen, thus benefitting the company. But the thought roiled my mind. He was half ruined already and another trip would destroy his usefulness. No! He would stay in St. Louis and I would have plenty for him to do.

I stretched, and then, unaccountably, I laughed. It was good to have old York back, safe and sound. I decided to go tell Meriwether. He had counseled patience and he was right.

I stepped into a splendid spring day, bright with promise and the fragrance of lilacs in the air. It wasn't far to the governor's office, and I wished it were longer, so I might stretch my legs.

I was in luck. The usual gaggle of petitioners was nowhere in sight, perhaps because it was noon, and Meriwether was alone.

"Governor, I have momentous and urgent and entirely amazing news," I said.

He looked alarmed.

"York's back."

He grimaced, and finally laughed in syncopation with my own gusts of delight. I sat myself in a chair without his invitation.

"And how is he?" Meriwether asked.

"Exhausted. He spent the whole of his visit manufacturing."

"Manufacturing?"

"Manufacturing labor, my friend. Labor."

Meriwether smiled crookedly. His pearly teeth were as white as ever, and I had long since dismissed Bates's vile accusations as the remark of a venomous man.

"Labor! Labor! Ah, that does exhaust a man," he said.

"He did quite a bit of manufacturing with the Corps of Discovery, but it didn't seem to wear him down any," I said.

No man on the voyage had found his way into so many lodges as York, and I was of the belief that he had single-handedly darkened the hue of every tribe we encountered.

"Remember how the Mandan ladies bid for him?" he asked. "They put their husbands to it: come visit my wife, they said, and old York was only too happy to comply." Meriwether laughed, and it sounded like old paper rattling in the breezes.

His eyes went dreamy. "Those were the days," he said, and I knew what he was thinking. Fresh breezes, a dancing sea of grass that made a mere mortal seem as small as an ant, the sparkling river, mysteriously carrying water from some place no white man had ever seen, silently carrying it endless leagues, across a continent, to St. Louis.

"He's older now," I added. "I expect I will have to feed him up, extra rations, good pork fat and beans to get him back into condition. The manufacturing business turns fat bulls into scarecrows."

Lewis grimaced again, and I thought maybe I should change the subject. He was more and more melancholic about his bachelor estate, and not even my efforts to cheer him, or introduce him to the Creole belles who drifted up from Ste. Genevieve to stay with their assorted cousins, seemed to lift his spirits.

"I wish I could do it all over," he said. "I wish I could start upriver with the Corps of Discovery again, and try it once more."

"What for?"

"To avoid the mistakes I made," he said.

"Mistakes are what a discovery trip is all about," I said. "I don't know of any anyway. There was not a decision, an act, a choice, that you would want to change."

He looked at me so desolately that I felt chilled.

Then he gazed out his window, and I sensed that old sadness was stealing through him again. I had seen it so often, but I had always seen his own vital force, his enthusiasm, his strong character triumph over the perfidy of his feelings. He could be melancholic for an hour or two, and then spring into action as if no gloom had ever filtered through his mind.

"You know, Meriwether, nothing prevents you from going upriver again," I said.

"Bates does. I cannot leave here with Bates undermining everything I am and every step I take."

"No, not even Bates keeps you here," I said. "If you need to walk that ground again, walk to the shining mountains, see the black herds of buffalo, then go walk it. Resign. I wish I could go with you."

He said nothing, but somehow I knew his mind was far upstream.

32. LEWIS

The intermittent fever afflicts more and more; I have had moments when I am delirious. Today, Monday, June 19, has been such a day. I saw Lisa and the last keelboat off on Saturday, but came only briefly to the levee because I am indisposed.

I have debated for weeks about seeing Dr. Saugrain again. I have dosed myself with my mother's simples rather than submit myself to another misdiagnosis. But now I'm at wit's end and scarcely know how to treat the disease. He is, after all, one of the most eminent physicians in America, and I thought I might consult him about doses.

I visited him at his chambers near me on Rue L'Eglise, and found him occupied with a Creole mother whose infant wailed pitiably through the varnished door. He bade me wait in his anteroom, and was in no hurry to see me. But at last he dismissed the woman and welcomed me coolly.

"Your Excellency," he said, without warmth.

"I am here about doses," I said abruptly.

He nodded, his sharp eyes taking in my entire condition in a glance.

"Sit yourself there," he said, rummaging among his diagnostic tools.

"I'm not here for an examination. I'm here because my

extract of cinchona does not seem to be controlling the fevers."

He grunted and ignored me.

"Open your mouth wide," he said, and peered in, using a small mirror to see what was to be seen.

"Quinine is not the only powder you are taking," he said. "You are taking heavy doses of mercury."

"That's because I need a purgative."

"Is it?"

He peered at my eyes. "Enlarged pupils," he said. "Which opiate is it that you employ?"

"Dover's powder."

"Ah."

He listened to my chest with his horn, and ran his practiced finger over the lumps in my face, examined my hands and feet, and looked at my nostrils.

Then he straightened, his small body radiating his special dignity.

"Your Excellency, it is time to face what must be faced," he said.

"It's ague. Malarial fever."

"If it was ague, the quinine would be sovereign. Do you suffer chills so violent that no blanket warms you and you shake for hours under a heap of them, and then suffer high fever and profuse sweating?"

I had no reply to that, and stared mutely.

"Then perhaps your self-diagnosis lacks science," he said archly.

He turned his back to me, perhaps to free me from that piercing gaze that seemed to unearth everything within my heart. He stared out the window, and then began softly.

"*Lues venerea*. Just as I have said, monsieur."

"No!"

"How much mercury chloride do you take?"

I started to reply, but he interrupted. "It is ten times too much. So much mercury in your brain; it ruins you even before the venereal does."

I started to protest, but stopped. He was all wrong.

He spoke gently now. "I can perhaps help a little. In the third stage, Governor, mercury does little good. It helps momentarily, yes. It provides less and less relief, and then no help at all. You are there, at that lamentable point, most regrettably. The disease advances on its own schedule, shall we say. I recollect cautioning you to keep the doses small; that would have been better for the sake of your mind. Now I would prescribe no doses at all."

"It's not the venereal," I said.

He simply ignored my protest. "How much of the powder?"

"I don't know. Whenever I need it."

"Two a day; three a day?"

"One at night."

"And how many by day?"

"I don't know," I replied.

"Nothing is gained by not knowing. Something is gained by knowing every fact, every dose, every risk."

"Two, three."

"I advised, Your Excellency, that you not imbibe spirits, because they hasten the disease. I trust you have abstained?"

"No, and don't speak of it again!"

He did not recoil from my biliousness, but let it pass.

"A gill, two gills a day, perhaps?"

"Wine and porter."

"A carafe or two?"

"I have no idea." I was utterly out of sorts and ready to throw on my stock and coat and escape. But in fact a great heaviness was stealing my resolve from me. I felt ashamed of my maltreatment of him.

"Forgive me," he said. I felt his hand on my shoulder. "I am merciless, but with a purpose."

I watched motes of dust play in the midday sun pouring through his window, and felt the ticking of the eternal clock.

"May we proceed, Your Excellency?"

I nodded.

"You ask about doses. Ah . . . The dose I recommend, I plead with you, is nothing of mercury. Nothing of the Peruvian bark. Nothing of Dover's powder or laudanum. Nothing of spirits or wine or ale. Sunlight, fresh air, putting aside that which worries you, vegetables . . ."

I knew I would not heed his prescription, but said nothing.

"You spoke to me once of your mother's simples, the herbs she gathers. Try them without the mercury, Your Excellency, but let science be your guide. Experiment. Observe results. Discard the failures."

"You have no cure, then."

"The disease sometimes cures itself. Pray that it will."

"You have nothing to offer me."

He stared again out the window. "No. Some physicians are experimenting with toxic metals. Poisons. Small doses of arsenic. I see little in it. I do not recommend it. *Mon Dieu!* The risk! Medicine is in its infancy. Someday there will be cures. I am a rationalist."

I sensed the man's helplessness.

I have an *incurable disease.* All that remained for me in this savant's lair was a schedule for my doom.

"What will happen?" I asked curtly.

"You might survive many years. Then again, you might not."

"Do better than that, Doctor."

He shrugged, that petite Gallic expression of submission I knew so well. "The disease attacks each mortal differently," he said.

"I am talking about me, not the human race."

He nodded. "When your mind is clouded, when your memory fades, when your judgment lapses, when your hand disobeys and your handwriting falters, when your phantasms and demons crowd your mind, you will know that *paresis* is upon you." He anticipated me. "Paresis is the madness often resulting from the final stage of *lues venerea*."

"I'll know? Some mad people don't know it."

"The paretic usually knows."

"And others? Will they see it?" I asked, for that was the crux of the matter.

He nodded.

"It can't be hidden?"

"Not to the discerning eye."

"And it will be visible in my flesh?"

He sighed. "It already is, Your Excellency."

"Will they be studying me, hunting for the lumps in my face, the oddity of my conduct?"

He stared out the window. "It is a cruel disease and the world treats its victims with utmost cruelty. They condemn the victim. They even laugh at him, for his indiscretions are naked before the world. The moralists rant. The gossips buzz. The ladies flee. Daughters receive lectures from their mothers about the secret vices of men and how to spot them. It is the snake in the Garden of Eden, slithering through good society, reminding them all that it could strike them dead. It is a pity, this barbarous intolerance, monsieur. No one pities the victim. No one tenderly assists him."

"What is done with such people?"

"They are hidden away by families. The uncle in the attic."

"The musty old bachelor."

He tried to reassure me. "Do not despair. You will have

good times. Maybe years. Live well and slow the progress of the indisposition."

I straightened. "I am a public man. What is your advice?" I asked directly.

"When the time comes to withdraw from public life, you will know, Your Excellency. It will be plain. But even after you withdraw into private life, you will have good days, time to write and think and prepare your papers. The disease will not kill you soon. It often takes eight or ten years from infection, and you have been infected only four."

"You are treating John Shields. How is he doing?"

The little Frenchman paused, trembled, and summoned his courage, plainly seeking words. "He is gravely ill, my captain. I do not expect him to last a month."

"Of *lues venerea*?"

The doctor nodded.

"The same as mine?"

"From his liaison with the Shoshones, yes."

I had no time at all. I thanked the diminutive doctor, dressed, and headed into the bitter sunlight, a doomed man, bearing his badge of shame for all the world to see.

33. LEWIS

I don't remember such a beautiful summer, the breeze so caressing and the mornings so aglow. The presence of death gilds the world. This July of eighteen and nine I have taken to walking the verdant bank of the majestic river, the mightiest artery of the republic, marveling that so much water from such distant country is rolling toward the sea. What small slice of it is from the headwaters of the Missouri? From the Jefferson River, where we left Louisiana to cross the continental divide?

What stories that restless water could tell me; of painted Indians warring on its banks; of shamans praying to their spirits; of fat beaver patiently building their dams of aspen; of countless buffalo drinking from it or paddling across it; of cottonwoods toppling into it; of dust storms turning it to mud; and of the bones of the dead that it rolls and tumbles to some great continental grave in the delta beyond New Orleans.

I walk through tender green timothy and bromegrass and orchard grasses and rustling leaves and thickets of brush and cattailed swamps, stirring up moths and butterflies, so that I might embrace a clean world and leave a befouled one behind me. I am finding sanctuary in nature.

I have always walked. On the great trip I walked while the others rowed and poled. My legs still sing under me, enjoy the rhythmic steps, sweep me along and never tire. I have spotted species of sedges and swamp flowers and lilies that tax my memory and might be unknown to botany; but now I do not pluck them. I reverence them alive and let their discovery await other eyes and other times. I have a horror just now of plucking anything to its death. I want to leave each bloom unmolested, and to see alertness in the eye of each creature. Life itself is the greatest gift.

Sometimes the past clasps me until I groan with memories. If I were to keep on walking I would arrive at the confluence of the Missouri, and if I never stopped, I might make the Mandan villages by fall and find a lodging with Big White; the captain and the chief united once again. I might taste succulent, tender buffalo hump again, and live in buckskin clothing that armors against the wind, and watch the savages howl and dance around their fires as sparks fly into the night. But the yearning passes, and I return to St. Louis after each hike, weary but uplifted by every natural thing I meet. For a little while, anyway, I will free myself from the webs of fate.

This is the river of death. I see mutilated catfish, their bellies chalky white, drifting toward the bayous. I have watched dead crows and terns and sparrows drift by, feathery on the water, en route to the sea. In time, the waters that flow by me will rifle every vault, melt every bone, and empty all the death of a continent into the Gulf of Mexico. I have watched the water flow through the ribby ruins of a buffalo, and watched the waters sluice the naked skeletons of cottonwoods and willows to the sea. All manner of things pass St. Louis, but death most of all.

I am reminded of these things but do not dwell upon them. For even as disease devours my flesh and eats my soul, I redouble my efforts to strengthen Louisiana. I have called a territorial council this summer. There are urgent matters to attend. The British furtively war upon us and mean to take us back into their empire. They have never believed their own defeat and will need another lesson.

The embargo has stopped our shipments of furs to Europe, so St. Louis languishes in debt and despair. Its warehouses bulge with rank-smelling peltries and skittering bugs, and some prominent citizens cannot afford the meanest tax.

I have seen Antoine Saugrain frequently, and he has gently and tenderly taught me the signs of my own decay: memory loss, lapses of judgment, difficulty with speech, an uneven hand that shows up in blots and tiny or oversized letters or crossed-out words, fits of unseemly passion, ranting, puzzlement, and above all, incoherence. I face those things. I, Meriwether Lewis, face *incoherence,* when I will blubber out words that do not connect and defy logic. I face the end of my very *self,* and that thought is more than I can endure.

He teaches me to understand my decline, for it is the only thing he has still to give me: the stigmata of my doom on my hands and feet, the cruel ciphers of the devil getting his usury for one voluptuous moment. That is the medicine the doctor portions out for me; that and a profound and sad affection he has formed for me, and a willingness to share in my desolation. The little doctor has become the physician of my soul. He charges but little now, but always manages to comfort me.

I do not always heed his counsel, and he has stopped chiding me. I take my powders when I need them because I am desperate for them, and I drink spirits at the balls and parties I attend to conceal my affliction and drug away the pain and fever when they pounce. The world sees nothing of any of this, for I still cut a fine figure, but no one, especially the women, has ever looked deeply into the eyes of their governor and seen the hell within.

Mr. Bates braced me again the other day. He has a catalogue of injuries which he writes down in the ledgers of his soul, and now that list is heavier than he can carry. He imagines himself a good official watching zealously over the public purse. I see him as an obstructionist, stopping my projects, quibbling about authority, finding fault with my every act, and spreading his toxins through St. Louis. He would have me leave for Washington so he might govern in my absence. I have no plans to go, but he has found the perfect way to force me: I will have to go east to answer his complaints.

"Do you think I don't know about your powders? I have friends all over St. Louis!" he snapped. "You have no secrets from me, sir. Not all your high connections can save you!"

"My ague?" I asked.

"Ha!" he snapped.

"Mr. Bates, do you want my office? Is that what this is about?"

"Never, sir. I am no usurper. I would be your loyal second, if you were but to consult me, but you never do."

"What can I do to reconcile us?"

"Nothing. It is a breach that cannot be bridged. You have earned my enmity, sir, and your very presence offends me."

I kept trying. "I assure you, sir, I am willing to listen and consider, and if I am misguided, I am willing to undo my arrangements."

He paused, nonplussed for once.

"Give me specifics, Mr. Bates. Would you care to discuss my diplomacy with the Upper Missouri tribes? Are you content with the agents? Do I coddle the hostile tribes too much?"

"I have no desire to press my views upon you; it would only stay your course."

I proceeded doggedly. "My appointments to office. You object to most of them. Pray tell me, what is wrong with, say, Boone?"

Bates drew himself up. "We have talked too much. I will not give you one bone to chew on. Go counsel with the high and mighty."

I saw how it would go. "Set your own course, then," I said sharply.

That is the polite expression of a complete rupture. Except for our official duties, we need have no other congress. He stalked out of my office, as if even that final caution was an insult to his prickly person instead of a way of accommodating each other while harnessed to the same wagon.

I stood at my desk, processing this latest bloodletting, and slowly took heart.

I plan to endure. I will heal myself and proceed. I have

let nothing slide and prosecute all manner of agendas to make this western border safe and secure and profitable, and a gem in the diadem of the republic.

I sometimes think the madness is upon me. I often walk to a place three miles up the river where there is a certain stony bluff that affords a view of the great blue Mississippi and the distant shores of the Illinois country rolling away. And there, I gaze upon life and death and think that the world is indescribably beautiful, that all of creation sings to me, every bumblebee and tern and eagle and field mouse and daisy. I go quite mad with joy, feeling the blood pulse in my veins and the moist earth-scented wind inflate my lungs, and the voice of the wilderness clawing my bosom.

And there I know I am a man, and will fight a man's fight, and will depart from a better world than the one into which I was born because I have set my gifts upon its altar. No matter that disease robs me of all but youth; my name will be remembered.

Someone will prepare the journals after I am gone and catalogue the plants after I am gone, and write a history of Louisiana after I am gone, and they will find my hand in it all, and none of it done on my account, but for Mr. Jefferson and the republic.

I never want to leave that sacred place where the world is inexpressibly beautiful, but the rain drives me off, or a passing fisherman breaks the spell and I am among people again. When I leave it is like descending a long path from a tabernacle to the mundane world, and I am no longer with the eagles, and at the end of the path is only Secretary Bates, and Dr. Saugrain.

34. CLARK

John Shields is dying. George Shannon sent word, and asked if I might go see the doughty private in the Corps of Discovery. I sent word that I would.

We in the corps look after each other, or at least those of us in St. Louis. We were bonded into a rare brotherhood by three years of trial and fire; now we have settled into our vocations. Some have married. A few, like Sergeant Gass, have gone east. Most have foolishly traded their warrants for three hundred twenty acres of public land, awarded by a grateful Congress, for a few dollars. Frederick Bates bought some of the warrants for very little. Several men have entered the fur trade and gone upriver. John Colter is such a one, George Drouillard is another, Shannon another, and it cost him a leg which had been amputated after the fight with the Arikaras.

I have watched over them fondly, and with a deep affection and pride. They were good men to begin with, and some of them had been transformed into exceptional men by our common ordeal. I try to watch over the Field brothers, Private Labiche, and all the rest, and I know Meriwether does, too. Never a letter goes east from either of us but that we don't inquire after those loyal and greathearted men.

I had heard Shields was sick, but the news that he is sinking shocked me.

"Are you sure?" I said to the black boy who had brought me the message.

"Mr. Shannon, he asks you to go right quick, sir."

I nodded.

Shields has a smithy at Fort Bellefontaine, a few hours'

walk from my office. He had traded his land warrant for a complete smithing outfit and is a respected gunsmith and blacksmith in the area, employing the trades he gave the Corps of Discovery. He had been a lean, muscular man with powerful shoulders and an iron grip. I could scarcely imagine such a Hercules sinking into the Stygian depths.

I saw nothing on my desk that required attention. The mid-July heat had already built, and I would be in a sticky sweat by the time I reached there, even if I should summon a carriage or a wagon. But I would walk. Walking keeps me hale.

I sent word to Julia that I might be detained and headed for the governor's lair, down the street, intending that we both should go and pay our respects to our corps man.

I found Meriwether studying a petition. The windows were open and he looked flushed by heat.

"Ah, Will!"

"You have a little time?" I asked.

He nodded.

"John Shields lies ill; they say he won't last. I have in mind paying him a call. Would you join me?"

"Shields? Shields?" Some strange light filled his eyes. "No. Busy, can't."

"I'll get a carriage and trotters, Meriwether. It won't be but three or four hours there and back."

"No!"

That rejection came so explosively that we stared a moment.

Then he retreated.

"I regret that I can't. Tell him so. Give him my heartfelt apologies and high regards. He's a good man. None better. He was our salvation several times when he made ironwork to trade to the Indians. If he dies, I'll grieve his passage.

If I can help find his heirs, count on me. If I can do anything . . ."

He subsided into a blank gaze. I did not know what was amiss, but Meriwether was acting strange again.

"You go; tell him his old captain honors him," Meriwether said. "He gave his life for the corps."

"He gave his life?"

"He wouldn't be so ill now if he hadn't come with us."

"What is it that he suffers?" I asked.

"Fevers."

I ransacked my memory. "You treated him and MacNeal and others with mercury for the venereal at Fort Clatsop."

Meriwether nodded curtly.

"Do you suppose it's the venereal?"

Meriwether shrugged.

"Well, I'll find out and do what I can. Will the army or the territory bury him?"

Oddly, Meriwether didn't reply. He had slipped into his own world, and was slumped deep in his chair.

"My regrets, Will. I'd see him if I could," he said.

I left him lost in reverie, went to my house, kissed Julia and peered at the sleeping infant, collared York, got a hamper of ham and bread and stew and jams from the kitchen, and we set off through a muggy morning for the cottage of John Shields, not knowing what we would find there.

We hiked north on a military road. The army had bridged Coldwater Creek, corduroyed over some marsh, and widened a horse trail into a wagon trace from the city to the fort that governed access to the Missouri River and did a lively Indian trade as well. Shields held a smithing contract there, and lived nearby.

York followed along behind me a few paces toting the hamper. We hadn't talked much since his return from

Louisville and I knew he was still looking for a way to be set free. He had been careful to fulfill his duties and to escape my wrath, but something between us had vanished.

The lifeless air seemed oppressive and forbidding.

I was perfectly familiar with Fort Bellefontaine, although it was a regular army post and not a militia site. And I knew Shields's cottage, so I headed there directly rather than paying my respects to Colonel Hunt, First U.S. Infantry, inside the post.

The stained log cottage baked quietly in the sun. Its shutters were open, letting light in and releasing silence to the world.

Someone must have seen us coming, because a door opened quietly, and a small composed woman greeted us.

"Gin'ral," she said, her glance sweeping me in. I heard Ireland in it. She was no doubt some noncom's wife, hired to look after the dying.

"We've come to see Mr. Shields, madam."

She nodded and motioned us in.

"I am General Clark."

"Oh, sir, I know, and I'm Mrs. Tolliver, and me man is Corporal Tolliver."

I glanced toward the bed. "How is he?"

"Oh, sir, you can see." She spoke softly and tenderly.

In spite of the open casement, I smelled death.

Shields lay in a narrow bunk on the far side, his eyes open but staring sightlessly. His mouth had curled into a permanent O, and his face had shrunk around his skull, save for some thick lumps along his neck and cheeks.

The woman started to retreat, but I stayed her.

"Madam, please . . ."

She stood back. York hung back, too, and I motioned him in. He put the wicker hamper on a rude table.

"I brought some ham and some other things," I said.

Shields didn't move; life was visible only through the light rise and fall of his chest. I took off my hat and stood here before the ruin of a splendid soldier and a fine companion of three years of travel. Here was a man who had gone the whole route, across the prairies, over the mountains, down the Columbia to the salt water, and all the way back, as valuable a man as we had with us.

"Who's attending him?" I asked Mrs. Tolliver.

"The little Frenchman," she said. "Saugrain."

"What does he say?"

"I ask him, and he just shakes his head. He comes up to my neck, sir, and I look down upon him. I say to him 'What s this malady, Doctor, that robs a good smith of life?' And he just pats my hand gallantly and says it is a certain fever of soldiers. Oh, may my man never catch such a thing!"

I stood over Shields again, trying to discover awareness n him.

"John, it's your old captain. Clark here. I'm here to wish you all the blessings God can bestow on a good man. You walked to the Pacific with me, did your job well, gave more than was asked of you. I remember you looked after your fellows loyally and faithfully, followed our command, used your abilities and trade to make the Corps of Discovery a uccess, and you stand tall now. You're the best of men."

I discerned nothing at all. Those eyes did not track me. I tudied that ravaged face, the lips that puffed oddly, the mouth caught in a death rictus, and I knew he was at the gates of eternity.

York edged close, uneasily, his eyes seeking permission rom me and from the woman. He studied Shields a moment and then exhaled deeply, a great long gust of sadness.

"Mastuh Shields, I am saying goodbye. You be a good man, you my friend, and I am wishing you get well, but . . ."

He stopped, fearful that I would rebuke him for being too

familiar. But I didn't. They were all brothers on that trip across the continent; strangers at first, brothers by the time we had returned. And York was a brother, too, the brother of us all.

I turned to Mrs. Tolliver. "Have his relatives been notified?"

"I think the colonel is seeing to it, Gin'ral."

"All right. I will do anything in my power to help. Please extend my apologies to Colonel Hunt, but I must return."

"Yes, sir."

We paid our respects a few moments more, and then left.

"Mastuh, what's he got taken him?" York asked.

"Perhaps Doctor Saugrain will tell me."

"You say he walked to the ocean, and he done all things right, and he help the corps, and he give all he got, and he don't need orders but just do it all without asking, and he be the best of men."

I nodded.

"I done that, too," York said.

35. LEWIS

We buried John Shields today, Friday, July 21, 1809. I wore my blue and white captain's uniform in honor of the man who served in my command. I looked dashing in it and my servant, Pernia, took pains to freshen it and black my boots and brush my tricorne.

They wanted me to do a eulogy and I agreed, though I would not have chosen to do so. There are things a man i required to do, and I do them without cavil. I rode to the post in Chouteau's carriage and took Will Clark with me.

All those from the Corps of Discovery round about St. Louis, save for York, were present to pay our respects to Private Shields, blacksmith, gunsmith, and carpenter, whose skills repeatedly saved us from disaster and starvation during that journey into the unknown.

Last night I went to my journals to refresh my memory. The man was our salvation. We had bartered Shields's skills for corn or other provender in the villages. He repaired the broken rifles and muskets of the tribesmen, or fashioned battle-axes and lance points out of sheet metal from a burnt-out stove, and in return we got what we needed to subsist ourselves. He had made nails and hinges for our winter posts, and carpentered tables and chairs and beds as well. He had been a fine soldier, swift to obey any command and eager to go the extra mile. A hunter too, and a gifted woodsman, comfortable in the wilds.

All this came back to me in a flood as I examined my entries. I turned finally to those of August 1805, when Shields, MacNeal, Drouillard, and I, in advance of the main party working up the Jefferson River, had ascended the eastern foothills of the Bitterroot Mountains and discovered the Shoshones, the Indians we wanted most of all to meet so we could barter for horses. They were shy as deer, and it took all our wiles to persuade them that we meant no harm. But at last we did meet Chief Cameahwaite and his hungry band, and boundless was our joy.

Their joy matched ours because Shields and Drouillard shot deer and pronghorn and fed them all. We all rejoiced in the lavender August twilight. They danced for us around a spark-shooting fire and offered us their tawny young squaws, and I well remember that night, though I have wished a thousand times since then that I had remained steadfast in my resolve. Only Drouillard stayed apart, for whatever reasons only that silent French and Shawnee scout and translator could say. And only Drouillard was spared what followed.

If I could take back that evening, blot away that eager, smiling, raven-haired, yellow-fleshed Shoshone girl with whom I could not speak a single word, repeal the eager smiles and caresses, purge every voluptuous second of it from my life, I would not hesitate to do so no matter the cost. From that moment onward, even though I ascended from triumph to triumph, I sank further and further into a hell beyond mortal reckoning.

My entry of August 18, 1805, caught my eye:

"I was anxious to learn whether these people had the venereal, and made the inquiry through the interpreter and his wife; the information was that they sometimes had it but I could not learn their remedy; they most usually die with its effects . . ."

I remembered why I had inquired so anxiously.

I sighed and put away the journals. I had garnered enough to offer the assembled veterans a glistening catalogue of John Shields's worth as a man. And I would do so boldly, concealing morbidity of my own soul from them all.

We assembled at the grave on a blistering afternoon.

There was the old corps, or some small portion of it. George Shannon, leaning into a crutch; John Ordway, third in command and a gifted sergeant, and now farming outside of St. Louis; Robert Frazier, private, living in St. Louis; Ensign Pryor, still in the army, a career soldier and skilled noncommissioned officer; William Werner, now one of Will Clark's subagents; and Will Clark, erect and commanding as ever. Of those in Louisiana, only York was absent, and I regretted that Will had excluded him.

Doctor Saugrain was there, enduring the heat in his black

suit, a tiny white-bearded presence at the head of the coffin, which rested on poles over the yawning grave. He had removed his top hat, his gaze sometimes shifting to me.

I saw, as well, one of the Creoles who had come with us, and had a troubled moment trying to remember his name. François Labiche? Jean Baptiste LePage, Pierre Cruzatte, who had put a ball through my buttocks? I think it was Labiche. I cursed my bad memory.

We are dwindling.

Potts is dead, killed last year by the Blackfeet though his partner, Colter, had miraculously escaped and I hear from traders returning to St. Louis that he is alive in the West, at Lisa's post. Gibson is dead, succumbing this year, like Shields, of the *lues venerea.* I remember dosing him heavily at Fort Clatsop. I heard of his death too late to attend the service, and I knew his relatives had hidden his sordid sickness from the world and hastened him into his grave. MacNeal has vanished, MacNeal, who was with me in the Shoshone village. I suspect he too has perished of the mortal disease that stalks us. We sought horses among the Shoshones, and instead bought death.

Bratton remains in the army, and so do Willard and Windsor. Joseph Field died in 1807 but his brother Reubin lives in Kentucky. I know nothing of Goodrich. Sergeant Patrick Gass is in the East, enriching himself with his journal and blackening me with every letter he writes to the press. Hugh Hall, Thomas Howard, Peter Weiser, Joseph Whitehouse, all gone from view, some dead I am certain.

I was sweating by the time the preacher summoned me to give the eulogy, and my damp hands blurred the notes I had scribbled, so I couldn't remember what I wanted to say about John Shields. Inside my blue tunic, I was drenched with sweat and I ached to tear it off and let some breezes cool my fevered flesh.

I felt my sweat gather at my brow under my tricorne, and traverse my cheeks, and drip relentlessly into my stock. I felt my armpits leak moisture, and knew it was sliding down my sides, dampening my linens. I felt as if I was standing on the brow of hell, feeling the heat, watching that fine old soldier John Shields slide into the eternal pit.

I gave him a good soldier's eulogy; he was brave, resourceful, obedient, courageous, honorable, an asset to our command. There were no parents and no widow and no children to receive my words; only a few old corpsmen with better memories than I have. So I didn't dwell on Shields's achievements for long; the words were more for us than for his family.

I spoke of what we had done, the odds we faced, the way we came together into an indomitable and well-knit force bonded by danger and brotherhood and sheer joy. I told those privates and sergeants and my officer colleague that we had done something grand, something that would shine forever in the eyes of the people of the United States, and John Shields had marched with us from the first step to the last.

Will spoke a few words, too, plainspoken and true, remembering the good soldier in John Shields and the brave companion of a thousand days of danger. Will looked grand in his Missouri militia uniform, a faint scatter of gray at his temples, his demeanor dignified and serious, his gaze welcoming each man present and acknowledging the gift of that man's attendance at the last.

We saluted. A trumpeter borrowed from Fort Bellefontaine played the dirge. Colonel Hunt and a few regulars stood at a distance, sharing the moment with us.

"Dust to dust," the preacher said, tossing some sand upon that plain plank coffin, the yellow shellac of the pine glowing in the hot sun. And then we lowered it into that yawning hole, a pit that looked all too familiar to me as I peered into its gloom. Who would the Stalker stalk next?

Will and I headed back together in the carriage.

"You look done in," he said.

"Hot in this uniform."

"You sure it's not fever?"

I didn't reply. For years I had blamed the ague, and now I could not.

"Why don't you stop for some refreshment?" he said. "I'll put Julia and the servants to it."

"I'll get to see my namesake?"

Will smiled. "Governor, the baby's fat and happy, and we're calling him Meriwether and he's old enough to respond to his name, and fixing to walk, and before we know it, he'll be walking to the Pacific Ocean and back."

Somehow, all that good news only deepened my morbidity.

I halted the dray horse before Will's house, tied up at the hitching post, and we escaped from the furnace of the sun into a close but cooler climate within.

He studied me. "Are you sure you are well?"

"No, I'm not."

He nodded, and soon was rousting out servants and Julia, making the whole house clatter to life just when it was lost in siesta to the heat.

I waited until I was bidden to the nursery, where Julia curtsied. She wore a shapeless white cotton dress that hid her from an old bachelor's admiration. I wondered if she might be expecting another child.

"Your Excellency," she said tonelessly.

The boy dozed restlessly in the moist closeness, a loose-knit coverlet over him. Meriwether Lewis Clark. New life following death, the endless cycle repeated. This child was as close as I would ever come to a son.

"He is a fine healthy boy," I said politely.

"We'll raise him up to be the image of you, Governor."

Julia looked uncomfortable, and her fingers played with the muslin of her dress.

"Please forgive me, but I think I will forgo your lunch," I said.

"Why, Meriwether . . ."

I retreated as swiftly as courtesy permitted, under the concerned and tender gaze of General Clark.

PART III

36. LEWIS

I stared at the letter from Washington, absorbing the bad news that had reached me this Friday, August 4, 1809. It came from a clerk in the State Department, one R. S. Smith, and with it came a voucher for eighteen dollars and fifty cents that I had submitted in February. The department, the letter explained, was returning the voucher because it lacked the authority to pay it.

The sum was to pay a translator, Pierre Provenchere, to render certain laws into French, something entirely necessary in a bilingual dominion. How could the Creoles know the law if it were not comprehensible to them? But here was this voucher and a note that blandly said I had gone beyond my authority.

Heat built in me. Clerks! They have no more vision than an earthworm. I fumed, reread the letter, and then began to worry about what else might befall me. I had signed hundreds of vouchers for necessary services. My signature as governor was all that any merchant or supplier required to ensure payment. And up to this moment everything I had signed, including the scores of vouchers for the Corps of Discovery, had been honored in Washington.

When I had submitted the voucher for Provenchere last February, I made a point of explaining the purpose of the expenditure. The French translations of the law were published and distributed for a felony trial. What could be more essential to the course of justice? Any reasonable official, any clerk in any bureau, would swiftly understand the need, the legitimacy. But not Smith.

I sighed, knowing that I would have to compensate Provenchere out of my own purse, and I would have to borrow again to do it. I did not even have enough to pay my manservant, John Pernia. The family estate in Virginia had not found a buyer and I was heavily in debt.

And was this the first? Would more come floating back to me? Was this the work of some conspiracy whose design was to ruin me? Was this Bates's spidery hand at work? He had threatened to protest my expenditures, and I knew he had done just that, appending little notes to each item announcing that it had been submitted over his protests. It doesn't take much of that sort of footnoting of a man's vouchers to ruin his credibility.

I slumped at my desk. If this was the first skidding snow in an avalanche, I was in grave trouble. And so were the merchants who had until now trusted me. What could I say to them?

I plucked up the letter and braved the heat, walking slowly toward Will's office. We had shared everything for years; now I would share this.

I waited in his antechamber while he heard out the petition of a Creole who wanted to go upriver to the Iowa country and trade with the Sauk and Fox tribes. I suspected that Will would turn the man down; the British had been stirring up the two tribes against us and that area was dangerous.

Then at last we were alone.

"Governor?" he said.

I handed him the letter. He frowned, studied it closely, and set it down. "Everything boils down to money," he said at last. He stood slowly, lumbered to a black iron strongbox, which was not locked, and extracted some national bank bills and some coin.

"I haven't asked," I said.

He grinned. "You were working up to it."

I withdrew my pocket ledger, borrowed Will's pen, and entered the debt. There were too many such entries in my ledger.

"What are you going to do about this?" he asked.

"I can't keep it a secret. Bates opens my official mail, and he knows about it, and it's probably all over the city by now."

"It's his doing."

"Yes, and I fear there will be many more of these."

Will nodded. He didn't try to comfort me or pretend that this would be an isolated incident. We both knew it wouldn't be. Not with the malevolent secretary appending his florid objections to my vouchers.

The general ran a gnarled hand through his red hair. "When it comes to money, I have learned not to trust the government, any government," he said.

"Did you ever resolve your brother's case?" I asked.

He shook his head. "George doesn't own ten cents to his name. The best we could do was switch the titles of a few properties to me. I am the nominal owner, and that's the only way we've beat off the creditors and lawyers and courts."

It was a grim tale, and I had heard parts of it many times from Will and his family. General George Rogers Clark of the Virginia militia had staved off British occupation of much of the trans-Appalachian west during the Revolution. Because of his determined generalship, and skill at keeping a militia army in the field when most of the men just wanted to go home and plant their fields, and Indian diplomacy, the republic now possessed the vast lands east of the Mississippi.

Operating as a general officer of the Virginia militia, he had signed scores of vouchers for munitions, clothing, arms, camp gear, footwear, horses and wagons, livestock, gifts for the always dangerous tribes, wages, and everything else to field an army in a wilderness owned by savages and British agents.

Then came the reckoning. The commonwealth shrugged off its obligations on one thin excuse after another, mostly having to do with lost records. Frustrated by the commonwealth, Will's older brother then appealed to the Continental Congress and was rebuffed: the debt was Virginia's, not the national government's. And then the creditors had moved in, claiming everything George Rogers Clark possessed.

The heap of debt set off a widening collapse, as the merchants who could not be paid by Clark in turn went bankrupt, and spread the bankruptcy to several removes from the old general. Will had spent much of his time before the expedition dealing with his brother's creditors and trying to salvage enough so that the whiskey-soaked general at Mulberry Hill could live in a modicum of comfort.

Somehow it had not embittered Will Clark; he was too great a man for that. But now, when I showed him my rejected voucher, I saw a deep and knowing cynicism bloom in his eyes. He had walked that path, and knew the thousand small cuts of officials and creditors and lawyers, and he knew exactly what probably was in store for me.

"We'll wrestle this together, Meriwether," was all he said to me. I had feared he might lecture me about my land purchases and living beyond my means, but he said not a word.

I was grateful for that.

"What are you going to do?" he asked.

"Pay Provenchere for the translation; let people know that a minor refusal is no ground for alarm."

Will smiled wolfishly. He didn't have to tell me what he was thinking: if Frederick Bates were not stirring up trouble, it might work. But Bates's busy tongue was already undoing anything I might say or do.

"I am an honest man! I will pay every cent!" I exclaimed.

Will's eyebrows arched and he scratched at his newly shaven jaw. "You might go talk to the man."

"He would not entertain my presence in his office. This is his design! His objections did this! He wants to ruin me! He'd stop at nothing! He and his Burrites, still smarting over their defeat."

"How do you know he was allied with Aaron Burr? I certainly don't know it."

"Why else would he be so determined to destroy me?"

Will grinned again. "Wants your office. Can't stand to be subordinate to you."

There was more to it, even if Will didn't think so. I saw threads leading back to shadowy men, leading back to Burr, and maybe General Wilkinson himself, men who wanted to turn the western country into their own satrapy to exploit and suck dry and then toss to the British, or the Spanish, when they were done. I saw design in it; men quietly maneuvering to fill their purses and assume the powers of state, men with stilettos and the will to use them.

But Will Clark, as was his wont, had reduced it to the boneheadedness of clerks and accountants, bureaucratic naysayers, and above all, a pompous, busy, mean-spirited, self-important man who thought himself misplaced as the second in command. One of us was wrong, I thought darkly, and it wasn't me.

"I suppose you had better make some plans," he said.

"Such as?"

"A trip east."

"What good would that do?" I asked truculently.

Will shrugged. "I prefer to sit down with a man and get to know him and get him to listen if I have something to say."

"Do you think James Madison would even see me?"

Will laughed easily, and that was answer enough.

"I want to talk to Secretary Eustis. He's the one I worry about. He reprimands me in almost every letter, and I don't like the tone of his correspondence."

"I worry about him, too. He's trying to trim down the army just when we're facing another war. We're fixing to hand the Louisiana purchase to the British if he doesn't send me materiel."

I glared out the window at unseen knaves. "I have tried to govern this territory on the best model, employing all the wisdom I could garner from Tom Jefferson, from my army experience, from my readings, and now this blowhard threatens to undo my every act!"

Will didn't reply; he simply rounded his desk and clapped me on the back, threw an arm around my shoulder, and let me know in that language of friendship that lies above and beyond words that I could count on him. I was suddenly grateful for this stately, dignified Virginian who looked more and more like George Washington as the years etched him.

"I'll wait and see. Maybe it will blow over," I said.

"My powers with the pen aren't much, but I'll come to your defense if you want me to," he said. There was a question in it.

"I'll fight my own fight," I replied.

"You're outnumbered," he said.

37. LEWIS

I downed a gram of Dover's powder to quiet my racing pulse, and waited for the opiate to steal my anguish from me. The letter on my desk this eighteenth day of August had catapulted my pulse and deranged my every thought.

I paced my chamber, some wildness keeping me from sitting myself down and reading the letter from Secretary of War Eustis a second time to measure its deadly impact. I pressed the lids of my eyes shut, wanting to drive out the sight of that awful missive, which had been written in mid-July but only now found its way to my hands.

Such was my agitation that the powder did not take hold entirely; no peace filtered through me, but only a leaden weariness that did not allay my anxiety at all, but perhaps even deepened it. I was tempted to take another gram, but put the thought behind me.

At last I felt my pulse slow, and my jumbled thoughts slow with my pulse, and I supposed that soon I could reduce the chaos of my heart to good order. Without the powder, I might have suffered an apoplexy beyond repair.

I seated myself again in the squeaking chair and let myself stare at the fluted white woodwork of my office, the seat of government of Upper Louisiana, a territory comparable to the *whole* of the original United States of America, though I don't suppose those back East ever fathomed that.

I watched the progress of my hands, sweaty and trembling at first, and spastic in their motions. They dried. I regained control of them. I could hold the letter without smearing the ink or straining my eyes.

It had been opened by Secretary Bates, who no doubt was even now trumpeting the tidings to his cronies, with many a joyous smirk and expression of hypocritical and pious horror. I reached to the cut glass decanter and poured a measure of ruby port and discovered as I lifted the glass that my hands were once again obedient to my will. I sipped, and again.

The letter from Secretary Eustis professed puzzlement about the expedition I had sent forth in May to return She-He-Ke to his Mandan village. Or rather, it expressed puzzlement about what the hundred and twenty trappers would do once they got above the Mandan villages. He said the government had no understanding of any of that, or where the commercial party was heading, or whether it would even remain in United States territory, and I should have inquired before acting.

This was official dissembling, the genteel lying of bureaucrats; he knew exactly what the trappers of the St. Louis Missouri Fur Company would do after they had delivered the Mandan chief to his village because I had thrice written Eustis in great detail about the arrangement, and what was required because the regular army would not do the job. I had enclosed a fair copy of the contract with the St. Louis Missouri Fur Company.

All this the secretary knew, but now professed ignorance, which is the venerable way of effete functionaries to say no, or rebuke underlings, or express disapproval. James Madison's pinchpenny secretary of war was not only no friend, but was now grimly undermining my every effort to secure the territory from the designs of the British, who continued to stir up the tribes against us.

I detected the Machiavellian hand of Frederick Bates in all this: those snide asides, those grandiloquent objections to my every voucher, those raindrops of dissent descending on the governor, all had their effect. His noose was tightening around my vulnerable neck.

The secretary of war wrote, in that dry, passive voice of his, that after his department had approved the seven thousand dollars for the expedition, "it was not expected that any further advances or any further agency would be required on the part of the United States."

He would, therefore, reject the voucher I had issued at the last moment for the additional five hundred dollars to purchase more gifts for diplomatic concourse with the tribes.

The voucher would be my own responsibility. I now owed every penny of it to the merchants who had trusted my signature on a government draft.

But Secretary Eustis wasn't done with me. "The President has been consulted and the observations herein have his approval."

So Mr. Madison was rebuking me, too. There was no sympathetic ear in official Washington. It was a vote of no confidence. It was a blatant if unspoken suggestion that I resign. No governor can govern without the power of the purse, and Eustis knew it.

It was, I felt certain, Frederick Bates's carefully executed coup d'état.

His office was but a few doors away, but I did not storm toward it. I reread Eustis's letter and resolved to fight. The first step would be a reply in this very day's post. I would again provide the exact details of the fur company expedition, the exact plans of the company after it had fulfilled its official function, and the exact costs. I have never been one to surrender under adversity, especially to the withered gray hand of bureaucracy, and so I wrote, the calmness adding to my lucidity, the powders subduing the clawing at my heart.

I explained to Eustis that the feelings his letter excited were truly painful, and I reminded him that I had always accompanied my drafts with detailed explanations of what the funds were purchasing. And I concluded, "If the object be not a proper one, of course I am responsible, but if, on investigation, it does appear to have been necessary for the promotion of the public interest, I shall hope for relief."

And I reminded him that "I have never received a penny of public money but have merely given the draft to a person who has rendered public service, or furnished articles for public use, which have been, invariably, applied to the purposes expressed in my letters of advice."

I fancied that it was one of the best of my letters to the secretary; and when I was done I signed it, sealed it with wax, and posted it myself rather than letting Bates see my correspondence.

But I was not sanguine about the effect of that letter. If I wished to retain office, I would have to go east, *at once,* and sit down with the president and secretary and anyone else who might help me, and make my case.

I dozed.

Will Clark startled me awake. I peered up at him, shaking the cobwebs from my brain.

"What's this about a voucher?" he asked.

So Bates had been telling the world after all. I handed the letter to Clark, who read it, frowning.

"This indicts us all," he said. "The fur company as well as your offices in setting up the expedition."

He had a steely set to his face I had seen only a few times before. An angry Will Clark was a force to be reckoned with.

"So Eustis is feeding you to the hogs," he said.

"Where did you hear about the voucher?"

"Ben Wilkinson. He asked whether the government would honor your warrants. He has several bills outstanding."

"I don't know," I said. "Who told Wilkinson about the letter?"

"He just passed it off as rumor."

"Bates," I said. "He's the one who received and opened it and placed it on my desk."

Clark grunted. "You can't answer backstabbers by writing letters. If you want to bend an official, look him in the eye. We'll both have to go to Washington."

I nodded.

He stared at me. "Are you indisposed?"

"Just tired."

"How soon do you think you can be off?"

"I don't know. A week, maybe. I hate to leave the territory in his hands."

"Bates is too hidebound to do anything. He's an absolutely rule-obsessed man. Put him in charge of anything, and he'd spend days trying to find a rule giving him the legal right to sneeze. You have no need to fear him."

Will could not have been more wrong, but I said nothing.

"You're indisposed," he said. "Maybe that's best. Go to your rooms and close the door and rest."

He left, leaving me to face my creditors. I drew my ledgers out of a drawer and began totting up my debts, which came to four thousand dollars. If more warrants were rejected, I would owe more. I needed cash, and fast.

There was one hope: I had never made use of my land warrant from the government, the sixteen hundred acres given me as my reward for leading the expedition. Land was cheap. There was more than enough. But maybe if it were auctioned in New Orleans, I might get two dollars an acre for it, a better price than I could obtain here. All right. I would take the warrant to New Orleans, and see what came of it. With luck, that might cover half of my debt—if Eustis didn't reject any more of my vouchers. I had the crawling fear that he would, especially egged on by Frederick Bates. If they wanted to ruin me, they could without much effort.

I drew up a list of creditors, and calculated. If I returned two of the farms I had purchased from Auguste Chouteau, I would cover my debt to him. If I placed the remaining farm in the hands of my creditors, and my several city lots, that would cover more debt. But there would be other debts remaining, such as the back salary I owed my servant, John Pernia. And the warrants. I didn't have enough to cover everything. I didn't have enough to afford a trip to Washington, much less the return to St. Louis.

No one had pressed me as yet. But with every commotion in the corridor, I expected one or another St. Louis businessman to burst in and skin my hide. That no one burst through my door was good. If I wanted to demonstrate my intent and my honor, I would go to them first, before they were forced to come to me.

I examined my ledgers, made my choices, and headed into the suffocating afternoon with the documents in a portfolio. I would see an attorney and draw up some papers empowering certain friends to handle my financial affairs. Then, in a day or two, I would face my creditors. Let no man say I am without honor.

38. LEWIS

I walked through dolorous August heat to the offices of Auguste Chouteau, merchant and entrepreneur, and the city's most prominent and powerful citizen. Some would have called it a fool's errand. My brow rivered water, and dark stains dampened my stock. But the discomfort was a small price to pay.

I entered his gloomy building, found him not present, and remembered that this was the hour of the petite nap; most of the Creoles encouched themselves for a little while in the afternoon. Still, the bells had tolled three, and so I waited in his chambers upon a brocaded divan he had placed there for visitors.

I bent my thoughts to other things to escape the discomfort of that stifling air, and remembered the faces. How many thousands of American faces had gazed upon me since my return? I remembered the admiration in their eyes, the smiles, and hearty congratulations. I remembered the curtsies of the women, their way of honoring a man of high rank.

I remembered the toasts raised by burghers in Virginia, learned doctors in Philadelphia, artists and politicians and poets, raising a glass to Meriwether Lewis, navigator of the wilds, conqueror of a continent, botanist, zoologist, stargazer, cartographer, youthful exemplar of everything good in the new republic, his reputation sterling, his name unsullied by any scandal.

Thousands of them, all expecting much from me because I had accomplished much. Expecting too much. I remembered their toasts, their joy, their poems penned in my honor.

I remembered their respect, the staccato applause of the United States Congress, Tom Jefferson's hearty public acclaim and his even kinder private words, in which he called me son, and told me that I had exceeded his every wish.

I remembered all that, and thought of my dilemmas, and knew that for the rest of my days I would focus on one thing: keeping my honor unstained. Whatever else happened, I would preserve my good name because the beloved republic required it of me. I would not disappoint Tom Jefferson, writing and gardening there in Monticello. I would not disappoint my mother. I had already disappointed myself.

The thought that I would surely disappoint them, or probably stain my name, or shame myself, brought pain to me so intense that I could not even bear the thought. The thought that I might have to peer into Tom Jefferson's eyes and see dismay there was beyond my endurance.

Chouteau appeared, disheveled and yawning.

"Ah! C'est vous!"

He waved me into his ornate and dark chambers, which lacked and needed light.

Wordlessly he motioned me to a creweled armchair, and poured some ruby wine from a decanter. Then he cocked an eyebrow.

"It seems my financial decisions have displeased Washington," I said.

"So I have heard, Governor."

"I am liable personally for some expenses mostly connected to the fur company."

"So I have heard."

"News travels fast. I received the letter only this morning."

Chouteau smiled.

"I am extended beyond my means."

Chouteau did not look surprised.

"If I return two of your farms, by my calculation, you will

be covered completely and have a gain too. My payments to you suffice to keep the third farm."

The phlegmatic merchant sighed, pursed his lips, and nodded. I had a sense that he had, this very morning, examined my debts and payments.

"I wish to return these to you, in exchange for canceling my remaining obligation due next May."

"You are a man of honor, Governor." The words issued from him in all sincerity.

That compliment brought me to the brink of tears.

We completed the transaction in a few strokes. He got his farms back; my debt was canceled, and he gave me a clear title to the remaining farm.

"There are some," he said, "who would use high office for aggrandizement." He smiled. "You, sir, have a loftier design."

I nodded, miserably. I had surrendered not only several thousand dollars of property, but my hopes for the well-being of myself and my family.

"*Alors,* there are others, *mon ami,* who use high office to ruin others, who whisper of afflictions, who claw at those above them."

He was talking about Bates, but in his own civil and oblique way that I had come to admire in this princeling of St. Louis. The assessment of Frederick Bates was not a kind one.

"Auguste, from the beginning, you and your family have helped me govern, resolved problems, generously assisted me in all my designs, and brought the government of the United States into harmony with the French in Louisiana. I am in your debt, and esteem you for your service and your friendship."

He absorbed that a moment. *"Merci, bien, bien,"* he whispered at last. I saw affection in his rumpled face.

I now had one farm in my sole possession, for one moment. I bade my host adieu after the shortest of visits, and headed up Main to the general mercantile of Ben Wilkinson, partner in the new fur company, brother of the army general who was up to his eyeballs in Burr's conspiracy, and no friend.

Wilkinson was more energetic, but somehow less formidable than Auguste Chouteau, and I found him bustling about his poorly stocked emporium, as if his sheer energy could cause goods to appear on his shelves.

"Ah, it's you, Meriwether," he said neutrally. "What can I do for you?"

I motioned to his cage, a raised and balustraded office overlooking the floor of his sandstone store.

"How much do I owe?" I asked, once we seated ourselves.

He donned spectacles and opened a ledger. "Considerable. There's the five hundred dollars of trading items that Secretary Eustis now rejects. Or so I hear. Is it so? I was thinking of asking you about it—"

"You'll be paid. Yesterday I appointed three friends to look after my debts. I'll give them power of attorney and they will sell such property as will pay my creditors."

"Who, may I ask?"

"Will Clark, and two of my Masonic friends, Alexander Steward and William Carr. The papers are being prepared, and I'll sign them Monday. They'll have a farm of mine and some lots as surety, and there will be more coming. I will not rest until every obligation has been satisfied."

"You're leaving us?" Wilkinson asked.

"I'm going to Washington to straighten out some financial matters. Some of them having to do with your fur company."

He nodded, and I knew none of this was news to him. "The rejected vouchers," he said.

"Yes, and there may be more. I cannot count on the Madison government honoring my warrants. I'm at sea, not knowing what will be accepted and what will fall to my own account, Ben. That's why I'm here. To protect you and the rest as best I can."

"Even Frederick Bates?"

"Even the secretary. I owe him a little, along with many others."

"So I am to press my claim with Steward and Carr?"

"Yes, but I hope you'll wait. If I can reverse the decisions in Washington I may not have to liquidate my holdings. I'll send my land warrant to New Orleans to be auctioned, and that will raise more."

"Does this mean you won't be back?"

I dodged. "I expect to settle this with the president and the secretary of war. It is hard to come to terms by mail."

"That's a long trip."

"Will and I are both going, but separately. Since your St. Louis Missouri Fur Company is at the center of the dispute, the general felt he has to explain things in person, just as I do. He will also see to his brother's affairs."

Wilkinson sighed, smiled, and shook his head. "Who would have thought it?" he said. His gaze slipped away from me, and I sensed all this had been much discussed, maybe even plotted. His closeness to Bates was well known to me.

I braced him: "The governor will pay his debts," I said. "Even when some others set out to ruin him."

That was further than I intended to go. It evoked a catlike grin in the amused merchant.

"Meriwether, old friend, rest yourself in peace," he said.

"I will remember that you are doing me a great service," I replied. "You've waited some while for payment, and now you'll need to wait a while more. I am grateful for your patience."

The kind words surprised him a little. He nodded.

A bleak wind was blowing.

I stepped outside into a different and crueler world, knowing there still were things that needed immediate attention. Raising some cash was one. I owed my manservant, John Pernia, two months' salary. I needed also to persuade him to come east with me.

I found him at my quarters, about to tote a load of my linens and smallclothes to the black laundresses.

He straightened up, the wicker basket in hand, a question in his dark face.

"Set it down, my good man, so we can talk," I said.

I waited while the dusky freeman set down his burden and gave me his attention.

"I would like you to come with me to Washington," I said. "It is crucial to me. I will entrust you with an important task, the most important you have ever been given."

He shook his head; I knew he was on the brink of resigning. A man cannot work for nothing for long.

"You, John, are at the heart of my plans. Come with me, and you will be paid everything owing you when we reach Virginia."

He might never know why I needed him; but someday soon he might.

39. CLARK

It is our custom to be at home Sunday afternoons, and entertain St. Louis. We put out bountiful viands and then await whoever comes, and there usually are a few dozen. Julia loves these occasions and swirls about welcoming the assorted militia officers, clerks and secretaries, old comrades from the Corps of Discovery, trappers, boatmen, merchants, and all their pretty spouses, mothers, aunts, children, and daughters.

This Sabbath, August 27, 1809, in the midst of this cheerful occasion, the governor's manservant Pernia arrived with a message.

He drew me aside. "The governor is indisposed, General, and regrets that he can't come. He doesn't know when he will depart for the East, but will let you know of his progress."

"How indisposed, Mr. Pernia?"

The servant squinted at me, reluctant to talk. His face was a mass of brown and liverish freckles, the result of the union of two bloods, and I saw him retreat into discretion. "I couldn't say, sir."

"Perhaps I should go see him."

"He didn't convey that request, sir, but if you want, I will tell him of your wish."

I smiled. The governor's manservant was not only loyal but protective. "Very good, Mr. Pernia. I'll go see him. Is he very sick?"

Pernia debated a response, and finally nodded. "When he doses himself with the medicines, sir, I know he's indisposed."

"I'll be along directly. I haven't seen him in a week, and I was wondering. Let me tell Julia, and I'll just duck out of here."

I left the governor's man waiting, while I cornered Julia.

"Meriwether's got the fever again. I think I'd better go check on him."

"But General—"

"Ah, Julia, they come to gaze upon your fair and willowy beauty, not see me. In any case, I'll be back directly."

She laughed. She was with child and it showed.

I took off with Pernia, hiking through a sultry August afternoon that threatened to explode in thundershowers. Meriwether's chambers were only a few blocks distant.

Pernia grew agitated as we drew close. "I'll just step ahead, General, and let him know that you wish to see him."

I ignored the servant. Meriwether and I had walked across a continent, shared a tent as well as a command, and he had no secrets from me, nor I from him.

The household was not locked, and Pernia let me in, plainly reluctant. "I'll go see the master," he said, racing through the cluttered parlor toward a bedroom at the rear.

This time I waited. I beheld several black leather trunks, their lids open, their interiors silk-lined. One contained his clothing: pantaloons, shirtwaists, hosiery, boots, red slippers, all neatly laid out by his servant. His two matched pistols rested in their case along with his ornate powder flask. I spotted his sword, which had traveled to the Pacific and back.

Another trunk contained the disputed vouchers and the journals, the battered ledger books stacked in orderly piles within. I itched to know what he had completed; whether some of those ledgers contained an edited version he would now take to Philadelphia and the printer, at long last.

Another, smaller chest contained an amazing assortment

of blue bottles and pasteboard boxes of powders, packets of herbs, and a store of spiritous drinks in tin flasks. Plainly, Lewis was taking east with him an array of medicines beyond my fathoming, enough to stock a small apothecary shop. I sensed that here was something I had only vaguely grasped about my old friend. How much of all these was he swallowing, and for what?

Pernia emerged from the gloom.

"He's indisposed, General," the servant said.

"I've seen him in that estate before," I said, overcoming the servant's reluctance. I pressed past the man and pushed through the door into Meriwether's bedchamber. A rancid odor smacked me, along with a fetid closeness. The governor lay abed, his face flushed. A nearly empty whiskey bottle stood at his nightstand, and I wondered if the governor's indisposition was nothing more than his occasional indulgence.

"Meriwether," I said.

He peered up at me from a flushed face, the red barely covering an underlying grayness of his flesh. "I'm fevered. Can't leave yet," he whispered.

"Have you seen a doctor?"

He shook his head.

"Should I fetch one?"

He shook his head again. "Nothing to be done. Fetch my mother."

"Your mother? Lucy Marks?"

He nodded.

"Meriwether, you are in St. Louis."

"Oh," he said. "Tell her to come."

Lucy Marks was in Ivy, Virginia, on the family estate. I pressed a hand to Meriwether's forehead. It was hot and moist.

"Close in here," I said. "I'll open a window."

"No! No, don't let them in!"

I paused. "Let who in?"

"I am indisposed," he said. "The fevers. Don't let any more in."

"Fresh air will do you good. Let me air the room."

"No, I beg of you, don't let them in."

I paused at the shuttered window. "Let who in?" I asked.

He stared at me from dull eyes, and said nothing.

The room oppressed me and I sensed that it was oppressing him, too, so I threw open the shutter and opened the casement. A breath of clean air filtered in.

He closed his eyes.

"You can close it in a moment," I said.

"Don't let Maria see me," he said. "Don't let her in."

"Maria? Maria who?"

"Wood," he said. "Pure and fair."

Maria Wood. He seemed to think he was back at Ivy, in his parental home. I wondered whether he was fit to travel at all.

I studied the array of medicines at hand. Dover's powder, calomel, Rush's purgatives, whiskey, wine, belladonna, ipecac, extract of cinchona, brown liquids I couldn't identify.

"Light hurts my eyes," he said.

That would be the Dover's powder, I thought.

"Meriwether, has a doctor prescribed all this?"

He didn't reply, but I knew the answer.

"I'll ask your man to apply cold compresses," I said. "Bring down the fever."

He nodded, and I bade him goodbye. I intended to check up on him daily. I had treated him many times on the expedition; now I would keep an eye on him.

In the parlor I braced Pernia. "He needs cold compresses. And less medicine. It's quite like him to think that if a little s good, more is better. He lays siege to his own body, with all this stuff. Mr. Pernia, please keep me informed. If the governor's not better tomorrow, I'll see to fetching a doctor. Who is it, Saugrain?"

"Yes, General."

"And take those blasted bottles and boxes away from him. Take everything away but the cinchona."

He hesitated, not wanting to offend the governor.

"For the governor's own good, Mr. Pernia."

Plainly I was intruding. My command had disturbed the man, so I clapped him on the back. "No man ever served better," I said. "A good man looks after his master just as you do."

"He desires me to go east, sir, but I'm not sure I should continue . . ."

"Continue?"

He looked trapped. "Without salary, sir?"

I chose my words carefully. "You are a good and loyal man. I am certain that the governor intends that you receive every penny owed you as soon as he reaches Virginia. His mother will see to it."

He nodded. Again I felt I was intruding in the private life of this old comrade of the wilds. But he lay ill and out of his head, and I was his friend, and no family but my own was there to look after him in St. Louis. Reuben was upstream with the fur company. So friends step in, without a thought, and Meriwether was as fine and noble a friend as I ever had.

"Mr. Pernia, your service to him as he heads to Washington would be invaluable. I can only say, sir, that without you he might not succeed. If you should run into any difficulties, contact me and I will do what I can."

I clapped his shoulder. "You've helped me, and helped him. I need to know how the governor's faring, and you can count on me as the governor's friend. It is not something to share with anyone else."

"Oh, never, General!"

"Good. You probably know what Doctor Saugrain prescribes and also prohibits?"

Pernia seemed to shrink into himself again. "Yes, but if I keep spirits from the governor, like the doctor wants, the governor, he gets upset and then I hear about it."

I nodded. A servant could no more keep spirits and powders from Meriwether than I could.

40. LEWIS

They fished me out of the river with their grappling hooks. They glowered at me, so I explained I had fallen in because I am not steady on my feet. The chill of the Mississippi shocked me back to my senses after my tumble overboard. I don't remember what happened before that. I must have been wandering the plank floorboards of this flatboat while the river boiled by.

The Creole boatmen began to examine me sharply as I dripped water, but I ignored them. I did not change into new clothing, but let the water cool my fevered flesh. The river is tepid anyway. I wrung the moisture from my pantaloons and settled within the cabin, on a crude bench that serves me for a bunk.

Pernia doesn't approve, and rummaged through my trunks to find a change of clothing. But I ignored him. I asked him for my pills but he is reluctant, and finally I rose and found the Dover's powder myself. I asked him to un-cork a jug of whiskey because I am shaking, but he seems almost truculent today, and glares at me. I am finding him more and more disobedient.

We traveled but little this Monday, September 4. The sun is so oppressive that the boatmen paused during the midday heat, unable to pole and row and steer the flatboat without wilting.

I am fevered as usual, and spend the lazy hours lying abed in the rude cabin. Pernia roams the deck the way a prisoner walks in the prison yard. He did not want to come. I do not want to make this trip.

In New Orleans I will board the next coaster heading east, and will round Spanish Florida and sail up the Atlantic coast, and in a month or six weeks, depending on the winds, I will enter the Chesapeake and be deposited in Washington, all by sea. That is, if the prowling British warships don't stop us. In my condition, that is the only way I can travel. My exertions are limited to walking the forty-foot flatboat for exercise, but the dazzle off the water is too fierce to permit it, so I huddle in the gloom of the cabin. Outside of this small sanctuary, I lose my balance and need support lest I topple again into the murky river that is carrying me on its shoulders to my destiny. I say destiny, rather than destination, knowingly.

I intended to start for Washington a fortnight ago, but fever stayed me, and also the wall of debt that rises higher and darker than the walls of a prison. I could not raise cash to travel. When I was feeling a little better, Will helped me organize my debt. We found that I owe, apart from my land payments, twenty-nine hundred dollars, of which I could readily cover only part by auctioning off my federal land warrant in New Orleans.

This oppresses me. I have subsequently enlarged my debt to purchase passage for myself and Pernia, and to buy the necessary medicines without which I could not hope to arrive in Washington.

The Creole boatmen have tied up here at Ste. Genevieve for the night, and gone ashore, leaving me to fend for myself. Pernia stays on, and has somehow commandeered a cold meal for me, though I am not a bit hungry. I can scarcely swallow the spirits and pills I require to allay my pain.

But there is so much worse afoot in my poor body: I am confused, and while I usually recover my senses, I remember my confusion and my hallucination, and it is as if I have returned from some distant and bumbling journey. I gazed backward this day, watching the bubbling wake of the flatboat as it rocked slowly along the turbid waters, knowing I cannot return to St. Louis. I did not say goodbye.

My last true friend, Doctor Saugrain, visited me several times those final days. He is humble and discreet, and reluctant to tell me how grave my condition now is. But he shakes his head slowly, and I did get out of him that it can no longer be concealed. If I arrive in the city named for our first president in this condition, I shall be found out. When I ask the little physician how long I might last, he shrugs gallantly. "Who knows?" he asks. "One year, ten years, yes?"

I could retreat to Ivy and become that legendary uncle in the attic, and wobble through a few more years hidden from a sharp-eyed world. I wonder what Maria Wood would think of me, could she but see me now.

Doctor Saugrain was firm the last time I saw him. "Have faith. Do not surrender to it. Do not, my friend, imbibe spirits, or swallow more mercury, or numb your soul with the Dover's powder. Stay yourself, my magnificent friend, and endure."

It was a parson's adieu, not a physician's. Live quietly apart, indulge in nothing, endure the pain of body and soul nd veil myself; let no mortal see the fumbling presence, he darkness of my vision, the lumpy thickenings that twist he flesh of my face, the mad eye, the hulk of a man. Coneal what is left of Meriwether Lewis, hide the pathetic runs from the world, place myself in the care of my suffering nother, and then die and be furtively buried in the family lot, well forgotten.

Doctor Saugrain told me months ago that I would know vhen I was losing my mind. The disorder is so slow and ubtle that its victim can observe the murderous progress f his own unraveling. Now that time is upon me, and yet I etain hope. Maybe my gifted mother, Lucy Marks, can rew the simples that might heal me. Ah, God!

Here I am, the governor of Upper Louisiana, on a trip east o talk to the president and secretary of war. The world nows it; I wrote letters and announced my intent, and they re expecting me. But what if I cannot talk? What if I am nad of eye? What if every word they say to me doesn't regster, and every utterance of mine is incoherent to them? I lon't want them to see me, nor my mother to see me.

It would be good to fall again off this flatboat. I am *no onger Meriwether Lewis,* and that answers all questions. If ve were to travel at night, I could design it. By day, with heir alert eyes following me, I cannot. But I might catch hem unawares.

It is dusk and the river men are in town after a miserable lay under the hammering sun. They deserve their pints in he local taverns. Only Pernia lingers here. The flatboat bobs ext to the levee, fastened by hawsers to pilings set in the nuddy shore. A thick plank bridges the gunnel and the rassy bank. We are carrying a cargo of stiff buffalo hides hat release sharp odors.

"Pernia, go enjoy yourself," I said.

He shook his head.

"I will be all right."

"No, sir, you won't be all right."

"If you lack money for a glass of porter, I have a little."

"No, Governor."

"I will need something to help me sleep."

He looked torn again, wanting to heed my every wish "Maybe you should not," he said. "I will fetch you some dr clothes. And a sheet will help. And I will hang up the netting."

Mosquitoes *were* whining everywhere; I was ignorin them, but Pernia was not.

He was being, as always, a faithful servant of his governor, and I forgave him his disobedience.

"I'm sorry to cause you such care," I said penitentially.

He gave me a hard look. "Maybe you try praying. Go make the fever go, maybe."

"I have no such beliefs. God is a Creator. He has put th universe in motion. That is all there is. I do not accept th idea of miracles."

"You a Christian, maybe?"

"Superstition."

Pernia made the sign of the cross. He was half Creole and the French had given him what little he possessed o religious understanding.

I lay back on my plank bench, feeling blood throb in m head. I would soon have a splitting headache unless I too some Dover's powder again.

"Why won't you give me my medicines?" I asked.

"They're bad."

"You go to town and enjoy yourself."

He shook his head doggedly. It was going to be anothe miserable night.

I lay on the hard plank, listening to the whine of mosquitoes, slapping at them, peering into the moist gloom a night things fluttered. I knew a lamp would attract moths.

I closed my eyes, knowing that John Pernia's devotion was good and important to me.

"John, if anything should happen, if I should take sick and perish at sea, what will you do?"

"Master Lewis, I will guard your trunks with my life. I will deliver them to Mr. Jefferson. I will do that, master, no matter what; for that is required of me."

"Only the journals need go to him, Pernia. The rest to my mother and brother in Ivy."

He nodded.

"But the journals go to Monticello, and I know you will guard them with your life. I am my journals. All that I was, all that I will be remembered for, are there on those pages."

He bustled in the gloom and I heard him opening and closing my several trunks until he found what he wanted, some mosquito drapery. He tied this awkwardly to various items, but it did hang over my pallet and did hold the whining mosquitoes at bay. A misty moon gave soft light, enough for me to follow his movements. He found my coat, rolled it up, and offered it as a pillow. I didn't want a pillow; I wanted the powder. I lurched up in my pallet, ripped aside the netting, and grasped the heavy jug, drawing it tightly to my belly.

He paused, sorrowfully, and then slid into that strange passivity he expresses in every motion when I overrule him.

"Get out, John. I will be alone now."

He retreated through the open rear, and into the soft light of the evening. I watched him settle on the transom, next to the sweep of the rudder. I pulled a cork and swallowed the harsh fluid, gasped, and swallowed again, until it burnt a trace down into my belly.

With luck, I might numb all species of pain, including the new one I have discovered, *Afflictus lewisensis.*

41. CLARK

It was time to report to Secretary Bates. Meriwether had left; I would be leaving on September 18, and the territory would be governed by the secretary alone.

I approached his office gingerly, having heard rumors o his current agitation, but little did I expect when I entered to experience the violence of his passions.

He spotted me at once, leapt from behind his waxed desk where no speck of dust resided without permission, and wagged his finger at me.

“You! You!” he cried. “You have come to rebuke me, and I will not stand for it, sir.”

I shook my head. “No, I just came—”

“I know exactly what you came for. It’s a canard. I have nothing whatsoever to do with the governor’s derangement Nothing at all. He brought it on himself, and it is the basest, vilest of lies and *insults* to say that I drove him to hi current estate because I covet his office. That’s what they’re whispering, sir, and I *despise* every malicious voice that is engaging in character assassination behind my back! I wil not tolerate it!”

He was livid. His eyes flashed. He windmilled his arm more dramatically than any actor playing King Lear. Since I could not speak without interrupting, I didn’t, but let him run on.

“Here is the *truth,* sir! I pity the man. I don’t wish to pu him out of office, wretched as his conduct toward me ha been. I am not so base as to conduct myself in such a *vil* manner. The canards floating about are contemptible, si nd I will push them aside. If any man says it to my face, I ·ill express my unalloyed contempt, sir."

I was grinning, and he took it wrong.

"Ah, so you mock me! You and your pitiable friend Lewis! am an honorable servant of the government, sir, abiding y its laws, unlike the governor, and I will not *tolerate* your ontempt."

I saw he was winding down, so I tried a tentative sentence: I'll be leaving for Washington on Monday and thought I'd eport to you, Mr. Bates."

"Report?"

"On the condition of the territory. On what's pending. On ·hat's in progress."

"Report! You'll report in Washington all manner of base anards about me, and I will *not* suffer it. I will defend myelf to the utmost, to the last, sir. You and the governor are oing to Washington to do me an injustice."

Bates was beyond rational argument, so I just scratched ny ear, rubbed my jaw, and smiled.

Oddly, he subsided, like a teakettle running out of steam o the lid no longer chattered.

"Actually," I continued, "I want to explain the fur comany to Secretary Eustis and the president. They've never rasped that the regular army wouldn't take Big White up he river, or bear the cost of it, and we had to find other neans. And while I'm there I'm going to try once again to et my brother's finances in order."

Bates was listening for a malign word about himself, or n fact any word, even a kind word, and when the expected eference to his person didn't emerge from my mouth, he ost interest. In fact I'm not sure he registered anything I aid.

"They've never given my brother, General Clark, a penny

for the debts he incurred. I've spent half my life trying t help him, and I'm not making much progress. So I'm goin to try again."

Bates nodded.

"Now, do you want my report?"

Bates strolled back to his chair and sat, slowly, his gaz suspicious.

"In my absence, you'll handle Indian affairs and the mi litia. You will also be assuming Meriwether's duties. Yo may wish to learn how things stand."

At last, he was receptive. I briefed him on my attemp to get cannon, shot, and powder from the secretary of wa the status of various tribes including the fractious Sauks an Fox, on our sources of intelligence about the Spanish prob ing our southwest border, the licenses to trade with variou tribes that had been renewed or issued, the condition of ou roads, the collection of imposts and taxes, the peltrie heaped in warehouses because of the embargo, and othe matters.

"I don't know just when I will be back," I concluded. "I'r aiming to return this fall if I can. Weather may intrude."

Bates was all sweetness and rose from the balls of his fe to his tiptoes. "I will look after the territory with *due dil gence,* General, and nurture our national interest to th utmost of my abilities and in the bosom of truth," he sai "You may count on me to do that which you would mo approve."

I didn't quite know what I had said or done to garner suc florid promises from the man. But neither had I ever unde stood what Bates had against Meriwether Lewis, apart fro envy. But I am good at smiling, and even better at shakin hands, and that concluded my duties.

That done, I hastened home to continue my arrangement I planned to leave Julia behind this time; she had a child care for, another coming, and a household to run. And I would not be leaving her for long.

I intended to travel by land, and to go only with my manservant. I could go clear to Pennsylvania by water if I chose, but traveling upstream in a keelboat would take much too long. Years ago I would have taken York especially for his good company, but he no longer offers company. He still does his duties punctiliously; I itch to fault him, but can find no fault. Yet matters have changed radically; he is a stranger to me, silent when we are together.

He would like to visit his wife again in Kentucky, but I cannot spare him the time this speedy trip.

Unlike Meriwether, I intended to travel light; a saddle horse and a packhorse would suffice. I have a good bay Tennessee walking horse that will jig me east, and some sound horses well trained to carry packs and York. I could be in the capital in a month, though I will spend time at Mulberry Hill with my family.

I found Julia couched on the daybed in our bedroom, embroidering. She doesn't weather pregnancy well.

"Where's York?"

"He took your horses to the farrier."

"Good. The traveler needs shoes." I sat down next to her. "Are you comfortable now?"

She laughed as if the question was idiotic, and that was answer enough. It was good to be among people who laughed. I realized just then I had never heard Bates laugh. And Meriwether's nasal whinny had vanished from his person months ago. I counted a good belly laugh better than a gill of spirits. Things were altogether too somber in official St. Louis.

"Julia, I hope you'll continue our Sunday open houses."

She nodded.

"Be my eyes and ears."

"General, I'll leave the affairs of state to the men."

"You'll hear more when I'm not around than when I am. Write me at Mulberry Hill."

"Will you have room in your bags for a few things?"

"A few. I'm packing light."

She wallowed to her feet and pulled some muslin from a drawer. It was bold crewelwork, orange, sea green, azure, enough to cover the seat of a chair. "This is for Harriet," she said. "Can you put it in oilcloth?"

Harriet Kennedy is her cousin, and I have a soft place in me for her. I promised I would. "She'll like it, and like word of you," I said.

"Will you get to Fincastle?"

"I intend to."

"Then I'll have a letter for the colonel. You'll take it, won't you?"

"Julia, I wouldn't miss a chance to see your family. I'll tell Colonel Hancock and everyone there that you're fine, our boy's fine, and Louisiana's fine."

"Are you going to Ivy?"

"Yes. I want to see Meriwether. And his family, too, but I want to check on him."

"Because he's indisposed?"

I nodded. Actually, I feared he might not be coming back to St. Louis, though I had never voiced that idea, even to Julia.

"What is the matter with him, Will?"

"He has a fever. It comes and goes."

"I hear it's affecting him. It's something horrible, isn't it? His mind's going, isn't it? Whatever could it be?"

I didn't illumine her. I was sure it was the venereal but I didn't really want her to know the nature of his indisposition. There are things to keep from a delicate woman. It has been clear to me for some while, but something I keep to myself. His vials and powders tell me much. The bills from Doctor Saugrain we recorded among his debts tell me more. But most of all, the ruin of his face, his eyes, his shuffling gait, his bewilderment, tell me the whole of it.

I marvel that I chose prudence all those days and nights with the Corps of Discovery. I cannot call it love or saving myself for Julia; I am an army man. I have ordinary virtues, and few enough of those. Just caution. Because of my caution, which stayed me for nearly three years, my life is full and blessed and complete.

Because of a moment of incaution, Meriwether is probably lost to public life. I need to know, and in particular I need to know whether that miracle worker, Lucy Marks, has any remedies. I will stop in Ivy not only to see an old and beloved friend, but to discover a verdict.

Julia caught me in my reverie.

She lifted a soft hand and pressed her fingers to my cheek. "I'll miss you, my general."

I am not a man who fancies up words to present to a lady, so I just smiled and winked. She hugged me, and I hugged her mightily.

42. LEWIS

We floated downstream in a searing sun, the distant shores lost in white haze, the September light so fierce that even the veteran river men squinted from bloodred eyes and wiped away tears.

I huddled in the cabin of this one-way vessel. In New Orleans it would be broken up for scrap, its planks sold along with its cargo of buffalo hides. Its derangement and mine were foreordained.

I too floated down the river of life, helpless in my makeshift body, a prisoner being taken where I would not go. Boulieu, whose flatboat this was, kept a sullen eye on me, his frown shouting invectives at me though he said not a word. The damp heat sucked life from my lungs. My man, Pernia, sat beside me in the choked gloom of the cabin, his furtive glances telling me that I was under guard.

I sweat from every pore, soaking my pantaloons and cotton shirt. I drank, defying their forbidding stares, finding my only solace in the raw Missouri whiskey in my jug. I was fevered again, but what did it matter?

Often the Creoles abandoned the tiller, and the flatboat careened ever southward, the torpid water slapping its planks; but other times when the channel veered into sullen swamps, or rounded a headland, they were all busy sounding and steering and studying the colors of the turgid water.

Yesterday at such a time I slipped to the larboard to relieve myself, and again I careened off the gunnel, the gloomy water inviting my company, but Boulieu spoiled the moment. I saw my face in the dark and mysterious waters. The ripples severed my image and mended it again, and I perceived myself as a boneless specter wobbling on the waters. Then I felt his harsh hand clasp my shirt and pull me back. He pushed me into the bilge and wagged a massive finger.

"Governor, I tie you up, *oui*?"

"Sunstroke," I said.

He grunted.

That was all he said, but he entered the cabin, found my jug, and pitched it into the river. I watched it bob, roll, and sink. I have more in my trunks, a flask of good absinthe. He did not know of my powders. He did not know anything about me except that I am the governor of Upper Louisiana and a noted man he was transporting to New Orleans, not perdition. He did not know that his plank boat and my body were one and the same prison.

Pernia helped me back into the shade, his mottled face fierce with shame. "You lie down; the fever don't go away if you're out in the sun."

I suffered Pernia's rebuke.

We came this afternoon of September 11 upon a curious loop of the river, and for a while bore north and west, the shoulders of the stream carrying me, for the briefest time, toward the Rocky Mountains somewhere beyond a hundred horizons. I thought of heaven. By late afternoon the heat had eviscerated me, the odd fetid smell of the river had nauseated me, and my imprisonment at the hands of Creole warders had driven me to distraction.

But then Boulieu himself was steering the stained and sordid scow out of the channel toward a settlement, odd little houses, innocent of whitewash or paint, with verandas on three sides to ward off the sun, mud lanes with silver puddles, rank green shrubbery choking the yards, and a stench of sewage redolent in the sultry air.

"New Madrid," Boulieu said, in answer to my unasked question.

New Madrid. We had come a long way.

My head was clear. There was something I needed to do, and swiftly.

The boatmen poled the flatboat into a grassy bank, tied it to some acacias, and stepped ashore while solemn boys in ragged pants watched suspiciously. One held a writhing garter snake.

"We stay here tonight," Boulieu announced to Pernia and me.

I stood dizzily. I hadn't shaven, wasn't clean, wore sweat-drenched and river-scummed clothes, and my innards felt as foul as my attire. But the heat was subsiding and my mind was as clear as the sky.

"Is there a merchant here?" I asked a boy, once I stepped out of the prison ship and onto a humped ridge of grass along the lapping waters. New Madrid was oddly bucolic and forbidding, a sleepy hamlet with chickens roosting on the main street, but as sullen as a thundercloud.

He must have regarded me as the equivalent of a pirate, but he pointed at a tired, whitewashed affair a block inland. I walked. Pernia followed silently, his disapproval manifest in his conduct.

The hand-printed sign announced a market whose proprietor was one F. S. Trinchard. I reeled in, unsteady on my feet and no less fevered.

A sallow young man rose from a stool behind the counter.

"Writing paper?" I asked.

He surveyed me, probably wondering if I were literate, and opened a glass case behind him. From within he extracted a sheet.

"Pen and ink bottle?" I asked.

He shuffled around, and placed the items before me, along with a blotter. "Half a bit," he said.

I was too weary to protest the inflated price, so I dug into my small coin purse and extracted a one-bit piece. I uncorked the black bottle, dipped the split quill into the bottle, shook it gently, and began my inscription:

Will

I bequeath all my estate, real and personal, to my Mother, Lucy Marks, after my private debts are paid, of which a statement will be found in a small minute book deposited with Pernia, my servant.

Then I signed it, blotted it, and handed it to the young man. "Please witness this," I said. He read it swiftly and signed his name.

"Thank you, Mr. Trinchard. I am fevered," I said. "It's a precaution."

"Glad to be of service, my good sir. Help availeth."

I patrolled his emporium looking for certain comforts of the flesh, found nothing helpful except some cinchona extract, and headed outside.

"Keep this safe," I said to Pernia. "It favors my mother. If anything happens, get this to her at all cost. Do not fail me in this."

Pernia took it. He could read a little, which was good. I watched him struggle through the text.

The whole business had wearied me, so that my sole desire was to return to the plank bunk and collapse there upon the splinters.

"You help me to the scow, and then you are free to go for the evening, John," I said.

"No, Governor, I'm right here looking after you."

He annoyed me. "I am quite safe."

He grunted something unpleasant that I took for rebuke.

The boys had vanished, but a pair of dowdy women in bonnets surveyed the flatboat. Then they, too, hastened away, leaving only a bullfrog for company.

Pernia opened the leather trunk that contained my journals, folded the will, and placed it within the leaf of the top journal, readily available. I watched.

"All right. Go have a mug of stout," I said. "Here's a bit."

"Master, this is a strange place and we don't know who'll steal. I'm staying here to keep an eye on things."

That was my Pernia, a man so loyal he shamed me. But he was also dissembling. He was really there to keep an eye on me, not my chattel. The Creole crew had vanished into a public house off a way that spilled light into the mucky street, leaving only Pernia to see to it that I . . . did not disturb the peace.

"Are you hungry? Thirsty, Governor?" he asked.

I wasn't hungry. "You could find some fresh water."

"There's a spring running from a pipe," he said.

He eyed me, left the flatboat, which was bumping softly against the bank, and in short order returned with a pot of fresh water. It felt cool down my parched throat. I sipped the chill water again, feeling fever slide out of me and my ruined body improve.

"Pernia, go buy me a quart," I said. "There's a public house over there." I pressed six bits into his hand, watching his face writhe in protest. But he did what he was paid to do, trudged through a somnolent twilight in an unpeopled village, and then he disappeared within. I tried hard to remember the name of this place, but it eluded me.

He returned wordlessly with a brown ceramic vessel in hand.

"They were fixing to throw me out," he said. "But I tell them it's for the master. He says it's a dollar a quart, so I says to him, fill it six bits' worth, and he does."

"You are a true and faithful man, Pernia."

I reached for the bottle. He seemed reluctant to surrender it.

"Maybe you should go to sleep, Governor."

"This will help me. I need it for pain."

He handed my bottle to me and shook his head. "I'll be here, outside, so if you're looking I'm right here."

That was both a jailor's warning and a servant's promise of service. He was too faithful, and I would need to devise some other path to gain my ends.

I uncorked the brown bottle, mixed the spirits with the cool spring water, and sipped regularly into the hazy night, slapping at mosquitoes when they whined close to my face. Sometime or other, the Creoles returned and settled on the deck outside the cabin, where my whiskey breath and the close air wouldn't afflict them. I wished I could remember the name of this place, but it did no good to think about it. The only reality was the fever which consumed me.

43. CLARK

River men carried us across the river to Cahokia on September 18, and York and I proceeded eastward through the Indiana Territory at once on two saddlers and with two packhorses. I gave York a rifle and powder flask, and we set off through forested wilderness that invited ambush from renegade Shawnee.

Up in Vincennes, Governor William Henry Harrison was negotiating a treaty with the tribes, but there were dissidents itching to fight the incursions of white men to the death, like the prophet Tecumseh. So we progressed cautiously, our gazes examining every sign of nature, from the sudden flight of birds to unnatural silences.

Both York and I were garbed in buckskins, which turned wind and weather well, and lasted better than fabrics. The trace was well traveled and there were shelters along the way, but there were also long stretches of thick hardwood forest that hid the sun and plunged us into gloomy cautiousness. The whir of an arrow would tell us we were too late and too few.

In spite of the danger, I knew York was enjoying himself. All this reminded him of the Corps of Discovery and his carefree days on the long trail. And of the years when the distinction between his estate and ours blurred in his mind, until he was simply part of the company.

I was thinking about it, too, and though neither of us spoke, we were well aware of the other's thoughts. I enjoyed the road, the acrid smell of a horse, the feel of a good mount under me, and the occasional moments when we dismounted, stretched our legs, checked the packs, watered and grazed the horses, or surveyed the ever-changing skies.

In fact that afternoon we scarcely said a word; nothing passed between us but my directions to him, which he acknowledged with a brief nod of his head, his dark face granitic and wary.

I have been irritated with him for months, in fact years, but now, as he rode beside me, my anger washed away in the soft September breezes. It was a fine time of year to travel, and the forests veiled the sun and kept us cool though the midday heat was oppressive.

The companion of my childhood and youth had experienced things unknown to most slaves, and had shown himself to be a worthy and hardworking member of our band of explorers.

Yet he spoke not a word.

Late that day I ventured to converse with him. "It is much like our trip west," I said.

He caught me in his gaze, his yellow eyes awaiting my direction.

"That was a good trip, and you were a part of it," I said lamely, not wanting to compliment him or inflate him. Why was I having such trouble talking to a slave?

He nodded as if it was all of no account, but I knew he was listening.

We paused a moment, when some mallards burst from a slough, and then proceeded silently until we had passed the place. He had lowered his longrifle, checked the priming, and was just as ready to defend us as any private in the army.

"We'll quit at the settlements," I said. About nine miles ahead were some farms clustered together for protection. They had been hacked out of forest land, but in between the stumps grew a rich harvest of wheat and corn, melons and squash. We would eat well this night.

He nodded.

I wanted to talk to the man but every time I tried, I stumbled into silence. He pretended not to notice my agitation, but I knew exactly what was going through his mind.

An hour later I fell into a familiar mode of dealing with him: "When we get there, you take care of the horses, rub 'em down and check the frogs and look for heat in the pasterns. I want a bait of oats if they have it, and plenty of good timothy. If any horse of mine lames up, you'll be sorry. Get our truck under roof, and find yourself a place to bunk."

His response was a sigh and a whispered "Yassuh." He kept his nag one step behind mine, which irritated me. I had to turn my head back to address him.

"You'll be wanting to see your wife in Louisville, but there won't be time. I need you. So put it out of your head," I said with a curt edge to my voice.

He didn't respond, but I could feel the hope leak out of him even as he slumped in his battered saddle. He had been counting on it; a swift trip to the tobacco fields south of

Louisville while I visited my brother and family at Mulberry Hill.

We traversed another three miles in total silence.

"Now, damn it, you know nothing about freedom," I said abruptly. We were crossing a broad meadow, the browning grasses waving gently in the low sun, the liberty of the place exhilarating after the imprisonment of the dark oaks and walnuts and hickory trees lining the trace like a prison wall.

"You know what it means? You'd have to take care of yourself. I make sure you're fed every day. I keep you in clothing. I put a roof over your head. I do that whether you're busy or idle or sick. Whether you're accomplishing my ends, or fallow. I do that in the winter and summer. I do that on days when I have no need for you."

His response was to tap the flanks of his nag with his heels and pull up beside me so he could hear all this better.

"If you were freed, what would you do?" I asked.

He said nothing, afraid to talk about such a dangerous subject.

"Go ahead, say what you are thinking," I said.

"Mastuh, I'd get me a horse and wagon and be taking goods from one place to another for hire."

"How would you do that? You can't read. You can't sign a contract. You can't do numbers. You'd be cheated. They'd say they'd pay you ten dollars and give you three and you couldn't do anything about it. They'd claim you spilled something, and try to take your horse and wagon from you."

He nodded. "Maybe I just do it for black peoples, not white peoples."

"You'd starve."

"Might be worth the starvin'," he mused.

"You'd be worse off than with me."

He didn't answer that, and suddenly I laughed. He carefully refrained from laughing, too, but I saw the corners of his mouth rise a little, and I reached across and clapped his shoulder.

What I saw then shocked me: there was more pain in his eyes than I had ever seen in him. Pain fit only for the dying.

I hated myself for it, but I knew what I would do, and I knew that I had to tell him then and there, walking across that lonely valley in wooded hills, in a land as dangerous as the one we traversed en route to the Pacific.

"I'll need you this trip and can't let you visit your woman. When I get back to St. Louis, I'll write the manumission papers. I'll do them in triplicate and file one, give you one, and put the other in the hands of Pierre Chouteau for safekeeping. I'll also publish it in the *Gazette*."

He stared at me, unbelieving.

"York, I'm freeing you."

He seemed bewildered. "You mean I don't have to work it off, the money?"

"I'm freeing you. When we get back."

"You mean I don't owe you nothing?"

"You'll regret it. You'll wish you never asked."

He sat there shaking his head back and forth, slowly, side to side, his lips parted, his eyes on some distant horizon.

I don't know what was impelling me, but I wasn't through. The farms were just ahead; I saw light spill from a cabin a mile away. I saw cattle in the field, with a belled cow announcing her presence.

"When we get back to St. Louis, I'll write your papers, and I'll give you a wagon and a dray. You can go into business. It won't be easy. You'll be competing with plenty of others and they might charge less. Hay and feed and pasture and oats cost money. Wagons break down; you'll need a wheelwright now and then. All of that costs money. You'll have to find a place to live, and that costs money. It's called 'rent.' You can own a house or rent one. You try to raise a family, and there's food to pay for, clothing to buy, furniture, cribs, blankets, diapers, coats, and all of it you'll pay for. I won't be providing it. And if you can't pay, someone will come and take it all away and leave you in the ditch looking for wild asparagus or maybe a mallard or catfish to live on or stuck in a shanty, chattering and cold when the snow flies."

I finally wound down as we penetrated the hamlet, and two curs set up a clamor.

"Mastuh Clark," he said. "You gone and make me a man."

"No, York," I said, remembering those years with the corps, "you made yourself a man."

44. LEWIS

On September 15 they put me off here at Fort Pickering along with Pernia and my trunks. It didn't matter much. For days they had stood guard over me; Pernia and the Creoles took turns as warders. The air on the river had been so thick and moist that I could scarcely breathe; the sun so blinding I couldn't bear to abandon the cabin. White haze obscured the distant shores, and I felt myself being carried to the sea in the prison of my body, detached from the world.

Sweet oblivion. To be aware was to suffer. I numbed the pain as best I could, blotted out the horror with powders, and the ghastly ruin of my body with spirits. They didn't stop me inside the cabin; they arrested my trajectory only at the gunnels of the bobbing flatboat, where one or another hung onto my shirt while I performed my ablutions. I lay drenched in my filthy cottons during the midday heat; lay chilled at night even though the air was sultry. My heart beat relentlessly, pumping life into the ruin of my flesh.

When we anchored at night they fed me broth and hung up the mosquito curtains around me, but little good those pathetic veils did. My arms and neck and face soon swelled with welts from ferocious insects, and only the powders were sovereign against the ache. I do not remember much of that journey, and don't want to.

Boulieu must have thought that a desolate and fevered governor was more cargo than he bargained for, because he took the tiller and made for the army post located on Chickasaw Heights in the Territory of Tennessee, on the left bank of the river. It was one of several posts commanding the river and its traffic, strategically located below the mouth of the Ohio.

Of all this I was only vaguely aware. We bumped against the levee under the mouths of iron cannon, and some hushed conversation ensued beyond my hearing. Then four privates in blue appeared with a litter, and they lifted me onto it, and several others began hoisting my trunks off the flatboat and into a mule cart. We ascended a steep grade, but for how long I don't remember. I only know I was threatening to slide off the litter.

So I was a prisoner of the army.

They deposited me in a whitewashed room walled with broad plank, barren and clean and so bright it hurt my eyes. A surgeon's mate examined me, took the measure of my fever, washed me, and then vanished. I heard mumbling in the hall outside my room. I discovered faithful Pernia hovering there, eyeing me solemnly. The room tumbled and whirled, and Pernia loomed over me and vanished. I wanted my powders and knew I would have to discover where they had taken my trunks. I was burning up again.

It didn't matter.

When I opened my eyes again I beheld a man of rank, his gold epaulets announcing his estate. I knew him somehow, and yet I didn't.

"Governor, I'm Captain Russell at your service," he said. "Gilbert Russell, commanding Fort Pickering."

I nodded.

"The river men have put you in our care," he said. "We've a surgeon's mate here, and he has examined you. Are you following me?"

I nodded.

"He's going to apply cold compresses to reduce your fever, which is elevated."

I nodded.

"Your manservant says you're en route to New Orleans, and then to the Chesapeake. My advice, sir, is that you will need some little while to recover from this attack."

"Thirsty," I said.

Russell nodded. The surgeon's mate brought a tin cup of cool water. I drank greedily.

"I would like my chattel brought here," I said.

Russell paused for just a moment. "Most of it, Your Excellency, will be brought directly. My surgeon's mate believes you are suffering from an excess of some things in your medical cabinet. We will ration those for your own sake. A glass of claret each day will suffice."

"But my pain—"

"We're up above the river, Governor, and it's cooler here. Clean linens and cold compresses and fresh air will restore you directly."

"I want my powders, my snuff. I'm a physician; I dosed the entire Corps of Discovery."

Russell sighed. "And so you did, sir, and brought your corps back safely. I am filled with boundless admiration."

"Is this an infirmary?"

"Actually, officer's quarters."

"Am I free to go?"

He hesitated again. "The boatmen and Mr. Pernia suggest, sir, that you were temporarily so fevered that you were acting against your own best interest. We have a watch stationed for your own safety. If there's anything you need, why, I am your servant in all else."

Even as he addressed me, my mind was quieting and the coolness of the room was comforting my burning flesh. I lay in a clean squared log bunk between muslin sheets. A breeze billowed through the open windows now and then. His talking wearied me. I nodded.

I remember little of the rest of the afternoon, except that the mate steadily applied cold compresses to my face and neck and chest, and so relentlessly that for the first time in a week I felt cool. I fashioned a vast longing for the powders, but knew I had no prospect of getting them, and lay cool and tense through this afternoon, while my faithful Pernia wandered in and out, studying me. I can imagine what he and the river men had told Captain Russell.

My mind clarified wondrously at twilight, and I was able to look about and see something of the post through the open window. Far below, the vast river glimmered, en route to the Gulf of Mexico and my rendezvous with a coastal packet, which would carry the prisoner, Governor Lewis, across the breast of the gulf, around the dangling organ of Florida, to my destiny.

I knew at once I wouldn't go.

Captain Russell visited me again that evening. It was very quiet. I heard nothing, not even crickets at their nightsongs. An assortment of enlisted men changed compresses every few minutes, cooling my body and mind.

"Would you like some claret, Governor?" he asked.

I nodded.

The surgeon's mate handed me a filled glass; a weighed and measured portion of wine. I struggled up in bed, took it, and sipped.

"Are you comfortable?" he asked.

"I'm changing my plans, Captain. I'm going overland from here."

He hesitated. "You're not fit, sir."

"I will be. I have my journals of the overland expedition with me. I fear that I might lose them if British men-o'-war stopped us. They'd love to get their hands on something like that. They are all ready for publication. All I need do is deliver them to my printer in Philadelphia. Years of work now ready to be set into type."

I wondered why I was telling him that. Had I lost all honor? But perhaps the end justified the means.

Russell nodded. "It's a prudent idea, Governor. The British would love a prize like that. And they'd make good use of the journals, too. The maps, the botany, the observations. But in your condition . . ." He let the rest of the idea slide away. "You know, the chances of being stopped by a British warship are very slender. I don't suppose they are more than one in a hundred."

"The British have intelligence, Captain. They would know of my journey."

"The sea is a restful way to travel," he said. "You need do nothing but recover your health in your cabin, watch the dolphins, and think about the future."

"I am already better," I said. "I'll go overland."

"Not alone, sir, not alone. In your condition, I could not let you do that."

I saw at once that the webs of fate binding me wouldn't be snipped so easily. I sipped the claret and smiled up at him.

"Is there anything you need?" he asked.

"I need to write a letter to Mr. Madison, telling him of my progress and my change of plans."

"I will supply the necessaries at once, Your Excellency. The post leaves early in the afternoon."

The captain visited with me a while more, and then suggested that I might wish to retire. It was yet light out, but sinking toward a Stygian night. He seemed formal, ginger in his dealing with me, conscious of rank. He bowed, saluted, and departed.

I dozed. A little later, an aide appeared carrying a small, burnished field desk of cherrywood, several sheets of vellum, an ink pot, and a dozen quills.

"The captain, sir, says you requested this," the corporal said.

I nodded. "Please light the tapers," I said.

The corporal nodded, vanished for a moment, and returned with a glowing punk. He lit one candle and then the other, and retreated.

I struggled to sit up in bed, and finally managed to pull the field desk to me, but my mind refused to work. Words had fled me. Phrases meandered through my mind, and I feared I would not be able to write one word.

For some infinity I tried to write Mr. Madison, the words forming aimlessly in my head and skittering away. It was necessary to send this letter; to let the world know I would head for Washington with intelligence of value for the president and his secretaries.

But after half an hour, or so it seemed, I had not managed

a word. I pulled the field desk off me, and blew out the tapers. Soon thereafter, in the close dark, I felt cold compresses on my forehead again. They might cool the fever of the body, but not the fever of the soul.

45. LEWIS

I awakened this morning feeling cooler. My fever had abated. I was not gladdened. A white blur of light probed through the window, but it did not hurt my eyes. I discovered Pernia sitting in a chair in a corner, as blurred a man as he always had been, for I knew him by his conduct, and not by his heart.

"Your Excellency—"

"Why are you here?" I asked.

"Governor, we're watching over you."

That seemed odd. "Was I that out of sorts?"

His glance slid away. "You were indisposed, sir. You look better now."

I had been abed a long time. "What day is this?"

"Friday, Governor."

"I mean the date."

"The twenty-second."

"And when did we arrive?"

"The fifteenth."

I measured that, slowly grasping that I had been in this bed for a week or so. I remembered phantasms, the tossing images, watchful soldiers, and the captain, yes, Russell. Captain Russell of Fort Pickering. Not Captain Clark. I remembered talking to Russell about my trip down the river, and my need to see the president, and my fear of the British on the sea, and the valuable journals I bore with me.

I looked about me, focusing eyes that refused to serve me. My trunks were collected in a corner, a black heap. A cherry field desk sat on a bedside table. Yes, I had scratched and blotted a letter to Mr. Madison. I remembered it clearly. It had required relentless effort, and neither my mind nor my hand was quite up to it. I had told the president that I would go to Washington overland; that sickness had delayed me. That I had important matters to bring to his attention. I wondered whether I might retrieve that labored epistle and do better.

"Was the letter to Mr. Madison sent?"

"Yes, Governor. I folded it, addressed it, and gave it to Captain Russell. He sent it in the next post."

I nodded. "Where are my medicines, John? I want to take some powders."

Pernia looked uneasy again. "The captain and the surgeon's mate have them, sir. They took away most everything but the Peruvian bark, for fear you might make, ah, your own employment of them."

"It was ague, then."

"They don't know, sir, but they kept up the quinine you'd been taking. They thought you were dosing yourself rather to excess, and it was afflicting your mood."

"I'll want my powders now." It was a command.

Pernia reluctantly shook his head, fearful to be resisting my direction.

I struggled to sit up, and found myself too dizzy and weak and bewildered to do so. I had been here a week and scarcely knew the passage of time. And yet I did remember most of it after a fashion, the darkness and light in succession, the parade of soldiers sitting there, one after another, never leaving me alone, the wild thirsts, the cold wet compresses, one after another, the nausea, the quaking of my limbs.

I lay in a dry cotton nightshirt. My freshly washed clothing hung from a peg in the whitewashed wall. I struggled to get up and dress.

"No, Governor. My instructions are to keep you in bed," my manservant said, reversing our customary relationship. "I think the captain would like to know you're . . . better."

"Back in my head, you mean. Yes, tell him," I said.

Pernia left the room, and I was alone at last. I found a thundermug and relieved myself. I was heading for my trunks when Captain Russell came in, followed by Pernia.

"Governor, I'm glad you're up," he said. "You asked to see me?"

I sank back onto the bed. "I have to go to Washington," I said. "I need to see the president."

Russell frowned. "You need to recover first. Then I'll help you."

"It was ague."

"Your Excellency, my surgeon's mate tells me it was many things, including the wrong medicines, and they had, frankly, affected your mind. Mr. Pernia's conveyed your request for your powders, and I'm going to say no for the time being. My surgeon's allowing you a glass of wine at evening mess."

The craving for some Dover's powder made me tense, but I could see I had no choice. I nodded.

"When are you going to let me go?"

"When you're back in health, and even then I intend to have someone accompany you. You're not up to traveling without assistance. I thought to join you, because I've some protested warrants too, like you, and we could make our cases together. But I can't get permission. They won't relieve me. So I'll need to find someone else."

"I can go alone; I'll have my man with me."

"Mr. Pernia is an admirable and loyal man, Governor, and he's looked after you for days, going without sleep to see to your safety. But you'll be traveling with someone who can keep an eye on you, when I can arrange it."

I sighed and sank back into my pillow. I was going to be taken where I would not go, watched night and day, treated as a prisoner of disease.

"Have you someone in mind?" I asked.

"Major James Neelly, sir, agent to the Chickasaws. He stopped here on the eighteenth and I've apprised him of your condition and the need for a traveling companion. He's willing to wait a few days until you are able to travel. I think you'll find yourself in good company. He's responsible, eager to serve the governor of Louisiana in any capacity, and beyond all that, an amiable friend who admires you boundlessly for your conquest of the continent."

I had never heard of him.

"I'll wish to talk to him in due course, Captain. But I wish it could be you accompanying me. I prefer regular army."

Major was an honorary title given to Indian agents. The man would no doubt be a civilian. Probably one of the innumerable parasites who sucked a living out of the government and the tribes they served. Maybe a rascal. No doubt avaricious, and probably a conniver. Maybe there would be some opportunity in all that.

"At any rate, Governor, I'm pleased to see your progress. My God, how greatly you worried us!"

"I hoped not to worry you at all," I said dryly, knowing he would not fathom my meaning.

I settled back into my bed and he left.

"You can leave now," I told Pernia.

"No, sir, the captain wants a man at your service, and I do a turn; another man will take the night turn."

So I would still be a prisoner. I settled into the pillow, wondering whether anything had changed, whether my life had somehow improved, whether I might better gather my strength and proceed to Washington, dissembling about my purposes, and retreat to Ivy and obscurity.

Nothing had changed. I hated my own dissembling. I had spent a lifetime, a happier time, holding my honor above all else. And here I was, concealing the dark design of my heart, even from my supine position in bed misleading those who were responsibly and affectionately looking after my body and soul.

Did they know? They must! The governor of Louisiana, the celebrated conqueror of a continent, the much-toasted contributor to botany and zoology and other branches of science, was losing his faculties, the victim of his own night of folly, his furtive dalliance with a dusky maiden far from prying eyes.

They could not help knowing. They would know what the calomel meant. They would know what those thickenings about my face meant. They would know, they would not keep it secret, and my honor and reputation would be thinner than an eggshell.

And in Washington they would casually suggest that I retire, and I would no longer hear from my learned colleagues at the American Philosophical Society, and the ruined man, Lewis, would vanish from sight, to the safe imprisonment of a cubicle at Locust Hill, a babbling idiot, kept by his aged mother and dutiful brother far from prying eyes and malicious tongues. Nothing had changed; and neither would my plans, though I would need to dissemble all the more.

"Pernia!"

My man jumped to his feet and approached me.

"I'm not going to Washington by sea. We'll take the Natchez Trace. I'll get horses somehow for the trunks. Now, do you understand your duties to me?"

He looked bewildered, so I enlightened him.

"You are to take my journals to Monticello, no matter what happens to me. If I take ill again, it shall be your bounden and sacred duty to deliver those journals to Thomas Jefferson. You will keep them dry, wrapped in oilskin if need be, and take every precaution for their safety. And my effects to my mother at Ivy. Have I your word?"

"Yes, sir, Governor, my word."

"Have I your oath, sworn before God?"

"Governor, I do swear it before God Almighty."

I fell back on the pillow and closed my eyes.

"Pernia, it all falls on you," I said.

I turned away from him. Not anyone, most especially my manservant, would I permit to see my face.

46. LEWIS

Captain Russell and Major Neelly have deemed me well enough to travel, and I have fostered their delusion. The Natchez Trace will be my route to wherever I am going. I have let them know that I won't entrust myself to a barque while the British prowl the coasts, and would go overland to the City of Washington.

That has taken some maneuvering. I've had to borrow a hundred dollars from Captain Russell to see me to Washington, which I secreted on my person, and also I have had to purchase two horses and tack from him, one to carry two of my trunks, the other to carry me. All of this came to nearly four hundred dollars. I've instructed Captain Russell to ship the other two trunks by sea. I will take the journals with me, plus a trunk of personal items, including my brace of revolvers and powder flask.

With a Virginian's eye I looked over the two horses, which seemed sound enough for my purposes, though neither was a handsome steed. I spotted no lameness or hoof rot or fistulas or other weaknesses, and believe that Captain Russell means to serve me well. Pernia will walk behind, being sound of back and foot, and will be my third beast of burden. The captain gave me a bill of sale, and I gave him a promissory note for $379.58 payable before next January 1.

Toward repayment, I wrote Major Amos Stoddard, who commands Fort Adams downstream, and asked that he repay a two-hundred-dollar loan if possible, and to forward the sum to me in the City of Washington. I have little doubt it will end up at Ivy.

I've had a chance to acquaint myself with Major Neelly, the Chickasaw Indian agent, these past two days. He is a smooth man, without a wrinkle of face or mind or soul, and his brow is innocent of all creases. I have little doubt that he smoothly extracts annuities from the War Department and smoothly distributes some small portion of it to the Chickasaws who reside only a few leagues from here. But perhaps I am jaundiced. My brother Reuben, after all, is an agent, appointed by Will.

I think Neelly will make a good traveling companion. He has shown genuine concern for me, and has expressed his admiration for my command of the Corps of Discovery.

And so, this morning, September 29, we set forth: Neelly and his slave Tom, my manservant Pernia, and myself, as well as a few others heading for the Chickasaw reservation. Both the major and his slave are mounted. They have pack animals as well. The heat still oppresses, though much of our travel is along a trace arched over by oak and maple, so that we progress through a perpetual twilight.

We bade Captain Russell goodbye at about ten o'clock, thanked him for his courtesies, and proceeded east by means of a cutoff from Chickasaw Heights to the trace, a considerable distance, I am told, barely settled, and buzzing with insects. We will have to have our horses and party ferried over the Tennessee River, which will cost my beleaguered purse considerable, but I no longer have choices.

In one of my trunks is my stash of medicines, and once free of the worthy captain, I swallowed some powders intended to release me from the pain that afflicts my mortal coil. I was at once set free. I recovered my flask from my trunk, and slipped it into my coat. I was now armed against misery and fever on the trail.

Major Neelly spurred his fine bay horse forward until he could keep pace with me, where the trace was wide enough to permit it.

"How are you faring, Governor?" he asked.

"I am making progress. It is a terrible thing, having to go clear to the City of Washington to settle accounts. Why will they not accept my word? Am I not an honorable man, Major?"

"I'm sure it's all a misunderstanding. I have the devil's own time getting my affairs straight with them."

"Will is following, you know," I said.

"Will?"

"General Clark. He's coming also. We've left the whole of Upper Louisiana in Bates's hands."

"Bates?"

"Secretary Bates. Acting governor, who this very moment

is penning letters to Secretary Gallatin, President Madison, and Secretary Eustis about my neglect, and my failure to imbibe his wisdom."

"Sir?"

"Ah, you wouldn't know about that, Major. No, not here, across the river. We are coming, Will and I, to set Washington right."

"You say General Clark is following?"

I nodded. "Right along," I said.

Neelly looked back, half expecting to see the general cantering up behind.

"Major," I said, "within those trunks rest my journals of the expedition, the ledgers kept by Will and me. Sir, I have instructed my servant to make sure those reach Mr. Jefferson at all cost. No matter what happens to me, those journals must go east."

"I'm sure you'll soon be fine, Governor."

"Will you promise it?"

"Governor, your manservant is as faithful as any on earth He'll see to it."

"No, Major, will *you* see to it?"

The major nodded. "I promise."

"Good. You are a patriot and a benefactor of science. In that trunk, sir, is a nation's claim to the territory it purchased, but also its claim to the Oregon country, the whole northwest. In that trunk, sir, are a few hundred descriptions of plants, birds, animals new to science. In that trunk, sir, is the defeat of the British fur traders. It contains priceles information, gathered by myself, about each tribe we met information that will seal the hold of our fur traders on those tribes; information that will keep the grasping British ou of the northwest. So I want more than a nod, sir; I want you pledge, your most solemn affirmation—"

"Governor, you have it. But what's this about Clark?"

"He's on his way, sir, and we'll deal with scoundrels and knaves and clerks, which are all one and the same."

"You made no mention to Captain Russell that General Clark would be coming."

"Ah! But he is coming, I assure you."

Neelly stared smoothly at me, his smooth smile concealing his true self and private thoughts. He could only be an excellent Indian agent, professing smooth affection for his Chickasaw charges.

I am sure Will is coming. He said he would come. He must be right behind now. Odd how it is that I don't see him. I need him to straighten things out. I am weary of sitting this horse. It may be sound, but it has a rough gait that doesn't improve my health. Horseflies attack us, big black flies that bite man and horse alike. I hear slaps behind me.

"What takes you east, Major?"

"Nashville. Business there. I will be picking up some items to distribute to the tribe."

"Will is coming soon," I said. "Then we will settle the protested vouchers. A great injustice, sir. I would be solvent now. I would be a landowner now. I would be laying the foundations for my mother and brother. Bates is a most difficult man, you know. Bates, can you imagine a man like Bates?"

He eyed me. "Would you like to stop and rest, Governor? There's a creek a mile ahead."

I closed my eyes against the sun and nausea. "Carry on, Major," I said.

The leaves along the trace had not yet colored and fallen, and so we traversed a green tunnel through a sweltering day. I was grateful for the shade.

I explained my grievances to the major, but I am not sure he grasped any of it. When we did pause to rest the horses or ourselves, he concerned himself anxiously with my care, and advised me that once we get to the Chickasaw reservation, we should pause to allow me to recover.

"I am well enough," I protested.

He did not reply, and I took it for disagreement.

We rode this whole day, and covered much ground, and scarcely met a soul. I have not made up my mind about this Indian agent. He is, by turns, solicitous of my health and eager to know what matters are much upon my mind. He calls my affliction the ague, and I wonder whether he means it, or if he and the others have agreed not to say what they must know.

Twilight approaches, and I know not whether we will find a stand where we might rest for the night. Such places are only a shade better than camping, mostly because we have a roof to turn the rain. But Neelly knows this road, and I leave the arrangements to him.

"Your Excellency, tonight we must make camp, but the skies are clear and I do not expect a soaking. From now on, though, we will find shelter. The day after tomorrow, we will arrive at my Chickasaw agency, and there you can take your rest until we're ready to travel again."

"Major, there is no need."

"There is a need, Governor. I am charged with looking after you, and I will keep my purposes before me."

"And what are those, Major?"

He looked at me gently, and I expected the smoothest from him. "Governor, I am taking it upon myself to deliver you safely and in the best health that can be managed. I do this because I want to, as well as from duty. You are a man I admire, the sort this republic elevates to positions of honor. Who is this man who is with me but a conqueror of a continent? And that is enough. I am pledged to bring you safely home. And I will be looking after you, along with your excellent servant Pernia. I'll do everything in my power to bring you safely to the capital, because I am honored to be in your company and honored to do you any small service I am capable of rendering."

I nodded. I found sincerity in every word. So Neelly would stick like a burr. I would have to think of something else.

47. LEWIS

We travel without Major Neelly now. Just my manservant Pernia, Neelly's slave Tom. Neelly stayed behind to catch two strayed horses at Dogwood Mudhole, where we camped for the want of a settlement.

The horses had been well picketed on good grass, but were freed in the night by parties unknown. They were nowhere in sight at dawn. Major Neelly was greatly puzzled by the disappearance.

"I could have sworn I hobbled them," Neelly said, upon discovering his hobbles resting beside his gear. "I must have imagined it."

In the night, I had untied those pickets and pulled off the hobbles, so that I could travel alone, save for the servants. We would leave the Indian agent behind.

This morning I proposed a plan: "Major, I'll proceed toward Nashville while you hunt down the animals, and I'll pause at the first stand I come to."

"Are you sure you're up to it?"

"I have Pernia," I said.

He nodded. I had been doing a little better for several days. We had stopped at his agency for two days, while I overcame the delirium that afflicted me. It was not my choice: as long as I was in his care, he decided these matters. But he did not take from me my necessaries, the snuff and the powders, by which I dulled the fever of soul and body. It was lying there abed in his Chickasaw agency that I decided what to do, and how to do it.

By the sixth instant I was, in Neelly's estimation, sufficiently recovered to proceed, and we continued west toward the trace, and were ferried across the Tennessee River in a flatboat, by an avaricious ferryman this morning. My horses and Pernia and my person cost me dearly.

This morning, then, my fate has changed. I travel alone sovereign at long last, east toward my sunset. Later we struck the trace, which burrowed like a tunnel through the golden forest, the air pleasant upon the cheeks, chill in the shade, but warm where the low sun struck my ravaged face.

I have been arguing with myself. Sometimes Pernia glances at me, because my debate rages even to his ears, as he trudges behind us. I go east against my will. Far better to go west, toward the future, toward the setting sun, than east, to Washington and exposure. I will not be the old uncle up in the garret of the family home at Ivy. I will not be that Lewis. I will be only the other Lewis.

The censor in me mocks me: you will defame yourself all the worse, he says.

But I rebuke my censor: one can choose a living death or one can choose a more honorable one that preserves the name of Meriwether Lewis for posterity. One death is tragic the other is vile. I prefer tragedy.

But this ghastly judge residing within me will not be stilled. "Ah, they will count it a coward's death, a shameful death, your weak character and melancholia forever on public display."

"Hush! You are wrong! What I must do requires all the courage I possess. I will preserve my name. I will not disillusion Mr. Jefferson. I will not disappoint my friends in the American Philosophical Society; I will not tarnish my honor; I will not mortify my family. I will not blacken the reputation of my Corps of Discovery. Let them call me a coward if they must, though what I intend is a sacrifice to honor. But I will spare my family, spare my friend Tom Jefferson, spare Will Clark, spare the corps. A good officer looks after his men; this is how I look after mine."

I heard laughter from that corner of my soul.

"You would not know what honor is," I said. "I will suffer shame, but preserve honor!"

Who was I arguing with? A phantasm, a nightmare, without flesh.

"You would not know what courage is, either," I continued. "You would not even know what pain is, pain of soul, pain of body."

Pernia said, "Are you all right, master?"

I smiled. "I am debating with myself," I said.

My manservant stared.

That grim judge occupying my heart would not be still. "You, sir, are a coward, deathly afraid of pain."

I acknowledged it. "Yes, I am."

"You won't succeed. You cannot inflict pain upon yourself. You will botch it. You cannot point a loaded piece at your bosom and pull the trigger."

He was nettling me. "I will do what I must do," I retorted.

This specter in my bosom laughed, and it sounded like a flight of honking geese late in the fall.

I turned inward. We proceeded through an autumnal mid-October day, with iron-belly clouds scudding low. I looked back, half expecting that Neelly would ride up with the two strays, but he didn't. Pernia and the slave followed behind my packhorse. I could not remember the name of the slave; only that Neelly owned him. My memory was flagging. I didn't doubt that someday I would not remember my own name. I suffered lapses constantly. I spent half an afternoon trying to remember the name of the officer at Fort Pickering, the man who would not let me have my medicines.

We were two or three days out of Nashville, but this country had yet to be settled. The dense oak and maple woods discouraged farming. I prefer open country, not this cloistering canopy. I pulled my flask and drank the harsh whiskey to settle my soul again.

Late this afternoon I espied a clearing ahead in a broad swale set in the oak-covered hills. It had been painfully hacked out of the dense forest, and at the far end of it stood a dogtrot cabin, that is to say, two cabins connected by roof in the manner of frontier dwellings across the South. And far beyond that, a log barn. And I discerned a yellowed corn crop rising among the black stumps that toothed the field.

Whatever the place, it would no doubt provide comforts for travelers such as ourselves. The trace ran along the very edge of the settlement, no doubt drawing trade.

I urged my horse forward, leaving my entourage behind.

At my arrival, a work-worn young woman in brown checked gingham emerged from one of the water-stained log cabins, and she was swiftly surrounded by urchins of stairstep ages.

I halted. "Madam, do you provide lodging?"

"Yes. Not fancy, but a roof. In there." She pointed at the other cabin. "That's where the children sleep, but I'll move them in here tonight. Are you alone?"

"My servants follow, with packhorses."

She nodded and pointed at the log barn. We negotiated a

price for myself, the servants, and the horses. A dollar and two bits in all, grain for the horses extra.

"I'm Mr. Lewis. And you?"

"Mrs. Grinder," she said. "My man's up at the other place . . . but he'll be back soon enough. Very well, Mr. Lewis, I'll shake out the tick and get ready. I'll have some supper in a little bit."

Grinder's stand, then. As I dismounted she vanished into the log cabin that would house me. The children shrank into the other cabin, which was redolent of stewing meat. Pernia and the slave walked up, and I steered them toward the barn.

"But put my trunks in there," I added, pointing to my quarters.

They unpacked the horse and carried my heavy luggage into the dark confines, while Mrs. Grinder finished her preparations.

"Where's my gunpowder, Pernia?" I asked.

"In your canister, sir."

"I want to recharge my pistols. I've neglected it. This is not a safe place."

Pernia eyed me uneasily, and then took my horses off to water and rub them down, as he always did. I entered my new dominion, alone at last. I had not been alone for a month. My two trunks rested in a corner. A not very clean tick lay on the puncheon floor, and I supposed it would have its complement of bedbugs. But that would not matter. I had escaped at last.

Twilight comes swiftly this time of year, and I knew I would not have to wait long for darkness to fall. I pulled off my shirt and put on my blue-striped nightshirt over my pantaloons. Mrs. Grinder invited me in and offered me some stew, but I refused. Her ragamuffins peered shyly at me, astonished at my odd attire.

"Give it to the servants, madam," I said.

"But you should have some, Mr. Lewis."

I dissuaded her. I was not a bit hungry and my fevers were mounting again. "I would take a little whiskey if you have it, madam."

Wordlessly she lifted a jug and poured a gill or so into a cup for me. But once I had it in hand, I didn't want it, and sipped but little.

"Madam, have you any gunpowder?" I asked.

"Gunpowder?"

"Yes. I wish to clean the damp powder out of my pieces and recharge them."

"Oh, sir, Mr. Grinder might, but he's not present now, and it might be a while."

I sighed. Would my intentions be defeated by that? I could not find my powder flask. Perhaps Pernia had it. Or perhaps it was in one of the trunks left at Fort Pickering. My two pieces were not loaded.

"Hidden it, have you?"

"Sir?" asked Mrs. Grinder.

"I was talking to someone else, my servant, madam."

She looked about, saw no one, and stared at me.

"You cannot know what it takes to do what I must do," I said.

"Are you indisposed, Mr. Lewis?" asked the poor woman.

"Madam, it's a very pleasant evening. I think I'll just sit outside and have a pipe before I retire, if that is suitable."

"Oh, of course, sir, of course. I just thought maybe something is amiss. If you're indisposed I have a few simples I might steep for you."

"No, madam, you look after your children, and trust the night."

She backed away, carrying her pot and ladle and a trencher intended for my use.

I watched her retreat, confused, toward the barn with the stew, and settled down on a bench outside my cabin door. I pulled out my old briar pipe and tamped some sweet tobacco into it, enjoying the soft sweet quiet of the fading day, the thickening blue of a lifetime.

48. LEWIS

It came down to duty. I could preserve, for the republic, the Meriwether Lewis they knew and celebrated, or not. I knew what I must do, but didn't know whether I could summon that mournful courage to do it. And so I argued with myself that soft Wednesday eve in the oak groves of Tennessee.

I hated this!

Oh, if only I might repeal three years; but how sad and feckless to think it. I paced and argued, but there was nothing to argue. The nation had built a shrine to me, and I had befouled it. Like the whited sepulcher, it contained corruption within.

I could not go east; I could not ride into the City of Washington without betraying the trust invested in me. I could not sully the Corps of Discovery, my loyal and stouthearted men. I could not beslime my mentor and friend Tom Jefferson. I could not open the floodgates of gossip. I could not babble my case to Mr. Madison or Secretary Eustis, for they would be listening to gossip and not to me. I could not bear the thought of entering into the presence of my mother, with her searching gaze and saddened mien.

I watched night settle and listened to the crickets. I heard the last of a day's toil in the cabin next door, and then the soft darkness settled over the farmstead. It was a gentle night, this eleventh day of October, soft and melancholic, the tang of the good earth in the night breezes.

There were black holes in a starlit sky, where occasional clouds obscured the universe. Even in that infinity, there was no place to go, no escape.

By the light of a stub candle, I stormed through my chattel and found the powder flask, which Pernia had artfully buried under my journals. I grasped the embossed canister and plucked it out of the trunk. In my other trunk I found my two brass-mounted Pennsylvania pistols, encased in a polished cherrywood box. I opened the box and beheld them in the drear rays of the candle. They were costly, reliable pieces, and had served me well during the expedition. They had put balls into grizzlies. They had comforted me in emergencies.

I lifted one, and felt the smoothness of the walnut stock and the coldness of the ten-inch octagonal steel barrel. I lifted the other, two old friends whose loyalty I did not question. The locks and frizzens were fine, the flints fresh. The pistols had been cleaned and oiled, and were ready for whatever use my eye and finger might put them to.

I charged each piece, pouring the full measure of good Missouri powder down the cold muzzle, patching a forty-four-caliber ball and driving it home, and then priming the pan. I hefted them. They felt fine, balanced, formed to my hand, and I pointed them here and there, at the candle, the floor, the wall, my trunks. Everywhere but at their target.

"You are a coward after all," said my censor.

I responded by pointing the pistol in my right hand at my forehead.

Could I not do what needed doing?

I paced again, the pistols putting authority to my every gesture.

"Mr. Eustis, if you will just let me explain. There was no way to execute Mr. Jefferson's design to return the Mandan without some expense. The regular army declined, so we created our own. But it will pay off, sir. And the presents we distribute along the river will ensure the safety of our western flank in the event of another war. The British never stop stirring them up! You will see, sir, how well it was spent. And now I am ruined. It's a burden hard to bear. Can you remedy this?"

No response rose out of the night.

"Who can say I lack courage?" I cried. "I faced savages with drawn bows intent on killing me. I braved roaring white rapids in a hollowed-out log of a canoe. I walked into savage villages even as I saw their warriors spread out and arm themselves and prepare to butcher me. I chose what rivers and paths to follow, often against the perceptions of the rest. I ate dog and horse and other meats that repel most men. I sat next to murderous men armed with long knives. I urged us forward when the faint of heart wanted only to flee. I faced angry bears and buffalo. I suffered a grave wound without complaint. Courage I have, for any good cause. And this is the best of causes."

All this I declaimed into the night, not caring who heard.

But there was only the hum of crickets. A wisp of smoke from Mrs. Grinder's fieldstone chimney eddied in.

And still I loved life too much.

"I am trapped! That is the sole reason!"

Then I thought of the unspeakable disease, of the shame, and thinking of the shame heartened me, and I thought I could do this thing if I could summon one swift moment of inner steel. Ah, that was the secret. One swift moment.

And still I could not.

I stepped to the door. Moist air met me. I saw no stars. The skies had been blotted out. I slumped to the stoop and sat dully, my mind purged of every thought. I knew nothing, scarcely knew my name, and could not even think of simple things. Maria Wood, she did not wait for me.

The calm eluded me. I had no more anodynes. I had snuff, and only a swallow of spirits. Violence was my only salvation.

I stepped into the inky black of the cabin, lifted the pistol in my right hand to my temple, and pulled . . .

49. CLARK

I have tarried here at Locust Hill some days with the governor's family, trying to make sense of it all. Mrs. Marks has welcomed me, along with Meriwether's half brother John Marks. I will stay a while longer in Albemarle County, where the family and Thomas Jefferson are quietly putting Meriwether's affairs in order. But soon I will go to the City of Washington for talks with Secretary Eustis and President Madison.

The news reached me in Shelbyville, Kentucky, only three days after I had departed from my own family at Mulberry Hill, Indiana Territory, and started east to untangle the financial affairs afflicting the Clarks and the governor and the St. Louis Missouri Fur Company.

The blurred story in the *Argus of Western America*, published in Frankfort, shattered my repose, and I read it over and over, trying to draw from it the information I wanted. But it was mute on all the essentials.

I handed the shocking paper to George Shannon, who was with me, and we stared at each other, scarce believing that our captain had left us, and by his own hand. My mind crawled with doubts, but at the same time I was not surprised.

I was so grieved and disquieted by the news that I didn't know what to do. There was in me a red-haired Clark itch to head south to the Natchez Trace and question all those at hand, rattle their teeth, bang heads together, and get to the bottom of it. Maybe they could tell me what had excited the governor's passion and caused this last desperate escape. But on reflection, I abandoned that course. The governor would have been in the company of his faithful manservant Pernia and others, and I would soon enough get the whole and true story.

I did alter my plans in one respect: I had planned to head directly to the City of Washington for talks with Secretary Eustis, with only the briefest pause in Albemarle County en route. Now I decided to sojourn with the governor's family and help any way I might. Meriwether had given me power of attorney to settle his debts and perhaps I might be of use even now.

In Shelbyville I wrote my brother Jonathan of the horrifying news, and said I thought the report was true. "I fear, Oh I fear the weight of his mind has overcome him, what will be the Consequence?" I concluded. Those last letters from Meriwether, posted en route, asking me to look after his affairs, persuaded me of the truth of it. I will destroy them.

Shannon and I started east again, sharing in all tenderness and simplicity our memories of the great captain who walked the banks of the Missouri while we poled and rowed our vessels into the unknown. There was Meriwether striding before us, pausing at a plant he had never seen, stopping to unlimber his instruments and give us our latitude and longitude, sending Drouillard out to make meat, all of his hunters and fishers somehow feeding us off the land every day. There was Meriwether, bravely treating with glowering savages with arrows nocked in their bows, handing out gills of whiskey along with rebukes and encouragement, for he was always the taskmaster, exhorting us to do better even while commending our successes and rewarding the men any way he could.

I was grateful to have one of the Corps of Discovery with me that long, sad journey east. We comforted each other as we proceeded on, Shannon always on horse, which he managed well even lacking part of a limb. We were remembering a man of unquestioned genius and honor, a man of such rare ability that he took us to the western sea and back without disaster, and left behind him a record of it all.

That brought to mind my deepest concern: what of the journals? Were they safe? Had he finished the editing? The matter had become so tender with him that I ceased inquiring, and I was utterly in the dark about them. Were they too lost?

There were moments when Shannon and I doubted everything we had read: maybe Meriwether had been murdered in a most vicious manner.

"The Burr devils got him, plain got him," he repeated, over and over.

Meriwether did not lack conniving enemies in St. Louis, the Burr conspirators as well as disappointed seekers of privileges and offices. Shannon in particular seethed with the idea that a foul deed had felled the governor. Suicide was improbable. Neither he nor I had ever seen the governor in any great state of melancholia; his nature was to fight on, through the worst of events, until he could see daylight again.

At times Shannon and I speculated: was the governor

simply murdered by the bandits infesting the Natchez Trace? Was this Neelly the instrument of an avenging cabal? Was this the work of the Burr conspirators, whose faltering scheme to detach Louisiana from the republic the governor had stoutly defused? Was the crafty General Wilkinson at the core of it? Might the governor's trusted manservant Pernia be a part of it? My mind seethed with possibilities, and yet, in the end, I believed the newspaper accounts were largely true. The governor took his own life.

I knew things about him I felt I could not share with my doughty friend: Meriwether had been overwhelmed by sickness, and he had all too generously dosed himself with anodynes, powders, snuff, draughts of spirits, whatever he felt might release him from the suffering of his mortal flesh. I had seen his accounts: of medicines he had purchased a plenitude. Of visits to the doctor, Antoine Saugrain in particular, he had accumulated an alarming number, and it was plain to me that something was radically amiss.

I thought of the unspoken thing, the *lues venerea,* which had afflicted him first on the Columbia and later at Fort Clatsop, and which he and I concealed from the corps and from the journal. I supposed he had the drips, but I was wrong. Had that vile affliction been his nemesis?

I perused more newspapers along the way. The fragmented and incoherent story had created a sensation everywhere. I learned that two balls had penetrated the governor, and that murder was a distinct possibility. All this aggrieved and disturbed me to the bone. I hoped the answers would come clear in Virginia, at least if Meriwether's manservant, or this man unknown to me, Major Neelly, had carried his possessions and information to the governor's family and to Monticello as I knew the governor intended. I could only hope, and hasten east as fast as Shannon and I could manage in nippy and often wet weather.

When we arrived at Locust Hill, on Ivy Creek, on December 3, Mrs. Marks and John greeted us tenderly, and swiftly brought from the servants' quarters the man I most wanted to see: John Pernia.

"Mr. Pernia's helping us with the estate. He's visited Mr. Jefferson and delivered the journals there," John Marks explained. "He's eager to talk to you, and has tarried here for your coming, just so he could deliver himself of an account of the governor's last hours."

That, indeed, was good news. While the servants hurried some hot viands to us, Shannon and I settled ourselves in the cream-enameled parlor, along with our hosts. In a moment, Pernia appeared.

"Oh, General, General," he said, clasping my hand. "What a painful matter this is! I have stayed here just so that you may learn of everything."

The mottled face of this Creole black man crumpled with feeling. Mrs. Marks and her son settled themselves on settees, all of us in that sun-drenched parlor, our sole focus the witness to Meriwether's death.

There unrolled, tentatively then more confidently, the account of the governor's horrendous last days, madness and delusion plaguing him, fever and sickness felling him, spirits and opium pills and snuff addling him. I listened to the story, believing it all. I already knew most of it.

"He says over and over to the major, to me, you are coming along right behind, and you are going to fix everything," he said.

"Was he . . . mad?"

Pernia sighed. "Ah, my general . . . Sometimes he was raging at the secretary of war for protesting his drafts. He says to Captain Russell that the journals were all written up and ready to publish. General, he never did write a word."

"Tell me about Major Neelly, Mr. Pernia."

"The major, he was no friend of the governor, and had certain failings, sir, but he saw his duty, and he respected the flag. He took care of everything afterward, doing it right and proper. Because of him, the journals are safe."

"Why wasn't he present at Grinder's Stand?"

"Now that be a strange thing, General. Two horses get loose of their hobbles the night previous; we hobbled them up for certain. The major did it himself, he being something of a horse fancier, and next morning two horses had strayed, one of the major's and one of the governor's. That's when the governor is pretty cheerful; he said he would go on ahead and stop for the night at the first stand he came to."

"Someone let the horses loose?"

"Someone did, sir. It was no mishap."

"Who, Mr. Pernia?"

The man looked reluctant to talk, glancing fearfully at Meriwether's mother. "The governor, *pauvre homme,* he had tried to throw away his life several times, and he be carefully watched for his own sake. I kept the vigil, the major watched, back at Fort Pickering there was a regular vigil, and that day, when the governor went ahead and the major stayed back to find the missing horses, that was the first time the governor wasn't watched. He got free."

"But you were with him, watching."

He looked discomfited. "I couldn't. The woman, Mrs. Grinder, she put us in the barn, sir, the people of color."

I nodded. "Was the governor murdered?"

Slowly Pernia shook his head. "All this that happened, it was the most plain thing, after his trying so much, so many times."

"Why didn't you come to him when you heard shots?"

"The barn was *très* distant, General. We didn't hear. I think the governor's powder was damp."

"Why didn't Mrs. Grinder go to him when he cried out?"

"General, she thinks him a lunatic, him arguing with himself and shouting half the night. She thinks only of protecting her children. Her man was away. She didn't unbar that door until the morning."

"How could a man shoot himself twice?"

"The first ball, it creased his temple and tore out bone and exposed the brain, not taking effect, and after a while he found the other pistol and put that ball into his chest. And still he lingered."

"Do you believe a man could do that?"

Pernia nodded. "In his condition, General, he would do anything he had to do."

"Where was Major Neelly?"

"He came up in the morning, sir. Maybe an hour or two after dawn."

"That's a strange hour. Was he present when the governor died?"

"Yes, sir. But it be too late. The governor is breathing his last."

"Did he have the missing horses?"

Pernia nodded. "He found one, his own, but not the other, and came up."

"How could he travel at night?"

"I didn't ask him, sir. It wasn't so dark. He maybe rode early, by moon, to catch up and press on."

"Then he was not far off at dawn. Is there the slightest chance that the major shot the governor?"

"No, sir, not as I know. The governor cut his arms to finish the dying. He lay there, bloody arms, sometimes aware of us, but he didn't accuse anyone from his deathbed. He didn't point a finger, he didn't say you or you or you did it. He didn't curse the major from his bed for all of us to hear. He could be doing that. He is aware enough. His eyes open."

"After he died, then what?" I asked.

Pernia looked uncomfortable. "The major set about digging a grave and getting a coffin. He put his slave to the digging, and me to get nails and all. There was no box, not in a hundred mile, and we got a few nails from a smithy and planks from a farm long ways away and a man there made a box from oak plank nailed up by himself. It be not much, but it's all we got. We buried the governor there, at Grinder's Stand the next day, all of us standing there, hats off to the governor, and the major saying the words."

"Then?"

"Then the major got the trunks and made an account of everything in them, the journals, disputed vouchers, clothing, weapons, and all, and we all set off for Nashville carrying the bad news inside us. The governor's purse was missing, and someone took it, maybe it got lost on the trail, the governor being so out of his mind, so there was no money for me.

"In Nashville the major gave me fifteen dollars to get here, for I had none, and sent the two trunks with me on the horse. And then he wrote the president—I mean Mr. Jefferson, and I brought the letter with me. He and I got the journals safe to Monticello, just as the governor wanted."

"And Mr. Jefferson has the letter from Major Neelly?"

Pernia nodded. "He read it while I waited, and then he brought me in and asked me things for a long time, and I answered everything for the president, best I knew how. I give the journals to him, just as my master wanted, and then I went to Washington and talked to the president about it, and came here with the horse and the other trunk, and Mrs. Marks kindly takes me in and bids me to stay."

There were strange circumstances. Missing money. Major Neelly a checkered man of dubious repute. The odd reappearance of Major Neelly soon after dawn. No one helping Meriwether all night. Two shots and yet a suicide.

But as I probed Pernia's story the rest of the day, and talked with Lucy Marks and her son, my mind kept returning to the overwhelming truth of it all: the disease whose name no one spoke had killed him.

50. CLARK

That December evening, beside the cold hearth at Locust Hill, Lucy Marks, John Marks, and I sat quietly, our hearts in Tennessee.

I would leave for Monticello in the morning.

"Are you satisfied?" I asked them. "I can ask for an investigation."

"Satisfied, General? Oh, no," Meriwether's mother said. "We'll never be satisfied, not with the reports so sketchy, and the accounts so jumbled, and so many self-serving stories."

"One word from Thomas Jefferson and the matter will be opened," I said. "The administration could scarcely refuse him. There's a good prospect that we can find out exactly what happened."

John Marks raised a hand. "We'd like to let it rest," he said. "Just let it be. My mother and I have come to that. It would be best for us, best for Meriwether, best for Mister Jefferson."

I nodded. I had come to that, too. Meriwether had done what he had to do, caught between terrible scourges, trying to salvage what he could for our sakes.

I had only eulogy to offer them, but eulogy was what each of us craved.

"He was a great man, a great American," I said, my soul

reaching out to these desolated friends. "I remember that great heart, that great mind, that great will, leading us through the unknown with all its perils. I remember his bright curiosity, his wonder at the world and everything in it; the way he marveled at a new bird, or a cloud, or a waterfall, or the way an Indian drew his bow. No man on earth was better fitted to lead, no man alive could have taken us to the ends of the earth and brought us back safely, save for Meriwether."

They smiled.

I knew that Mrs. Marks, even in her grief, was aglow with pride. "You do him honor," she said gently.

"The world will always do Meriwether Lewis honor," I said, "because he earned it."

"Yes, both of you," she replied. "You together."

AUTHOR'S NOTES

The mystery of Meriwether Lewis's death probably will never be solved. The evidence is too tangled, too contradictory, and too old. For generations there were two opposed theories: he died of suicide induced by depression, or he was murdered.

The suicide theorists argued that he had twice tried to kill himself en route to New Orleans and had made a will, and was depressed by his debts. They cite Jefferson's observation that melancholia ran in Lewis's family. The murder theorists argued that a suicide doesn't shoot himself twice, and there were plenty of people with plenty of reason to kill him, and Lewis showed no sign of manic-depressive disorder or any sort of depression.

A few years ago a Seattle epidemiologist, Reimert Thorolf Ravenholt, M.D., examined the journals and other material and concluded that Lewis had contracted syphilis during his 1805 contact with the Shoshones, and by 1809 the result was paresis, the mental deterioration induced by virulent third-stage syphilis, which led him to his death. Dr. Ravenholt pursued this thesis in three brilliantly argued papers that can be downloaded at his Web site, Ravenholt.com. I recommend in particular "Trail's End for Meriwether Lewis," presented to the American Academy of Forensic Sciences in 1997.

This is not the place to debate the issue. Suffice it to say that I found Dr. Ravenholt's analysis the most persuasive and the only one that adequately explains events and fits much of the evidence. But the other theories are plausible and have serious advocates, and must not be dismissed, though the murder theory seems weakest to me. There is too little known, and too many contradictions, to come to firm conclusions. Of all the mysteries of American history, this one invites the most caution.

We might learn something if Lewis's remains are exhumed and tested for mercury and evidence of syphilis, a disease that can affect bones. They might also offer clues as to the direction the two shots took, the size of the ball, and so on, and thus throw light on the question of murder.

I chose to construct the novel around Dr. Ravenholt's superb historical and medical analysis, and also upon a penetrating monograph called *The Character of Meriwether Lewis,* by Jeffersonian scholar Clay Straus Jenkinson, who brilliantly examines every facet of the complex, troubled, courageous, and sometimes repellent man who died on the Natchez Trace in 1809.

I believe that Meriwether Lewis took his life at Grinder's Stand, not because he was depressive by nature (I doubt that he was depressive at all), but because he was desperate and hopeless and fearful that his scandalous disease could no longer be concealed from the public. He feared that the national hero would soon be the national disgrace. By killing himself, he might yet preserve honor, not only his own but that of the entire Corps of Discovery.

Had he not killed himself, he might have lived years longer, even though his syphilis, probably complicated by malaria, was steadily destroying him. He knew he would soon become the demented, degenerate husk of the magnificent man he once was, and that was more than a man of his pride and sensibility could endure. Desperate circumstances father desperate acts.

As I examined the question of Lewis's disease, I found myself discarding the murder theory, and also abandoning the much-publicized idea that Lewis was depressed. Lewis was trapped. He was a courageous young man who was caught in a vise that was steadily squeezing him to death. He could not arrest the course of the disease or halt the decline of his reputation. He turned to one remedy after another, but nothing would heal him. He probably overdosed the mercury and further addled himself. In the space of only three years after his return, his health and spirits were ruined.

And so this novel was born. I came to share Lewis's horror and despair as I walked beside him. I admired and pitied him. Here was a good man, a greathearted American hero, desperately struggling against an insidious disease that was destroying not only his body but his very person. Here was a Homeric story worth telling. I resolved to tell it as a stark chronicle of decline. Lewis never surrendered. His suicide was a last act of defiance of the disease that was robbing him of his soul.

There are no full-scale biographies of William Clark, but his life can be pieced together from various sources, including *Lewis and Clark, Partners in Discovery,* by John Bakeless, and *William Clark, Jeffersonian Man on the Frontier,* by Jerome O. Steffen.

Other useful works include *Meriwether Lewis,* by Richard Dillon, *Undaunted Courage,* by Stephen E. Ambrose, and *A History of the Lewis and Clark Journals,* by Paul Russell Cutright.

There is a vast Lewis and Clark literature, too extensive to be listed here, as well as several excellent editions of the Lewis and Clark Journals, including the majestic and exhaustive new one by Gary Moulton.

A novelist dramatizing history must sometimes depict events for which there is no historical record. The funeral of John Shields, in this story, is such a scene, and there are others. I have also arbitrarily chosen among various spellings and decided which of the many conflicting accounts to use in the novel.

I am indebted to my editor, Dale L. Walker, for awakening in me a fascination with the Lewis question, and offering shrewd and thoroughly researched insights into the various possibilities as well as research material. And I am grateful to archivists at the Missouri Historical Society for pointing me toward various sources about William Clark.

RICHARD S. WHEELER
NOVEMBER 2001